No More
Lonely Nights

Also by Nicole McGehee

Regret Not a Moment

No More Lonely Nights

A Novel

Nicole McGehee

Little, Brown and Company

Boston   New York   Toronto   London

First Edition

The characters and events in this book are fictitious. Any similarity to real persons, living or dead, is coincidental and not intended by the author.

Library of Congress Cataloging-in-Publication Data

McGehee, Nicole
    No more lonely nights : a novel / by Nicole McGehee. — 1st ed.
      p. cm.
    ISBN 0–316–55854–0
    I. Title.
PS3563.C36373N6 1995
813'.54 — dc20   94–37442

10 9 8 7 6 5 4 3 2 1

MV–NY

Published simultaneously in Canada by Little, Brown & Company (Canada) Limited

Printed in the United States of America

To my mother, for her stories;
to my grandmother, for the memories;
to my husband, just for love

Acknowledgments

This book would not have been possible without the help of my mother, whose fascinating stories of her youth in Egypt inspired my imagination. She revealed far more than a daughter has a right to expect, though I'm sure there are still volumes that have not been told. I would also like to thank my Aunt Odette and Aunt Lucette, as well as my cousin, Viviane, for recalling their memories of Egypt — the way it was then.

I offer thanks to my editor, Fredrica Friedman, for her superb advice, insight, and thoughtfulness. Robert Ducas, my agent, I thank for his encouragement and his efforts on my behalf. Finally, to my poor husband, Michael, who, because of me, never gets enough sleep, thanks for the late nights poring over the manuscript, for the inspirational critiques, and, most of all, for making my dreams yours.

BOOK ONE

CHAPTER 1 ⤫

Alexandria, Egypt

1956

DOMINIQUE had never loved Stephen so much as at that moment, when she knew she would never see him again.

As she approached the top of the gangplank, she pivoted on her kidskin high heels and searched the throng on shore, as if she would find him there. But the only familiar figure was that of her mother, Solange, who raised her hand in a regal salute. Dominique raised her own gloved hand in return, trying valiantly to make her wave jaunty. It was hard, though. She was only twenty-one and she was leaving behind . . . everything.

Her eyes panned the raucous harbor, trying to commit it to memory. Against a backdrop of once-grand buildings was a scene that would fit nowhere but the Middle East. White-robed porters shouted to each other as they hauled baggage to the ship. Pushcart vendors — each with an umbrella to keep out the blistering sun — hawked food, copper goods, and Oriental rugs to the milling crowd. Luxurious European cars blew their horns at the donkey wagons that jammed the roadway.

Amidst the dust, noise, and confusion, the immaculate white cruise ship that would take Dominique to her new life in America seemed strangely alien. As it swayed softly with the incoming tide, Dominique put a hand on the teak railing to keep her balance. She should board, she told herself, but still she lingered on the gangplank.

Dominique closed her eyes and inhaled deeply as the scent from a falafel cart wafted up to her. Would she ever again smell the familiar blend of cumin, hot oil, and pepper? Her throat tight with nostalgia, she opened her eyes for one last look.

Suddenly her body grew rigid as her gaze locked on a man strolling a few yards from the ship — one of the ubiquitous khaki-uniformed soldiers who patrolled the waterfront. At once, Dominique pulled down the net veil of her hat and hurried up the gangplank.

A crew member dressed in crisp whites stepped forward to greet her. With a bow, he offered a steadying hand as Dominique stepped onto the polished deck. Then his eyes landed on the face beneath the net veil. There was a barely perceptible pause. Until now, he hadn't had a good look at her. Having seen her husband, he'd never expected someone so young — certainly not so striking. But it was verboten to stare at attractive passengers — especially when they were married. Recovering quickly, he gave her the deferential smile that he always accorded first class guests.

"Good morning, Mrs. Renard. Welcome aboard the *Golden Gate*." He raised his voice to be heard over the celebratory crowd on board. Champagne corks popped and waiters rattled by with glasses and trays. Long, curly streamers sailed through the air and landed unnoticed on richly clad shoulders. Cries of, "I'll miss you! Don't forget to write!" Enthusiastic waves to those on shore.

The handsome crewman leaned toward Dominique and said solicitously, "Your husband's found a place for you at the rail, if you'd like to watch the departure." He gestured toward the bow of the ship, farther away than the length of a football field. "Would you like someone to show you the way?" He pointed to a column of young men wearing red jackets with brass buttons — like bellhops in fine hotels. They stood at attention, waiting to escort passengers to their staterooms or relieve them of their bon voyage baskets.

Dominique smiled nervously. "Thank you, that won't be necessary. I'll find him." The truth was she felt awkward at the prospect of being alone with the man she had married in a rushed ceremony two hours earlier. As she made her way past the gleaming expanse of polished brass and wood, she wondered about Anton. What would they talk about? She barely knew him.

We'll manage, Dominique firmly told herself. We'll be fine. She forced herself to focus on the pleasant excitement around her. The atmosphere was that of a huge, carefree party with hundreds of fascinating strangers. Dominique was already catching bits of conversation in French, English, Arabic, and Italian. She wondered if she and Anton would make new friends on board. She hoped so, for she knew no one in America other than her sister, Danielle.

Finally Dominique spotted the back of her husband's sleekly groomed gray head. She eased into the space beside him and murmured a greeting as she pulled a stream of confetti from the shoulder of her fawn silk suit.

He turned to her with a welcoming expression. "You said your good-byes?" Anton Renard spoke to her in French, their native language.

Dominique nodded and returned his smile.

Anton squeezed her elbow in a proprietary way and leaned close. "Ready for your new life in San Francisco, darling?" He brushed a strand of her auburn hair from her face.

Without realizing it, Dominique inched away from him. "Of course!" She tried for enthusiasm. The feeling of strangeness would fade, she reassured herself. It had to. Anton was her future; it was time to let go of her past. Forget Stephen.

The earsplitting shriek of the ship's klaxon broke into Dominique's thoughts. She leaned against the rail and longingly focused on her mother as the *Golden Gate*'s crew pulled up the gangplank.

Solange Avallon waved, a majestic, controlled motion. Even in the heat of the Alexandria sun, she looked cool in her ivory linen suit. She carried in her gloved hands a parasol of matching fabric — nothing frilly for Solange. And it seemed the crowd around her sensed that it was in the presence of *someone*. No one jostled her. No one stood close to her. She commanded respect. Dominique studied her mother with a mixture of admiration and hurt. Why couldn't Solange, just once, act as if she would miss her? What a contrast to Dominique's tearful parting from Nanny. The old woman — more family than servant — had been too overcome with emotion to accompany Dominique to the ship. But if Solange experienced similar feelings, they didn't show.

Heat stung the inside of Dominique's eyelids. It was wrenching to leave her mother, even though their relationship had never been harmonious. She bit her lip and determinedly stifled her unhappy reflections. Instead, she tried to cheer herself by thinking of her sister. Danielle wrote that she loved America. Eight years before, she had moved to New York with her husband, Ronald Marks, an American officer she'd met on the Avallon family's annual trip to France. Danielle's engagement had been as sudden as Dominique's. But then, Danielle had been in love with her husband.

Well, Dominique would learn to love Anton. She was grateful that he was taking her away from Egypt. She gave him a brief, sidelong glance, then once more turned to gaze at her mother. *Why* was Solange so determined to stay in Egypt after all that had happened? The country just wasn't safe for Europeans anymore! But Solange insisted she wasn't worried. The deputy minister of Egypt himself was her protector. The ugly incident that was chasing Dominique into exile was an aberration, and Solange would simply be more cautious from now on. Still, she had insisted that Dominique go. And what reason was there to stay, since there was no future with Stephen?

Dominique looked guiltily at her husband, as though he could read her thoughts. But he was absorbed in conversation with the man on the other side of him. So, for just a moment — for the very last time, she vowed — Dominique closed her eyes and allowed herself to succumb to her memories. Memories of Egypt. Memories of Stephen.

CHAPTER 2 ⤸

Cairo, Egypt

Eight months earlier

DOMINIQUE'S present to herself on her twenty-first birthday was to apply for a job with the Royal Air Force. All her friends worked for the British.

"You'll practice your English," said the serious-minded ones.

"You'll meet so many handsome officers!" said the rest.

Not that anyone Dominique knew *had* to work. In fact, her mother vehemently opposed the idea.

"What do you mean *work?*" Solange demanded in French as they wended their way through the rose garden that dominated their walled back yard. Looped over her left arm was a round, flat basket that she used for cut flowers; in her right hand, a pair of shears. Now she waved the shears in a gesture of dismissal. "Women in the Avallon family don't work! When your father died, he left us very well provided for."

Dominique unconsciously turned and looked back at her family's imposing Belle Epoque home. It was in the Garden City district of Cairo — a neighborhood of quiet, shady streets, vast lawns, and high walls; an enclave built by Europeans to remind them of the elegant world they had left behind in the grand capitals of the Continent.

The Avallons' closest neighbor was the Italian embassy. A block away was the British embassy. But neither outshone the Avallon house, with its long windows, high ceilings, and marble corridors. The home was a monument to all that was graceful in French architecture.

And though Henri Avallon had been dead twelve years, the house was maintained as perfectly as it had been during his lifetime, thanks to Solange's watchful supervision of a retinue of well-trained servants.

"Dominique, pay attention to what I'm saying!"

Dominique turned back to her mother with an absent expression.

Solange gave her a look of exasperation. "Oh, for heaven's sake, it's much too hot to stand here and discuss this! We'll go into the courtyard." Solange turned and strode decisively up the brick path. Dominique stared after her mother, then, bracing herself, hurried to catch up.

As the two women passed under a stone arch marked by a lacy iron gate, they left Europe behind and entered a tiled inner courtyard that was unmistakably Arabian. An oasis of tropical plants and cool fountains, it was perfumed by a jasmine vine that spanned the second story colonnade. Exotic flowers like oleander and hibiscus flourished, thanks to regular watering by two gardeners.

Solange placed her basket on a wrought iron table and, with a curt motion of her hand, assigned Dominique one of the matching chairs. Dominique complied as Solange, too, sat down and rang for the butler. Seconds later, a broad, white-robed man appeared, almost blocking from view the veiled woman shadowing him. They approached the table with noiseless, gliding steps.

Solange looked up and handed the man her basket of flowers. The man took the basket and, in turn, handed it to the black-robed woman, who bowed and backed out of the garden.

"Lemonade, please," Solange said in Arabic.

"*Aywalla'*, Madame Solange," he replied in a mix of Arabic and French. He too, then backed silently from the courtyard.

Solange brushed her hands together as though she had accomplished a challenging task, then fixed Dominique with a baleful look. "Now, about this ludicrous notion . . ."

The scorn in Solange's voice made Dominique's jaw clench — and it made her all the more resolute. Nevertheless, she wanted to avoid another of the arguments that regularly punctuated their stormy relationship. Fighting to maintain her composure, she said, "Mother, this is 1955. A lot of women work. I *want* to keep busy."

Solange's eyebrows came together in an angry V.

Dominique hurried on, before her mother could argue. "I want to practice my English and my typing." She spread her hands palm up in front of her. "Why did I learn them if I'm not going to use them?" Her sentence ended on an upraised note of exasperation.

Solange stiffened. "Keep your voice down," she hissed, as the butler returned with a tray bearing a pitcher of lemonade and two glasses. The women remained silent until he poured the drinks and retreated into the house.

As soon as he was out of sight, Dominique impatiently leaned forward and picked up where she had left off. "Why did you force me to have the English tutor all those years when you don't even speak the language? Why did you send me to the American College? I'll forget it all if I don't use it!"

Solange opened her mouth as if to fling back a retort, then paused with a look of uncertainty. She averted her head and reached for her lemonade.

Dominique knew she had hit her mark. Solange, who spoke French, Italian, and Arabic, insisted that English was the language of the future. The British had been the military power in Egypt for as many years as Solange had been alive. More important, America had emerged from World War II as a superpower. So although Italians, French, and Greeks dominated Egypt's commerce and fashion, Solange was convinced both her girls should speak flawless English.

Dominique watched her mother carefully, guessing her thoughts.

Solange — moving so slowly that Dominique knew she was playing for time — took a sip of her lemonade, then another. Finally, she replaced her glass on the table. A shrewd gleam came into her eyes. She crossed her arms over her ample bosom and tilted her chin up victoriously. "We go to Alexandria every summer and France every spring. So you won't have time to work" — she paused and gave Dominique a knowing look — "unless you intend to give up those vacations."

Dominique made a sound of impatience. "We just came back from Alexandria and we're not going to France until next spring. I can quit then. I just want to see what it's like to work."

Solange's eyes flared. She had clearly run out of patience. "I forbid it!" she cried.

Dominique's chair scraped angrily on the tiles as she shoved it backward and sprang to her feet. "I'm twenty-one now. You can't stop me!"

Solange's palm slammed down on the table, rattling the glasses.

"Then I wash my hands of you! Don't come to me for money, because you won't get any!"

"I don't want it! I intend to pay my own way!" Dominique cried.

That didn't end the dispute, though. Another heated exchange came a few days later, when Solange learned that her daughter would be working not in Cairo but a hundred kilometers away, in Ismailia.

"Why can't you stay here in Cairo? You can take classes at the American University. It's simply unbelievable that you have a home like this," said Solange, with a sweep of her hand, "and you want to go and live in a flat with two other girls."

Dominique looked around the formal sitting room. Solange seemed in her element among the ornate Louis XV furniture, the Persian rugs, and the heavy draperies. But Dominique found them oppressive. She found living with Solange oppressive. "It's not just two other girls, Mother. It's Paulette and Jean."

"Jean!" Solange said scornfully. "That British girl. British girls are like prostitutes. They're almost as bad as Americans! She'll have men running in and out every hour of the day. She'll ruin your reputation!"

Dominique gave her mother a sardonic look. "I'll take that chance."

"You'll take *any* chance! That's your trouble!"

○◇ ○◇ ○◇

One week later, Dominique threw open the glass doors of her new apartment in Ismailia and stepped onto the balcony. She took a long, satisfied breath, then moved to the banister, shivering deliciously as the breeze from Lake Timsah ruffled her linen dress.

Looking down at the tree-shaded street below, she decided that Ismailia deserved its reputation as the prettiest — and cleanest — city in Egypt. It was not a resort on a scale with Alexandria or the French Riviera, but its charming little hotels and picturesque avenues were more approachable.

Dominique leaned on the railing between two vivid flower boxes and dreamily gazed at "her" street. Tiny boutiques, their doors thrown open to the sunshine, beckoned passersby with local crafts and baked goods. Outdoor cafés decorated the street corners.

Dominique turned her head at the sound of a horse's hooves. Jingling down the road was a quaint, brass-trimmed open carriage, a line of cars patiently crawling behind it. Dominique grinned at the sight. In Cairo or Alexandria, there would have been shouts, curses, a ceaseless wail of horns. The carriage halted in front of the red striped awning of the café opposite. A man and woman in British military uniforms hopped out to cries of welcome from a group at a sidewalk table. It was just past teatime and the café's little white tables were filled to capacity. There were groups of women and groups of men and many couples, all in Western dress. Their conversation mixed with the lively clatter of dishes as waiters bustled through the crowd. The scene was so inviting that Dominique had an urge to hurry downstairs and join in. She could leave a note telling her roommates to meet her there when they came home from work. Then they'd go out to dinner to celebrate their first evening together. And stay out as late as they liked! Dominique was struck by the heady realization that she no longer had to account to her mother, nor even to poor Nanny, who worried so much. Her life was beginning!

⌒ ⌒ ⌒

"You're very fast," said the British sergeant who had given Dominique the typing examination. "They could use you in the typing pool, but . . ." He narrowed his eyes and studied her. Normally, he'd try to make time with a girl this attractive, but this one was too rich for his blood — didn't take a genius to see that. Look at that dress: one of those plain navy numbers that screamed money. Kind of hinted at the hourglass shape underneath, but didn't cling enough to let you know for sure. He'd like to see her without it. She'd be a handful, even though she was just a tiny thing.

The sergeant shifted his attention to her face. Oh, yeah, she was a firecracker, all right! Lips a little too full, nose a little too long — but the combination was *pow!* And then there were her eyes. Reached out and grabbed you, those eyes did. Told you there was spice behind that rich-girl finish. Smarts, too. What color were they, anyway? The same as that stone in his mother's good ring. Topaz, that was it. Dominique Avallon's eyes were like topaz. And they tilted up at the corners in a way that made her look exotic. Or mysterious. Or something else that got him going. Stood out against that auburn hair like flames. Of course, he didn't go for redheads as a rule. They usually had freckles — not his cup of tea. But this one had skin like golden honey.

Girl's too special for the typing pool, the sergeant decided. She's the kind the top brass like.

"Group Captain Hampton's secretary just got married," he told Dominique. A group captain was the equivalent of a full colonel in the U.S. military — an exceedingly high rank. "He needs a new girl. I'll send you over to him." He sighed inwardly. Hated to see her go. A looker like this broke up the monotony of his day.

Fifteen minutes later, Dominique paused in front of the open door of Group Captain Stephen Hampton's office. She peeked inside as she tapped the glass panel that comprised the upper half of his door.

Hampton was bent over his desk, sun-streaked hair the only visible feature. At the sound of knocking, his head shot up, revealing an aristocratic face deeply tanned from years in the tropics. Serious gray eyes brightened as they landed on Dominique.

"Good morning, sir. I'm Dominique Avallon. I believe Sergeant Williams phoned?"

Hampton's features at once settled into an expression of businesslike civility. He stood up and came from behind the massive oak desk to hold out a chair for Dominique. "Ah, yes, Miss Avallon," he greeted her in his upper-class British accent, "I hope you didn't have any trouble finding me."

Dominique sat down as she murmured, "None, thank you."

He was so unexpectedly young! He couldn't possibly be more than thirty-five. Dominique watched him return to his place and sit down. Despite his youth, he had a commanding presence. Dominique had the impression that he was one of those rare individuals who never raised their voices nor addressed others impolitely. Probably he never had to. His orders would be followed, whether or not he was in uniform.

Dominique continued to study Hampton as he read her paperwork, his brow furrowed in concentration. She was usually outgoing and would have tried to engage the officer in small talk, but there was about him a cool reserve that held her at arm's length. It was hard to imagine Group Captain Hampton ever being flirtatious, despite the split second of interest she had detected in his first glance.

"Your scores for typing and grammar are excellent," he said, not taking his eyes from the paper.

"Thank you," Dominique replied. She watched his face as he scanned the rest of her application. She could discern nothing from his expression.

Finally, he raised his eyes. Dominique saw them linger on the gold watch dangling from her wrist, then travel to the saucy Paris creation she wore on her head. He looked back down at her file.

"It says here that you speak Italian, French, English, and Arabic. I assume you read and write English fluently, since you graduated from the American College. Do you read and write Arabic and Italian as well?"

She shook her head. "Italian, yes, but only a little Arabic." Europeans living in Egypt were rarely fluent in Arabic. They attended mostly French schools, learned English or Italian as a second language, and used Arabic mainly with the household help.

"Hmmm." Hampton's reaction was noncommittal. With Hampton's eyes focused on the papers on his desk, Dominique was free to look around his office. It was large, of course, as befitted a group captain. On a credenza behind him were perhaps a dozen photographs. There was one of Hampton standing in front of an airplane.

He must be a war hero, Dominique speculated. That was why he had attained high rank at such a young age. She looked at the left pocket of his uniform. It bore many decorations, but she didn't know the meaning of most of them. Still, an unfamiliar feeling of awe crept over her.

She turned her attention back to the photographs. There was one of a woman and two children. The woman was young — a classic English beauty. Dominique looked at Hampton's ring finger. He wore no wedding band. But there were many married men who chose not to. Dominique went back to studying the photos. The largest was of Winston Churchill and it bore an inscription, but Dominique was too far away to read it. The rest of the photographs appeared to have been taken in England, perhaps at Hampton's home. It was a large Tudor-style estate in the country — smaller than the manor of the Avallons' cotton plantation outside Cairo, but impressive nonetheless. In one of the photographs, Hampton held the bridle of a horse. The two children from the first picture sat on the horse's back. There was a pond surrounded by irises in the background. In another photograph, a middle-aged couple sat on the terrace of the house.

Hampton looked up, then at the picture. "My parents," he said somberly. "They were killed in the war. Their home in London was destroyed by a German bomb." Despite his economy of speech, Dominique could sense in Hampton a profound sadness at their loss.

Her heart warmed with real sympathy. "I'm so sorry. It must have been a terrible blow to lose them both at once." She thought of her own father, dead when she was only nine. Dominique still missed him.

She blinked and shifted her gaze to another family photo. "Your wife and children?" she asked in a subdued voice. "They're lovely."

Hampton turned to face the credenza. He picked up the photo of the two children on horseback. "Lily and James," he said fondly, "eight and ten."

"You must miss them terribly."

He sighed. "I do. But they're away at school now. I usually manage to get leave when they're on holiday."

Dominique thought they seemed young to be at boarding school, but the English insisted on sending their children away at early ages. On the other hand, she wondered if her own childhood had been any better. True, she had remained at home with Solange, but Nanny had actually raised her. Solange had seemingly had a thousand more interesting things to do with her time. Dominique wondered if Hampton's wife was the same way. He hadn't mentioned her even once.

"Have your children been to Egypt yet?" Dominique asked. She didn't want to come right out and ask about his wife. Not a second time.

"Last year. They were fascinated, but quite put out that I couldn't spend more time with them. Unfortunately, our governments were in the midst of negotiating the Anglo-Egyptian Treaty." Egypt had been a British protectorate since the turn of the century, but the treaty provided for the gradual evacuation of British troops from the country. Egyptian president Gamal Abdel Nasser wanted the evacuation to be immediate rather than gradual; the British wanted a longer transition. However, both sides had agreed that the British would be granted permission to use their Ismailia base on the Suez Canal in times of war.

"Not *our* governments. I hold a French passport," Dominique reminded him.

"Yes, of course." Hampton looked back down at the last page of her file. "You've a strong French accent, but it appears that your English is quite perfect."

Dominique's eyes met his steadily. "I hope the accent is not a problem?"

Hampton looked disconcerted. "Certainly not! Charming, in fact," he said hastily.

She tilted her chin up and nodded approvingly, as though she couldn't possibly have conceived of a different answer. British and American men often commented on the allure of her accent, and she had dated her fair share of both nationalities.

Hampton cleared his throat and pointed at the papers in front of him. "I see your home is in Garden City. Lovely place. Why do you want to work here?"

Dominique dimpled mischievously, her irrepressible frankness rising to the surface even in a job interview. "To escape my mother!"

Hampton laughed at the unexpectedly honest answer, and Dominique laughed with him. He was handsome when he relaxed, she noted. And he seemed nice, despite the constraint of his demeanor. She liked him, she decided.

Hampton leaned forward in his seat and rested his elbows on his desk. For the first time, he concentrated his gaze on Dominique. "How does your mother feel about your working here?"

She met his eyes with a defiant expression. "She is not particularly pleased."

Hampton raised his eyebrows. He didn't need any trouble with the European community. The British already had their hands full with Egyptian unrest.

Dominique sensed his misgivings, but offered no further explanation. She knew she was well qualified for the job and was certain he would give her a chance. And, if he didn't, it wasn't a serious matter. She could always go back home, dreary though the prospect was.

Hampton looked back down at her application and studied it for a moment. "Avallon . . . Avallon . . . ," he murmured. Then his head snapped up, a light of recognition in his eyes. "Avallon — as in Avallon Cotton?" he asked.

"Yes, of course. I thought you knew." Dominique was a little surprised. Her surname was usually recognized at once by Europeans in Egypt.

Hampton, as flustered as his British self-possession would allow, automatically stood in a gesture of respect. "I'm so sorry. I didn't at once recognize . . ."

Dominique remained seated. She looked up at him, amused. "It doesn't matter. It has nothing to do with my qualifications for the job."

"Quite" — Hampton faltered, as though thrown off balance by her carefree attitude — "but surely you understand that it may be a bit awkward to have you as a subordinate."

Dominique's eyes danced. "And surely there are members of the British aristocracy who work under you."

Hampton smiled with her, then nodded in acknowledgment and sat down again. "You're an able debater, Miss Avallon, and you make a good point. On the other hand, *you* are a civilian, not a junior officer. I'm not sure it would work —" He cut himself short as he gave Dominique a speculative look.

Her smile disappeared and her expression became earnest. "I'd like the job and . . . I think I can help." Her eyes went involuntarily to the pile of papers in Hampton's "in" box.

Hampton grimaced at the overflowing stack. With a sigh, he turned back to Dominique. He looked thoughtfully at her, then once more at the piles on his desk. "Well . . . you're certainly capable of dealing with the backlog here. And there's no real reason not to at least try . . ." He clapped his hands palm down on the desk in a decisive gesture. "Let's give it a go, shall we?"

Dominique removed her white gloves and put them in her pocketbook. She removed her navy blue and white straw hat and looked questioningly at Hampton. "Where should I begin?"

The group captain looked at her with a startled expression. "Now? Don't you need to get settled or . . . fill out some forms? . . ."

Dominique laughed merrily. His confusion was endearing. "Please! I've spent all morning filling out forms. Besides" — she gestured at his desk — "you have enough work to last me at least a few minutes."

Hampton chuckled, then cut short the sound by clearing his throat. "Your desk is just outside. I believe you'll find supplies in it." He was all business now. He paused. "By the way, do you take dictation?"

"Not shorthand, but I can type as fast as you can speak."

"Hmmm . . . perhaps we can use that table for the typewriter." He gestured at a small table against the wall with an empty vase on it. "We'll put you in here for the morning. I'm sure you can understand that I don't fancy pacing up and down in the hall outside as I dictate to you. There's not much privacy there, I'm afraid." Secretaries along the corridor sat in built-in alcoves directly outside their superiors' offices. The alcoves, while providing some sound insulation, had no doors, so anyone in the hall could see into them.

"Of course," Dominique said in a tone as crisp as his. "I'll get the chair." She put down her hat and purse and stood.

Hampton sprang to his feet. "Here, let me help you."

⌒ ⌒ ⌒

Dominique picked up the ringing telephone on her desk. "Group Captain Hampton's office."

"*Bonjour, c'est moi.*" Paulette was whispering — she had a job in the typing pool, and her conversations could be overheard — but her excitement came through anyhow.

"Hello!" Dominique replied in French. "Ready to go to lunch?"

"Sure. But it'll just be me. Jean has another date with her captain."

"Good for her!" Dominique laughed.

"Anyhow, I'm not calling about lunch. I've found a wonderful way to celebrate the end of your first week working for the Royal Air Force."

"What's that?"

"How about a date for dinner and dancing tomorrow night at the French officers club?" Paulette giggled. The French officers club, which was in Ismailia, was far more popular than the British officers club, which was on the base, twenty minutes from town.

Dominique's eyes sparkled at the prospect. It would be the first date of her life that didn't have an eleven o'clock curfew. "Who are they?"

"Two very handsome British lieutenants." Paulette sighed. "I'm not sure which one I like best."

"They're not married?" Men far from home frequently lied about that, Dominique had discovered.

"They're only twenty-four and they're not wearing rings. But, of course, I didn't ask them!"

"Why not?"

"Dominique! Come on. It's just dinner and dancing. Anyhow, who cares? There aren't many British wives on the base, you know."

"So what?" Dominique shot back. "That doesn't mean the husbands should cheat."

"You're such a prude! Everyone here dates whomever they want and you're the only one I've *ever* heard object to it."

Dominique knew this was true. For as long as there had been European military in Egypt, there had been local liaisons. Those in charge cast a blind eye on the behavior of men far from home.

As though Paulette could read Dominique's thoughts, she said,

"You know, their situation here is tense. President Nasser is on the radio every day telling the Arabs to rise up and murder the foreign imperialists. They're being forced to give up everything they've worked for here over the past century. There are constant run-ins with the Egyptian police. Who can blame them for trying to find someone to make their time here a little easier? And a lot of it is innocent. They just want to look across the dinner table and see a pretty face. What's wrong with that?"

Dominique tried to see it from her friend's point of view. It was true that the base was cloaked in an air of taut expectancy. Tension crackled in the dispatches Dominique's boss received from the Home Office. Egypt's President Nasser alarmed London. He was trying to extend his power in the Middle East beyond his own country. He was meddling in the affairs of Jordan and the Sudan, areas traditionally in the British domain. Although the British had agreed the previous year to phase out their military presence in the Suez Canal, it was an agreement that left the British military uneasy. They were trying to maintain a fine balance between cooperation and capitulation, and the strain was apparent in the hostility of the Egyptians, the self-righteousness of the British.

"I understand about the stress as well as anyone," Dominique said softly, "but that has nothing to do with what's right for me. I don't want anyone else's husband."

"Well, then, I'll give you my friend's phone number and you can ask for his life story," Paulette retorted. "I'm not going to," she said with finality.

Dominique couldn't help but laugh at the conviction in Paulette's tone.

Paulette seemed to sense her weakening. "Come on, Dominique. Please! They're absolutely dreamy. And I'm almost positive they're not married."

Dominique was tempted. They were young, she reasoned, so they probably weren't married. And it *was* only dinner. "Well . . ." Dominique drew out her answer to tease Paulette. ". . . All right." Dominique smiled. In reality, she looked forward to the evening. Her first date as a free woman!

"Wonderful! They said they'd pick us up at the apartment at seven-thirty."

"You already told them they could? Without asking me?" Dominique's stern voice belied the happy little flutter inside her. "They'll think you're desperate."

"No. They're the ones who are desperate. Do you know how many men there are on this base for every woman?"

"No. But I'm sure you'll tell me. Only save it for lunch. I have to go."

◌◌ ◌◌ ◌◌

The sound of violins floated on the night air as Dominique and her three companions emerged from their car in front of the French officers club. Dominique's step quickened with pleasurable anticipation as she took the arm of Lieutenant Edward Wentworth-James. She was pleased with her blind date. In his uniform, he looked like an idealized version of a British officer: tall, blond, and blue-eyed. Paulette's date, Harry Spencer, could have been Wentworth-James' brother, so closely did they resemble each other; only Harry's hair was light brown rather than blond and he was slightly taller than his friend.

Wentworth-James smiled down at Dominique and led her through the marble-pillared lobby into a courtyard. As they waited at the entrance for the maître d', Dominique gazed in appreciation around the lush garden. The whole place twinkled. Votives flickered on each white-clothed table, scattering stars of light on the fine crystal and china. Date palms rustled in the breeze and cast dancing shadows on the colorfully painted tiles below. Dominique turned her head as a table of revelers nearest the entrance burst into laughter. They all looked so glamorous. The men in their uniforms, the women in their wide, rustling gowns of taffeta, tulle, and lace. Dominique felt giddy with the loveliness of the evening.

As Dominique and Paulette preceded their escorts through the courtyard, heads turned, for they made a striking pair. Paulette was a gamine brunette with twinkling blue eyes and a wide, resplendent smile. That was her face. Her figure was that of a ballerina, with a swanlike neck and long, slender limbs to match. She wasn't curvaceous, but her strapless blue gown with its wide petticoats made the most of what she had. Dominique wore pure white, setting off her golden skin and hair to advantage. Her gown was a Grecian-style one-shouldered chiffon that flowed behind her with every step. Her only jewelry, a coiled diamond snake with emerald eyes and a ruby tongue, which she wore on her upper arm.

Dominique tried to retain a look of practiced composure as they were led to a table near the edge of the parquet dance floor, but she had to restrain herself from humming along with the sixteen-piece orchestra playing "Stardust." Since her debut at eighteen, Dominique had been permitted to date, but there had always been Solange in the background, measuring each prospect as a potential husband, stationing Nanny by the door to ensure that the curfew was honored, insisting on the presence of at least one other couple so that her daughter should never be alone with her date. Now, for the first time, Dominique felt like a sophisticated woman instead of a sheltered girl. Grown up . . . finally!

As the foursome arrived at their table and were seated, Dominique gave Paulette a subtle nod of approval.

"Well, it was jolly of you ladies to join us," said Dominique's date, as he unfolded the white damask napkin and placed it on his lap. "Shall we order champagne to mark the occasion?" Edward asked with a wide smile.

The women agreed, and soon the group was conversing easily. When the champagne arrived, they clinked their glasses together in a toast to new friends, then set about studying their menus.

"I say, Dominique." Paulette's date, Harry, closed his menu and laid it on the table. "I understand you're secretary to Group Captain Hampton."

"Yes, I've been working for him for a week," Dominique replied, enthusiasm apparent in her tone.

Edward looked up from his menu with interest. "He's top flight. A hero in the war, you know. A fighter pilot," he said with admiration. "He set the record for downed Luftwaffe. Then went to the Pacific theater. I don't think the kamikaze had anything on him! That's why he's already a group captain — and only thirty-one years old!"

So he's even younger than he looks, Dominique mused.

"Nothing of the braggart about him, though, for all his decorations," Harry remarked.

"Too bad they've moved him from flying to policy," Edward said. "But I suppose he's needed for that, given the situation." His face turned grim.

Paulette ignored the sudden pall. She giggled. "Hampton's very good looking, don't you think, Dominique?"

A mask of indifference came down on Dominique's face. "I never really noticed."

Paulette rolled her eyes knowingly. "I'll bet," she said sardonically.

Dominique gave her a look of annoyance. "I told you I'm not interested in married men."

Edward threw back his head and laughed. "Well, you'd better watch yourself, because he may become interested in you."

Dominique's icy gaze stilled his laughter. "He has two children and a very attractive wife. I'm sure he's not interested in outside romances."

Edward rubbed his jaw in a classic gesture of skepticism. "That's not what I hear."

Paulette leaned forward conspiratorially. "Tell! Tell!"

Dominique sat back deliberately in her chair and crossed her arms.

"I wouldn't want to offend Dominique," Edward teased.

Paulette made a sound of protest. "She wants to hear, too! She's just too stuck-up to show it."

Edward leaned toward the table and, with a wicked grin, said, "I won't go on without Dominique's permission."

Dominique stared at the group. They looked back at her expectantly, tauntingly. She lifted one shoulder indifferently. "Don't let me stop your childish games."

Edward leaned even farther forward and lowered his voice to a whisper. "Well, they say that the boy — James, I think his name is — really isn't his. That his wife found herself a . . . diversion, shall we say, while he was in the Pacific."

"Why didn't he divorce her?" Paulette whispered, her face flushed with enjoyment.

"No one knows. Maybe because he didn't find out until the youngest was conceived."

"How does he know that one is his?" Paulette asked.

Edward replied with a shrug. "But he hasn't exactly been in mourning."

"What do you mean?" Paulette's breath grew shorter in anticipation.

Edward glanced at Dominique. She looked away pointedly and feigned a yawn. He grinned and continued, "He keeps company with a very dishy blonde. Lieutenant Amanda Smythe."

Dominique had to suppress a start of recognition. The woman

phoned Hampton every day, her manner always peremptory. Dominique had wondered why she was so unpleasant.

"Well, well, speak of the devil," said Harry. He raised one eyebrow as he fixed on a spot near the entrance.

Dominique turned to look. At the entrance of the courtyard stood Stephen Hampton, the epitome of masculine authority in his officer's dress uniform. Beside him was a tall, stunning blonde, also in dress uniform. Dominique felt a twist in her stomach and realized that she was angry. Well, of course, she told herself, I'm disappointed in him. I thought so highly of him. He seemed so reserved and proper. Now it turns out that he's just like all the other soldiers who cheat on their wives when they're away from home. And that nasty woman!

As if on cue, Amanda Smythe turned toward Hampton and possessively snaked her arm through his. She looked up at him with a coy smile and said something in his ear. He was rather more stiff in his manner, but nonetheless smiled down at her as he replied.

"Well, whatever Mrs. Hampton's up to in England," said Harry, with a lewd wink, "the group captain obviously believes that what's sauce for the goose . . ."

Dominique tore her eyes away from the couple with difficulty. "I still think it's wrong," she said with disgust in her voice.

Paulette shrugged. "Who knows what goes on in a marriage?"

"I believe we've hit a sore point," Harry drawled, looking at Dominique. "Perhaps we'd best change the subject. Why don't we order?" He raised his hand for the waiter.

After they had ordered, Edward invited Dominique to dance. Her good spirits returned as they joined the people streaming to the dance floor. She smiled up at her escort as he took her in his arms and moved into an accomplished fox-trot. "I love this song," Dominique sighed. "It's from an old Fred Astaire movie, isn't it?"

"*Swing Time*, I think." Edward turned her expertly, then led her into a few more intricate steps. "And you dance as well as Ginger Rogers!" he smiled with enthusiasm.

Dominique loved to dance, loved the caress of the gown as it swirled around her legs. She closed her eyes and gave in to the rhythm, her face aglow with enjoyment. The orchestra segued into a Latin tune. "Oh, my favorite! A rumba," Dominique said in delight.

Edward's face echoed her pleasure as Dominique's hips began to sway to the Latin beat. No English girl would have dared move *that* way. Dominique's dancing was entirely unselfconscious, yet mesmerizingly uninhibited. She was thoroughly involved in the song when she heard a familiar voice over her shoulder.

"Good evening, Miss Avallon, Lieutenant." Hampton stood next to them on the dance floor, the blond beauty at his side.

Edward Wentworth-James snapped to attention as Dominique turned to face Hampton. She was radiant from the dancing, her golden skin illuminated by a pink flush, her upswept hair in a halo of tendrils around her face. Hampton's gaze lit briefly on her bare shoulders, then quickly moved upward. Without taking his eyes off Dominique, he said, "At ease, Lieutenant." In her peripheral vision, Dominique saw Wentworth-James drop his arm, but her attention was focused on Hampton. Everyone's was — he had that effect, not only because of his rank, but because of an innate nobility, a way of carrying himself that would have distinguished him in any company.

Hampton turned to the blonde and said, "Lieutenant Amanda Smythe, Miss Avallon. You've spoken a number of times on the telephone, I believe."

The lieutenant gave Dominique a frosty smile. "Oh, yes, the one with the accent."

Dominique shifted her gaze to the woman, then smiled, too, but her expression was devilish. "Accent?" she said innocently. "I should say that you British are the ones with the accent."

Lieutenant Smythe's face froze. Edward coughed uncomfortably. Stephen Hampton chuckled, "Touché, Miss Avallon. We tend to forget that we're visitors here. And unwelcome ones at that."

"Unwelcome perhaps," Lieutenant Smythe said haughtily, "but nonetheless the only effective authority in a country of heathens."

Dominique was used to the British expressing such views and she had a ready answer. In an exquisitely polite tone, she said, "These heathens, Lieutenant, created one of the greatest civilizations known to man. And one of the richest. But, of course, you know that" — Dominique gave a sly smile — "since your people took all the treasures back to London and put them in the British Museum."

Lieutenant Smythe's face turned red. She pivoted toward Hampton, her profile to Dominique. "Are you going to allow her to insult us this way?" she demanded.

Hampton turned his hands up in a gesture of amused helplessness.

"I'm afraid I have no authority over a French civilian, my dear. Especially when she's the best secretary I ever had."

Lieutenant Smythe inhaled sharply at Hampton's response, then turned and glared at Dominique.

Dominique, her eyes flashing gold in the candlelight, regarded Smythe with an ironic stare. It was laughable that this woman thought the British military had any power over a member of the Avallon family.

Smythe's expression went from anger to uncertainty, finally settling into disdain. "I'd like to sit down now," she said imperiously to Hampton.

In a lilting voice, Dominique said, "It was a pleasure to meet you."

The other woman's eyes snapped. She turned and walked away stiff-backed.

Dominique looked at Hampton with a defiant expression. If he upbraided her, she would defend herself. She didn't have to put up with Amanda Smythe!

But instead of anger, Hampton wore a look of amusement. His eyes widened comically and he murmured, "I'm in hot water now."

Their gazes met and held, sharing the humor. Dominique's nostrils flared with suppressed laughter. Hampton's mouth twitched at the corners. "Well . . . ," he said. His eyes danced as they darted from Dominique to Edward, then back again. "I'll see you Monday, Miss Avallon."

Fizzy bubbles were cavorting in Dominique's head. It took everything she had to suppress a grin. All she trusted herself to say was, "Monday."

∽ ∽ ∽

Dominique arrived at the office before Hampton. She had discovered in her first week that if she didn't, she'd never complete all the work he generated in one day. And that was important to her. She wanted to prove that she could do well in her job, no matter how much Solange denigrated it.

As she went through the letters Hampton had left in her "in" box, she realized that she had already learned enough to draft replies to most. Two, however, required Hampton's review and she took them to his office.

As she walked in, she spotted a mug of coffee on the credenza, a leftover from Friday. Ugh! Cold coffee. Wrinkling her nose, she picked it up, then paused thoughtfully as she noticed the photo behind it: Winston Churchill. She had never had the opportunity to read the inscription. It said: "Stephen, I have always known you would bring honor to your country, as your father did before you. You are one of the brightest stars of the British Empire. We are proud."

So they actually knew each other, Dominique thought. Hampton had never mentioned it. She realized that he never mentioned any of his accomplishments. On the contrary, he was always quick to point out the good points in others and to praise his subordinates for their work. Even in front of Lieutenant Smythe, he had called her, Dominique, the best secretary he ever had. She smiled as she thought of the incident three nights before. She had seen a new, unexpectedly humorous, side of the group captain. It charmed her.

In fact, as Dominique reflected on her first week with Hampton, she realized they had worked together very companionably. He had shown no impatience at the inevitable mistakes she, as a newcomer, had made. He was a gentleman. Which brought her musings full circle. Why the poor choice of women in his life?

She picked up the photo of Hampton's wife and children. Serena Hampton had the same cool, blond beauty as Amanda Smythe. They were both undeniably striking. But surely Stephen wasn't so shallow as that!

Dominique started and looked up as she realized that, for the first time, she had thought of him by his first name. She should stop immediately, she chided herself, or it would one day slip out.

Her eyes returned to the photograph of Hampton's wife. What an awful woman to have cuckolded him while he was at war. And to present him with a child upon his return! Why had Hampton accepted such treatment? Of course, he, too, was wrong to commit adultery. But still, Dominique felt sorry for him. And perhaps there was a reason he could not divorce. Perhaps his wife refused to let him and he was too gentlemanly to accuse her of infidelity. That would be like him, Dominique thought. She couldn't imagine him doing anything vengeful or petty.

She moved to the picture of Hampton with his children. He was smiling broadly, his teeth gleaming white against his tan, his sun-streaked hair giving him the look of an outdoorsman. Had she really thought him overly somber only one week before? How could she have failed to notice how truly handsome he was? She had failed, she reminded herself, because his looks were overshadowed by the manner in which he carried himself. He was a leader, and that came through as his most prominent characteristic. It was a quality that commanded respect. It made Dominique proud to work for him.

She thought, once more, of his easy demeanor Friday evening. So unlike him. It seemed like a mood confined to that time and place — a momentary aberration, almost unreal. And what of her behavior? What had come over her? She'd been intoxicated with the evening, with her freedom. She had felt irresistible, witty, reckless. Now she felt embarrassed, as though she had been drunk and indiscreet.

Dominique sighed and replaced the photograph on the credenza. She'd drive herself crazy if she dwelled on the incident. Work was the best cure for introspection.

When Hampton arrived a half hour later, Dominique was at her desk.

"Good morning, Miss Avallon." He smiled down at her.

The sight of him flustered her. Not just because of Friday night. But because only a few moments before she had been speculating on the most private aspects of his life.

She stopped typing just long enough to hand him a pile of yellow slips. "You have several messages," she said, then quickly resumed typing. Had she put his photos back in their correct places?

"Thank you," said Hampton. He perched on the corner of Dominique's desk and read through his messages. "Have a nice time Friday night?" he asked as he studied the papers in his hand.

Dominique stopped typing and looked up. She'd been dreading this. In the unmerciful light of Monday morning the delicious verbal sparring of Friday night seemed like insolence. After all, Lieutenant Smythe *was* her boss' friend. And though Dominique owed her no particular sign of respect, she owed Hampton at least the respect he had always shown her.

Hampton's eyes flickered toward Dominique, then back to his messages. She barely caught a glimpse of his expression. Amusement? Curiosity? Or was it annoyance?

She answered warily, "I had a very nice time, thank you."

Hampton arranged his message slips in a neat pile, then put them in his briefcase. He latched it and stood up. Now he focused his entire attention on Dominique. "You're quite a dancer," he said dryly.

Dominique's cheeks burned. Her hands slid off the keys of her typewriter and dropped helplessly to her lap. "Thank you, sir," she responded automatically. Why did he stand there looking at her? Why didn't he go into his office?

Hampton tilted his head to one side, as though puzzled. "You seem awfully subdued this morning, Miss Avallon. I must say it's quite a change from your mood Friday night."

Here it was. Dominique braced herself for his rebuke. But, after all, Smythe had provoked her — had deserved Dominique's retort. Still, perhaps a small apology was in order. Dominique hadn't been wrong, but her manner could have been less challenging. Keeping her eyes down, she said, "I hope I wasn't too . . ." She didn't know how to finish.

"Provocative?" Hampton completed the phrase for her. He let it sit there for a moment. "Well, I can't deny that you provoked Lieutenant Smythe, but, as for me" — his eyes were merry — "I enjoy a provocative exchange."

For the first time since Hampton's arrival, Dominique looked directly at him. As on Friday, he revealed a manner so uncharacteristically approachable that it perplexed her at the same time that it fascinated her. His mask of aloofness was slipping, and it was intriguing to peer behind it. It gave Dominique a small thrill, as though they were sharing a secret. Tentatively, she smiled.

In return, he flashed the same brilliant smile he wore in the photo on his desk.

Dominique caught her breath. Was he was flirting with her? Impossible. Their working relationship was too proper for that. She'd make a fool of herself if she got carried away by the mood of the moment. She gave him a questioning look.

Hampton let out a soft exhalation of laughter and, without another word, turned and went into his office.

A few minutes later, Dominique heard him whistling cheerfully. The tune was the rumba from Friday night.

⟲ ⟲ ⟲

It was three weeks later, a fine morning in September, that Dominique saw the headline that was to change her world.

Nothing about the morning presaged trouble. The sun was already high in the cloudless blue sky as Dominique waited at the bus stop for the shuttle to the base. Vendors with pushcarts passed by chanting their wares: ripe, juicy fruit, hashish, and fresh-baked bread, warm and aromatic from the oven. The street, by no means as crowded as Cairo, nevertheless stirred with a lively sprinkling of people, for many businesses opened from eight to two, then closed until five o'clock or, sometimes, until the following morning.

With a sense of contentment, Dominique inhaled deeply of the morning breeze. It was still fresh from the dramatic drop in temperature that was a nightly occurrence in the desert. Her buttercup-yellow dress fluttered around her legs and she had to keep her hand atop her matching hat lest it be carried away by a gust of wind.

Everything appeared peaceful and calm. Not until Dominique reached her desk and picked up the British military newspaper did she see the headline: "Nasser Snaps Fingers at West, Buys Arms from Soviet Bloc." A chill snaked up Dominique's spine as she stared at the red print bannered across the front page. Egypt's president, whose request to purchase arms from the United States had been stalled for months, had instead turned to the Soviets for help. The article went on to say that the British had exerted tremendous pressure on the United States to refuse Nasser's request, claiming that his threat to seek arms elsewhere was a bluff. A letter from Winston Churchill to U.S. president Eisenhower had been leaked to the press and reprinted worldwide. "You can't give them arms with which to kill British soldiers who fought shoulder to shoulder with you in the war," Churchill had written.

Dominique's mouth went dry as she imagined the consequences of Nasser's defiant reaction. But she didn't have to imagine, for they were spelled out in the article. First was the unadulterated joy of the entire Arab world, which had come to hate the French and British powers that controlled it. Second was the immediate hostile reaction of the two European powers. Officials from Britain's cabinet universally condemned the move and issued thinly veiled threats. The French foreign minister portended "possibly disastrous consequences."

As Dominique turned the page, she was greeted by a photograph that took her breath away. It showed a crowd of Arabs — tens of thousands of them — crammed into the streets surrounding the Council of Ministers building, in which Nasser had an office. They carried signs proclaiming him their savior. But what drew Dominique's eye were the burning effigies as tall as ten men — three of them, dressed in the flags of France, Britain, and the United States. A close-up photo showed the gleam of ferocious, lusty pleasure in the eyes of those nearest to the burning symbols.

Dominique dropped the newspaper and cradled her forehead in her hands. Seconds later, she heard Stephen Hampton's voice coming through the closed door of his office. She looked over her shoulder in surprise. He was never there before her. With a worried glance at his door, she removed her gloves and hat and deposited her purse in her desk drawer. Then she approached his office, ready to knock. But as she lifted her hand, the sound of other raised voices stopped her. She heard the phrase, "untenable situation."

"The Communists won't let this —" There was a loud report, as though someone had slammed his palm down on a table. Dominique jumped, then backed to her desk. Her stomach twisted with apprehension. What would happen now? She stood frozen as she considered the possibilities.

Then the door swung open. Voices floated out. She saw two officers emerge, one in the uniform of an army major, one bearing the same rank as Hampton. She hastily sat down at her desk and busied herself with the morning mail. One of the officers turned to address a parting remark to those still inside. Dominique gave him a sidelong glance, longing to know more about what she had read.

"Then it's agreed. We won't react until we've consulted —" The second officer cleared his throat and shifted his eyes in Dominique's direction. She quickly returned to shuffling the envelopes on her desk.

The two officers stepped back inside Hampton's office and closed the door, then re-exited seconds later, this time accompanied by two more men. Dominique didn't look up to bid them good-bye. As soon as their footsteps faded down the hall, she stood and went into Stephen's office. He looked up in surprise as she closed the door behind her.

Her brow was crinkled with worry. "I know there are things you aren't supposed to tell me," she blurted out, "but I have to know. Are the British going to act against Nasser? Is there going to be another Black Saturday?"

Neither she nor any other European would ever forget the last nightmarish battle between the British military and the Egyptians.

Black Saturday had occurred just before the revolution of 1952, but for the British and other foreigners living in Egypt, Black Saturday had been far more of an upheaval than the revolution that had followed. The ouster of King Farouk had, after all, been a peaceful coup led by Nasser and other young military officers. But Black Saturday had been a brutal scene of pillaging and murder, a crazed mob engaging in a bacchanalian feast of blood, revenge, and abandon.

Dominique felt a wave of nausea grip her as she thought of that day on January 26, 1952. It had started with a clash between the British and the Egyptians over access to the Canal Zone. Many Egyptians had been killed, which had driven activists in Cairo into a frenzy of rage. Foreign businesses had been looted and wrecked. Nightclubs, hotels, and bars frequented by foreigners had been burned to the ground. Most horrible of all had been the savage massacre of nine British civilians at Cairo's Turf Club. Four of them were disemboweled, one trampled to death.

Dominique shuddered as she thought, for the hundredth time, how easily she could have been one of the murdered. She had frequented so many of the places that had been torched, as had all her European friends. It was the good luck of the Avallons that the wedding of a relative in Paris had caused the family to be out of the country.

Now she wondered if another such horror was imminent. Ismailia, despite the presence of the British base, seemed so much more peaceful than Cairo that Dominique had managed to forget about the anti-European demonstrations that frequently disrupted the Egyptian capital. She took a step toward Hampton. "My mother," she whispered. "You know she lives in Cairo. Near the European embassies. If the demonstrations turn into riots again . . ." Her lips were stiff; she couldn't make herself go on.

Stephen stared at Dominique. His expression was sympathetic, but he remained silent, as though trying to formulate a response. Finally the answer came. Simple and, Dominique believed, truthful. "I don't know what will happen."

Dominique paled. She had wanted reassurance. With Hampton's air of quiet authority, she would have believed him had he told her that everything would be fine. Instead, his answer frightened her.

Stephen got up and came around his desk to stand in front of Dominique. He leaned close and said softly, "If Nasser does nothing further, we won't provoke him. But there are other factors in the equation. The Israelis are just across the Canal and that's eating away at him." Hampton paused and straightened. He looked Dominique in the eye. "The situation is dicey."

Dominique regarded him with an expression of profound concern. A hundred questions plagued her, but Hampton's veil of reserve warned that he had divulged as much as he could. She stared into his eyes, trying to read the subtext behind them.

His voice, more reassuring now, soothed her. "It's not time for alarm yet," he said. "I'll let you know when it is."

Dominique regarded him gravely. There was no question in her mind that he would keep his word. She gave him a decisive nod. "All right." For a moment, they stared at each other, then Dominique turned to go.

Stephen's voice stopped her. "You could leave now, you know."

Dominique turned back and gave him a questioning look.

He took a step toward her and continued. "You're under no obligation to stay, and I would certainly understand."

Hampton stood so close that Dominique could feel his breath on her hair. And standing so close to him, she felt safe. She had the idea, irrational she knew, that she would always be safe in his presence. She met his gaze steadily and said, "No. You said the situation was dicey. You didn't say I ought to go. Besides, I'll learn more if I stay here than if I quit and return to Cairo."

Stephen's face registered admiration, then relief, at her decision. "I'll have to count on you more than ever now."

Even in her alarm, Dominique found it hard to suppress a thrill of pride. That a man like Stephen Hampton should trust her and rely on her was immensely gratifying. And there was more — a feeling of alliance and shared confidence. "I'll do my best," she promised.

Hampton lightly touched her arm as he might have a junior officer whom he was trying to reassure. Despite the innocence of the gesture, a hot jolt went through Dominique. Her stress at the morning's events had turned her into a jumble of nerves. She had a sudden, crazy urge to bury her face against his chest and receive the warm comfort of his arms around her.

"Try not to worry too much." His voice was soft, almost tender.

Dominique squared her shoulders. Somehow, Hampton's faith in her made her feel brave — almost as brave as he thought her. "I won't worry," she assured him in a calm, clear voice.

But that night, Dominique could barely sleep. She jumped at every sound from the street below. Earlier in the day, she had worried about a military clash between Egypt and Britain. But now she began to consider what could happen to individuals who displeased the Egyptian government. The police could swoop down in the night with trumped-up charges and drag a person to jail. There would be a trial, but everyone would know the outcome in advance. Guilty. Always guilty. It had happened to the father of one of her school friends. And to one of the professors at the American College. The professor had finally been released after two years. Dominique had been aghast at his appearance when she had encountered him in the park one day. His black hair had turned white and his posture had become stooped and crooked. Torture and privation had transformed him from a vital intellectual into a feeble old man.

Dominique wondered if such a thing could ever happen to her or Solange. She tried to push the thought from her brain. Of course it couldn't! They weren't involved in politics. And her mother socialized with many in high office. The deputy minister of Egypt visited Solange almost every day. Nothing could possibly happen to them!

ᴇᴏ ᴇᴏ ᴇᴏ

Stephen stood up from his desk and yawned. "You must be exhausted," he said to Dominique, who sat at the small typing table on the other side of the room.

She looked up from her proofreading and gave him a philosophical smile. Since the crisis had erupted five days before, they'd worked progressively later, and at an unforgiving pace. But until tonight they'd adjourned by eight — plenty of time for Dominique to go home and change for dinner. Most evenings, she dined in restaurants, as there were always men anxious for her company. But tonight Dominique had broken her date, uncertain of when she'd finish work.

She shifted in her seat. How many hours had she been in the same position? She longed to freshen up, but didn't want to take the time. Her hair, which had started the day in a decorous chignon, now tumbled on her shoulders. Her lipstick was gone, revealing the natural rosiness underneath. And her skin, unpowdered since morning, wore a faint glow. Her sophisticated veneer had given way to her own natural beauty. But if someone had told Dominique how lovely she looked, she would not have believed it. She felt weary and tense. A long, hot shower would have been bliss.

Stephen looked at his watch. "It's past eight-thirty. If we don't get something from the mess now, we'll miss dinner entirely."

Dominique stood up and discreetly rotated her ankles. "Tell me what you'd like. I'll bring up a tray."

Hampton grimaced. "Anything except one of their beastly stews."

Dominique laughed. "English cooking . . ." She shook her head.

Stephen's gaze lingered for a moment on her dimples, then on her tumble of auburn waves. He averted his eyes and, in a deliberately casual voice, said, "Horrid stuff, English cooking. I'm afraid Egypt has spoiled me." He shrugged in a good-natured way and strolled over to the map on the wall, keeping his eyes focused on it.

"And what about the weather?" Dominique teased. "Won't you miss the sun when you go back to England?"

"Don't remind me!" Hampton groaned. He put his hands on the small of his back and stretched.

Dominique followed the movement with her eyes — the pull of fine linen across his broad chest, the glimmer of bleached down on his muscled forearms. With his tie loose and his sleeves rolled up, his maleness suddenly seemed overwhelming.

Dominique dragged her eyes away from him and bent to pick up her handbag. "I'll be back in a few minutes," she murmured.

When Dominique returned with the tray, Stephen was back at his desk going over the report. She placed a roast beef sandwich and a small pot of tea in front of him and, before he could thank her, took her own plate to her desk in the hall. They'd never before eaten together and the etiquette of the moment felt awkward to Dominique. She ate hurriedly, then went to the washroom to pin up her hair and brush her teeth. By the time she returned to Hampton's office, he was finished eating.

When he saw Dominique, he stood up. "I'd like you to compile some data from the files in this drawer," he said, pointing to the right side of his desk. "You sit here so you won't have to keep going back and forth. I'll work at your desk."

Dominique's face lit eagerly. It was the first time he had allowed her access to those files and she was pleased at the new sign of trust.

He smiled at her expression. "You've done excellent work," he said. He stepped aside and made room for her. Gingerly, she sat in his chair.

She could feel his body heat in the soft leather that enfolded her. It was a troubling sensation.

ᕲ ᕲ ᕲ

The next night, they worked to unify the data they had independently gathered. Stephen, at his desk, began a first draft of the report. Dominique sat at the small table in his office and edited. He accepted all her revisions and commented on their excellence. "Your English tutor certainly did his job well," he remarked appreciatively.

"And you doubted me!" she reminded him of their first interview. "You see? My accent doesn't mean I have poor grammar."

Hampton gave her a crooked grin. "I never said I didn't like it. No red-blooded male can resist a French accent!"

Dominique laughed gaily. His comment made her feel feminine and pretty, aware of the power of her charm. For a moment, she forgot he was the group captain. His gaze was that of an appreciative male and she responded to it. Then she caught herself. She lowered her lids to hide the coquettish light in her eyes. "I'd better get back to this report," she said amidst their fading laughter.

A few minutes later, Dominique looked up from her work to find Hampton staring at her. She blushed and saw it reflected in the pink that flooded Hampton's cheeks as he quickly looked away. Could he be attracted to her, Dominique wondered? A shaky excitement made her pulse hammer. She stole another glance at him, but he was bent over his desk in an attitude of concentration. She had better concentrate, too, she chided herself. She picked up her pencil and went back to the report.

As on the previous evening, Hampton sent Dominique to bring back dinner. This time, they gobbled their food as he paced up and down in his office and dictated a section of the report. The next two evenings followed the same pattern. Dominique brought up sandwiches from the mess and they ate as they worked. Until Friday evening, when the contents of Stephen's sandwich dropped onto the Oriental rug.

His brows came together in an expression of annoyance, but Dominique couldn't suppress her laughter at the sight of Hampton holding two pieces of bread, while the roast beef, cheese, and tomatoes lay in a tight little pile on the floor.

Hampton looked at Dominique and his frown turned into a grin. She could see the tension ease from his face. Nevertheless, he declared emphatically, "This is uncivilized and, I'm sure, not at all what you're used to, especially on a Friday evening. Surely, we can afford half an hour to eat in a proper fashion. Let's go down to the officers' mess. I'd enjoy a chance to — Oh" — he stopped in confusion — "you've finished your sandwich." Stephen's face fell.

Dominique, flustered, looked at her empty plate, then back at Stephen. Disappointment washed over her. He had said, "I'd enjoy a chance to . . ." To *what?* Dominique wondered. To get to know her better? To have a break from work? She wished he'd finished his sentence. She wished she hadn't already eaten her sandwich. She thought of saying that she was still hungry, then realized that she would look overeager. She could offer to have dessert while he ate, she thought. But a piece of chocolate cake was stationed accusingly at her elbow.

"Well," she teased gently, "*I* haven't been doing the talking."

Hampton smiled. His cheeks carried a trace of five o'clock shadow and his tailored uniform showed a few wrinkles, but that only made him look more virile. "Next time, then," he said.

When? Dominique wanted to insist. The offhanded phrase tantalized her. She wished the report weren't almost finished. There might never be a "next time."

Now Stephen was pacing up and down again, clearly ready to resume dictating. Oh, she was a fool! He'd meant nothing, absolutely nothing, by the comment. She was his secretary. He was her employer. That was all, she told herself firmly. Besides, Stephen Hampton was not the man for her. He was married. He had a mistress. And yet . . . he was fascinating. Dominique was intrigued by the mysteries behind his discreet facade.

On the following Monday, Dominique's routine returned to normal. She left the office each evening at four-thirty, went home to change for dinner, then danced till midnight. Like the people around her, Dominique attacked her social life with the sort of frenetic hedonism born of tension. Restaurants and clubs were full every night with lavishly gowned women and free-spending men. Parties were frequent, with a seemingly endless supply of liquor and delicacies served by white-jacketed waiters. The atmosphere was one of a perpetual New Year's Eve.

The British had promised to withdraw from the Canal Zone, their last base in Egypt, by June 1956, and there was a sense of an era ending, of chances slipping away, of good-byes and tears amidst the frivolity.

Then, one evening in mid-October, as Dominique was preparing to go, Stephen approached her desk and announced in a tight voice, "Field Marshal Waterhouse is coming from London the day after tomorrow. There's concern that these Israeli-Egyptian skirmishes are going to blow up — maybe even close the Canal. I need to prepare another big report and I'd like your help."

The gravity of his voice made Dominique's pulse quicken, but so did the prospect of working late with him. "Of course," she said. She looked at her watch. "I just need to make a phone call."

Hampton was apologetic. "I hope I haven't ruined your evening. We should be no later than seven-thirty or eight. Most of the information I've already sent off in dispatches to London. It's just a question of summarizing it in a risk assessment."

Dominique's brow furrowed with concern. "There must be considerable risk if the field marshal is coming here on such short notice."

"I don't think anything will happen until the Israeli elections in November, but we have to be prepared."

Dominique paled. "For war?"

Hampton was silent. His eyes met Dominique's — sympathetic, anxious, and . . . something more. He took a deep breath. "I don't think it's reached that point. We'll probably just see more of the same for a while. Border raids and the like. That's what I intend to say in my report." His voice dropped. It came out raspy and tender, like a lover in the dark. "I haven't forgotten my promise to you. I'll let you know if I think something's going to happen. I wouldn't let anything —" He stopped short. His eyes locked with Dominique's. "I wouldn't allow your family to fall into jeopardy," he concluded formally.

Dominique held her breath as she focused implacably on his face. After a moment she said softly, "I know." Her trust in him was total, she realized.

An odd light came over Stephen's face. Dominique could see he was touched by her faith in him. She followed him with her eyes as he went back to his office.

It was a little more than an hour later that she heard the sharp sound of high heels marching down the hall. Lieutenant Amanda Smythe brushed past Dominique without a word and entered Hampton's office. She slammed the door so hard behind her that Dominique was afraid the glass panel would shatter.

The woman's voice, shrill and angry, rang out. "We've been planning this for weeks! You can't cancel now!"

Dominique couldn't hear Hampton's response — didn't want to hear anything at all. She got up and went to the ladies' room. When she returned, she saw that the door to Hampton's office was still closed. She averted her eyes as she saw the blurry figure of Amanda Smythe pass behind the door. Dominique started to type, trying to ignore the drama going on just a few feet away. It was almost ten minutes more before the door opened again.

"Fine." The lieutenant's high-pitched voice still registered displeasure, but the fury was gone. "I'm not at all happy about this, Stephen, but I'll see you at eight-thirty. Don't be late."

Dominique kept her head down as the lieutenant passed. But she still felt her glare.

Seconds later, Hampton emerged from his office. Dominique continued to type, not wanting to meet his eyes. She was embarrassed for him — embarrassed to have witnessed such a private scene.

As if reading her mind, Hampton addressed the matter directly. "Can you stop typing for a moment, Miss Avallon?" His voice was subdued.

Dominique stopped and looked up at him. She focused on a place somewhere over his left shoulder. This was mortifying. She hated the woman for humiliating Stephen. He was so dignified and reserved. Such public ugliness must be unbearable for him.

Hampton looked down at his feet, then at his secretary. "I'm sorry you had to hear that."

She couldn't meet his gaze. She replied hastily, "I really didn't. I was down the hall most of —" She paused when she saw the understanding smile on his face.

Hampton said gently, "That's a generous lie, Miss Avallon." He was silent for a moment as he studied her face, his eyes soft. Then he nodded, almost imperceptibly. "You are a true lady," he said.

Her heart ached at the open simplicity of his declaration — at all that it implied. She wanted to cry, "Why do you put up with her? You deserve so much better!" It was almost a physical labor to suppress the words.

Dominique's eyes locked with Stephen's. She swallowed, and the sound filled her ears. She sat motionless, unable to speak.

Stephen held her gaze, wouldn't release it. His eyes were bright silvery gray, like clouds after a storm. Dominique's nerves tingled with the impact of his regard. When he spoke, she was almost startled by the sound. "Miss Avallon, I'm sure I've disrupted your plans this evening. When we finish, would you permit me to drive you home so you don't have to wait for the shuttle?"

Heat rose in Dominique, starting in a place near her stomach and filling her chest, then her head. It took great effort to answer calmly, "Yes, sir, I would."

When Dominique and Stephen emerged from the office at seven-thirty, the sky was dusky blue. Dominique lifted her face to the fresh air, glad to be liberated from the stuffy office. Directly in front of the entrance sat Hampton's military car. His driver held open the door to the back seat. Dominique started to enter, but Stephen caught her by the elbow. She turned and looked at him questioningly.

He smiled. "It's such a fine night. I'd like to take my own car if you don't mind." He pointed to a sporty red Jaguar roadster parked some yards away. The top was down and Dominique could see the sparkling tan leather interior.

She grinned back at him. "That would be wonderful."

Hampton dismissed his driver and led Dominique to the convertible. He held the door open for her as she got in, then went around to the other side. He turned his head to look at her. "You should take off your hat, or it may blow away."

"Oh . . . I hadn't thought of that." Dominique reached up and removed the tiny round cap pinned to her curls.

"I think there's a scarf in the glove box if you'd like to cover your hair," said Stephen.

"No, thank you," she said, too quickly. Dominique suspected that it was Lieutenant Smythe's. She didn't like to think about that.

"Right, then. We're off," Stephen said briskly. The engine growled to life, then settled into a contented purr. Dominique watched Stephen's hands as he put the car in reverse, then shifted into first. They were strong-looking, but long and elegant.

As they started to drive, the wind mussed Stephen's hair. It made him look younger, Dominique thought, as she covertly studied his face. She felt the sudden urge to run her finger down the smooth line of his aristocratic profile, as a blind person might to discover the features of a loved one. She quickly averted her eyes and looked straight ahead.

The car slowed at the base checkpoint and Dominique spoke. "I live nearby." She gave him rapid directions. "You'll be back by eight-thirty."

Stephen gave her a puzzled look.

Dominique reminded him, "For your appointment with Lieutenant Smythe." She tried to keep her tone neutral.

"Oh, yes," Stephen said indifferently.

They drove the rest of the way in silence. Dominique was excruciatingly aware of Stephen's body. Each time he moved his legs to depress the clutch or step on the gas, she could see the muscles of his thighs through the thin, tropical-weight wool of his slacks. His left hand on the stick shift was so very near that her pleated pink skirt, buffeted by the wind, once blew over it. She hastily pulled back the material and secured it under her right knee.

Dominique wished she could think of something witty or intelligent to say, but she was tongue-tied. Nor did Hampton look at her or speak. He seemed deep in thought. Occasionally he whistled a few bars of a tune, then abruptly stopped. Dominique remembered the day in the office when he had whistled the tune of the rumba from the officers club.

Before she realized it, they had arrived at her apartment. Hampton eased the car to the curb and stopped. He took one hand off the steering wheel and turned the upper half of his body to face Dominique. For a moment, he contemplated her.

Dominique held her breath, wondering what would come next.

Finally, Hampton said, "Thank you so much . . . for your help."

Dominique was overcome with disappointment. But what had she expected? she asked herself. She knew he had a date at eight-thirty. And even if he didn't, *what had she expected?*

She realized, with a start, that she hadn't answered him. She was simply staring into his eyes. Hastily, she looked away. "I didn't mind helping," she said. She gathered her purse and hat. He didn't move from his place. Did he intend to open her door or did he have something more to say? With her right hand, she reached across her left shoulder and unlocked the door.

Stephen looked startled by the action. "Oh, excuse me. . . ." He hastily got out of the car, then came around to her side and held the door open. He politely extended his hand to assist her.

Dominique reached for his hand. Even before they touched, she felt the vibration, like an electric current. It sizzled through her. It was impossible that he did not feel it, too. She stood and found herself just inches away from him — almost in his arms. His scent teased her. A mixture of sandalwood cologne, leather, and soap.

Suddenly, two images flashed in quick succession in her mind, like slides on a projector screen. She saw Stephen's wife, then Lieutenant Smythe. Both tall, blond, cool beauties. She compared them with herself: diminutive and unquestionably Gallic. Her heart sank. He wouldn't be interested in her. She wasn't his type at all.

She spoke automatically — words she didn't even hear. "Thank you for the ride." With a halfhearted smile, she turned and started to move away.

Then she heard his voice. Not loud at all. "Dominique. . . ." Like a caress. "Wait, please."

She spun around to face him, her eyes alight. "Yes?"

He stepped toward her. "Would you" — he paused, as if debating whether to go on. "Would you have dinner with me this evening?"

Dominique's pulse thudded in her ears. "Yes," she answered. She didn't even think about fetching a wrap from her apartment. She was afraid he would change his mind in the interim. She just got back into the car. She wondered, only briefly, what he would do about Lieutenant Smythe.

ɢ∿ ɢ∿ ɢ∿

They went to the Majestic, a convivial downtown brasserie. As they entered the etched glass doors, they were hit with a wave of sound. The restaurant was crowded with French and British military, and the roar of conversation echoed off the wood floor and high ceiling. Tables were closely packed, but there were dark red velvet booths separated from each other by panels of etched glass.

As soon as they were seated in one of the semicircular banquettes, Stephen ordered a bottle of light, dry Sancerre for them to sip. Then he excused himself. Dominique guessed he was telephoning Lieutenant Smythe.

When he returned, he slid into the booth, leaving a discreet amount of space between them. He looked at Dominique and smiled conspiratorially, his eyes silver in the light from the brass chandeliers overhead. He wore a look of exhilaration that made Dominique's pulse race. What had he told Lieutenant Smythe?

Dominique didn't have time to dwell on it, because Stephen turned the conversation to her. "There's something I've been wanting to ask you from the first time we met," he said, still smiling.

The room was so noisy that Dominique had to ask him to repeat himself. Stephen edged closer and spoke more loudly. "You said you came here to escape your mother?"

He remembered? A thrilling sort of tension made Dominique's heart pound faster. She leaned forward and raised her voice over the din. "Mostly that. Yes."

Stephen cupped his ear and edged closer until they were side by side. "Surely, she didn't finance such a move for you?" he said, now able to speak in a normal tone.

Dominique took a sip of wine to calm herself. She was reeling at the fact that she was actually having dinner with Stephen. She could feel the warmth of his leg, though it was not quite touching hers. It made it difficult to focus on their conversation. The last subject she'd expected Stephen to bring up was her mother. "No, you can be sure Mother's not helping me," she said with a crooked smile. "I've saved some money from birthdays and the like. And, luckily, I found a job immediately."

"Your air force salary can't possibly afford you the lifestyle you're used to."

Dominique shrugged. "I take the shuttle to work. I share my apartment with two other girls. And ..." She was going to say that she dined out most nights, courtesy of the British Air Force. Then she thought better of it. She continued on another tack. "And I have enough clothes to last me a long while. Anyhow, I told my mother I'd quit my job next spring when it was time for us to go to France."

Stephen looked startled. "That's disappointing!" His features settled into a scowl.

"But you — the British, I mean — are pulling out of the Canal next year, aren't you?" Dominique looked down, then reached for her glass and twirled it absentmindedly on the tablecloth. Talking about the future with Stephen disturbed her because she knew that after next year, she'd never see him again.

But Stephen's next words lifted her spirits. "As you know, there's some discussion about how quickly and completely we'll pull out. Nasser, of course, wants us all gone by March. We'd like to keep a small force here for several more years." He sighed. "We're negotiating."

They were interrupted by the arrival of the waiter with their appetizers, escargots in garlic butter. When he left, it was Stephen who spoke first. "I've been wanting to do this for some time." He gave her a sidelong look.

Dominique stammered, "I . . . you never . . ."

Stephen shrugged and stabbed an escargot with his fork. "I didn't want to spoil a good working relationship." He put his fork down and looked squarely at Dominique. "But I was afraid — with things as they are now — that if I didn't take the opportunity, I might lose it altogether."

Dominique stopped with her fork halfway to her mouth. "I don't understand. I thought you said there was no cause for alarm yet." She heard the sound of metal on china before she realized she had dropped her hand to the table.

Stephen's smile faded. "That doesn't mean that my stay here is indefinite. We may not get what we want from President Nasser. Things are changing every day. I don't know how much longer I'll be stationed here."

Dominique's stomach flip-flopped. Her fingers released their hold on her fork. It slid from her hand and lay askew on the edge of her plate. "I would think you would be one of the last to go," she said in a constricted voice.

Stephen's jaw tightened. His expression was tense. "I'll probably be one of the last sent back to England, but there's trouble all over the Middle East. I may be assigned elsewhere in the region."

Dominique looked down at her plate, trying to hide her dismay. Suddenly the sight of the snails swimming in garlic butter made her feel ill. She pushed the dish away and took a sip of wine, trying to cover her distress. She was so happy working with Stephen. Why did things have to change?

"In any event," Stephen continued, "we've worked together for almost two months and . . . how shall I say this?"

Dominique held her breath and lifted her gaze to his. Stephen's expression relaxed — his eyes flamed with warmth. He drew closer and said, "I wanted to know you better." He paused. "You are . . . unique." Very briefly, he brushed her hand with his index finger, then withdrew. "When I first saw you, I thought, 'This won't do at all.'" He gave her a mischievous smile. "I was certain your looks would be a distraction."

Dominique regarded him skeptically. For the second time that evening, she mentally compared herself with the two blondes in his life.

Stephen gave her a questioning glance. "You don't seem convinced."

Dominique said nothing. Solange had indoctrinated her with the notion that she was less than attractive, but Dominique had learned enough about the allure of confidence to hide her insecurity. She didn't fish for compliments to bolster her ego, because she felt it betrayed weakness. Instead, she met Stephen's eyes with a challenging look. "Then why did you hire me?"

"Don't you remember the state of my desk?"

They both laughed at the picture his words conjured.

Then he continued. "When I saw your application, I knew you were smart. But I expected you to be frivolous and . . . well, like any other debutante. I didn't expect to be able to trust you. I didn't expect you to be so conscientious or capable or —"

With a flash of irritation, Dominique protested, "I haven't been pampered, if that's what you mean."

Stephen grinned. "Come now!"

Dominique's face softened. "My father pampered me, if you want to use that word. . . ." Then her features grew hard and she said in a flat tone, "But my mother never did. I may have everything in the material sense, but . . . we're constantly at odds."

Stephen gave her an understanding look. "You'll get over that."

Dominique looked skeptical. She sighed. "I don't know. . . ." She loved her mother, but she wondered if it was possible that she and Solange would ever truly *like* each other. Then she shrugged. It was better not to dwell on the subject. It always upset her.

She searched her mind for a new topic. "Tell me about your children," she said.

Stephen smiled broadly, his eyes crinkling at the corners. "Why, they're perfect, of course."

"Just like their father," Dominique joked.

Stephen's smile faded. "I miss them," he confessed. "I feel guilty that we spend so little time together."

Stephen paused as the waiter cleared their appetizers and brought out their main course, roast pigeon. He opened a bottle of Bordeaux, which Stephen tasted and approved, then left the couple alone.

Dominique picked up her fork and cut into the succulent meat. "There's something I have to ask you," she said in a troubled voice.

Stephen's expression turned grave, a reflection of her tone.

Dominique picked at her food halfheartedly. She was too preoccupied to appreciate it. "It's about your . . . wife." Her face turned crimson. What would he think of her for asking such a question on the first occasion they were alone socially? Should she have waited? But until when? It would be coy to pretend that this was just a friendly dinner. It was much more than that, and they both knew it.

Stephen nodded and put down his fork. He looked as though he were bracing himself. "You're right. I need to explain." He took a deep breath. "It's the old cliché. You've heard it a thousand times. I stay with her because of the children. We essentially have no marriage."

Dominique shook her head. "I haven't heard it a thousand times. Because I've never . . . gone out with someone who was married." She gave a short, self-mocking laugh. "I don't approve of it." She put down her fork as Stephen had done, and pushed her plate aside.

Stephen turned to her and took her hands in his. "I know. You don't need to tell me. It's one of the reasons I" — he stopped short. "These past weeks . . ." Again he faltered.

Dominique's eyes were riveted to his. No one else in the room existed. *"These past weeks . . ."* He didn't need to finish the thought. She knew! It was the same for her. Respect had turned into liking. Liking had sparked curiosity. Curiosity had led to attraction. And all of it had been fueled by the roller coaster of tension at work. There was a sense of something about to happen. And when she worked late with Stephen, there was a feeling of alliance and common purpose more binding than mere sexual attraction.

Stephen's hands tightened around Dominique's. He searched her eyes, as though trying to predict her reaction to what he had to say. Finally he spoke. "It's much too soon for declarations. I'm afraid you'll think I'm not serious."

Dominique bit her lip. She was torn. A part of her longed for Stephen. Another part shrank from the involvement. If she were strong, she would tell him to take her home at once. She would forget about him, resign, and never see him again. There was still time to escape.

She withdrew her hands from his. "This is going too fast. I'm . . . I'm confused. You seem like such a good person. I've never respected anyone as much. But it's difficult to reconcile with . . ." Dominique let her sentence fade.

Stephen gave her a sad smile. "It would be easier to blame everything on my wife, I know."

Dominique looked down, ashamed. She wanted to blame his wife. To have an excuse she could live with.

Stephen put his index finger under her chin and lifted her face. "My wife is a victim of loneliness. I went away as soon as we were married and have been away ever since. Serena doesn't care to leave England. I can't blame her, really. Some of my posts have been beastly." He sat back and took a sip of wine before continuing. "We've both done things that were wrong." His voice was resigned. "The children . . . I think they need to know I'm somewhere about. She . . . Serena . . . is often . . . preoccupied. She has her interests. I'm afraid the children would feel quite isolated if I weren't part of their lives. I go home for holidays. They come to my posts during the summers. I'm not sure Serena would be so generous if we were to divorce."

"Can't you get a post in England?" Dominique asked.

Stephen smiled bitterly. "I've had that. I'm afraid things didn't work out. Serena insists that the children go away to school. How can I argue when I know I could be sent off and she'd have to deal with them on her own? So, with the children away, we end up alone together much of the time. And I'm afraid there've been too many ruptures to make that a happy circumstance."

Dominique nodded. Her questions were answered, but there was little comfort in what she had learned. His wife wasn't a lunatic, a drunk, or a witch. They simply didn't love each other. Rumor was that Serena had strayed first — Dominique didn't dare broach that subject. Couldn't Stephen have divorced her then? Fought for the children? Perhaps even brought them to live with him? On the other hand, Dominique knew that courts seldom awarded custody of children to fathers. It seemed an impossible situation.

"Stephen?" Dominique had one more question. "Did you ever love Serena?"

Stephen thought for a moment. "When we married I was eighteen.

I was going off to war and I wanted her more than anything in the world. But as to whether or not I loved her, I honestly don't know."

Dominique searched Stephen's eyes. "Have you ever been in love?"

There was a long, tense silence. Stephen didn't take his eyes off Dominique. His face was serious when he replied. "Two months ago, the answer would have been no."

⌒ ⌒ ⌒

When they left the restaurant, the night was a clear, midnight blue. It was too chilly to drive with the top down, especially as Dominique had brought no wrap.

She watched in silence as Stephen pulled up the little tan canvas. When she got into the car, she was shivering. Her teeth chattered as she rubbed her arms.

"I'm sorry," he said, "I didn't notice how cold it was." He removed his jacket. "Here, put this around you." He reached around Dominique and she leaned forward in her seat so he could drape the jacket around her. Her arms burned where his fingers brushed her skin. Never before had the simple touch of a man had such an effect on her.

Once again they drove in silence. When they arrived in front of her apartment, Stephen got out and opened her door. "I'll walk you upstairs," he said.

Dominique nodded. When they reached her apartment door, she turned to face Stephen. He was standing so close, he seemed to tower over her. She looked up at him. "Thank you. I had a . . ." She couldn't think of anything adequate to say.

Stephen reached for Dominique's hands and pulled her close. The movement dislodged his jacket from her shoulders and it dropped to the floor. Both of them ignored it. He ran his hands up her smooth arms. This time when she shivered, it wasn't from the cold. He cupped her face in his hands and looked at her for a long moment. Ever so softly, he rubbed his index finger in the little space between the top of her spine and the bottom of her hairline. The feeling was so deliciously sensual that Dominique thought she might faint. As though in a hypnotic trance, she drew closer to him; closer, until she could feel the buttons of his shirt against her breasts through the thin silk of her dress. She closed her eyes. She felt the warmth of his breath as he drew closer. And then he kissed her. His lips were sweet and hot. Dominique opened her mouth, wanting to taste him. His arms tightened around her as they pressed together. He moaned, then his mouth glided off hers and onto her neck. Dominique was sure that if he let go, she would be unable to stand, so she clung to him — abandoned herself to him completely.

This was what she had secretly wished — not just this, but more! And there was nobody to stop them. No Nanny standing guard at the other side of the door.

Suddenly Dominique felt like a trapeze artist without a net; free, yet frighteningly aware of danger. Her mind screamed a warning. Stop! She pulled away. She was breathless, her face flushed with desire.

Stephen stared at her, his expression startled. He looked as intoxicated as she.

Then he slowly released her. "I have to leave," he said, his voice thick. He bent down and picked up his jacket.

The withdrawal of his touch brought Dominique jolting back to reality. As she stepped back toward the door, she stumbled and reached behind her for support. Seeing her falter, Stephen caught her by the waist. She found her footing and righted herself. She rested her palms on his chest and looked up at him. "This doesn't seem real," she said, her voice shaky. "Will it still be the same tomorrow?"

Stephen released Dominique's waist. His eyes roved over her features.

She looked back at him, her pupils dilated with yearning. She was all eagerness and promise.

"Dominique, don't you know?" he said tenderly. "For me, it will always be the same."

⟳ ⟳ ⟳

When Dominique arrived at the office the next day, Stephen was already there. His face lit when Dominique walked tremulously through his office door. He stood up and came around his desk to greet her, but stopped a few feet away from her. They stood facing each other.

"I don't think we should touch here," he said, as the sparks flew between them.

Dominique, breathless, balled her hands into fists. He was right, of course, but she so wanted to feel his embrace. "No, of course not," she murmured.

"I'd like to see you tonight."

Dominique's heart leapt. "Yes."

"And . . . this Saturday. What about a trip to the beach?"

He wanted to see her as much as she wanted to see him! Dominique struggled to suppress a giddy burst of laughter. "That sounds . . . wonderful," she whispered.

Over the next week, Dominique realized that the calls from Lieutenant Smythe had stopped. Clearly the woman had vanished from Stephen's life, though Dominique never knew how he had managed it so quietly.

Just as Stephen had been open about his relationship with Smythe, he was open about the role of Dominique in his life. They dined together almost every evening. Weekends were taken for granted — there was no question of either of them dating another person. Every moment seemed precious. When Dominique saw Stephen's car pull up in front of her house, her pulse raced with excitement. When they parted at the end of the evening, she felt as though she were losing part of herself. There was a physical void when she was apart from him. And she rarely was.

Stephen introduced her to his friends, and they seemed to welcome Dominique, to genuinely like her. Invitations no longer came for him alone. It was "Stephen and Dominique."

"He's had it tough," explained the wife of an American diplomat who was a close friend of Stephen's. "Serena gives him a dreadful time. And as for that stuck-up bitch Amanda," she said with typical American frankness, "no one could stand her. We can see he's a lot happier with you. It's obvious he's crazy in love. He can't take his eyes off you." She smiled wistfully. "My husband hasn't looked at me that way for years. But," she continued cheerfully, "we're happy for Stephen. For both of you."

Dominique was shocked at the American woman's openness — she spoke as if Stephen and Dominique were married — but it made it easier for Dominique to say what was on her mind. "You don't . . . blame me?" she asked hesitantly.

The American flipped her wrist nonchalantly. "For what? People have to be realistic. In a situation where there are long separations from a spouse, and where the marriage isn't happy, who's to blame for the consequences?"

Dominique thought of Solange. Solange would find someone to blame and it would most certainly be Dominique! She shuddered to think of the uproar if her mother ever learned that she was in love with a married man — and that he was in love with her.

⤧ ⤧ ⤧

The ballroom of the French officers club was awash in scarlet poinsettias. Banks of them obscured the murals on the walls and were reflected in the mirrorlike parquet of the floor.

Dominique and Stephen stopped short just inside the entrance and gasped at the holiday display, their eyes widening at the extravagance of the scene. Now Dominique understood why ladies had been requested to wear Christmas red. Women on the dance floor spun to the music, their red gowns flying in circles about them, rubies and other precious stones sparkling against their bare skin. The effect was magical.

Stephen smiled down at Dominique. "Your dress matches the poinsettias."

Dominique laughed and smoothed the skirt of her full, crimson velvet gown. Its portrait collar plunged to a low V in front and back, creating the perfect setting for the diamond and ruby necklace she wore, so delicate that it looked like the dewy silk of a spider's web. The bottommost stone glittered enticingly at the apex of her lush cleavage.

Stephen gazed at the stone, then followed it with his eyes to the even more inviting sight below. He leaned close and squeezed her hand. "I'm so proud you're with me."

Dominique looked up at him, radiant with love. She tried not to think of their impending separation: he would return to England until after the New Year, she to Cairo. She got a knot in her stomach every time she thought of the three weeks without him. He had become such a fixture in her life that she could barely imagine it. Yet she knew he was eager to see his children and loved him for feeling that way.

The time would go quickly, she tried to reassure herself. There would be much required of her as Solange prepared for her annual New Year's Eve gala. And then there would be a full calendar of invitations.

In any event, there was no use spoiling tonight's beautiful party by brooding about Stephen's departure. Dominique laced her arm through his and let him lead her through the crowd to their reserved table at the side of the room.

Amidst greetings and friendly kisses, the couple finally arrived at their table for two. Once seated, they were barely noticeable in the hubbub around them, and they liked it that way. They ordered champagne and settled back to listen to the orchestra. It was playing the lively "Shall We Dance" from *The King and I*. Stephen lightly drummed the tabletop in time to the music. Dominique couldn't keep from tapping her foot. The waiter reappeared a few moments later and filled their glasses with a flourish.

When he had gone, Stephen lifted his glass and said, "Happy New Year, darling." He uttered the words with zest, his spirits obviously high.

"Happy New Year." Dominique matched his tone. It was impossible not to feel cheerful when the room glittered with such life and fun — and when she was with Stephen. He looked resplendent in his dress uniform, his shoulders broad and square, his face brimming with male vitality, his limpid gray eyes sparkling. She remembered with amusement her initial impression of him. How could she have ever considered him distant?

A look of secretive excitement came over Stephen. He leaned across the table and took Dominique's hand. "I have a special Christmas gift for you," he said softly.

Dominique grinned at Stephen. "I brought your present, too." She withdrew from her clutch a small box and slid it across the table to Stephen. "You first."

Stephen at once recognized the name of the store embossed on the gold box. He asked with endearing enthusiasm, "Is this what I think it is?" He slid his finger under the seal and carefully removed the lid. "It is!" He withdrew an intricately detailed crystal paperweight in the shape of a book, which he had several times admired in a shop near Dominique's apartment. Stephen held up the translucent object so that the light from the chandelier overhead passed through it. He smiled. "I don't have to tell you that I love it, because you know it already."

Dominique flushed with pleasure.

Stephen returned the paperweight to its box and moved it to the middle of the table, where it would be out of harm's way. Then he reached into his breast pocket and drew out a satin-covered jeweler's box. Without a word, he placed it in front of Dominique.

Her eyebrows shot up in surprise at its unmistakable shape. Ever so slowly, she reached forward and opened it. Embedded in soft white satin lay a diamond solitaire. For a moment, Dominique could do nothing but stare. It seemed alive with fire, its facets reflecting each light from the chandelier, each flicker of the candle on their table.

Dominique raised her eyes to Stephen. There was no misreading the intention behind the ring. One part of her soared at this evidence of his love. The other part, the stronger part, shrank from it. She slammed the box shut. "I'm sorry," she said, heartsick, "I can't accept this."

Stephen looked dumbfounded. "What do you mean?"

"No, Stephen, *what do you mean?*" Dominique hardened her voice to cover the shaky feeling inside.

Stephen stared at the box. With quiet determination, he said, "I mean to marry you."

Dominique's reaction was immediate. She shook her head in a rapid, panicky movement. "We can't do that!" she cried.

Stephen's eyes bore into her. "We can't keep on this way!" He was emphatic. "We're together *more* than most married couples. We hate being apart. It's like the best sort of marriage, except —" He stopped and looked away with a sound of frustration.

There was only one thing missing, but they both knew the rules. Dominique couldn't have spoken of it if Stephen had been looking directly at her. But to his profile, she was able to say, "I'm grateful you haven't pressed me about that — "

He turned then, and the expression on his face brought her to a dead halt. For the first time, Dominique saw the fighter pilot he had once been. His mouth was taut and strained; his eyes, gray steel, unwavering; his nostrils pinched. In his temple, a vein throbbed. He was almost frightening in his intensity. And he seemed devastatingly powerful. Did he know how much she wanted him, too?

"Dominique, I'm not a boy anymore." His voice was as steely as his regard. "This is torture and I can't keep pretending otherwise." He leaned forward and took her hands in his. Something he read in her eyes softened his expression. "I know what your upbringing has been. For God's sake, it's practically medieval how young women are raised here!" He swallowed, then went on in a calmer voice. "Look, I want to marry you more than anything in the world. It's the only way for us."

Dominique couldn't suppress the euphoric drumming of her pulse at his words. She wondered if Stephen could feel it pounding where his fingers brushed her wrist. "If you were free!" Dominique's voice was fervent. "Or maybe if it was just your wife. But" — her eyes grew moist — "I remember when my father died. And . . . I can't put another child through that kind of loss." Stephen opened his mouth to protest, but Dominique continued hurriedly. "I know it's not the same situation, but . . ." She straightened and withdrew her hands from his.

Stephen looked wounded by the action. "But you know how things are! This is inevitable!" he argued.

Was it? What a mess if he left his family! What a quagmire of hurt feelings and accusations. Stephen would find it more odious than he would ever admit, Dominique knew. "You're lying to yourself — and to me — if you say that you could leave your children," she said dully. She picked up the box from the table and placed it directly in front of him. It was the hardest thing she'd ever done.

Stephen blanched. He sat perfectly still. When he spoke, his tone was one of absolute conviction. "I'm going to work this out."

Dominique's face was tight, frozen. "Put the box away, Stephen. Please. This is already too difficult."

Stephen's expression was implacable. "Look, I don't want to embarrass you with a scene so I'll do as you ask for now." He glared at the box for a moment. Then he snatched it from the table and, with an angry, jerky motion, returned it to his breast pocket. "But this isn't the end of the discussion!"

∾ ∾ ∾

Dominique and Stephen stood in the dark of the stairwell whispering their good-byes. It had become a nightly ritual, the secret caresses in the obscurity of the hall. A ritual of almost unbearably delicious tension for both of them. Tonight, though, Stephen's proposal and their impending separation lent a special poignancy to their lovemaking. Dominique leaned against the wall, abandoned to the sensuality of his touch, knowing in her heart that he would stop before he went too far. Never had she allowed a man to touch her as Stephen did, but she trusted him. Softly, he traced the curve of her neck, the graceful line of her shoulder with his tongue. He folded down the bodice of her dress, freeing her heavy, firm breasts.

Dominique moaned with desire as Stephen brushed her nipples with his fingers until they were erect against his palms. She arched her back, straining against him, hot with unfulfilled lust. He bent and ran his tongue over her breasts, over her nipples, sending chills through her. His hand lifted her skirt, then his warm fingers brushed against her thighs. Slowly, excruciatingly slowly, he moved upward until his hand covered the piece of silk between her legs. He moved his finger back and forth in a hypnotizing rhythm until the sheer cloth was moist. Dominique pushed against him, burning with the desire to feel him inside of her. She said thickly, "I want to go with you tonight."

Stephen, panting, pulled away from her. His face was covered in a thin sheen of perspiration despite the coolness of the evening. He studied her face. Her expression was wanton, her pupils dilated. "Are you sure?" he asked in a voice unsteady with desire.

She nodded. She saw the struggle on his face. She knew his conscience was telling him to say no, but he took her arm and opened the door to the stairwell. They hurried to his car. In silence, they drove to the base.

Dominique had been to his villa no more than a half-dozen times. Usually they only stopped there briefly to fetch something Stephen had forgotten. It was as though they knew that to be alone together was too much of a risk.

As Stephen pulled the car into the courtyard, Dominique felt her heart pound with fear. *What am I doing?* she asked herself. *Becoming the mistress of a married man?* It was suddenly all so sordid. She turned to look at Stephen. He looked like a stranger to her. A stranger who wanted to use her in a way that was wrong. Oh, and she wanted it, too! But now it seemed like a terrible mistake. Stephen turned off the engine and faced her.

"Stephen, I — " She stopped. How could she say no at this point?

Stephen looked at her knowingly. "You've had second thoughts, haven't you?"

Dominique looked down at her hands, ashamed. She didn't reply.

"It's all right," Stephen sighed, and started the car. "I have, too."

CHAPTER 3 ∾

"I'M TIRED of you moping around," Solange declared. "You'll come to the Renards' luncheon with me tomorrow or go back to Ismailia. But this moping must stop."

Dominique looked up from the book she was reading. She lay on a chaise lounge in her mother's game room. The room in which Solange spent most of her time was occupied by four elegant gaming tables, each inlaid with different, complementary patterns of Italian marquetry. At the end farthest from the sitting area was an intricately carved billiard table. Solange didn't play billiards, but her men friends did. Solange was a card player, canasta being her game of choice. At this she was an expert. In the absence of a partner, however, she enjoyed solitaire in all its forms. Now she sat at a table near Dominique and rearranged her cards according to the rules of her current round of solitaire.

"I don't mind going back to Ismailia," Dominique said indifferently.

Solange lifted her head and glared at her daughter. "That's out of the question!" she said, in direct contradiction of her previous statement. "You'll be here for the New Year at least. We have the deputy minister coming as well as three more of that awful Nasser fellow's people."

"If you find the president so awful, why invite his ministers to our house?" Dominique said, her voice scornful. "And why are you friends with the deputy minister."

Solange's lips tightened in annoyance. "You know as well as I that he's been in the government for years. It's only because he has an unimpeachable reputation that he managed to survive Nasser's coup. Why *shouldn't* I like a kind, honest man like him? They're rare enough." With an impatient stroke of her arm, Solange gathered the cards on the table into a pile. She looked up and met Dominique's inquiring gaze. "As for my being polite to the rest of Nasser's henchmen, how do you suppose we've managed to keep everything we own?" Her tone was sharp.

Dominique swung her legs to the floor. "What do you mean?"

Solange made a noise of exasperation. She picked up her cards and began to shuffle with the skill of a croupier. The gems on her long, tapered fingers flashed with her movements. "You don't appreciate what you have, Dominique. You don't even understand it." Her hands stopped for a moment and Solange focused her gaze on Dominique. "Don't look down on things you don't understand," was all she said.

After a few moments, Solange spoke again. "The Renards have a cousin from America visiting. He's very pleasant. He'd like to meet you." She dealt the cards into yet another version of solitaire.

"Mother, you're always trying to play matchmaker. I'm not looking for a husband! And I wish you'd stop doing it for me," Dominique said, irritated. She pulled her feet back onto the lounge chair and leaned into the down-filled cushions.

Solange frowned. "This . . . this working for the British has made you even more impertinent! You won't listen to anyone!" She glared at her daughter. "You have to face reality. Most Europeans have left Egypt. If you could find a husband in America, you could become a citizen. You could leave here and you'd be safe."

Dominique looked at her mother sharply. "Have you had trouble?" she asked in an urgent voice.

Solange leaned forward, her face creased with exasperation. "Do you have your head buried in the sand? You've seen the anti-European riots! You've seen them take the property of our friends!"

"But no one's ever bothered us!" Dominique argued. "You just said you were friends with —"

Solange threw her pile of cards on the table, effectively cutting off Dominique. "You idiot! You want to be grown up, but you're too much of a child to see the truth. The word 'friend' means nothing. It's a matter of political expediency."

A sliver of fear, no more than a suspicion, snaked its way into Dominique's conscience. She approached the table where her mother was sitting and stood in front of the older woman. "Are you worried?" Worried, not frightened. Her understatement was deliberate. She didn't want to use the word "frightened." It was much too strong.

Solange stared at her, silent.

Dominique was shaken by her expression. "Why didn't you ever say anything!" she gasped.

Solange sprang to her feet. "Because you're my child!"

Dominique stared at her, uncomprehending. She had never in her life seen Solange express fear. It didn't seem real. And what exactly was the threat? "Tell me!" she insisted, her voice rising.

The strength seemed to drain from Solange and she sat back down, her posture weary. "Nothing's happened . . . not to me." She sighed. "And our friendship with the deputy minister makes me feel somewhat more secure. But . . . things are changing. You know that as well as I." Solange raised her eyes to her daughter and returned to the central point. "I want to see you safely married in America. I can offer your husband a good dowry. You could go quickly and I'd have one less worry."

"Mother." Dominique sat down opposite the older woman. "Why don't you go to France for a few months until the trouble blows over?"

Solange gave a rueful half-smile. "Because, my dear, they won't let us take our money out of the country. I've been putting aside some cash just in case, but —" Solange cut herself short. A veil fell over her features.

She was silent a moment, then she fixed Dominique with a severe gaze. "Anyhow, you have to think about settling somewhere permanently. This isn't a place to raise a family anymore." She sighed. "It won't be as easy for you as it was for your sister." She gave Dominique an appraising look. "You haven't Danielle's beauty. It's a shame your nose is so long. And your hair is quite impossible."

Dominique felt as if she'd been struck. It seemed as though every time her mother revealed a side of herself that was halfway human, she immediately countered it by saying something awful.

Solange saw her expression and gave a little sniff. "Oh, don't be so sensitive, Dominique. You're quite presentable enough to find someone. But" — she paused — "you'd be lucky to get this Anton Renard. He's in the import-export business in America, just as his people are here. It would be a good match."

Dominique thought of Stephen. Of course, it was out of the question that she confide in her mother. The very hint of such an affair would drive Solange into a fury. Dominique knew she could offer no excuse to avoid meeting Anton Renard. "All right, Mother." Dominique's voice was resigned. "I'll come with you to the Renards'."

👓 👓 👓

"I told you to wear your blue silk," Solange said as Dominique descended the stairs the next morning. Dominique was wearing a chic black two-piece ensemble with a white crepe de chine shirt. The look was sophisticated, but severe, and it made Dominique appear even more mature than usual.

"I didn't *want* to wear the blue silk," said Dominique as she drew on her white kid gloves. "I detest those puffed sleeves. They're too childish." Dominique turned to the Venetian mirror that occupied almost an entire wall in the entrance foyer. She carefully arranged her curls around a small black hat tilted at a piquant angle.

"You look like you're going to a funeral," Solange remarked with disgust. Solange wore bright red, a color that contrasted magnificently with her ash-blond hair. Her nails and lipstick were painted a matching scarlet. Solange was not slender, but she always clad her generous curves in elegant couture originals. She was a handsome woman, and she had the proud bearing of one who knew it.

"I *feel* like I'm going to a funeral," Dominique remarked dryly. She turned from the mirror and walked toward her mother. "Like a lamb being prepared for slaughter."

Solange marched impatiently to the front door. "Don't be ridiculous! You really are the most trying person. Danielle never spoke to me as rudely as you do."

The butler held open the door as the two women exited. Dominique paused before the door of the waiting car, held open by the driver. She answered Solange, "That's because you never spoke to Danielle as you speak to me."

Solange made a sound of annoyance with her tongue. She put her hand on her daughter's back and nudged her. "Get in! We're late."

The women sat together in cold silence as the car crawled through the dusty, traffic-choked street. Dominique had almost forgotten the overwhelming barrage of Cairo's noise and humanity. It was a startling contrast to the pristine little town of Ismailia.

She looked out the car window as they passed one of the city's ubiq-uitous coffee houses filled with dark, chattering men — never women. Several men lounged around a handful of rickety tables carelessly plunked down on the sidewalk in front of the establishment. At each table was a water pipe, a tall, bubbling contraption with a long, flexible stem used mostly for smoking hashish. The cloying smell of the drug filled the air.

Solange held her handkerchief over her nose and made a sound of disgust.

Suddenly Dominique and Solange uttered startled cries, as from beneath the car came a high-pitched squawk and the panicked flap-ping of wings. A second later, a chicken, clucking with outrage, cata-pulted itself away from Solange's Rolls-Royce. The women looked at each other and laughed with relief. Then they settled back in their seats.

Through the car's open windows, new smells drifted in and settled upon Dominique, thick as the dust from the desert. She wrinkled her nose as, from a dark little doorway, came the acrid odor of urine. As the car turned the corner and emerged onto a broader avenue, a line of flower vendors filled the car with a more pleasant aroma.

But they had no sooner started to merge with faster traffic than the Rolls came to a screeching halt, just in time to avoid running over the donkey and rider that immediately preceded it. It was noon and loudspeakers throughout Cairo announced to Muslims that it was time for prayer. Buses stopped and their passengers got out. Men climbed down from their farm carts. Cars stopped. Everything came to a halt while the pious unrolled their prayer rugs and knelt in the direction of Mecca. The streets were a mass of prostrate humanity, though many less-religious men continued to step around the devout. A chant filled the air, the roar of tens of thousands praying in unison.

Solange looked impatiently at her watch. Her driver, too, knelt near the car. She sighed, resigned to the delay.

After a few minutes, the relative quiet that had settled over the city exploded into an eruption of car horns, shouted conversation, and die-sel engines. Coppersmiths working in the shops that bordered the street resumed their banging. The buses rumbled to life. Solange's driver got back into the car and tried to ease through the congestion.

"It takes an hour to go a few blocks," Dominique commented. "Not like Ismailia."

"We would have avoided this if you hadn't lingered so much this morning," Solange remarked peevishly.

Dominique turned away from her mother and looked out the window. They were entering one of Cairo's main boulevards, the Shari' Qasr el Nil. The street contained many of the city's most exclusive boutiques, but was also sprinkled with luxurious apartment buildings and hotels. Dominique winced as they passed Groppi's and she saw the burned rotunda where Nanny used to take her for tea before the revolution. Groppi's had been one of the city's most popular gathering spots, serving picture-book pastries in the afternoon. At night there had been dining, dancing, and concerts underneath a stained-glass ceiling. But with the burning of the rotunda during the revolution, and the subsequent emigration from Egypt of many Europeans, Groppi's chic clientele had disappeared. Part of the restaurant had reopened, but a rough element frequented it. Dominique reflected that too many such changes had taken place in Cairo. It was true that the monarchy of King Farouk had been corrupt and that Nasser had a vision of improving the lot of Arabs, but so much that was lovely had been destroyed. And now tensions were high once more. There were more gun-toting soldiers on the streets than at any time since the revolution. More seizures of private businesses in the name of the government. More xenophobic propaganda.

As Dominique's gaze lingered on the fading grandeur of Cairo's landmarks, she wondered if all European influence would eventually be wiped out. Did the new regime think there was nothing of the old worth salvaging? She tried to shake off her dark thoughts as the car stopped in front of an imposing old apartment building. A uniformed doorman hurried from beneath a beige and blue awning to open the car door for the ladies.

Solange and Dominique stepped into the blistering sun for only a moment. Then they hastily entered the building through brass-framed double doors. The vast foyer was blissfully cool, thanks in part to the marble floor. An elevator attendant asked Solange whom they were visiting, and they were taken to the eighth floor.

The Renards' apartment was the only one on the floor, and the elevator opened directly into their foyer. The whole Renard family stood in front of the elevator and broke into exclamations of welcome as the two ladies stepped out.

Dominique was swept into a series of perfumed embraces, the air beside her cheeks the recipient of one double kiss after another. And then, as if on cue, the mass of humanity parted to reveal Anton Renard. It's like the parting of the Red Sea, Dominique thought wryly, and they think he's the miracle.

Anton's aunt took his elbow and propelled him toward Solange and Dominique. He bowed over Solange's hand and politely shook Dominique's.

Renard, older than Dominique had expected, wore a black suit with a stiffly starched white shirt. His tie was deep burgundy with no pattern. His graying hair was styled in a vaguely 1920s manner: parted almost in the middle, with soft waves falling on his high, pale forehead. But the whole thing seemed held in place with some sort of unguinous substance. Nevertheless, his features were pleasantly regular, his dark eyes graced by long, curling lashes. To Dominique, he seemed attractive enough, but stodgy. He's old enough to be *Mother's* next husband, she thought with amusement.

The wave of Renards surged around Dominique and Solange and propelled them into a drawing room. The furniture was ornate, with a great deal of crimson upholstery and gilt. Heavy red velvet drapes were drawn against the midday sun. Dominique was directed to sit in a fat little tufted chair, while Anton was urged into its twin. Trays of hors d'oeuvres were brought in by servants and circulated among the guests. Dominique noticed that everyone in the room pointedly ignored Anton and her, presumably in the hope that they would strike up their own conversation. And this Anton obligingly did.

"It is nice to see my family after so many years," he began.

Dominique smiled politely. "It must be." She studied the man before her. He appeared to be close to forty-five. He was slight, only a few inches taller than Dominique, but his suit was well cut and made him appear nicely proportioned. His expression was cautious, but friendly. Dominique wondered if he felt as pressured as she did. But no, he had arranged the meeting. That was the way things were done in Egypt, even among Europeans. A man expressed his desire to marry. The family suggested suitable brides. The eligible women's families were approached and meetings arranged. Then, often in as little time as a day or two, a verdict was pronounced, a dowry agreed upon, and a date set. Of course, love matches did occur and were growing increasingly common, but it was rare that two young people were willing to defy both families in the name of love.

"I understand that your sister lives in America," Anton ventured. He took an hors d'oeuvre from the servant and placed it on the small plate that had been given him earlier. Dominique watched as he bit the minuscule treat in half. The gesture seemed unnecessarily prim.

"My sister lives in New York," Dominique replied. "Have you ever been there?"

"No. Only San Francisco." Anton dabbed at his mouth with his napkin.

"Oh? How long have you lived in America?"

"Twenty-four years. I went there when I was twenty."

"And you've never had the desire to explore other parts of the country?"

"I prefer to sleep in my own bed and to eat my mother's cooking."

Dominique raised her eyebrows. "You live with your mother?"

Anton gave a slight smile, devoid of warmth. "It's temporary. She lived with my sister and her husband until last year. But they are undergoing ... difficulties at the moment. That leaves only me. Mother speaks no English. She couldn't manage on her own."

"By now, you must speak excellent English," Dominique remarked.

Again, he gave her a lifeless smile. His eyes were so dark that they were unreadable. "It will never be as good as my French, I'm afraid. I don't really like English."

Dominique cocked her head in surprise. "How do you get on? Work?"

"I do very well," Anton replied with a self-satisfied expression.

Lunch was announced and, as Dominique expected, she was seated beside Anton. I'm surprised they didn't set up a table for two in the drawing room, she thought. She decided to enjoy the lavish meal that was served, even if she had no interest in Anton Renard. The Middle Eastern specialties the cook had prepared were delicious. Dominique noticed that Anton plunged in without the restraint he had shown earlier. In fact, he fairly wolfed the food down, leaning forward over his plate. At one point, a drop of sauce landed on his tie. He appeared not to notice as it was absorbed into the red silk.

When the meal was over, the company returned to the drawing room. Dominique watched as Anton took a seat next to Solange. When it was time to go, he once more bowed over Solange's hand. Then he hurried to Dominique's side.

Dominique smiled politely and held out her hand. "It was a plea-sure to meet you. I hope you have a nice trip back to America."

"Thank you." This time he bowed over Dominique's hand, too. "We will see each other again. Your mother has graciously given me permission to call on you."

If he noticed Dominique's look of astonishment, he gave no sign.

ᵔ ᵔ ᵔ

As it turned out, Solange had invited Anton to her New Year's Eve party. But Dominique barely spoke to him at first, so occupied was she by the other three hundred guests. The deputy minister came, of course. He had been almost a daily visitor for the last five years. Dominique watched him and her mother with a smile. She knew that Solange had refused several offers of marriage since the death of her husband. She said she preferred to remain independent. But Domi-nique suspected that the deputy minister had proposed many times.

Paulette and Jean also came with their families, neighbors of So-lange. The three young women giggled in the corner about their love interests in Ismailia.

"Do you miss Stephen?" Paulette asked breathlessly.

"Of course," Dominique said in a wistful tone.

"He'll be back next week, won't he?" asked Jean.

Dominique nodded.

Paulette grinned. "Everyone's talking about this relative of the Re-nards. They say he's here to find a wife. Are you supposed to be the victim?"

Dominique rolled her eyes. "That's what Mother wants."

"I met him earlier," Jean said, "and he's not half bad."

Paulette's eyes widened. "Is that true, Dominique? Is he good-looking?"

Dominique shrugged.

"Hmmm, maybe I should have a look at him," Paulette said specu-latively.

Dominique smiled. "Be my guest."

But Solange was careful not to seat any other single young women next to Anton during the midnight supper. His eyes lit with pleasure when he saw that Dominique would be next to him. He scanned her appreciatively, taking in her elegant black gown with its gold satin halter neck and bodice. The gold of the fabric made the highlights in Dominique's hair shimmer in the candlelight.

"You look lovely this evening," Anton told her.

Dominique smiled — civil, but not warm. She didn't want to encourage him.

Anton looked attentively around the room. "Your mother certainly spares nothing in her entertainment," he commented. "Even the flowers are magnificent!" Solange had cleared two drawing rooms and her game room of their usual furniture in order to set up thirty-six tables for eight. They were covered with Belgian lace tablecloths and matching lace-trimmed napkins. At each place — set with Limoges china and Christofle vermeil — were four Baccarat crystal goblets: one for sherry, one for white wine, one for red wine, and one for champagne. Solange, like most French, did not serve water with dinner.

Dominique had never considered the scale of her mother's entertaining. A party for three hundred only occurred once or twice a year, but Solange was no less extravagant when she entertained on a smaller scale, which she did weekly, with scintillating dinners for twelve to twenty guests.

Dominique said, "Mother loves parties."

"You must enjoy them, too," Anton said, leaning back as a footman placed a serving of cream of chestnut soup in front of him.

Dominique picked up her soup spoon. "I'm not here much anymore," she announced, feeling quite grown up and independent.

Anton paused, his soup spoon poised above the dish, his head tilted questioningly.

"I live in Ismailia now. I work for the Royal Air Force."

Anton couldn't have looked more shocked if she had confessed to being a stripper. "You . . . work?" His lips tightened in disapproval. "Your mother doesn't object?"

"Oh, she does," Dominique replied breezily. She laughed at Anton's expression.

"In my family," he intoned, "young unmarried ladies do not work."

Dominique smiled. "Well, to each his own."

Anton lifted one eyebrow and seemed about to argue. Then, apparently thinking better of it, he nodded politely and said, "Indeed."

As the soup plates were cleared, Dominique turned to chat with the man on the other side of her. He was a former beau of her sister, Danielle, and an old friend of the family. She soon found herself laughing gaily at his remarks.

By the time the dinner was over, Dominique felt a little tipsy from the wine. When she heard the orchestra warming up in the ballroom, she wished Stephen were with her. How wonderful it would be to see in the new year with him. Instead, she found Anton trailing behind her as she made her way to the romantically lit chamber.

Once they started to dance, however, she began to enjoy herself. Anton's dancing was smooth and competent. She smiled at him. He wasn't so bad. She could see how her friends might find him attractive.

"I wonder," he asked, "if you'd have dinner with me one night next week?"

Dominique stiffened. This was too much! She had no intention of encouraging this man. "I'm sorry," she said with as much sincerity as she could muster, "I return to Ismailia at the end of the week and I have too many people to see here before then."

Renard's face fell. "That's disappointing," he said gently.

Dominique felt a pang of guilt at her unequivocal rejection. "Well," she said with a friendly expression, "perhaps another time."

෨ ෨ ෨

"Trouble's brewing," Stephen confided to Dominique.

Dominique looked up from the file cabinet with an expression of alarm.

Stephen, at his desk, held up the cable he had just finished reading. His brow was creased with worry. "There were demonstrations yesterday in front of the British embassy. The mob was quite abusive."

"But that's right near my house!" Dominique cried. She hurried to Stephen's side and leaned over his shoulder to read the wire. She had to know more! She hadn't spoken to her mother in over a week and she hadn't seen her since a month before in January.

Stephen swiveled to face Dominique and handed her the dispatch. Her expression grew frantic as she read it. "Don't worry," he soothed her. "It's just a crisis we have to weather. It will turn out all right in the end."

Dominique looked up sharply. "That's not what the newspapers say," she argued. Things were getting worse, not just in Egypt, but in all of North Africa. A few weeks before, mobs in the nearby French colony of Algeria had launched a random attack against Europeans. Victims had been ripped from their cars, then slashed with knives and razors. Dominique had read with nausea of a terrorist attack on a French family that had left a pregnant mother disemboweled, her unborn baby torn from her womb and placed in the empty cavity of her stomach.

"They hate us!" Dominique cried. She threw the wire back on Stephen's desk. "They want their country back! And I'm not sure we can blame them."

Stephen exploded. "Can't blame them!" He shoved his chair backward and stood up. For a moment, they were nose to nose. Then he began pacing. "That's the stupidest thing I've ever heard. Why, we've brought this country into the twentieth century!"

"Whether or not that's true, they want us out now!"

Stephen whirled to face her. "And we're complying for the most part. But the Suez Canal is vital to our interests — the entire world's." He threw his hands in the air in an uncharacteristic gesture of agitation. "We must maintain at least a presence here."

Dominique's eyes shifted to the map on the wall. "I don't know as much about politics as you do," she said uncomfortably, "just what I read and hear."

Stephen stopped pacing and looked at her. The expression on his face turned gentle. He sighed and jammed his hands into his pockets. "Dominique, I may as well admit it. Things *are* serious. I'm going to have to go back to England for consultations."

"Oh no!" Dominique took a few steps toward Stephen, then stopped, remembering their rule against contact in the office. "When?"

Stephen looked down and sighed. "End of the week."

Dominique swallowed. "For how long?"

Stephen lifted his head. His gaze was tortured. "I don't know. Maybe . . ."

Suddenly, the significance of what Stephen was saying hit her. She felt sick to her stomach. "How long, Stephen?" she repeated hoarsely.

"I . . . don't . . . know." He struggled with each word as though loath to pronounce it.

∽ ∽ ∽

That evening Stephen took Dominique to his villa on the base. They needed to talk privately, he told her. Seriously.

As Dominique entered the cool, white building, she knew her first peace of the day. Though she and Stephen had spent no significant time at his home, each time she entered it, she was struck anew by its simple beauty. It was furnished in the ultracomfortable British colonial style, a mixture of fine down upholstery and artifacts native to the host country. Cool floors of marble, teak, and tile lent an air of serenity to the sparsely furnished rooms.

Stephen showed Dominique into the main salon, the most Arabian of all the rooms, with its groupings of low, fluffy sofas and small brass-topped tables. A manservant brought in a tray of sweet mint tea and cakes. He set it on one of the small tables beside the couch, then withdrew. Stephen threw open the wall of French doors and let the perfumed breeze from the garden waft in, stirring the long sheer curtains. Then he led Dominique to a sofa that faced out over the courtyard and its merrily burbling fountain.

They sank into cushions that enveloped them in a soothing embrace. Still, Dominique had too much on her mind to relax completely.

"I spoke to Mother this afternoon," she blurted out as Stephen poured the tea.

Dominique saw him hesitate for a moment, then smoothly continue his pouring.

"She wants me to quit. She wants us to go to France for a few months. She thinks things will calm down after the summer." She didn't mention that Solange had once more urged her to consider marriage to Anton Renard.

Stephen turned and handed her a cup. He took a sip of tea as he studied her, his face inscrutable. Then he nodded slowly. "You should go," he said in a voice barely louder than a whisper.

It was the last thing Dominique expected to hear. She tightened her grip on the teacup. "You mean, you think we're in danger?" How else could he stand the thought of such a long separation? Was there something he wasn't telling her about his own impending absence? Could it be permanent?

Stephen leaned closer to her so that their shoulders touched. "I want you to go," he repeated. "I'll find a way to meet you in France."

Dominique turned the upper half of her body so that she was facing him. "Tell me exactly why you think I should go," she said, trying to keep her voice calm. The months apart stretched endlessly, agonizingly, before her.

Stephen didn't answer. Instead, he got up and pulled a silken cord that hung on the wall. Seconds later, the servant reappeared.

"I won't be needing you anymore today," Stephen told him. "Thank you."

The servant bowed and withdrew from the room with a backward step, not turning until he was in the hallway.

Dominique waited tensely for Stephen to explain, but he remained standing, his head cocked like a hound, until a distant click alerted him to the servant's departure. He let out a long exhalation and returned to his place on the couch, loosening his tie as he settled in. Though they were now alone, he spoke softly. "A wire came in after you left today. The United States is threatening to withdraw its financial support for construction of the Aswan Dam. Nasser's angered them with his nationalistic rhetoric. He won't declare himself an ally of the West, which of course means Britain and the U.S." Stephen lowered his voice to a whisper. "Nasser's threatened to nationalize the Suez Canal if the U.S. withdraws its financing."

"Can he do that?" Dominique exclaimed. "The Canal is owned by British and French shareholders! Wouldn't that be an act of war?"

Stephen shook his head. "Not because of the nationalization. Look how many businesses and assets he's seized from Europeans in the four years he's been in power."

"But the Suez Canal was a European project! Unless it's kept safe, every ship passing to or from Asia will have to go all the way around Africa!"

Stephen looked somber. He took a long swallow of his tea. Then he stood up and crossed the floor to a butler's table that held several crystal decanters. "I'd like something a little stronger, how about you?"

Dominique shook her head impatiently. She wanted to hear what Stephen had to say. "Would it be an act of war?" she repeated.

Stephen poured two fingers of whiskey. He took a sip, then came back to stand in front of Dominique. He looked down at her with a grim expression. "Yes."

The color drained from Dominique's face. She plunked down her teacup on the low table beside her, suddenly too shaken to hold it. "Then . . . what?"

Stephen took a deep breath and sat next to Dominique. "I don't know yet. That's why I have to go to England."

"Oh, Stephen!" Dominique was chilled with fear. "Maybe Mother and I shouldn't travel. What if we're in France when all this breaks out? How will we get back? What will happen to our home, everything we own?" She remembered her mother's warnings during the Christmas holidays. Would they end up like many of their friends? Penniless, forced to flee the only home they'd ever known?

Stephen put his arm around Dominique and drew her to him. "Sssh, it's not time to upset yourself yet," he said soothingly. "It's likely this whole thing will blow over. And if there is an . . . incident, you'll have plenty of warning."

Warning to do what? Dominique felt utterly helpless.

Stephen could see the distress written on her face. He drew her closer. "Listen, I want to talk to you about something different," he said. Dominique raised her eyes to his, her expression troubled. He continued. "I want you to agree to marry me," he said firmly.

Dominique drew away from him. "No! We've already discussed that."

"Dominique, be reasonable! Are you prepared to end our relationship here and now?"

"What do you mean end it?" Dominique's voice sounded a note of panic.

Stephen grabbed her hands and gripped them tightly. "Serena wants to see me when I'm in England," he said deliberately. "She wants a reconciliation. And if Nasser succeeds in getting rid of us, I may be transferred there. Don't you see?"

Dominique stared at him, trying to absorb his words.

He continued, his voice urgent. "Events will force us apart unless you agree to marry me!"

"But . . . your children?"

Stephen released Dominique. He put his elbows on his knees and cradled his head in his hands. Finally he spoke. "I have to make a difficult choice. And I'm asking you to make one, too." He lifted his head and gazed unrelentingly at Dominique. "I love you."

Dominique put her hand on Stephen's arm. "But if Serena's willing to try a reconciliation and you divorce her now, she may never let you see the children again."

"I have to make her see reason, that's all!" Stephen chopped the air with a downward stroke of frustration. He turned imploring eyes to Dominique. "And I have to make you see reason." He covered Dominique's hand with his. "Please, Dominique!"

She was in turmoil. How could she give him up? But how could she do something that was counter to everything she believed? As long as she didn't cause the breakup of his family, she could rationalize their affair. She could tell herself that she was doing no harm. But if he divorced . . . The very idea was frightening in its burden of responsibility. The image of Stephen's children flashed in Dominique's mind. Why, they were almost the same age she had been when her father had died. She remembered her shock, her utter inability to accept that he would never return. She remembered the pain and loneliness. How could she inflict that on two innocent children? She would never be able to live with herself if she did such a thing.

"Stephen, I love you, but it's . . . wrong. How would you feel about me if I were responsible for your children hating you?" Dominique wrung her hands. "You would end by hating me! It would be nothing but misery for us!"

Stephen drummed his fist on his forehead. "Dominique, why think of the worst possible outcome? Why can't you believe it will all work out?"

Dominique leapt to her feet. "It hasn't so far, has it?" she cried. She leaned toward Stephen. "You're deluding yourself. I'm not refusing you for some wonderfully noble reason! I wish I were! I just don't want you to . . ." She clenched her teeth, trying to choke back tears. "I don't want everything we have . . . made ugly." She held his eyes with hers. "I don't want us destroyed by fights and court battles and resentment!"

Stephen looked up at her, his eyes glassy. He reached for her wrists and eased her down beside him. Silently, he wrapped her in his arms. He sighed, a deep, tremulous sound. For a long time he was silent.

Dominique's heart constricted with pain. She didn't trust herself to speak.

Finally Stephen murmured into her hair, "Then I owe it to the children to give Serena one more chance." His voice was full of misery.

Dominique pushed him back so she could see his face. It was ravaged with grief, and the expression on it made her lose control. She choked, burying her face in his shoulder.

"Don't . . . don't cry!" Stephen said, but even as he uttered the words, Dominique could feel the tremor of emotion that shook him. She encircled his neck with her arms and clung to him as tightly as she could. Her tears burned a path down her face.

Stephen, in return, gripped her so tightly that he almost squeezed the breath from her, but she didn't care. She wanted to melt into him, to become him, so that they'd never be separated. Her head dropped so that her cheek, wet with tears, rested against his.

"I don't want us to end!" Stephen's voice sounded far away, like that of a drowning man.

Dominique couldn't stand to see his anguish. She closed her eyes and felt the tender heat of Stephen's lips on her neck. She felt lost . . . drugged with a surfeit of feeling. Each caress transmitted his emotions like an electrical impulse humming over her skin.

The thin cloth of Dominique's blouse chafed at her as though it were made of steel wool. If she didn't feel his skin against hers, she'd go mad with wanting. She fumbled with the buttons on her shirt, her fingers trembling with impatience. Stephen slid the thin garment from her shoulders, kissing the honeyed skin where it had lain. Dominique fell back into the soft cushions of the couch, abandoning herself to the pure, shattering feeling that encompassed her.

Stephen's embrace became more urgent. Searing. He bent his head and ran his tongue over the dark shadow of her cleavage. His hands cupped her breasts, then caressed them through the delicate lace of her bra. Dominique held her breath, her body quivering. Stephen gently drew off her brassiere, and her nipples hardened in anticipation of his touch. She pressed her naked breasts against the cloth of his shirt. He drew in his breath sharply and tightened his grip on her, then sat back and threw off the garment. A moment later, Dominique sighed, reveling in the masculine feel of his wiry chest hair against her tender skin, then moaned as his thumbs covered her nipples, teasing them with soft, butterfly strokes. He lifted up her arms and, with one hand, gently pinioned her wrists above her head, then lowered his tongue to her breasts. She pushed herself against him, willed him to spread her legs and touch her there, where she was already soaked with desire. She knew he wanted to. She could feel the hard length of him pressed against her thigh.

Without quite knowing how it happened, she felt the silk of her stockings slip from her legs. Somewhere at the edge of her consciousness, she heard zippers and buttons, but the sounds were like fuzzy background noise. Then her ears roared with a rush of blood as Stephen's naked body came to rest on top of hers.

He moved so gently. He caressed her with the lightest possible touch. Caressed her until she was rocking against him, crying out for more. She felt as though a thousand pinwheels were whirring about her head. She was sensation, only sensation.

Stephen sighed and buried his face between her breasts. Then, as if he could resist no longer, he placed the tip of his member at the soft folds of her labia and pushed. At first, she pulled him unreservedly into her. And then she felt the pain. Despite her excitement and her love, despite her overwhelming desire, the pain was sharp. But Stephen was beyond stopping. He pushed into her, oblivious to her cries.

Then Dominique realized that the pain was diminishing. The throbbing soreness was becoming throbbing of a different sort. She found herself moving instinctively to Stephen's rhythm. As he moved faster and faster, so did she. She was straining toward satisfaction, every muscle of her body taut. The weight of his body on top of hers was bliss. She rocked her hips ever more wildly.

The motion was too much for Stephen. The muscles inside her squeezed the last bit of control from him. With a long groan, he pushed into her.

Dominique felt him shudder. A drop of sweat from his forehead fell onto her chest. And then the pinwheels began to spin faster, faster. She held her breath, tightening against him until the pinwheels exploded into stars. Spasm after delicious spasm shook Dominique's body as Stephen held her close.

She clung to him, her love for him flooding her heart. She felt bound to him with an intensity she could never before have conceived. She couldn't imagine letting go of him. Couldn't imagine separating from his touch.

Her heartbeat was beginning to return to normal when Stephen eased to his side and cradled Dominique's head in the crook of his arm. She turned her face to his chest and closed her eyes. Soft wool glided comfortingly over her as he pulled a throw over them. She felt as though they were in a refuge, safe from the realities of the world. She wound her arm around his waist and pulled him as close as she could. The cool breeze of evening shimmered over her face, but she was warm from Stephen's heat. Protected and whole.

Stephen put his free arm over Dominique and hugged her to him. "I love you," he whispered hoarsely.

Dominique's throat constricted. The words had new meaning for her now. She felt a tight knot of sorrow. How could she do without Stephen? How could she let him go? She wanted to renounce everything she had told him earlier. Renounce both their families. She wanted to flee to a place where they knew no one, where their pasts didn't matter. She had thought she could walk away from him, thought she was strong enough to end it, but the very notion caused her physical pain, like a knife twisting in her heart.

Dominique's fingers tightened their grip on Stephen and she felt his responding squeeze. She slid her hands over his chest, which gleamed with a fine sheen of sweat. Every breath filled her with his essence. It was as though part of her had slipped into him and no longer belonged to her.

Stephen turned his face to Dominique, then eased his arm from under her head. He propped himself on one elbow and fixed her with a look of such intensity that Dominique felt it vibrate through her. "Dominique," he said in a voice that betrayed his struggle, "I can't leave you." He reached forward and stroked her hair.

Dominique gazed into his eyes. They were smoky in the light of dusk, magical in the love they conveyed. She closed her eyes, unable to bear the heat of his emotion — and frightened by her own.

"Look at me!" His voice was harsh.

She opened her eyes, startled by his rough tone.

He suddenly sat up. He dropped his legs to the floor and leaned over Dominique. He grasped her shoulders and lifted her into a sitting position. In his eyes was a look of urgent desperation. "You can't leave me now!"

For one wild moment, Dominique let her imagination take her to a time and place where she was actually Stephen's wife. She thought of sleeping in his arms each evening, waking with him each morning. Being part of his daily life, part of his family.

Family. She inhaled sharply as the word entered her consciousness with a jolt. Suddenly, Dominique was shivering, as though with a fever. She wrapped her arms protectively across the front of her bare torso.

Stephen gripped her shoulders more tightly and forced her to look into his eyes. "Don't think about the obstacles!" he cried.

His words, the temptation he dangled in front of her, had the opposite effect. She braked her impulses as sharply as though she were in danger of catapulting over a cliff. Dominique slumped, suddenly drained of the vigor that Stephen had transmitted to her. If he had not been holding her, she would have collapsed back into the cushions. "We wouldn't be happy that way, Stephen." Her voice was leaden.

"We've talked about it. We've agreed." She shook her head with each word.

Stephen opened his mouth as though to argue, then a change came over his features. His brow furrowed and he closed his mouth without uttering a word. Releasing Dominique, he dropped his head into his hands, his knuckles white with strain.

She reached forward instinctively to comfort him. When he felt her touch, he raised his head, and the pain on his face shocked her. "Stephen!" she cried.

He pulled her close. Dominique could feel his heart thudding, thudding against her breast. A choked sound came from him.

Dominique was stunned to feel wetness seep into the crevice between his cheek and hers. It wasn't possible that Stephen was crying! It was absolutely counter to his stoic nature. The realization was shattering. Dominique crumpled. Her own tears spilled over and mingled with his. Sobs choked her throat so that her whole body shook, and the sound was trapped in her throat.

They gripped each other, as though dying, sinking in quicksand, helpless to do anything but surrender as they cried together. How long they held each other, Dominique did not know. She was unaware of her body — only emotion. Finally, though, her tears slowed. Her soul was left with a heavy, numbing sadness. She eased her hold on Stephen and, with a deep sigh, he released her.

They lifted their heads. Their eyes met and held. Stephen reached forward and brushed a strand of hair from Dominique's damp face.

Dominique held his hand against her cheek. She turned her face and caressed his palm with her lips. "We can't go through this again, Stephen. We can't see each other anymore," she said in a low voice.

Stephen winced. His eyes pleaded with her, still reflecting a spark of hope. "Unless you agree to marry me."

Keeping her eyes open, Dominique gently kissed him. As she drew back, their gazes locked. Inches apart, they sat completely still, hypnotized. It was as though they didn't dare move for fear of breaking the spell. Then Dominique eased away ever so slightly. "Good-bye," she whispered.

Stephen lifted his other hand to her cheek. He pulled her closer, so that her face was just inches from his. He fixed her with a look of utter conviction, then said in a clear, calm voice, "You are my last love."

CHAPTER 4 ∞

"KEEP an eye on the valises!" Solange exhorted her driver from the back seat. "This place is full of thieves." The trunk of the Rolls was open, but held down with leather straps, thanks to the number of trunks she and Dominique were taking on their trip to France. The car inched its way through the crowd near the Port of Alexandria. There were so many people that it was impossible to move faster.

The older woman turned to her daughter. "Your cousin Emile said that last time they cut the straps and snatched two of his valises as the car was moving!" She shook her head in outrage and increased the motion of the silk fan she held in her hand.

The car jerked to a halt as three French sailors spilled drunkenly out of a bar and onto the street in front of them.

"Disgusting!" Solange hissed, "and at ten in the morning! Roll up your window, Dominique."

"Mother, it's stifling," Dominique protested. Her pink linen traveling suit already felt damp. "Look, they're already gone." Indeed, they had disappeared into the throng on the sidewalk.

Dominique moved closer to her open window, trying in vain to catch a breath of cooler air. She said wistfully, "I'll be glad to get out of Egypt for a while. Demonstrations every day in Cairo and" — she looked around at the once-grand buildings — "this city has become . . ." Her sentence drifted off as she was carried back to pre-revolutionary days, when Alexandria had been one of the most cosmopolitan vacation spots in the world, offering as many attractions as the

French Riviera: gambling, dancing, world class entertainment, fine dining, and boutiques stocked with Parisian clothes.

"It's become positively seedy!" Solange declared. "Look at that garbage over there. And all those broken windows." She pointed at an ornately constructed public building, then clicked her tongue as if to say, "What a shame!"

Dominique's eyes followed her mother's gestures. A one-armed beggar crouched in a doorway, a basket of his meager belongings at his feet. Farther on, more beggars sat immobile, cups stretched forward in a perpetual gesture of entreaty. Dominique had the urge to jump from the car and place money in each cup, but she knew Solange would upbraid her. "Don't get near them," she'd say. "Who knows what diseases they have!"

Dominique turned her eyes back to the road, trying to gauge the distance to their ship. Its giant smokestacks rose in the distance. Behind the ships, on a hill overlooking the harbor was the stunning image of the Fort of Qaitbay. The fifteenth-century sandstone structure looked stark white against the deep, cloudless blue of the Alexandrian sky. The fort was like a picture-book ideal of a medieval castle, with its crenelated walls and turrets.

"The buildings are still lovely if you don't look too closely," Dominique remarked. Laid out by Europeans for Europeans, modern Alexandria, until the revolution, had been admired for its broad avenues and Belle Epoque architecture. Now the grand buildings crumbled with neglect and the exquisitely landscaped avenues were choked with weeds.

"Alexandria is still beautiful," Solange acknowledged, "but the time has come for me to sell the beach villa, if I'm to get anything at all for it." She sighed. "Though I can't imagine who will buy it with the town deteriorating as it is." Her face became pensive and her hand slowed its agitated fluttering of her fan.

"Sell the beach villa?" Dominique turned to her mother in surprise. "But it's miles from here! The neighborhood is still lovely." Why, the villa held her fondest childhood memories. Memories of summer, when her father had for three months taken a rest from work and spent his time squiring Solange and their daughters around Alexandria.

"I don't know how long it will be lovely," Solange said with a resigned shrug. "It's best to sell while I still can."

Dominique regarded her mother with a pained expression. Everything was changing! Everything was slipping away. She closed her eyes and thought of the Alexandria of her childhood. Unlike Cairo, where the lives of adults and children were strictly segregated, Alexandria meant family outings and endless lazy days lived in bathing suits instead of starched school uniforms. There had been boat excursions and garden parties, musicales and the theater. And when their mother and father had outings of their own, Dominique and Danielle would rise at dawn and drag Nanny to the beach until dusk. As they approached adolescence, Nanny had insisted they travel a mile down the promenade to the beach that was exclusively reserved for women. The sisters didn't mind at first, because there had been a marvelous ice-cream pavilion adjacent, built to resemble a circus carousel. As they grew older, however, they would tell Nanny they were going for a walk, then hike back down to the beach frequented by both men and women. Dominique smiled now as she remembered Nanny's good-natured resignation at her charges' small adventure.

The old woman had left the week before to visit her sister in Marseilles before she rendezvoused with the Avallon women in Nice. Dominique missed Nanny's comforting old face; her heart lifted at the prospect of seeing her again.

As the car approached the customs building, the cacophony outside grew louder. Dominique opened her eyes and saw that smokestacks from three ocean liners now obscured the horizon. Smaller boats, like toys beside the huge vessels, bobbed on the calm cerulean water of the harbor. Alexandria had been the most important port in the Middle East before the revolution. Now Beirut had gained ascendancy. But ship traffic was still heavy. Tugboats were already circling the luxurious French ship Dominique and Solange would board, preparing to guide it out of the harbor.

Dominique thought the scene would have been cheerfully frenetic had it not been for the scores of Egyptian soldiers who stood about glowering, their guns at their sides.

But as soon as the car pulled to a stop in front of the government customs house, Dominique's view of the soldiers — and everything else — was blocked by the mob of porters who converged on the Rolls. They all spoke at once, a disorderly chorus of Arabic. Solange's driver impatiently shooed them away. The valises were *his* responsibility. When the porters had retreated a few feet — and looked as though they would be held at bay by the driver's warning expression — the servant opened the door to the car and handed out the ladies.

"Let's hurry up and get on board," Solange said, taking Dominique's elbow. The two women entered the government building and went to the desk belonging to the cruise line. Solange showed her tickets and was directed to a passport checkpoint. She glided confidently through the crowd until she reached an Egyptian officer dressed in the uniform of a lieutenant. She addressed him in Arabic, *"Sabbah el-Khair."* Good morning.

The lieutenant nodded coldly at her. His eyes stared at a distant point somewhere over her shoulder. "French citizens?" he barked. Solange nodded. *"Aywalla'."*

The lieutenant clapped his hands and another man, this one dressed in the uniform of a customs policeman, hurried to his side. "Check them," he ordered, still not looking at the women.

Dominique felt a prickle of apprehension, but tried not to be unduly alarmed. After all, procedures seemed to change with each voyage she and Solange took. And she was thankful they had not been turned over to the army, which was responsible for most of the affronts to foreigners, but instead to customs, whose police didn't even carry guns.

The policeman, a rotund, worried looking man with a disproportionately large handlebar mustache, gave Solange a pleading look and directed the ladies to follow him.

"What is this?" Solange demanded loftily of the army lieutenant. He turned away and picked up a telephone. Solange looked dumbfounded. Never had she been treated with such a lack of respect.

She rounded indignantly on the policeman. "What is this?" she repeated.

This man was more human. He looked apologetic as he said, "Routine check."

Suddenly a look of understanding crossed Solange's face. "Aah . . . ," she said. She smiled winningly at the young man. *"Baksheesh?"* she offered. "Perhaps there is a permit we neglected to purchase? How much is required?"

The little man was furiously shaking his head even before Solange finished her sentence. "No, no," he whispered, casting a frightened glance at the nearby officer.

Solange followed his gaze and lowered her voice. "How much does he want?"

"No, no!" the policeman grew more agitated. His mustache jumped with each exclamation.

Solange stared at him, puzzled. She had never before encountered such a reaction. *Baksheesh* — tips or bribes, depending on the viewpoint — had for centuries been an accepted way of life in Egypt. The practice occurred openly and was considered a necessary expense of any transaction with the government.

"You must come!" the policeman explained, his voice imperative.

Now Dominique grew worried. She thought of the money they had hidden in their brassieres — the only means by which they had been able to take out enough for their trip.

Solange cast another glance at the back of the lieutenant, as though debating whether to insist on speaking to him. He appeared engrossed in his telephone conversation. She turned back to the policeman. "Very well," she agreed. "Let's get this ridiculous thing over with." She turned to her daughter. "You wait here for the bags."

"Madame," said the policeman, "your baggage is in our possession. And your daughter must come also."

Solange frowned. "What do you mean, young man? I haven't time for delays. We have to board that ship!" She gestured with her fan in the direction of the boat.

The policeman stared at Solange for a moment. "You will follow me, please," he said. Without waiting for a response, he turned and began to push through the crowd. Solange let out a noise of exasperation and followed him. They were led down a narrow hall lined with crooked pictures of President Nasser and his cabinet, then into a tiny, stifling room with no windows. Once beige, the walls were now pocked and graying.

Solange and Dominique gasped when they saw that their valises lay open on a battered wooden table. Two customs police were buried up to their elbows in the contents, rifling through the clothes, indifferent to the havoc they created.

"What is this!" Solange's voice rang out.

The policemen turned to face the arrivals, smirks on their faces. One of them, a gangly man with an acne-scarred face and a gold tooth, moved toward the women with an insolent expression. He didn't answer Solange, but rather sauntered to the door, looking the women up and down as he walked. Mother and daughter kept their eyes stubbornly ahead as he moved behind them. They both started when the door slammed shut.

Dominique felt the man's eyes on her. It made her flesh crawl. But she kept her gaze straight ahead on the third policeman, who had so far remained silent. He was clean-shaven, with blunt, Germanic features. Dominique thought he must be of mixed blood, for his hair was red. Though there was nothing sharp about his features, his sly expression and his red hair reminded her of a fox.

From behind Dominique, the gold-toothed one, who seemed in charge, addressed the women's escort in a gruff voice. "They're loaded. Jewels, furs, everything."

He wandered back in the direction of the table, but not before taking a detour to circle Dominique like a farmer inspecting a prize heifer. As he drew near, Dominique's spine stiffened. What gave him the confidence to treat them so arrogantly? What did he have planned for them? She knew they had discovered nothing wrong with their baggage, so he had to be bluffing. Taking out his anti-European sentiment on them. He was just a sadistic bully, Dominique concluded, and the best way to deal with bullies was to stand up to them. She turned to face the man squarely. "What is it you want?" she asked icily.

The man leered at Dominique and walked over to one of her trunks. He dipped his hand in and picked up a pink silk camisole. He held it to his nose and, with an exaggerated look of appreciation, inhaled the Chanel No. 5 that wafted up from it.

Dominique's head whipped in Solange's direction, expecting to see outrage on her mother's autocratic features, but Solange seemed paralyzed with shock, her eyes fixed on the gold-toothed man. What was wrong with her? Why didn't she object?

Solange's inaction galvanized Dominique. She stalked toward the policeman and snatched the garment from his dirty hand. "You've no right!" she spat.

Solange drew in her breath sharply. The plump man winced. Fox-face, who had not spoken, gave Dominique a dangerous look. The gold-toothed man reacted as though she had slapped him. His expression darkened frighteningly. Dominique involuntarily bit her lip and took a step back, suddenly afraid *he* would hit *her*. But his reaction chilled her more than if he had shown anger.

Ever so slowly, as though he were savoring each move, the man reached for the garment in her hand. His eyes locked onto Dominique's as he gave the camisole a tug. Dominique was dumbstruck. Her fingers offered no resistance as the silk slipped away. The policeman's black eyes remained fixed on Dominique's. She wanted to avert her gaze, but was afraid to. She felt, irrationally, that if she kept her eyes on him, he would eventually back down. He was just trying to scare them. He would let them go when he grew tired of the game.

But the game didn't seem to tire him at all. He lifted the filmy camisole and held it to his chest with both hands. Then with a motion so deliberate that it appeared to be in slow motion, he pulled each half in opposite directions. There was the pop of a seam, then the high-pitched sound of the material being torn in two.

Solange made a noise of distress, but Dominique kept her eyes on the man in front of her. He crushed the two pieces of material in one hand, then held his balled fist in front of Dominique's face.

Dominique jumped back. The look of hatred on his features was like a physical assault. This was much, much more than a game to him!

With a broad, angry sweep of his arm, he threw the silky pieces of cloth at her feet. Dominique recoiled as one of them slithered over her shoe like a snake.

The policeman gave her a malicious smile that bared his gold tooth. He looked like a jackal, Dominique thought, a grinning jackal. Without turning from her, he reached behind him and snapped his fingers. He barked a one-word command and his companion handed him another silky garment from Dominique's trunk. Gold-tooth held it up in front of him like a magician about to do a handkerchief trick, then he put one end of the fine cloth between his teeth. His lips curled into a snarl as he jerked his head one way, his hand the other, and tore it in half, like an animal savaging its prey.

Dominique's mouth went completely dry as she watched the evil glint in his eye grow brighter. Her throat was so tight she felt that if she tried to speak, she would choke.

The policeman took a step toward Dominique.

She stepped back. She felt clammy all over. Clammy with terror and stifling heat.

With an exaggeratedly casual gait, Gold-tooth continued to saunter forward as Dominique backed away. Until she felt the wall stop her with a thud. Her whole body shook as she plastered herself against it. She wished she might disappear through it, like a ghost. Never had she felt such menace directed toward her.

Gold-tooth lifted his hands and placed them palm down on the wall on either side of her head. Dominique was surrounded by the rancid smell of his sweat. His filthy breath, a mixture of cheap tobacco, garlic, and unwashed teeth, assaulted her. It crept into her nostrils, her mouth, and her eyes like a noxious vapor. The room started to spin around her. Her knees trembled so wildly that she was sure she would collapse. But she was filled with horror at the thought of being unconscious and helpless in front of these men.

"Leave my daughter alone!" Solange's voice, shrill with fear, resounded in the little room.

Gold-tooth whirled about in fury and shouted in Arabic at the other two men. "Arrest her!" he cried. The eyes of the plump one widened in fear. He looked indecisively from the leader to Solange. But the other, more arrogant man briskly moved toward Solange, withdrawing his handcuffs from his belt as he approached her.

As Dominique saw Fox-face reach for Solange with his grimy hands, a hot surge of outrage doused her fear. Inflamed beyond reason, she rushed past Gold-tooth. She shoved the second man as he was about to clamp the handcuffs on the struggling Solange. "Leave my mother alone!"

Fox-face lost his balance and fell back against the table. He uttered an oath of pain as his elbow caught the edge, and he tumbled to the floor in an undignified heap, the handcuffs clattering down beside him.

For a moment, the room was dead silent. Then Fox-face scrambled to his feet and started toward Dominique. Gold-tooth jerked his arm back. The red-haired one looked at him, then at Dominique. Through clenched teeth, he said, "She can't get away with that!"

Dominique, panting, glared at each soldier in turn. None of them moved. But the hostility that radiated from them was heart-stopping. How would she and Solange ever escape now! Dominique's mind tried to make sense of the panic rising in her, but before she could compose her thoughts, Gold-tooth spoke.

"So . . . you like to fight. . . ." He smiled and said in a pleasant tone to Fox-face, "Give me the handcuffs, Mustafa."

"You don't know who you're dealing with!" The words spilled desperately out of Dominique. "We're very good friends with the deputy minister. He'll punish you for this!" Her voice rose shrilly, bordering on hysteria.

Fox-face sniffed with disbelief. "Hah. . . ." Then his eyes brightened with a lascivious gleam. "They say you French make the best whores," he jeered, as he cast a conspiratorial look at his comrade.

The more timid of the three injected in a worried voice, "Amir, maybe we shouldn't —"

"Shut up!" boomed Gold-tooth without taking his eyes off Dominique.

The little man fell silent.

"The handcuffs, Mustafa." The leader snapped his fingers impatiently. Fox-face dropped the metal objects into his hands.

Dominique was transfixed. With horrified fascination, she saw the policeman start to move toward her, his partner close behind.

"Don't come near me!" Dominique cried in a voice so strident that the two men stopped in their tracks.

For an instant, she felt that reason might somehow prevail. She tried to control the twitch of fear on her face. "On what grounds do you propose to arrest us?" she demanded with bravado. Her tongue was so thick that, like a drunk, she had to concentrate in order to enunciate clearly. She tried to pronounce each letter as though it were a word unto itself.

Gold-tooth sniffed in derision, obviously unaffected by her performance. "Those jewels and furs. You're taking far more than your allotted currency limit out of this country if you count their value."

"But no one does!" Solange leaped from her chair. "They're our personal belongings. We're allowed to take what we like!"

Dominique's eyes shifted back and forth as she followed the exchange. She was petrified at the thought of the cash she had stuffed into her brassiere. Her breath came in short ragged gasps. She sensed catastrophe and wanted to bolt. But, of course, there was no place that was safe. She felt like an animal in a trap.

As if reading her thoughts, Gold-tooth turned to Dominique. She held her breath as she tried to gauge his expression. Fixing his gaze on Dominique's breasts, he said to Solange, "Your daughter is very beautiful."

Dominique froze. She stared straight ahead, no longer daring to meet the policeman's eyes. She wanted to dissolve into the filthy floor, out of sight of the men. If they touched her, she would lose her grip on reality. She would scream and scream and — But no! Stay calm. It was her only chance. "Leave me alone!" she said roughly.

That only fueled Gold-tooth. Dominique heard him take a step closer to her. Once more, she could smell his unbathed body. Combined with the heat of the room, it made her gag. But she didn't dare show it. Didn't dare do anything.

Like a vulture circling the dead, Fox-face joined his companion, circling Dominique as he exhaled a terrifying chuckle. The policemen's movements were slow, unhurried, clearly savoring Dominique's debasement.

Dominique kept her head steadfastly down, refusing to meet their gaze, but she could feel their excitement growing. It vibrated through the room. Gold-tooth stopped directly in front of Dominique. Her heart pounded through her chest. She knew the policeman could smell her fear.

"Mustafa," he said, his voice low but nonchalant, "hold the mother. I don't want any trouble from her."

Dominique's head shot up. Her eyes met Solange's. Solange opened her mouth, then closed it. Her eyes were huge with dread as Fox-face approached her.

Dominique cringed as he came to stand behind her mother. But all he did was place his hands on Solange's shoulders. "Don't move," he commanded. And somehow, his calm, the absence of the handcuffs or any other object of force, were more frightening than any previous action. It was as though the policemen knew they didn't need force because they could do what they pleased to the women and suffer no consequences.

Dominique swallowed and looked back down at the floor. She had to think of a way to escape this nightmare! But how?

And then she saw a hand enter her field of vision — the hand of the gold-toothed policeman. As though she were watching a cobra, Dominique stood immobile, her gaze fixed on the hand. Ever so slowly, the man extended his fingers and clawed a handful of her skirt. She saw him lift the flimsy cloth.

She jerked back, but the policeman was quicker. He roughly grasped her wrist and yanked her arm toward the pair of open handcuffs.

Blind panic surged through Dominique. Her limbs struck out uncontrollably, flailing in every direction. Her legs struck flesh, wood, plaster. Her fists rained down on the man. Then she was slammed against the wall. A rough hand reached up her skirt and grabbed hold of her leg. She heard her stockings tear and, without knowing what she did, she threw her knee straight up, hitting bone so hard that she thought she had shattered her kneecap. She screamed with pain and collapsed to the floor. She was vaguely aware of the room in chaos. Of khaki uniforms converging on her. Of Solange's screams, and objects flying, scraping, slamming.

Then she felt Gold-tooth's weight grind her into the floor. In revulsion, her body heaved up against his, trying to dislodge him, but he was too strong. She frantically turned her head, searching for escape. She saw the feet of Solange and another policeman caught in a struggle. And she saw the handcuffs, there, just beyond her reach. She heard Gold-tooth take off his belt and unfasten his slacks. And then his hand grasped his member.

Now was her chance! With every bit of strength she could muster, she arched her back, then released her limbs like a rubber band. They swung upward in unison, throwing the man off balance. She scrambled away from him and reached for the handcuffs. She was almost there, her hands touching, but not grasping the metal.

Then arms circled her waist in a grip of iron. She lost her hold on the handcuffs, but kicked behind her like a mule.

"Aaagh! You whore!" she heard him scream behind her.

She wriggled across the dirty floor and grasped the handcuffs. But as soon as her hands closed on them, a foot crushed her wrist. She looked into Fox-face's eyes as he smirked down at her. Like a cheetah, she lunged forward and sank her teeth into his ankle. He doubled over in anguish and Dominique's wrist, hurt but not broken, came free. Without looking behind her, she swung the handcuffs wildly. Metal hit flesh. A cry. Blood splattered over her arm and onto the floor. She turned and looked behind her.

Gold-tooth lay writhing on the floor, his hand clutched over his left eye, blood pouring between his fingers.

"You put out his eye!" screamed Fox-face. The plump one ran to Gold-tooth and pulled his hand from his face to see the injury.

Dominique crouched in the middle of the floor like a mad woman, swinging the handcuffs in a circle around her head.

Solange, her face bloodless, was backed into a corner clutching her torn clothes about her.

Gold-tooth, still on his back, whimpered. His flaccid penis lay inert on his thigh. Fox-face ran to his side and knelt beside him.

Dominique rose on trembling legs. Her whole body shook uncontrollably. Afraid to take her eyes off the policemen, she blindly reached for the wall behind her. She didn't have the strength to stand on her own. Her left hand made contact with the hard surface, while in her right she still clutched the handcuffs. Like a person trapped on a narrow ledge, she cautiously inched her way toward her mother, all the while keeping her eyes fixed on her attackers.

Fox-face had pulled his handkerchief from his pocket and was holding it to Gold-tooth's eye. Dominique was within a foot of Solange. She reached her bloody hand forward. Solange closed the gap between them with one step and grasped her daughter's hand. Suddenly, Fox-face looked up at them. His face turned dark red with fury. He hoisted himself to his feet and faced the women. Dominique jerked the handcuffs upward at the same time as the rotund policeman cried, "No! Enough!"

Dominique kept her hand raised threateningly as she led her mother toward the door. "We're leaving now," she rasped.

Fox-face's eyes bored into her. He gathered his breath and let forth a stream of spit that landed at her feet. "You haven't heard the last of this!" he glowered.

๑๑ ๑๑ ๑๑

Solange slid the note across the breakfast table to Dominique.

Dominique picked up the thick, cream-colored stationery, which bore the official seal of Egypt, as well as the seal of the deputy minister. He had responded quickly. The incident had occurred only two days before.

It had all been a terrible mistake, Solange was assured by her friend. He was so sorry she had missed her boat. The customs officers would be severely punished, the women would receive an official apology.

Dominique made a sound of disbelief and threw the note on the table. She pushed back her chair and stood up. "That was no mistake, Mother!" Dominique moved away from the table and began to pace back and forth across the Persian rug of Solange's sitting room. Solange followed Dominique's movements with her eyes. "Those policemen may not have recognized our name," Dominique continued, "but I don't think it would have made any difference if they had. They knew we were French. I'm sure they understood our background." She stopped pacing and faced Solange, whose expression reflected her daughter's fretfulness.

The muscles in Dominique's face were so tightly strained that the tendons of her neck protruded. "I don't see how we can ever feel safe again! What will they do next? Steal our business? Throw us out of the house?"

"The deputy minister says he'll see to things," Solange said. But her voice lacked her usual conviction.

Dominique folded her arms across her chest. She said scornfully, "You saw how much his name meant to those men! Officials come and go in Egypt. Half of the ones who helped Nasser with the revolution are in jail now!"

Solange didn't argue. Both women were silent for a few moments.

Solange suddenly stood up. "Leave, Dominique!" she blurted out. "Marry Anton Renard and go to America!" She turned her palms up. "He's an attractive man from a good family. And I'll give him twenty percent of Avallon Cotton."

Dominique let out a bark of mirthless laughter. "It would be foolish for him to consider that a good dowry. How will he get the money out of Egypt?"

Solange lowered her lids. "There are ways. When the cotton is sold, we can have the money paid into a bank account in California instead of here. By November, he'll have the first year's income. And it will be very handsome," she said with a nod of assurance.

Dominique tilted her head to the side and studied her mother. "You've discussed this with him, haven't you?"

Solange turned away and went to the window. She pulled the curtain aside and looked out. With her back still turned, she answered, "Yes. And he's agreeable." She whirled to face Dominique, her features set in an expression of impatience. "I don't understand why you won't say yes. He wants to marry you." She took a few steps toward Dominique. "You're almost twenty-two. You should be married."

Dominique thought of Stephen. If only he were free! She envisioned herself as his wife. She imagined herself in England, far away from the turmoil of Egypt. With all her heart, she longed for what she could not have. It was like a physical hunger. For a moment, she had the wild impulse to call him, wire him, somehow contact him and tell him she had changed her mind.

But she knew that he had returned to Serena. Dominique's heart ached as she realized that, in pushing him away from her, she had irrevocably given up any claim to him. If she went to him now, she would cause nothing but disruption and heartbreak.

Solange interrupted her thoughts with a sound of exasperation. "Ouf! What are you waiting for? To fall in love? It will come after marriage, as it did for me, as it did for my mother! You think all your friends married for love? No! They allowed their parents to arrange things, just as you should! Look at that friend of yours — Jean — the stupid British one. Or Paulette. They haven't married yet. And why? Because they want to marry for love!" Her hands moved up and down with each word in typical Gallic fashion. "You all think it's so modern. So much more noble. But soon there won't be any Europeans left in Egypt for you to marry! Do you understand?"

"Then why are you staying?" Dominique cried. Could the danger be so great if Solange was determined to stay? Wasn't she afraid of another incident like the one two days before? What if the money in their brassieres had been discovered? Dominique blanched at the thought.

"Dominique, stop worrying about me! I wouldn't be happy if I left. Everything I've ever known is here. My business, my whole life!" She brought her hands together in the middle of her chest.

Dominique took a step toward her, her expression agitated. "But you may not be safe!" She remembered the terrible riots of 1952, the demonstrations in front of the British embassy that were now a weekly occurrence. Most of all, she thought of the attack in the customs house. It seemed like a horrific nightmare, too implausible to have actually occurred. Yet no matter how hard Dominique scrubbed in the shower, she felt she couldn't wash away the smell of the policemen, the feel of their hands. She knew she would never feel safe until she was far, far away; until she was *positive* they — or others like them — could never again harm her. Why didn't Solange feel the same way? "Mother, how can you think of staying after what happened?"

Suddenly, the energy seemed to drain out of Solange. Her arms dropped to her sides. She repeated, "You make leaving sound simple. And it could be, for you. You'd be leaving with a husband, who already has a business. You speak English, so you'd make friends. But I don't. My life is here. My friends are here." She averted her eyes. "The deputy minister is here." She shook her head and sighed, then returned her gaze to Dominique. "I don't want to start over. But you" — she waved her hand toward her daughter — "you're young — you can make a new life for yourself in America. And you won't ever have to worry again about things like those . . . those *animals* in the customs house." She paused, then leaned forward, her expression urgent. "*Please*, Dominique, you've never been afraid to take chances. Don't throw this one away!"

CHAPTER 5 ∞

DOMINIQUE started as Anton took her elbow. Lost in thought, she'd momentarily forgotten where she was. The ship had moved quickly, and Alexandria was nothing more than a distant cluster of sand-colored buildings against a background of pure, deep blue. Suffocating homesickness filled Dominique as she watched the skyline disappear.

Anton exerted a gentle pressure on her arm, a signal for her to come away from the rail. Dominique turned and faced him, suddenly realizing that this stranger, her husband, would be the only familiar face in her new world.

"Shall we go below and get settled?" Anton murmured. Without waiting for a response, he pulled her closer and steered her through the crowd toward their cabin.

Not yet! Dominique wanted to cry. She wasn't ready to be alone with him! She slipped away from his grasp. "I . . . I . . . need to pick up some Dramamine from the gift shop," she stammered, backing away. She tried to gloss over her reaction with a conciliatory smile.

Anton gave her a brief, impatient smile in return. Then it vanished. "Our cabin is extremely comfortable. And" — he gestured at the placid blue sea — "the water is calm. You won't have trouble." He took a step toward Dominique and once again reached for her elbow. "Come along," he commanded. "The steward will have unpacked by now. We'll have a drink and relax."

Dominique didn't want to argue with her husband on their wedding day, but his persistence made her contrary. "I'll be there in fifteen minutes," she said decisively.

Anton looked annoyed. There was a moment of silence that threatened to erupt into an argument. Dominique unconsciously squared her shoulders and took another step away from him.

"Fine," Anton conceded, composing his features. "Don't take too long," he added in an imperious tone.

Now that she'd won her point, Dominique felt more generous. She smiled at Anton and made an effort to sound affectionate. "Only a few minutes." Avoiding his gaze, she turned and hurried away, conscious of his eyes following her.

Free of Anton, Dominique breathed deeply of the warm, soothing breeze that ruffled her hair and made her pleated skirt dance. The salty ocean tang brought back memories of so many delightful trips — France, Italy, Greece. But this was her first passage on an American ship. She looked around curiously. So far, it appeared as fine as any she'd seen. She smiled approvingly as she entered the teak-paneled main foyer. A line of small boutiques glittered along the concourse, each offering luxury items for the amusement of the *Golden Gate*'s passengers. The display windows beckoned Dominique closer. There were evening gowns and perfumes and fine leather goods. Dominique lingered as she spotted a vivid yellow silk scarf with a geometric design of green and royal blue along the border.

She checked her watch. Ten minutes had already passed! Remembering her promise to Anton, she decided to hurry in and buy the scarf, then return to the cabin. The Dramamine was completely forgotten.

Dominique entered the shop and was greeted by a pretty young woman. "May I help you, ma'am?"

"I'd like to see the scarf in the window, please," Dominique said with a smile.

The shopgirl quickly brought it to her. "It's perfect with your hair!" the young woman exclaimed.

Dominique stood before a full length mirror and artfully draped the scarf around her neck. It *was* perfect. "I can never resist yellow," she confessed. She opened her handbag. "How much?" It hadn't occurred to her to ask before — she had never had to.

"Forty dollars, ma'am."

Dominique reached into her handbag. Her eyebrows drew together in puzzlement as she peered inside. Then the color drained from her face and her mouth opened in surprise. Where was the brown envelope she had put there yesterday?

"My money!" she gasped. Two thousand American dollars had disappeared! It was the same money that Solange had hidden away for their aborted trip to France. But this time, by virtue of Anton's American citizenship, it had been easily exchanged for dollars and legally taken from Egypt under the assumption that it was money he had brought with him from the United States.

"Oh no!" exclaimed the saleswoman. She shook her head. "The port has so many pickpockets."

Dominique wheeled away from the mirror. "It can't be that! We went right from the car to our stateroom."

"Did you have your bag with you all the time?"

"Did I?" Dominique closed her eyes and tried to concentrate. She, her mother, and Anton had boarded the *Golden Gate*, then Dominique had accompanied Solange back to the dock for their final good-bye. But she was certain she had left her purse in the stateroom, thinking it would be safer there. She couldn't imagine that any of the crew had tampered with it. Not on a ship like the *Golden Gate*.

"It has to be here!" Dominique cried. She hurried over to a glass display case and emptied the contents of her purse onto the countertop. Out tumbled a gold compact and lipstick set, a handkerchief, a brush, Dominique's passport, her marriage certificate, and her birth certificate. Everything was there but the money. She impatiently swept the items back into her purse and closed it. "I have to go to the stateroom," she said, her voice urgent. "Maybe my husband found it." She turned to go.

"Would you still like the scarf?" the young woman asked hesitantly.

Dominique put her hand to her neck, where the scarf lay draped over her collar. "Oh, I forgot." She looked over her shoulder at the young woman. "Yes, yes. Just charge it to Mademoiselle Dominique Ava — I mean Madame Anton Renard."

Dominique hurried to her room and burst through the door. Anton was sitting on a green velvet sofa, reading a newspaper. "Anton!" she cried, her hand still grasping the doorknob, "my money's gone!"

Anton folded the newspaper slowly and neatly. He remained seated. His face was stony, unreadable. He looked pointedly at his watch. "You've been almost half an hour." His tone was accusatory.

"Anton! Did you hear me?" Dominique scurried into the room, flinging the door shut behind her. "I'm missing two thousand dollars! We have to call the purser!" She looked around the well-appointed suite for the phone. It rested on the mahogany end table at Anton's side, but he made no move to pick it up.

Instead, he slowly rose to his feet, all the while brushing nonexistent wrinkles from his suit. "I have the money," he announced in a matter-of-fact tone.

Dominique closed her eyes with relief. "Oh, thank God! Where did you find it?" She held out her hand for the money.

Anton looked coolly at his wife. He allowed a few seconds to elapse. Finally, he spoke. "You didn't misplace it. I took it for safekeeping. I'm head of the family. I handle the money."

Dominique gaped at him, caught between astonishment and indignation. Her outstretched hand dropped to her side and, in the next second, contracted into a fist. "How dare you!" she cried, moving closer to Anton. "How dare you open my purse and take something without my permission!"

Anton took a step forward, too, so that they were face to face. "Don't be ridiculous." His voice was harsh. "Your money is my money."

"No it's not!" Dominique shot back. "You were given a dowry, but this money is mine! Now give it back!" she demanded, holding out her hand.

Anton's face flooded crimson. He pointedly ignored Dominique's outstretched hand. "You're my wife!" he said between clenched teeth. "I decide how we spend our money. And whether you like it or not, that's the way it is. In America, in France, and in Egypt!" he finished victoriously.

Dominique's reflex was to hurl back a denial. She opened her mouth to speak, but no words came. The horrible fact was that Anton was right and Dominique knew it. And knowing it, she had no retort for him. Furious, she glared into his self-righteous face, but it was like being confronted with a solid rock wall. There was nothing she could say to persuade or convince, no way to win her point.

Anton seemed to mistake her speechless outrage for capitulation. His expression relaxed, anger giving way to condescension. "You will have to adjust your outlook, now that you're my wife," he intoned pompously. "With all due respect to your mother, she has allowed you more independence than is good for a young woman. I can't blame

her entirely, of course — she's had no husband to take you in hand."
He put a thumb in the pocket of his vest and continued in a smug
tone. "But you'll find that marital harmony is the result of a wife yield-
ing to the greater wisdom and experience of her husband. And, my
dear" — he gave her a significant look — "that's even more true in our
case. Don't forget, I'm over twenty years your senior."

A dozen conflicting thoughts collided in Dominique's mind. She
wanted nothing more than to wipe the self-satisfied expression off her
husband's face. In one breath, he had criticized her, her mother, and
the manner in which she led her life. He had no right to judge her
or Solange!

But another part of her sounded a warning. She hardly knew this
man, yet she had to live with him — had promised to. He was taking
her away from the danger of Egypt, the sad and frightening memories.
He was offering her a chance to start anew. And, no matter how chafing
she found his approach, it was not much different from that of the
husbands of her friends.

She thought of her neighbor, Odette, whose husband forbade her
to go out without a male servant or family member for fear that she
would be accosted by other men. And Paulette's sister, who didn't buy
clothes without her husband's approval. Dominique knew scores of
women who tolerated their husband's philanderings, viewing them as
a male prerogative. If a woman philandered, however, her husband
could conceivably murder her, and the general view would be that he
was rightfully defending his honor. Male dominance was unques-
tioned in the Middle East, and the French and Italians who lived
there originated from countries almost as paternalistic.

Dominique stared up at her husband, not sure what to say. He regarded her with an air of tried patience, as though she were an unruly
child. It was a look she had often seen on Solange's face. And she was
tempted to throw out a caustic remark, to argue, as she so often had
with her mother. But she knew she wouldn't get her money that way.
All she would accomplish would be to create hostility at the outset of
her marriage.

So, for now, she clamped her mouth shut and turned away, vowing
to assert her independence when they settled into their new life together.

ᏉᎯ ᏉᎯ ᏉᎯ

"So . . . you're still here."

Anton's voice woke Dominique. The room was dark and he appeared as a shadowy form hovering over the bed. She squinted at the alarm clock on the night stand. Seven-thirty — evening already. Then she remembered. They'd argued. She'd turned away from him, silent, mentally exhausted, wanting only to be rid of him. He, too, had seemed anxious to escape. Mumbling something about cocktails, he'd hastily withdrawn. Dominique had taken off her suit and lain down, too drained for anything else.

Now she sat up and rubbed the sleep from her eyes. "What time is dinner?" she asked. She was refreshed from the long nap and her stomach growled with hunger.

"Eight thirty. We've plenty of time," Anton said.

Dominique eased her legs over the edge of the bed. "I'm going to have a shower."

"You can do that after," Anton said.

He's used to getting his way, Dominique thought. Already she could hear the rustle of his clothes as he undressed. "Lie back down," he commanded.

Dominique started to protest, then changed her mind. Maybe it was better to get it over with, since there was no way to avoid it. She did as he ordered, but made no effort to undress or get under the covers. Anton, apparently, didn't care. The mattress creaked as he moved to join her. She turned her head in revulsion as his whiskey-laden breath hit her full in the face. But he wasn't drunk. With the same economy of motion he might have used to open a window, Anton gathered the hem of her slip and pushed it up around her waist. His voice was collected as he said, "Would you please remove your panties?"

Astounded by his methodical approach, Dominique's first instinct was to balk, but her desire to finish as quickly as possible made her obey. She left on her slip, though. She didn't want to be nude in front of Anton.

When she lay down again, Anton mounted her. The soft, hairy feel of his thighs on hers was startling — Stephen's had been hard and muscled. In the dim room, Dominique couldn't see much of Anton's physique. Nor did she want to. He felt surprisingly underdeveloped. Stripped of his well-tailored suit, it was clear that his shoulders were barely wider than Dominique's; his waist was thick, almost gelatinous in texture. But his skin was cool and dry, betraying no sign of passion. She wondered what he expected of her in the way of response.

For a few seconds, Anton groped feebly at her breasts, still covered in her lacy white slip and brassiere. An impulse of kindness made Dominique roll to her side so that he could unsnap the bra. There was no point in being uncooperative — Anton was her husband and this was only the first of many such episodes, she was certain. It was best to resign herself to the inevitable and try to make it as successful as possible. Solange's words echoed in her memory: "You don't love Anton now, but you'll learn to, as I did your father."

Dominique closed her eyes and tried to muster a pinpoint of tenderness for her husband. But his gestures were so hopelessly clumsy, so lacking in fire, that they were distracting. Nevertheless, Dominique was dismayed to discover that he was immediately ready to penetrate her. Without making any attempt to excite her, Anton inserted his member. Every muscle in Dominique's body rebelled against the intrusion. She went rigid, crying out at the friction against her dry skin.

"It always hurts the first time," Anton explained, his tone apologetic but dismissive. He thrust himself more deeply into her.

Dominique squeezed her eyes shut and resolved to endure it. She wanted to be anywhere but there. Her mind fled to Stephen. She could withstand the experience if she imagined him in Anton's place. The memory of his lean, hard muscles and warm, bronze skin made her relax a little. But she had no time to immerse herself in her fantasy, for Anton finished almost at once. He stroked perhaps a dozen times before he shuddered silently and collapsed on top of her. For a few seconds, he remained in that position, then he rolled off her and hurried into the bathroom. Dominique clamped her legs together in involuntary disgust. The encounter had in no way resembled lovemaking. Dominique wondered if Anton had any real desire for her or if he, too, was simply performing a dreaded duty. He had mentioned more than once that he wanted to begin a family.

Dominique vowed to obtain contraception immediately.

ᢁᡎ ᢁᡎ ᢁᡎ

Dominique gripped the armrest on the inside of the taxi door as it plummeted down the steepest road she'd ever seen. Every so often the automobile would veer alarmingly, the result of hitting a cable car track. The driver would jerk the wheel back, and the taxi would resume its jangling progress.

Anton studied his bride with a look of amusement. "Lucky it isn't raining," he remarked, "or it would be even worse."

Dominique smiled weakly and tried to relax. It wasn't that she didn't like San Francisco. From the time the boat had entered the choppy waters of San Francisco Bay that morning, Dominique had been awed by the dramatic surroundings. Everything about the city was exhilarating, from the brisk wind that chased the final wisps of late morning fog, to the green mountains and vast bridges that punctuated the landscape of the bay. But the city was so strange — unlike any she had seen before. She was acutely aware of being a foreigner, of being thousands of miles from home.

As they rose to the crest of the hill and turned a corner, Dominique blinked, not believing the vision before her. Rising surrealistically from the street was a Chinese pagoda — in the middle of an American city! The taxi turned again and entered a narrow street lined with busy shops, many with their doors thrown open to attract passersby. Stands filled with vegetables, fruit, and fresh seafood spilled into the walk. An old woman in a pointed straw hat scurried out of a fish market carrying a pole across her back with a bucket suspended at each end. It was like something out of a painting!

"The Chinese like their seafood *very* fresh," Anton joked, following her gaze. "There are some wonderful restaurants here." He smiled. "This is a little out of our way, but I thought you'd like to see the city."

"Oh, yes!" Dominique said enthusiastically. She gave Anton a look of polite appreciation, as she might have given an acquaintance who had done her a favor. He still seemed almost a stranger to her. Though they'd spent three weeks together on the ship, Dominique knew very little about her husband. Other than the initial dispute over money, their relations had been civil, but distant. They had spent little time together during the day: Dominique enjoyed the beauty treatments and shops (charging her few purchases to their stateroom), while Anton played cards or billiards. When the weather was warm, Dominique would settle cozily into a lounge chair with a novel, often chatting with neighbors. Anton preferred to socialize at the bar. In the evenings, they dined at a table for eight, so there was no chance for intimacy. Anton didn't seem to mind; indeed, he showed little interest in

Dominique. He danced the requisite dances with her, told her she looked nice when she dressed for dinner, and carefully confined his toiletries to one corner of the bathroom. Otherwise, their contact was limited.

"It's a shame you don't like cards," he'd commented once as he dressed to meet his group. But his tone betrayed no genuine regret.

If Anton had been less indifferent, Dominique might have felt more guilty about her daydreams of Stephen. She tried to stifle them. But they came unbidden to her, surprising her, ambushing the course she had set for herself.

Now, as she gazed out the car window, she forced herself to mentally focus on Anton. They would be arriving home soon. His home. Her new home. She would meet his mother, whom Anton had written with news of their marriage. Dominique pragmatically anticipated that Madame Renard would be pleased by her son's match. After all, the old woman had, according to Anton, encouraged him to return to Egypt to find a wife. And he had found a wealthy one.

Anton's voice broke into Dominique's introspection. They were in the financial district now, he told her. Dominique looked up at the skyscrapers that flanked the street. Each area of the city was so different from the last! A few more blocks and they were in the downtown shopping district. Then the sophisticated department stores and hotels of Union Square gave way to gingerbread Victorians trimmed in bright colors. They turned again and encountered a series of splendid mansions overlooking the sea. This was the most beautiful neighborhood Dominique had seen so far. "Are we close?" she asked hopefully. She leaned forward and looked at the vista below: blue water tipped with whitecaps, misty mountains, and careening seabirds. She felt her heart quicken in excitement. She could live here! This neighborhood seemed familiar, with its grand European-style architecture: generous bow windows overlooking the water, sweeping terraces, and imposing porticos.

"Nothing's very far in San Francisco," Anton replied.

Dominique settled back in her seat, feeling less apprehensive. San Francisco was really quite lovely.

They came to a vast park, an oasis of green. The kind of deep, vivid green reminiscent of England. Dominique saw mothers pushing strollers, lovers walking hand in hand. "What a huge park!" she exclaimed.

"Golden Gate Park," Anton said proudly. "We're almost home."

The car traveled south and they exited the park. Soon Dominique spotted row after row of stucco houses painted a lively variety of colors, but mostly white, cream, pink, and yellow. Their tile roofs reminded Dominique of Italy. Each little home had a neat green lawn bordered with colorful flowers. The area was well tended, obviously comfortable and respectable, but unmistakably several rungs down the economic ladder from the neighborhood that had impressed Dominique a few moments before.

The taxi slowed in front of a white house with second floor awnings of dark blue. Like its neighbors, it had a patch of crisp, green lawn and several rose bushes. Anton smoothed his hair and put on his hat. He turned to Dominique. "This is it," he announced, not meeting her eye.

Dominique's smile froze. She looked from the modest house back to Anton, dumbfounded. There was nothing wrong with the house, nothing to cause Dominique to shrink from it. But Anton had given the impression that he was very well off, and this certainly wasn't the house of a wealthy man.

The taxi driver opened Dominique's door. Mechanically, she stepped out. Her high heels sank into the damp grass and she looked down in dismay as the wetness seeped into the delicate kid of her pumps. She lifted her foot carefully, so that her shoe would stay on, then stepped forward. A high-pitched bell sounded a warning and she stopped just in time to avoid a young boy speeding down the sidewalk on a red bicycle with training wheels. The boy passed her in a *whoosh* of air, then turned around and yelled over his shoulder, "Sorry!"

Dominique couldn't help laughing. "Okay!" She said the first American phrase she could think of. She would have to get back into the habit of thinking in English. On the boat, Anton had spoken only French to her.

Somehow, the exchange with the little boy cheered Dominique. She stepped onto the sidewalk and took a good look around the neighborhood. It reminded her of the idyllic small towns she'd seen in Mickey Rooney movies. It was a world away from what she had expected of Anton, but, she decided, it was charmingly American. The prospect of living in a place so different from the one she was used to made her feel adventurous.

Eager to see the inside of her new home, Dominique turned and watched Anton pay the driver. She shivered as the wind whipped through the fine wool of her dress. If this was what San Francisco was like in May, she would need to buy heavier clothes.

Anton came to Dominique's side and took her arm. "The driver will get the bags."

Dominique noticed that he didn't ask her how she liked the house. In fact, he continued to avoid her eyes. She followed him through a hip-high picket fence, then up a stone walk. There was a small porch in front, but it was devoid of furniture or flower urns. Dominique would have festooned it with wisteria or jasmine or whatever grew in San Francisco's chilly climate. Yet this place was oddly sterile.

As though reading her thoughts, Anton said, "This is just a temporary rental. We had a house on Nob Hill before, but things took a downturn." His tone was not apologetic; rather, it warned Dominique to accept the situation without comment.

"How long have you lived here?" she asked as she mounted the steps.

Anton shrugged and mumbled something unintelligible. He searched in his pockets for his keys, but before he could find them, the door was thrown open.

Anton's mother stepped onto the porch and flung her arms around her son. Anton hugged her back, holding her close for a few seconds, then kissing her with genuine feeling. Dominique was surprised at the emotion he displayed. Pleased. Perhaps there was more to Anton than she thought. The affectionate exchange between mother and son gave Dominique the chance to study Madame Renard. She was a short, wiry woman with dark hair almost entirely devoid of gray. She might have looked almost as young as Anton were she not wearing the sort of shapeless black dress common to older women in Mediterranean countries.

After a few moments, Anton gently disengaged himself from his mother's grasp. The woman released her son with obvious reluctance, but she allowed him to turn her toward Dominique. She continued to smile as she regarded her daughter-in-law, but the glow disappeared.

"Mother, this is my wife, Dominique Avallon."

Dominique extended her hand. *"Enchantée, Madame Renard,"* she said warmly.

The older woman's eyes showed no responding warmth, though she kept her smile in place. Her gaze dropped to Dominique's handmade shoes, then rose to take in her ivory wool dress, her windblown curls and fashionable hat. When her eyes met Dominique's, their expression was calculating. Her fixed smile widened slightly. She stretched her hand out to meet Dominique's and squeezed it in a grip of surprising strength. "How do you do?" Though uttered in French, her words had none of the welcoming lilt of that language.

An awkward silence fell over the trio as they waited for the taxi driver to struggle to the porch with the last of the bags. Dominique searched her mind for a topic. "Anton tells me you prefer to speak French. That will be good," she said in a gracious tone. "I don't want to forget my own language now that I'm in America."

"I don't speak English," Madame Renard said blandly. She turned to lead the way into the foyer.

On the left was a straight wooden staircase, on the right, a living room decorated with old-fashioned fussiness. Dominique stopped under the arch that marked the entrance to the living room and waited for the other two, now occupied with hanging Anton's raincoat in the hall closet.

She couldn't imagine that the living room reflected her husband's taste. A pair of beige drapes trimmed with small brown pom-poms blocked most of the sun from the wide window that overlooked the front yard. Perpendicular to the window was a frilly-skirted sofa covered in brown, pumpkin, and gold flowered chintz. Opposite the sofa, two dark brown Victorian armchairs with antimacassars draped over their backs. They flanked a fireplace that appeared never to have been used. Dominique's eyes traveled upward. In a place of honor over the mantle was a still life of poor quality.

Dominique tried to stifle the depression that threatened her. After all, the house was clean. The hardwood floor gleamed and there wasn't any dust. With the drapes thrown open, a few nice paintings, and some bright pillows, the house could be inviting.

"My room's this way." Anton picked up two bags and indicated the direction with a jerk of his head. Dominique started to follow her husband up the stairs, as his mother silently watched the pair.

Anton stopped, one foot on the step above. "Will you bring up one of the bags?" he said over his shoulder to Dominique.

They had no household help? It was a concept totally foreign to her. In Egypt, all but the poorest had servants. But perhaps the same wasn't so in America. Dominique's only reference point, once again, was the movies. In most of the films she'd seen, a uniformed woman with a white pinafore hovered in the background. Dominique tried to recall if Danielle had ever referred to domestics in her letters. She couldn't remember.

With each moment that passed, Dominique felt more out of place, but she didn't want to show it. She turned and looked at the bags lining the foyer. Mechanically, she went and picked one up.

At the top of the stairs, she and Anton turned into a narrow, dim hallway. They passed a large bedroom with several windows. Dominique glanced inside, noting a white chenille bedspread and a run-of-the-mill bedroom set — headboard, bureau, and end tables in matching wood. Then they entered a smaller room.

Dominique stopped in the threshold and gasped. It was a world unto itself, a cavern of treasures. A canopied double bed draped with extravagant maroon brocade dominated the space. It was beautifully complemented by end tables of rosewood and walnut marquetry upon which rested silk-shaded chinoiserie lamps. Opposite the bed, a burled walnut chest of drawers — obviously a valuable antique — was decorated with items that revealed its occupant's sybaritic bent: a sterling silver brush, comb, and hand mirror; a brass-trimmed mahogany case containing three Baccarat decanters labeled "port," "whiskey," and "sherry"; a mirrored tray of men's colognes; and a tooled leather box for cuff links and studs.

Anton watched his wife with a smug expression. She could see that he enjoyed her astonishment. "I hope you don't mind that I've given Maman the bigger room."

"No . . . ," Dominique said vaguely, still trying to take in her surroundings. She did a one-hundred-eighty-degree turn, noting the gilded wall sconces and fine paintings. When she stopped, she was looking into the hall. The door opposite must be the bathroom, she thought. She crossed to it and looked inside. Black and white tile dating from the 1930s; old, worn-looking fixtures. The space was only slightly larger than her shower at home, and a rack of drying nylons told her that they would share it with Anton's mother. But, Dominique tried to rationalize, it was clean and contained all the necessities. She'd have to get used to it, she told herself firmly.

She crossed back to the astounding bedroom. "Anton" — she hesitated — "are these all things you brought with you from your other house?"

Anton emptied the contents of his valise on the bed and looked up with a puzzled expression. There was a second of silence. Then he said, "Oh, yes, yes." He straightened and brushed past Dominique. "Put those things away. I'll get the trunks."

She stared at Anton's departing back, still a little bewildered. Why was his room the only one containing items of value? Didn't he care about the rest of his house? And wasn't a man accustomed to such resplendent surroundings also used to having servants? Before Anton reached the staircase, Dominique ventured a question. "Anton . . . . " He turned, his expression one of elaborate patience. Dominique continued, "Don't you have help?" The change on his face stopped her cold.

His brows drew together and his complexion darkened. He came back to where she was standing and gripped her upper arm, leading her back into his room. "Things are expensive in America!" he said in a low, fervent voice. "I told you I had a downturn! As soon as we get the first payment from your mother's cotton, we'll be able to do more."

Dominique tilted her head and gave him a look of bewilderment. "But Anton, when you proposed, I never thought we'd have to depend on Avallon Cotton stock!"

He pointed an accusing finger at her. "You've had it easy all your life. You've been spoiled," he declared, his voice rising. "And I don't intend to coddle you. You can ask your mother to send you more money, but don't complain to me!"

Dominique recoiled. He couldn't have surprised her more if he'd punched her. In a split second, he'd changed from welcoming to antagonistic. Until now, Dominique had supposed that he was at least attracted to her, a much younger woman. Did he find nothing admirable, alluring, or even likable about her? Was it only Solange's money?

She faced him squarely, her hands on her hips, her eyes snapping with indignation. "I am *not* complaining, I am merely asking a question, which you've now answered! And I am *not* going to ask my mother for more money!"

Anton looked taken aback by the strength of her tone. With an air of wounded dignity, he said, "I would have hoped for my wife to be supportive. My business has succumbed to . . . difficulties. You're well off. . . ." His sentence tapered off. He was silent for a moment. He tugged at the knot of his tie as though it were too tight. Then he resumed. "After all, it isn't unusual for a wife to help her husband when there's trouble."

Dominique studied her husband. "What trouble?" she asked suspiciously.

Anton's eyes shifted away from hers. "Well, the business has been difficult to reestablish. You see, I —"

"What!" Dominique had no patience for a long, oblique explanation. She looked around at the exquisite bedroom, at her husband's suit. Everything was of the best quality. "How do you pay for . . ." She swept her hand downward in a gesture that clearly indicated his clothes. Then she threw her arms wide to indicate their surroundings.

Dominique saw the same sly look on Anton's face that she had seen earlier on his mother's. "I have savings . . . investments," he said cryptically.

Dominique regarded him steadily. In Egypt, it was not uncommon for well-off men to live on their investments and never work. Like European aristocracy, they spent their days playing polo, golf, or cards. But now that she'd seen Anton's home, she could hardly believe he was wealthy enough for such a life.

As though reading her thoughts, he said defensively, "I want to work, you know. I just need some money to get my business back on its feet."

Dominique's eyes narrowed. "And you thought I would provide it?"

Anton shifted his feet. At first his expression was sheepish, but Dominique could see that whatever shame he felt he quickly suppressed. The cold mask fell back into place. "We are married. What's yours is mine now."

Dominique raised her eyebrows sardonically. "Well, I'm sorry to disappoint you, but unless you want some of my dresses, you've already taken all my assets." She was now thankful that she'd been too frightened by the customs house incident to risk bringing any important jewelry from Egypt.

"Well. . . ." Anton hesitated. "Then we'll just have to wait for the cotton money. It's only a few more months."

But Dominique had already decided she wasn't going to wait for anyone to give her money. "In the meantime," she announced, "I'm going to find a job." She prepared herself for an onslaught of protest. She remembered Anton's shock and disapproval of her job with the RAF.

But, surprisingly, Anton protested not at all. He shrugged and said, "Suit yourself." Then, as an afterthought, "But remember, I handle the money."

∽ ∽ ∽

Dominique turned her face toward the feeble light and opened her eyes. Everything was smoky. With a gasp of surprise, she jerked to a sitting position. Her eyes were wide open now, but she had no idea where she was. She looked around. The sheets beside her were rumpled and there were oily stains on the pillow. Suddenly, she remembered. Anton's hair pomade. She shuddered and averted her eyes until she was once more gazing out the window. The fog, it was so thick! Dominique had never seen any like it. Fascinated, she swung her legs over the side of the bed and padded to the window. The grayish white cloud obscured everything. It seemed hard to believe that the day before had been bright and sunny.

She turned to the gold Florentine clock on Anton's nightstand. It was already past nine! With sudden vigor, Dominique moved to the closet. She selected the first casual dress she came to, a pale yellow cotton shift, then hurried downstairs, eager to search the newspaper's Help Wanted section.

When she reached the living room, she found Madame Renard in one of the brown armchairs. The older woman had a pair of glasses perched on her nose and she was mending a shirt of Anton's.

"*Bonjour*," Dominique said.

The old woman raised her head and returned the greeting with a lukewarm smile. Once again, Dominique was acutely conscious of the woman's scrutiny.

Dominique tried for a friendly tone. "Have you had breakfast?" she asked.

"I don't eat breakfast. Anton already had his. He's gone out. There's some coffee left, I think. And there's some bread if you want to make toast."

Dominique smelled bacon and noted that she was offered none. But she didn't care, she was used to the French-style breakfast of bread, jam, and café au lait. "Thank you," Dominique said. She passed through the living room, then the small dining room behind it, and leaned into the swinging kitchen door.

Madame Renard's voice stopped her. "By the way . . . " Dominique stepped back into the dining area and looked attentively at the older woman. "I made Anton's breakfast this morning. But in the future, I'm sure you'll want to get up and make it for him."

Dominique raised her eyebrows. What was she supposed to say to that? She decided on the truth, though she knew Madame Renard would disapprove. "I'm afraid he wouldn't like that. You see, I have no idea how to cook."

Madame Renard put down the shirt she was mending and removed her glasses. She gave Dominique a penetrating look. "Anton told me of your background. I'm afraid it hasn't prepared you for life in America. I warned my son —" She stopped. After an awkward pause, she said with a trace of sympathy, "Anton tells me that your father died when you were a child."

Dominique came forward until she was standing at the threshold of the living room. "Yes, I was nine." Her voice grew somber, as it always did when she spoke of her father's death.

Madame Renard tilted her head. "Of course I understand that you were not brought up with a man in the house. But surely a woman of your mother's breeding has told you what's expected of a wife."

An icy calm settled over Dominique. For the second time in as many weeks, she — and Solange — were being criticized for her failure to behave as Anton's subordinate. She bit the inside of her mouth, determined not to lose her temper, but equally determined to stand up for herself. "Frankly, Madame Renard, your son led my mother to believe that he was a wealthy man with an active business. Mother — and I — assumed that my life here would be very much as it was at home."

The older woman regarded her daughter-in-law steadily. She showed no sign of surprise.

Dominique continued. "As I'm sure you know, the payment to Anton when my mother's cotton is sold will be very generous. And he'll continue to profit from his stock. Furthermore" — she walked slowly toward her mother-in-law — "he took two thousand dollars from my handbag as soon as we were married." Dominique stopped and crossed her arms. "So, to put it bluntly, Anton has profited from this marriage while I —" She hesitated, afraid she would go too far. This was her mother-in-law, after all. She owed her some respect. In addition, what good did it do to criticize Anton to his mother, who adored and depended on him?

Madame Renard's lips tightened until they were nearly invisible. "A woman's duty is to look after her husband. These are things that every wife does for her husband and you'll need to learn. You don't intend to neglect that, I hope," she challenged.

"I'll do my share," Dominique replied at once. "But I won't be the maid here," she warned. "And I'm going to find a job."

Anton's mother leapt to her feet. "Your first duty is to your husband! If working is an excuse to neglect —"

"I'll do my share!" Dominique cut in, her voice rising. She fixed the other woman with a level gaze.

Madame Renard threw the shirt she was holding on the chair and strode from the room.

Dominique's stomach churned with tension. It occurred to her that, so far, she had found little in her married life to recommend it.

After the first few bumpy days, however, Dominique discovered the key to peace with Anton: the promise of money. She quickly found a job as a secretary in the international currency department of San Francisco's largest bank, and she looked forward to going to work each day. As soon as she hopped aboard the cable car that whizzed her downtown, she felt more alive. The atmosphere in the financial district throbbed with vitality. Everyone walked purposefully, eager to get on with their work. And when Dominique entered the sprawling marble lobby of her bank, she felt as though she belonged. She quickly made friends, and one in particular, a pretty Chinese-American named Susan Lee, became her daily lunch companion.

Anton, on the other hand, took little interest in her job except on Fridays, payday. Then he waited outside the bank for her and collected the cash she had in her purse, leaving her enough for the next week's lunches and nylons. What he didn't know was that Dominique had opened an account and was depositing almost one third of her fifty-dollar paycheck in it. It was her secret way of rebelling.

As for the disputed housework, Anton's mother prepared the evening meals and made the beds. After dinner, the women took turns cleaning up. Dominique would then retire to the bathroom to wash and set her hair for the next day. Anton would either remain in the living room with his mother or, just as often, go out to play cards.

Sunday was the family's day for major house cleaning. The first time, Dominique, in her ignorance, allowed Anton's mother to "teach" her. This meant that Madame Renard hovered over Dominique, every so often issuing laconic criticism. The next Sunday, Dominique insisted that they would finish more quickly if they divided the tasks. So Anton's mother dusted, vacuumed, and changed the sheets, while Dominique scrubbed the bathroom and kitchen and swept. She even persuaded Anton to haul the basket of wash to the basement laundry room on the grounds that the job required a man's strength.

It was the only work Dominique ever saw Anton do. He disappeared from the house before she left for work, but what he did all day, Dominique didn't know. He occasionally brought home a new item of clothing for himself — a silk tie or a set of handkerchiefs. These he would carefully place between layers of tissue in his bureau.

One evening, as Dominique watched this meticulous procedure, she asked him, "Have you ever thought about decorating the rest of the house? I feel a little guilty that our bedroom is so much grander than your mother's."

"You shouldn't," Anton said flatly. "Hers is bigger."

His shortness made Dominique wonder if he begrudged his mother the master bedroom. But why should he? It was his house. It had been his choice to give it to her. Dominique changed tacks. "But wouldn't it be nice to redecorate the living room?"

Anton shrugged. "We'll see in November."

It was a constant refrain. Anton made it clear that almost every aspect of their future depended on the cotton money. Dominique didn't like that, but she knew there was nothing she could do about it. And she couldn't help looking forward to the day when Anton would start his new business and they would no longer depend on her dowry. She imagined that when he was busy again — earning a living, feeling productive — he would be less withdrawn. It was this hope that made her daily life with him bearable.

Nights, though, were more distressing. Dominique read as late as she dared, but all too often, when she turned off the light, she would hear Anton's voice in the dark.

"Lift up your nightgown," he would instruct. It was a frequent ritual, an odiously frequent ritual. Dominique had learned to insert her diaphragm before going to bed, as routinely as she brushed her teeth, all the while dreading what was to come. Oddly enough, it wasn't Anton's touch that was so objectionable, it was the sickly sweet smell of his hair pomade. It would assail her nostrils as he rose and fell on top of her. The smell had begun to symbolize all that repelled Dominique about Anton. It was greasy and suffocating — a failed attempt at order and refinement, like Anton's entire life. So she turned her head away and imagined he was Stephen in order to get through the invasion.

Afterward, her mind would drift to thoughts of divorce. What if Stephen were free? What if his reconciliation with Serena hadn't worked? To see him again, just *see* him . . . But then what? Dominique had been indoctrinated since childhood to believe that marriage was permanent, divorce unacceptable. How could she face her family if she left Anton? He might be lazy, but he didn't abuse her. She might not like the fact that he had taken her money, but it wasn't unusual. Besides, marriage demanded compromise.

Then an event occurred that changed everything.

Dominique was home one Saturday in July enjoying her solitude. Anton had gone to play cards and his mother was at the market. The sun sparkled through the living-room window, urging Dominique outside. She threw open the front door and stepped onto her porch, inhaling the warm, fresh air. Her next-door neighbor looked up from his roses and waved his pruning shears in greeting.

"Hello, Mr. Vitalli." Dominique smiled with pleasure. The old man was a masterful gardener and the sweet fragrance of his blooms perfumed the air.

"Gorgeous day!" Mr. Vitalli called back.

Squinting her eyes against the sun, Dominique peered at the flower-filled terra-cotta pots that lined Mr. Vitalli's stairs. She wondered if Anton would give her money to buy flowerpots for their own house; she wouldn't use her own savings.

The ring of the telephone interrupted Dominique's thoughts. She turned and hurried into the house, wondering if it was Susan, from the bank. They had talked about seeing a movie that afternoon. She eagerly picked up the phone, which rested on a table near the couch. The voice that greeted Dominique was that of a stranger. The woman spoke in rapid French, clearly mistaking Dominique for the elder Madame Renard.

"Bonjour, Madame Renard, c'est Marie. Pourrais-je parler à Anton?"

Dominique replied in French. "This isn't Anton's mother, but I'm Madame Renard. He's not here, though. May I take a message?"

Silence.

"Hello, are you still there?" Dominique asked.

"You're Anton's *wife?*" The woman sounded stunned.

"Yes," Dominique said impatiently. Was this an old girlfriend?

"May I take a message?" She leaned over and picked up the pencil that lay near the phone. Dominique was disturbed to hear the woman burst into laughter. "Why are you laughing?" she asked uneasily.

"Welcome to the club!" said the woman with cynical cheer.

Dominique's grip tightened on the phone. Her mind was racing ahead. "The club?" Her voice rose anxiously. She dreaded what was to come.

"How much did he take *you* for?" the woman asked with bitter amusement.

Dominique's pulse roared in her ear as she pressed the receiver closer. "You were married to him?" she asked in a voice that was deceptively calm. The eraser of her pencil shot across the room as her thumb mashed into it, tearing it from its anchor. Dominique slumped into the couch, yanking the phone from the table to her lap. "Tell me!" she commanded, too distraught to phrase it politely.

The woman let out a mirthless bark. "I was his second wife. He ran through the dowry of the first one in five years. A Canadian . . . Montreal I think. Her father owned hardware stores or something like that. My father has vineyards in Bordeaux."

Dominique listened in stunned silence — at the pit of her stomach, a grinding anger.

The woman went on. "And you? Not from France, I'll wager; he keeps a distance between wives so their families don't find out about him."

"Egypt," Dominique whispered. She thought of Anton's hands on her at night, his loose, white body — of what she had endured out of a sense of duty! She squirmed with revulsion. She had been so worried about keeping her word. Worried about staying with the husband she had married for convenience. She had thought she *owed* him. And now she was faced with a betrayal so vile that it was almost unimaginable!

"Ah, yes. . . . Anton has family in Egypt," Marie was saying. "Unfortunately, he has family in many countries and I don't think any of them know about his schemes."

Dominique thought of the Renards. She and her mother had known them for years. They couldn't have known about Anton! *Couldn't* have betrayed her, too! Dominique shook her head vehemently. "What schemes?" she rasped.

Marie's voice filled with disgust. "He's a con artist! He robbed my father of the last of his savings! But the sickening thing is, he didn't do anything illegal!" She spoke fast, clearly relieved to talk about it. "Father was almost ruined by World War II. But he had enough for a dowry to ensure that I 'married well,' as he put it. He thought Anton was a good match. The Renard family is highly respected in France. Anyhow, it wasn't until after the marriage that I realized Anton had a gambling problem. When I told Father, he hired a private detective to find out just how much he was losing, and how often. That's how I discovered his first marriage."

"Gambling problem?" Dominique said dully. She was going to be sick to her stomach. She didn't trust herself to say another word.

"Ha! You didn't think he was playing cards for pennies, did you?"

Dominique cradled her head in her hand. It was spinning, the room fuzzy. "I hadn't really thought about it," she said weakly. Solange played cards every day and there had never been a money problem. Dominique tried frantically to think if there had been other clues she'd missed. But what? "I don't understand." Her tone was suddenly belligerent. She wanted to find a gap in Marie's story. Wanted to believe that Anton was no longer gambling away his money. "If he keeps losing money, how can he afford this house? All those nice things?"

"The house!" Marie's voice was incredulous. "It isn't his, it's his mother's!" She paused. "Does he still have that fancy bedroom?" Her voice was filled with scorn. At Dominique's silence, Marie continued. "Paid for with my father's money!"

Dominique caught her breath. "What about Anton's business?" she choked.

"I see he didn't change one line of his story," Marie said dryly.

Dominique was frantic — her knuckles white from grasping the phone so hard. She had to get away from Anton! Her muscles twitched with the urge to throw down the phone and *run*. No! That wouldn't help. Slow down and *think*, she commanded herself.

"Are you all right?" The woman's voice pierced her conscience.

Dominique took a tremulous breath. "I . . . I don't know. . . . I don't know what to do. . . . I . . ." She was silent for a moment, then she blurted out the thought that was uppermost in her mind. "I have to get away from him!"

"That would be my advice," the woman said sympathetically.

But how could she leave? She imagined herself going upstairs, packing her clothes, going to a local hotel. But she had only five dollars in her handbag. And the bank wasn't even open on Saturdays. She would have to go to a cheap hotel, the kind that demanded payment in advance. Until Monday, she could do nothing. And then what? Her confused mind was unable to focus. She needed time to think.

Dominique appealed to the woman. "Please! I know you're angry at him. I know you called to talk to him. But please don't let him know you spoke to me. I need some time to plan. Do you understand?"

"I certainly do!" the woman said fervently. "But be careful. Be smart. Just because you leave him, don't think you're finished. As long as he thinks he can get money from you, he'll keep trying." She paused, then said sourly, "Anyhow, I only called to tell him to stop pestering me. He already cost me my job. I'm going back to France and he'll never get another penny from me! We'll see how he likes that!" she snarled. Then she let out a satisfied chuckle. "But knowing that you'll have your revenge is delicious. I hope you get the best of him."

With fumbling movements, Dominique placed the phone back in the cradle. She held the cold object on her lap and stared straight ahead like a sleepwalker. She wanted to leave. Now. Never come back. But as she considered her alternatives, envisioned the consequences of leaving, she realized it was too soon.

You've made a mistake. Don't make it worse! She had to be cunning, more cunning than Anton. She had to plan carefully, to look after herself. "Be smart," Marie had said. What was the smartest thing to do?

She could try putting aside more money, but whatever meager amount she could save would last only a short while. She would have to ask Solange for money. If only she could call her! But telephone communications in Egypt were primitive. Dominique would never get through on the first try. The operator would have to call back. And what if Anton or his mother were home by then? A wire wouldn't do either; it would cost far too much to explain everything. And she *had* to explain everything so that Solange would be as outraged as Dominique. A letter would be best. In the meantime, though, every instinct told Dominique that she had to conceal from Anton what she had learned.

Dominique bolted up decisively. She would write the letter and mail it before Anton or his mother returned. And she would warn Solange to send her response to Dominique in care of the bank. After everything else he had done, Anton would hardly shrink from opening her mail.

∽ ∽ ∽

Dearest Dominique,

The turn of events you have described is, of course, disastrous. I had such hopes for your marriage to Anton and your new life in America.

As you requested, I have refrained from contacting his family here; however, I am most anxious to discuss this with them as soon as possible. It is inconceivable that such fine people could have known about his past. This is a matter I cannot leave unresolved.

It distresses me that I can be of no help to you. Foreigners' assets here are more closely watched than ever, and we are now forbidden to send any money out of the country. In fact, cash withdrawals at banks are limited to an amount that barely enables me to cover my household expenses.

You will have read that the British spent the month of June evacuating the Suez Canal Zone. No one knows what the Nasser government will do next. Our friend the deputy minister fears for his position, as he is considered one of the "old guard" and not well looked upon by some influential members of the new regime. Extremists in the government are urging the president to nationalize the Canal, which, as you know, would be perilous. Britain and France would almost certainly go to war to defend their access.

Cousin René's textile manufacturing plant was nationalized right after you left. He was promised compensation, but the terms are laughable. In exchange for an operation which brought him millions a year, he has been given Egyptian government bonds with various terms of maturity. In effect, they have stolen the factory. René hopes to emigrate to France, but the government has told him he must continue on at the plant to train the new director. He and his family will be arrested if they try to flee.

For the first time, I, too, am uneasy about my prospects here. I have insisted that Nanny go to her sister in France. But I suppose I will die here. I don't wish to leave, despite everything. As long as I remain, I believe I'll be able live as I always have. It is those foreigners who seek to leave who fall under government suspicion.

I hope by the time you receive this letter you will have found a solution to your dilemma. Divorce is a drastic measure and one to which our family has never resorted. I know that what Anton has done seems hei-

nous, but reflect carefully whether you wish to be a divorcée. Life can be difficult for a woman alone, most particularly for a woman without financial resources. Sometimes even the worst of husbands can smooth a woman's way in the world. I gather that you fear no physical threat from Anton. You might consider at least waiting until the November cotton sale. Since that takes place overseas, I feel confident I will be able to forward him the profit to which his shares entitle him (I regret now that I did not put them in both your names, but, of course, it is the husband who manages the money). Perhaps that will make your life with him easier.

I know this is not the answer you were anticipating and that the situation appears hopeless, but if you could view it through my eyes, through the perspective of greater experience, you would perhaps understand why I am not certain that divorce is the best solution. I know that things are more liberal in America, but I must remind you that divorce is still considered a disgrace among our people — a last resort born of desperation. I beg you not to act with your usual impetuosity.

Love,
Your mother

Dominique reread the letter twice as she leaned against the partition in the ladies' room. She had shut herself into the little stall, wanting no interruptions from curious co-workers. Now, in shock, she kicked down the toilet lid and collapsed onto the seat. She was stunned by the hatred — the sheer, desperate hatred — for Solange that boiled through her. With trembling hands, she tore the thin paper into tiny pieces, clutching the debris in her fists. Overwhelmed with despair, she closed her eyes.

She had waited five weeks for the letter in her hand. Five weeks with a husband she despised. It had been endurable only because she had been sure that help was on the way. She had counted on Solange. Now Solange wouldn't help! But the final blow, the most wounding, was that Solange seemed to assign some blame to Dominique. The letter's closing line stung. "I beg you not to act with your usual impetuosity." Was it impetuous to want to leave a liar and a swindler? Was Solange so afraid of disgrace that she would ask Dominique to endure the marriage? There *had* to be a way to get money out of Egypt. Dominique opened her clenched fists and looked at the tiny pieces of paper in her hand. A dull, gnawing pain started in her stomach. She clenched her fists and huddled close to the wall, her teeth chattering. It was hard to think logically. Rocking unconsciously to and fro, she tried to regain control of her emotions. She inhaled deeply in an attempt to calm herself. In. Out. A few more breaths and she was able to think more coherently.

Where could she go? How could she start a new life with less than two hundred dollars? Today was Friday, so she could take her entire check and decamp. But even that would add only fifty dollars to her meager savings. What she needed was a place to stay until she could save more. But the idea of even one more day with Anton was too detestable to contemplate. On the other hand, if she left, he would surely make trouble for her at the bank. He would insist that she stay with him until November as insurance for the payment of her dowry.

She had to leave San Francisco! And that meant she had only one possible refuge. Her sister, Danielle. But Danielle had a family now. What if they didn't have room for her? Dominique jumped to her feet. She would call right now and ask.

Moving with frantic haste, she jerked open the door of the stall so hard that it crashed against the wall. Oblivious to the noise, she rushed from the ladies' room. When she reached her desk, she realized she was still clutching Solange's shredded letter. With a vigorous swipe of her hands, she brushed the bits of paper into the trash. Only after she sat down and picked up the phone did she hesitate. What if Danielle refused? What if she, too, advised Dominique not to divorce? And how would Danielle's husband, Ronald, react? Impossible to say. The last time Dominique had seen him, she had been thirteen. Only a sketchy image of him remained in her memory — a swaggering American naval officer with sunshine blond hair. Her sister had met him in Alexandria just after World War II, at a time when all Americans had been regarded as heroes. They had fallen in love and married quickly. Danielle had been eighteen, young by American standards, but just the right age for marriage in Egypt, even among Europeans. Then they'd gone back to America, where Ronald had entered the field of advertising.

Now, as Dominique sat at her desk, her hand frozen on the telephone, she realized that so much time had passed that she couldn't predict what sort of welcome she might expect from either Danielle or Ron.

Suppose, though, that she simply showed up in New York. They could hardly refuse her a place to stay for a few nights. Dominique was confident she could find a job as quickly as she had in San Francisco. That was the way to do it, she decided boldly — present them with a fait accompli.

∾ ∾ ∾

Dominique carried her valise to the phone booth of the New York Port Authority bus terminal and closed the door on the cacophony of the station. She dialed Danielle's number, her stomach fluttering with anxiety as she waited for the call to go through.

"Hello." A weary male voice came over the telephone line. It didn't sound like anyone Dominique knew.

"Hello, is this the Marks residence?" she asked tentatively.

"Yes, this is Ronald Marks." More inviting this time, with a note of expectation.

Dominique made her voice as pleasant as possible. "Hello, Ronald, it's Dominique. How are you?"

There was a pause. "Oh, hi. Okay I guess." His voice sank, his disappointment almost palpable. "You want to speak to Danielle?" He didn't wait for a response.

Dominique heard him lay down the receiver. In the background, a child cried. "Danielle!" the man bellowed. "Phone!"

The receiver clanked a few more times, then Danielle, sounding short of breath and harassed, said, "Hello?"

"*Danielle, c'est moi.*" Dominique automatically reverted to the language they always spoke together.

"Dominique! How are you!" The fatigue in Danielle's voice was replaced by excitement.

"Fine. Fine. But, listen, I have something important to tell you." Dominique wanted to get it over with. She was bone tired after the endless hours on the bus. She was dying for a hot shower. All she wanted was to be with Danielle and relax.

"What is it?" Danielle sounded alarmed.

Dominique blurted out, "I've left Anton." She held her breath as she waited for her sister's reaction.

"What!" Danielle's voice was sharp, unbelieving.

"He hasn't called looking for me?" Dominique asked apprehensively.

"No . . . I don't know, we were at Ron's mother's this weekend." Danielle sounded stunned.

"Danielle, I need your help." Now the words spilled out of Dominique in a torrent. "Anton lied about everything. He's been married twice before. He finds wealthy women and he —"

Danielle interrupted. "Where are you?" she demanded, sounding worried.

Dominique didn't answer for a moment. Then, in a small voice, she said, "In New York. At the bus station." Then the torrent of words resumed. "I should have warned you, but I was afraid you'd try to talk me out of it, and I didn't have anyone else to turn to! I'm sorry to be a burden, but can you put me up for a while? Just until I find a job. It won't be long. I found one right away at the bank in San Francisco. Of course, I can't use them as a reference since I've quit so sud—"

"Come right away," Danielle interrupted her. "We sold the car so we can't pick you up. I'll meet you at the subway stop."

Dominique eagerly fished a pencil from her purse. "Give me the directions."

∽ ∽ ∽

It was bliss to be with family again! To share fond memories and a common background. To find refuge. Now that the excited greetings, the initial hugs and kisses, were out of the way, the sisters were chattering at high speed about their lives. Their rapport was as comfortable as it had always been — as though they'd never been apart.

As she and Danielle emerged from the stale-smelling subway station, Dominique paused, bombarded by impressions. People rushing by, carelessly bumping into them. Loud voices, strange accents. Car horns. High-pitched police whistles. Trucks clattering down the narrow street. And the heat. August mugginess that was a mixture of steam and diesel fumes. It came off the pavement in waves. It was at least twenty degrees hotter than San Francisco. "God, this reminds me of Egypt," Dominique said in wonder.

"Egypt!" Danielle laughed as she bent over and unfolded a metal frame cart with wheels. She efficiently strapped the suitcases on. "Everyone here uses these for groceries," she explained.

Dominique looked around, catching her breath. Despite the clamor, she could see that Danielle's neighborhood was very pleasant.

The street was lined with small trees planted at curbside. Elegant apartment buildings, their doors trimmed with brass, bronze, or wrought iron, rose high to create a shaded walkway. "This is nice," she said.

"I insisted on buying in the Upper East side," Danielle said knowingly as the sisters walked from the subway station. She fixed Dominique with a look of conviction. "It's better to have the worst house in a good neighborhood than a good house in a bad neighborhood."

Dominique laughed. The advice, delivered with the utmost solemnity, reminded Dominique of the young girl who had each week carefully saved a portion of her allowance. Not like Dominique, who had frittered hers away on chocolates and trinkets.

"You look wonderful!" Dominique complimented her sister.

"You think so?" Danielle preened a little. "I've been dieting."

"You're crazy!" Dominique said. "You're perfect just as you are."

Indeed, at age twenty-seven, Danielle was in the full bloom of young womanhood — she exuded sex appeal. With the eclectic panache of a fashion model, she played up her good looks. Her makeup was perfect, if dramatic. Her dress was tailored in all the right places to show off her figure. And even on a walk to the subway, she wore high heels. Dominique noticed men turning to stare as they passed. Doormen tipped their hats to Danielle, and even the newspaper boy, hawking extras on the street corner, stopped in mid-sentence to give her the once-over. Dominique was used to attracting attention herself, but when she was with Danielle, she was certain the focus was on her sister.

Danielle, however, seemed momentarily oblivious. She peered at Dominique, as though there were no one else on the busy street. "And you! The last time I saw you, you were a kid." She shook her head slowly from side to side and made a clucking noise with her tongue. "I remember Mother was always so worried about how you'd turn out." Danielle chuckled. "She must be proud of you now!"

Dominique wrinkled her nose. "I don't think so," she said darkly.

Danielle looked sharply at Dominique. "There's nothing wrong between you?"

Dominique shrugged and told her about Solange's letter. "You know, at first, I really hated her."

Danielle looked troubled. "But if she's not allowed to send money . . ."

Dominique sighed. "I know, I know. Don't worry. I've had a few hours to think it over. I can't blame her for being afraid to try. But what really makes me furious is that she actually suggested I stay with that parasite!"

Danielle chuckled at the vehemence in Dominique's tone. "She's just old-fashioned about things like that. How can you blame her? She's lived all her life in a culture where a man is allowed to have four wives!"

Dominique gave her sister a sidelong glance. "I'm used to her criticism, but I was afraid you might feel the same way," she said quietly.

Danielle didn't immediately contradict her. After a moment, she said carefully, "I understand why you left. But I think Mother's right about one thing. It's hard for a woman to be on her own. I know I wouldn't want to be."

"But we're not talking about a husband with a snoring problem!" Dominique said in a frustrated tone. "Anton's mercenary and he's dishonest."

"I know, I know," Danielle soothed, "but you asked my opinion and I told you."

Dominique made a noise of exasperation. There was no point in arguing. The only way to prove them wrong was to find a job, get a divorce, and make a new life for herself — a happy life. But it seemed that the two people closest to her doubted her ability to do it.

And what of her brother-in-law? He hadn't come to the station. Did that mean that he, too, disapproved? She asked Danielle, "Does Ron mind my staying with you?"

Danielle kept her eyes straight ahead. "I'm sorry he couldn't come," she said obliquely. "He's waiting for an important phone call."

"Danielle. . . ." Dominique waited until her sister looked at her. "Does he mind?" she insisted.

Danielle looked trapped. "He doesn't really understand. . . ."

Dominique was beginning to feel more and more apprehensive, but before she could probe further, Danielle suddenly stopped her with a hand on her arm.

"We're here."

Dominique looked up at an unimposing yellow brick building. Its only decoration was a green canopy over the entrance. It was inarguably the plainest structure on the block. Not at all what she would have pictured from Danielle's letters.

Danielle led Dominique to the glass doors, but made no move to open them. Instead, she brought the luggage cart upright and faced her sister with a grave expression. "Before we go in, I have something to tell you."

Dominique tried not to be alarmed at her sister's ominous tone.

Danielle took a deep breath and continued. "Ronald's lost his job." Hastily she added, "It's not his fault. He's very good." She wrung her hands, but her gaze was level. "But advertising is a cutthroat business and people can get fired for the slightest reason."

Dominique put a hand on her sister's arm. "I'm sure he'll find something soon."

Danielle gave her a skeptical look. "It's been three months." She paused. "We're . . . he's . . . very concerned. You can imagine!"

Dominique was silent. Clearly, she couldn't have come at a worse time. She hung her head. "It never occurred to me that you might be in trouble, too." She raised her eyes. "Why didn't you write to me about this?"

Now it was Danielle's turn to look down with a shamed expression. "Ron didn't want anyone to know. And" — her voice rose bravely — "we'll be fine. I just wanted to prepare you in case he's not as . . . well, . . . as welcoming as he ought to be."

Dominique impulsively took her sister in her arms. "Oh, Danielle, I'm so grateful to you. And I won't be a burden. I'll find something right away. I promise."

Danielle patted Dominique's back comfortingly. "You *know* I'm glad to help."

Dominique had to struggle to keep from crying with a mixture of relief and tension.

Danielle squeezed her sister sympathetically. "Well," she said with a forced smile, "let's go in." She stepped away from her sister and unlocked the lobby door, then held it open while Dominique wheeled in the cart. "The doorman's only here during the day," Danielle said apologetically, "but we're lucky to have found a doorman building at all."

"It doesn't matter." Dominique's voice was warm. A few minutes later, the elevator opened on the seventh floor and the sisters stepped into a long hallway. It was painted a dim green and carpeted in a darker shade. They walked in silence almost to the end of the corridor before Danielle stopped. She turned to face her sister. "This won't be what you've been expecting," she confessed in a low voice.

Dominique's expression was understanding. "It will be better than where I came from," she said with gratitude.

Danielle nodded nervously and turned toward the door. Then she turned back to Dominique. "Let me just prepare you," she whispered. "Ron has changed."

Dominique looked into her sister's eyes and saw disillusionment. She smiled sadly. "It doesn't matter," she said and squeezed Danielle's arm affectionately.

Danielle turned the key, then inserted another in the lock above it. She pushed open the door and motioned for Dominique to go in first. Dominique stepped into a small, parquet-floored foyer that led to the living room. She heard the television. She saw Ronald's profile, less defined than before, a little soft under the chin. He wore a white dress shirt with the collar unbuttoned and the tie loosened. His attitude was one of utter weariness.

Dominique smiled politely and stepped into the room, her sister close behind her. "Hello, Ronald," she said.

His brooding figure looked incongruous in the cheerfully decorated room. The place was smaller than Anton's home, but more inviting, with comfortable, modern furniture and bright accents. Everything was positioned to make the most of the limited square footage, and the windows were enhanced by a jungle of plants.

Ronald turned his head partway toward Dominique. He didn't seem able to tear his eyes from the flickering black-and-white screen. Dominique saw that he was watching "The $64,000 Question." Finally, though, he focused on her. He gave her a half-smile. "Hiya, Dominique. How're you doing?"

He was still handsome, Dominique saw, but his demeanor was different. Gone was the swagger, the rakish spark that had made him so attractive.

Dominique continued in a soft voice. "Thank you for having me. I know it's an imposition, but I hope it —"

"Look" — Ron's smile faded and his tone became belligerent — "I don't like this stuff of running off and leaving your husband. I don't want any part of it. If it were up to me, you'd be on your way back home." He brushed his hands together as though he were ridding them of dust. Then he turned back to the television.

"But he —" Dominique felt Danielle nudge her. She turned her head toward her sister, a questioning look on her face.

Danielle smiled with false cheer. "Do you mind helping with dinner? The girls have had theirs. They go to bed at seven-thirty. So it's just us," she explained.

"Of course," Dominique murmured, confused.

"Just put the cart anywhere," Danielle said briskly. Then she added in a more apologetic tone, "You'll have to sleep on the couch. We don't have anyplace else."

Dominique looked back at her brother-in-law. He appeared absorbed in his television show. She hadn't expected jubilation at her surprise visit, but she hadn't expected surliness either.

⚏ ⚏ ⚏

"I'm sorry about last night." Danielle took Dominique's hand. The two sat on a bench in the playground opposite Danielle's apartment. Monique, the two-year-old, slept in her stroller while four-year-old Lana played on the seesaw with another girl. It was a hot, dusty afternoon, but the park was a cool refuge.

Danielle continued. "Ron usually isn't like that. He's just under a lot of strain. In the advertising business, if you compete for a big account and don't get it, you can be fired. These people move from one agency to another every other week."

Dominique gave her sister's hand an encouraging squeeze. "Then he's sure to find something."

Danielle removed her hand from Dominique's and clenched it in her lap. "He looks every day until he's exhausted." She gave her sister a look of appeal.

Dominique turned halfway in her seat to face her sister. "Danielle, let me give you some money for my upkeep." She didn't have a dime to spare. Not if she was to rent a room. But she felt guilty about relying on Danielle and Ron when they, too, were worried about money.

"Don't be silly!" Danielle protested. "I wouldn't take your money."

"But just a few dollars for —"

Danielle held up her hand. "Stop! You're insulting me."

Dominique looked down at her lap. "I don't think I should stay more than a few days," she murmured.

Danielle gave Dominique an understanding look. "I can handle Ron."

Dominique studied her sister. She grinned. "You can handle anything. I don't know how you manage. You have two small children. A house to keep up. You cook and clean every day. You have troubles of your own, but you still look like a movie star."

Danielle grinned at the compliment. Then she furtively looked around. She leaned close to Dominique and said in a whisper, "Before Ron lost his job, I used to put aside a little of the grocery money for myself. Sometimes I'd buy clothes with it."

Dominique tilted her head to one side in puzzlement. How could Danielle outfit herself so stylishly on money left over from groceries?

Danielle leaned even closer to her sister. "I've been saving since we married. I always like to have a little security. In the beginning, I asked Ronald to give me a few dollars to open a bank account in my name. But he didn't think a wife should have a separate account. So . . . I started setting aside a little each week. I don't have much because I *did* sometimes spend it." Danielle pointed a warning finger at Dominique. "A woman always needs a little money of her own." There were a few seconds of silence. "Besides," Danielle continued, a defensive note in her voice, "I earn that money. I work hard around the house. I work hard to find the best values. Why shouldn't I have something to show for it?"

Dominique saw the logic of Danielle's words, but she wanted to believe that love and trust went hand in hand. She said, "But if you love each other . . . shouldn't your things be Ron's and Ron's things be yours?"

Danielle's brow furrowed. "You have to look out for yourself, no matter how much you love someone. You should realize that from your own experience. After all, you wouldn't have had the money to get here if you hadn't been saving, too."

"But I gave Anton plenty of money! Besides, I never loved —" Dominique halted abruptly and blushed. Her sister didn't know about Stephen Hampton and she didn't fully understand the circumstances behind Dominique's marriage to Anton.

Danielle gave her a penetrating look. "And you think *I'm* hard-hearted?"

Dominique turned her palms up. "I made a mistake, but one day I'll fall in love and marry someone I can trust." She shook her head. "I hate the thought of having to keep secrets."

Danielle smiled indulgently. "Well, I'll be the first to congratulate you." She patted her sister's knee. "But until then, we have to worry about getting you back on your feet." She paused and raised her eyebrows sardonically. "Why don't you let me lend you some of my tainted money?"

Dominique burst out laughing. "Oh, you're awful. I never said it was tainted! Anyhow, I have about two hundred dollars left. Isn't that enough to rent a place of my own until I find a job?" Dominique knew she should make the move soon. It was clear that her presence was causing trouble between Ron and Danielle.

Danielle gave her sister a worried grimace. "I don't know" — she pushed herself to a standing position — "but I'd feel better if you'd let me give you what I have. Ninety-five dollars. Pay it back when you can."

Dominique stood and hugged her sister. "You're wonderful. I'm so sorry for the imposition, but I *would* feel better if I had a little extra, and I promise to pay back every cent with interest." She released her sister and stepped back, fixing her gaze on Danielle's face. "And I'll start looking for a place tomorrow," she said softly.

"You don't need to be in that much of a hurry." Danielle smiled.

But, as it turned out, she did. Ron was waiting for them, his face stormy, when they returned. "Your husband called," he barked as soon as they walked in the door. He stood in front of them, his hands on his hips.

Dominique put her hand to her throat and froze. "What did he say?" she asked, her lips pale.

Ron signaled with a motion of his head for Danielle to put the girls in their room. Then he turned and walked into the living room, sinking into his usual spot on the couch. Dominique followed him cautiously, like someone trying to avoid a trap.

In the background, Danielle closed the door to the girls' bedroom. She appeared a few seconds later, pausing tentatively at the threshold of the living room.

"Both of you sit down," Ron said gruffly.

Dominique pulled out one of the stools that rested beneath the counter dividing the kitchen and living room. Danielle took the armchair opposite Ron.

"He says he's going to fight the divorce," Ron said stonily.

Dominique sprang up. "How can he? I can get all sorts of evidence about his gambling and his swindles. Everything!" He wasn't going to stop her! He couldn't.

Ron gave her an impatient look. "Do you have the money to pay a detective? Or a lawyer? Are you sure this stuff even matters to the courts?"

With a sinking heart, Dominique met Danielle's eyes. They exchanged a look of distress.

"That answers my question," Ron said bluntly.

"I may have to put off the divorce until I can afford to hire an attorney," Dominique said quietly. As long as she never had to see Anton again, she could bear the delay. But she didn't intend to go back to him, no matter what!

"He's probably just waiting until he gets the dowry," Danielle said in an acid tone.

Dominique's face lit up. "That must be it! He'll lose it if we start divorce proceedings before November. Oh, but I don't care. Let him have the money! I just want to be rid of him."

Ron crossed his hands over his chest and glared at Dominique. "Look, I don't want any trouble here. I know your sister wants to help you. . . ." He looked at Danielle and, for a second, his eyes softened. Then he turned back to Dominique and his expression grew set. "But I'm not about to get in the middle of a fight between you and your husband. I don't know what your deal was with him and I don't want to know." He dropped his voice. "You're going to have to leave."

Danielle stood up. "This is my house, too!" she cried. "Dominique doesn't have to leave just because you say so."

"I don't want any trouble!" Ron boomed. He ran his hand over his face. Dominique could hear the scratch of his whiskers against his palm. "We have enough trouble as it is." He finished, in a voice that was quieter but still vehement.

Even in the midst of her own worries, Dominique couldn't help thinking of the strain he was under. Not only did he have to worry about supporting himself, but also his wife and two children. She was offended by his tone, but sympathetic to his position. In some ways, she was better off than he.

Danielle opened her mouth, an argumentative look on her face.

"Danielle!" Dominique said, her voice commanding. She took a step forward so that she was in the middle of their line of sight. She met Ron's eyes with a dignified expression. "I'll go tomorrow," she said.

CHAPTER 6 ∽

DOMINIQUE tiptoed up the stairs to her rented room, wincing in anticipation of a telltale creak from a floorboard. She was three days past due on the rent and she didn't have the money to pay the landlady, Mrs. Parsons.

She eased open the door to her room, then closed it silently behind her. She leaned with her back against it, her arms at her sides, palms flat on the surface, in a posture of utter fatigue. Her eyelids dropped and she let her head fall forward. But her feet were throbbing too much for her to remain standing. Taking off her raincoat, Dominique went to the little pine table and chair in the center of the room. She slung the raincoat over the chair's back and, without stopping, walked to a musty green sofa bed that dominated the cramped room. With a long sigh, she sank into it.

Dominique knew she would be more comfortable if she took off her shoes, but she was afraid to look at the sore on her heel that had been festering for two weeks. It felt damp, so she knew it was oozing. And there was a scratchy, swollen sensation as though her shoe had worn a hole in her nylon and was in direct contact with the wound. She grimaced as she thought of it, but she knew she had to tend to it. It hurt too much to be left alone. Dominique leaned forward and ever so tentatively removed her shoe. For a moment, it stuck to the wound, then suddenly came loose. Dominique yelped as the pain shot up her leg. When it had subsided, she braced herself and looked down at her heel. The sight of it made her gag. It was much worse! The protective bandage had been shoved upward by her shoe so that the wound was completely exposed. Pieces of skin mixed with coagulating blood to form a sticky, infected mess.

Dominique unfastened her garter and slipped the stocking down her leg. As she reached the wound, she cringed and bit her lip. Then, in one motion, she pulled the stocking off, almost crying out with agony. After a few minutes, she removed her other shoe and hobbled over to the only sink in the apartment — the one in the bathroom.

Underneath the sink was a basin in which Dominique soaked her feet each night. Now she filled it with warm water and placed it on the floor. Using the closed toilet seat as a chair, she plunged her feet into the water.

The warmth was soothing, for it was cold in her room. The air outside already had a distinct chill, although it was only October. Dominique knew that her raincoat wouldn't be warm enough in winter, but she couldn't afford a wool coat.

After the water in the basin cooled, Dominique hoisted herself up and padded into the other room. It was an all-purpose space, serving as living room, dining room, bedroom, and kitchen. From the closet, she withdrew her hot plate and plugged it in. It was against house rules to have a hot plate, but Dominique had no other option. She couldn't afford to eat out — could barely afford to eat at all. When she opened her cupboard, the sight of her meager rations depressed her: two cans of beans, a package of dried spaghetti, a can of tomato sauce, and a jar of instant coffee. On the window ledge, Dominique knew, there remained two eggs and a half-pint of milk. She thought she could make the food stretch a week, but after that . . . what? She had already borrowed far too much from Danielle. Whatever Danielle saved, she gave to her sister, but that didn't amount to more than a dollar or two each week, even though Ron had finally found a job.

Dominique suppressed tears as she surveyed the near-empty cabinet. *It doesn't do any good to cry.* Her stomach rumbled with hunger and she reached for a can of beans.

As she waited for it to heat, she couldn't stop herself from dwelling on meals she'd had in the past. She had taken so much for granted! Had been so unaware of her good fortune! Her mouth watered as she recalled the teas she and Danielle had enjoyed at the Negresco Hotel in Nice. She closed her eyes and envisioned the terrace overlooking the sparkling aqua Mediterranean Sea. The platters of tiny sand-wiches — cucumber, watercress, or smoked salmon. Warm, rich scones with clotted cream and preserves bursting with fruit; miniature eclairs filled with custard, and luscious strawberry tarts.

Dominique was startled from her reminiscence by the sound of the beans boiling. She rushed to turn off the hot plate, then poured half the contents of the can into a dish. Once settled at the table, she ate very slowly — it made the food last longer. When she finished, she was still starving. The rest of the beans were meant for the next day, but Dominique was tempted to wolf them down. If she did, though, nothing would remain by the end of the week. Then what would she do?

If only she could find a job! But people thought that her accent meant she couldn't read, write, or speak English properly. It wasn't enough that she excelled at typing and spelling tests — she had to compete with applicants who had no accent. Even her fluency in French and Italian were of no use. There were many bilingual Americans in New York and they had the added advantage of an American accent. It seemed no one wanted someone with a strong foreign accent answering their phone.

It had been so easy to find a job in San Francisco. She didn't understand why it was so difficult in New York. Not a day passed that she didn't look. On Sundays, she buried herself in the *New York Times* employment section. Weekdays, and even Saturdays, she marched from business to business.

In September, she had taken a temporary position in the office of a dress manufacturer, and that had provided some income. But the regular clerk had returned from her honeymoon, and that had been the end for Dominique.

There had also been instances in which she had almost been offered a position, but was asked to supply references. What references? She had walked out on her job in San Francisco. So she put down on applications that she had worked for the Royal Air Force in Egypt, but verifying that was too much trouble for prospective employers.

After dinner, Dominique washed and dried her dishes, then put them away in the cupboard. She went to the green couch at the opposite end of the room and picked up a novel someone had left on the subway. Curling her legs under her, she settled into the corner and tried to read, but the steady roar of traffic from Lexington Avenue distracted her. She closed her eyes and sighed. Her foot was beginning to throb again. Dominique knew it was infected, but she couldn't afford to go to a doctor. She lay down, shivering, and clamped her eyes shut, a pillow clutched to her chest.

"This can't go on," Dominique whispered. Again and again she repeated the phrase, like a chant. Abruptly, she stopped. "I must be going crazy," she said aloud. That struck her as funny and she started to laugh. The sound was loud in the silence of the desolate little room. She laughed and laughed. She laughed hysterically. Her sides began to hurt, but still she couldn't stop. Tears streamed down her face, but she kept laughing. And laughing, her mouth in a deformed rictus. Her laughter rose in pitch and volume. It didn't sound anything like her, and she knew it. She tried to stop, but couldn't. The sound poured out of her, uncontrollable. She snorted as her inhalations grew deeper. She was having trouble catching her breath. A sliver of fear, like a knife glittering in the dark, stabbed at her. She was beyond reason. She knew it, but she couldn't help it.

And then, mercifully, a loud banging at the door brought her back to reality. The sounds coming out of Dominique abruptly stopped.

"Hey, what's going on in there?" Dominique recognized the shrill voice of Mrs. Parsons.

Dominique held her aching sides as she got up from the couch. "Nothing, Mrs. Parsons, I was just listening to a show on the radio."

"Open up. I need to talk to you," came the gruff answer.

"Yes, ma'am," Dominique said. She smoothed her hair and opened the door.

"Rent's late," said Mrs. Parsons without preamble. The woman had stringy gray hair, harlequin glasses, and a set of false teeth stained by nicotine.

"I'm sorry, Mrs. Parsons. I have a little money I can give you right now, but I can give you all of it on Friday."

Mrs. Parsons' eyes narrowed. She placed her hands on her hips. "Look, sister, I rented you this place 'cause you promised to pay your rent on time."

Dominique was going to point out that she had paid a month's rent in advance. She opened her mouth to argue, but then thought better of it. Arguing was her natural reaction, but arguing would only antagonize Mrs. Parsons. It was better to be conciliatory. "Yes, I know," Dominique finally said, "and I'm so grateful to you for that. I haven't found a job yet, but I'll be seeing my sister on Friday, and I'm sure she can lend me the rent money."

Mrs. Parsons gave Dominique a skeptical look. "How much you got now?"

Dominique sighed with relief. The question meant that she had at least a few days' reprieve. "I can give you half." That would leave Dominique just enough for the subway to Danielle's on Friday, plus a little extra lunch money. She had to stop at midday for at least a bowl of soup, or she felt light-headed.

"Well . . . ," said Mrs. Parsons, scanning Dominique from head to toe, "I can tell you got class. You're just on hard times. I'll let you stay til Friday, but you got to give me some security." She looked pointedly at Dominique's gold watch.

Dominique followed her gaze and winced. She couldn't possibly give up her watch! She needed it for appointments, to know the time when she woke up in the mornings. Besides, it was surely worth hundreds of dollars. She couldn't give it to Mrs. Parsons as security. She didn't trust the old woman.

"Mrs. Parsons," Dominique pleaded. "I need this watch while I'm looking for a job. But . . ." She looked down at it again. Something caught her eye. Her wedding band. Dominique grasped the ring and wiggled it off her finger. She held it out to Mrs. Parsons. "I can give you this. It's platinum," she said quietly.

Mrs. Parsons took the ring and studied it, a gleam of acquisitiveness in her eye. "Okay . . . ," she said grudgingly, "that'll have to do. But you'd better have that rent on Friday. You get me?"

⨏ ⨏ ⨏

Dominique awakened with a leaden, unrelenting feeling of dread. Tomorrow was Friday. She had no money left, no job prospects, and almost no food.

The only thing to look forward to was her weekly visit to Danielle's. Thankfully, the visits were less strained now that Ronald had found a job. It seemed to lift the tension that had been hanging over the household. At the same time, he made it clear he had not changed his views on Dominique's desertion of Anton. She wondered if Ronald was subconsciously afraid that Danielle would one day do the same.

Nevertheless, the visits were a welcome respite. Dominique could enjoy the warmth of her sister's support for a few hours — and have a decent meal.

She put on her robe and headed to the bathroom to wash her face. A knock on the door interrupted her in mid-stride. Mrs. Parsons about the rent again, Dominique thought with a sinking feeling. But it was only the man next door. "Phone call for ya," he shouted through the closed door.

Dominique stood up, hope lighting her features. Could it be about one of the jobs she'd applied for? She hurried into the hall and picked up the phone.

"Hello?" she breathed into the receiver.

"Dominique, have you seen the newspaper?" Danielle sounded upset.

"No, I —"

Danielle cut her off. "Israel's invaded Egypt! There's talk of England and France getting involved. They want the Suez Canal back under their jurisdiction. Dominique" — Danielle's voice rose frantically — "what's going to happen to Mother?"

Dominique had the dizzying feeling of catapulting through space. Her only clear thought: something terrible was going to happen to Solange.

"Dominique!" Danielle cried. "Are you there?"

"Yes. I . . . I don't know what . . ." Her mind raced in circles. She felt infuriatingly powerless.

"What can we do?" Danielle moaned. "I've sent a wire, but it will take at least until tomorrow to get an answer. And that's assuming that everything works like it's supposed to. Which it never does!"

Adrenaline surged through Dominique, every muscle tensed for action. They had to do something more! "Can't you get through on the phone?" If only Dominique could afford a long distance call. . . .

"I tried! Nothing. You know how the phones are there. They never work even in normal times." Danielle was close to tears with frustration.

Dominique wracked her brain. There *had* to be a way to get news. Suddenly, an idea. "Maybe the French embassy could tell us something!"

Danielle pounced on the suggestion. "I hadn't thought of that! I'll call them right away. I'll ring you back when I learn something."

"If that doesn't work," Dominique said, her brain shifting into gear

now, "try the British embassy. They can at least give you some information." The words spilled out of her with urgency.

"What about the Egyptian embassy?" Danielle asked anxiously.

"No! French citizens are their enemies now. It would be dangerous
to draw attention to Mother." She paused. *Think. Think.* There had
to be other avenues. "If the first two don't work, try the U.S. State
Department."

"All right. This may take all morning. I'll get back to you as soon
as I can." Danielle sounded better now that she had a mission.

"Danielle . . . I . . . I can't wait here. I have to go out to look for a
job." It was agony to think that she would have to be in suspense all
day. "Will you call me tonight?"

"Yes, of course." Danielle was silent for a moment. "Oh, Dominique, I'm worried!" she cried.

Dominique closed her eyes and leaned against the wall. "I am too."

"Well . . . I'd better get started," Danielle said. Dominique heard
her stifle a sob. "I love you, Dominique," she choked.

"I love you, too," Dominique whispered.

Dominique hung up slowly. She walked back to her room on
shaky legs.

❧ ❧ ❧

Dominique knew she had done badly on her interviews. She had been
so preoccupied by the news from Egypt that she'd barely been able
to focus on questions put to her. She had interviewed at a real estate
company, a bank, and a dime store.

The real estate company and the bank had given her short shrift,
maybe because of her accent. Her rejection at the dime store had been
for an altogether different reason. The personnel manager, a no-
nonsense man in his forties, had coolly assessed her from head to toe,
then thrown out the verdict that she looked too "highbrow" for his
store.

"My customers wouldn't feel comfortable asking you for help. Try
Saks."

Now Dominique sat in a Chock Full O'Nuts coffee shop resting
her foot and nursing a bowl of soup. As she ate, she pored over the
classified ads. She had already responded to most of the job notices

for which she was qualified. No matter how many times she studied the page, new ads refused to appear, she reflected with black humor.

She put down the classified section in disgust and picked up the front page. Her eyes went automatically to the article about the Suez Canal. She'd read it so many times that she knew it by heart. Trying to stop herself from compulsively reading it once more, she folded it and put it aside. Instead, she picked up the society page and scanned the pictures of glamorous parties. They reminded her so much of home! She closed her eyes and sank back in her booth. Impossible to remember the good times without thinking of Stephen. It struck her like a blow, her loneliness for him. Had she done the right thing in refusing to marry him? At the moment, it seemed like a huge mistake. She sighed as her memory took her back to the Christmas party when he had proposed to her. Their conversation replayed itself in her mind. Her reasons for refusing him had been sound — she'd done the right thing. But why did it have to hurt so much?

She shook her head impatiently. What good did it do to dwell on the past? There were enough problems to cope with now. She sat up and tried to focus on the newspaper. The front of the society section was devoted to coverage of a fashion show organized for charity by the ultra-elegant Saks Fifth Avenue. An ironic snicker escaped her as she recognized the name mentioned by the dime store's personnel manager a bare half hour before. As she read the article, she noticed that the menu, touted as the last word in stylishness, seemed awfully dull compared to those served in her mother's home. And the crowd in the photographs was undeniably well dressed, but in a staid sort of way. It occurred to Dominique that anyone attending that party would surely be dazzled by an evening at Solange's.

Dominique couldn't seem to stop thinking about Solange. She shook her head. Solange would be all right, she tried to reassure herself. Now it was time to concentrate on looking for a job. She turned back to the newspaper. What had she been thinking about? Oh yes, Solange's parties.

Solange's style of entertainment required a lot of hard work, even with a houseful of servants. Just the right atmosphere had to be created with flowers, candlelight, wines, seating, and music. One had to check the work of each person to whom a task was delegated. Solange always said that a large party was like a complex puzzle. If an element was omitted, the whole could be ruined.

Dominique wondered who handled the logistics for events she read about in the newspaper. In Egypt, individuals sponsored charity events; here, it seemed that commercial establishments were largely responsible. She scanned the article. No one was credited with organizing the event. She speculated, therefore, that the store's staff must have done it.

Abruptly, she folded the newspaper and stared into space. *Why can't I do that!* She had helped Solange a thousand times with parties bigger than the one at Saks. Bigger and more extravagant! She was perfectly qualified for that sort of job. Adrenaline pumped through Dominique as she thought of the possibilities. How better to use her languages and her knowledge of protocol? She knew all about hired help and proper food service, the correct height for centerpieces and the intricacies of place settings. She knew which wines went with which foods, the differences among the world's best caviars, the proper format for engraved invitations. She knew to order soft music for dinner and more energetic tunes for after the meal. She knew about party favors and decorations.

Instead of settling for a routine job, she could have an interesting career using the skills that had been drummed into her from adolescence. It gave Dominique a charge to think of relying on her own resources. All at once, she realized that she had never before done so. She thought of her time at the RAF. How independent of Solange she had wanted to be! But the independence had been short-lived. In the end, she had returned to her mother's home. And she had allowed herself to be pushed into marriage with a man she didn't love. Why? Because it had been the safest, easiest course. Even now — though she lived alone — she counted on Danielle for financial help and food.

Dominique was tired of feeling like a beggar, tired of reacting instead of acting. She needed a goal, not just a means of getting by from day to day. And her new plan gave her that. It made her feel she could succeed.

She threw down a few coins and gathered up her raincoat and purse. Enough of being turned down for mundane jobs! It was time to go after something at which she would truly excel. But first, she had to devise a strategy. She would get started that very afternoon. She was glad, anyhow, for an excuse to go home and wait for Danielle's call. It was hard to concentrate on anything when she was so anxious for news of her mother.

A half hour later, Dominique scooted up the stairs of her building as fast as her sore foot permitted. As soon as she opened the door leading into the vestibule, she heard the phone ring. Maybe it was Danielle!

She hobbled up the four flights of stairs as the phone shrilled insistently. Dominique was afraid it would stop before she arrived. Danielle, though, knew to let it ring many times. Finally grasping the phone, Dominique cried, "Hello?"

"I got through to her," Danielle said at once. "I called and called and finally I got through."

"What did she say?" Dominique asked breathlessly. Her heart drummed against her ribs.

"It's worse than we thought. We'll probably see it in tomorrow's papers." Danielle's voice had the staccato tone of a person in shock. "England and France have bombed Egypt. They may invade. The Egyptians have been arresting foreigners all day. They've told Mother she has to leave. Immediately. She's coming here to live with us. They've taken the business, the houses, the car — everything. She's allowed to bring clothes. But no jewelry. No furs. Nothing valuable."

"But" — Dominique was aghast — "what about everything in the house? All the family things?" She heard Danielle take a deep breath, as though bracing herself.

"She has to leave it all. She's allowed to take the clothes she can fit in a few suitcases. That's it."

"Oh, my God!" Dominique slumped to the floor as she tried to digest her sister's news. She was too stunned to take in the full import of it.

Danielle was silent. Then she began haltingly. "Dominique, I know I'm awful . . . I know I should be grateful that Mother's getting out alive — and I am — but how are we all going to live in this little place?" she cried. "You know how Ronald was with you. And that was only temporary. Now he's going to have Mother on his hands. He's going to hate it. He's going to make my life —"

"Where is he now?" Dominique asked urgently.

"He was so angry at me, he just stormed out of here. And he blames you, too. He says that if you had stayed in San Francisco where you belong, Mother could go to you!"

Dominique felt like she'd been kicked. "Ron's being a brute!" she shouted. "Why do you put up with it?"

Danielle's own temper, as hot and edgy as Dominique's, erupted. "So I should leave and end up like *you?*" she shot back.

"Dominique was struck dumb. Danielle's words echoed the thoughts Dominique had had in the coffee shop, but they hurt coming from her own sister. How could Danielle say such a thing to her? She felt humiliated and furious at the same time. Before she could respond, her sister cried, "I'm sorry! I didn't mean to say that! You were brave to leave Anton. You were!"

The apology did nothing to ease Dominique's hurt. She didn't trust herself to speak.

"Dominique!" Danielle's voice was almost hysterical. "Are you all right? I didn't mean what I said!"

In a small, distant voice, Dominique said, "I'm sorry I've been such a burden. I thought it would be easier."

"I know. And I know Ron's being unfair. But, Dominique . . ." Danielle beseeched her to understand. "I still love him. He's great with the girls and he . . . he loves me. He really does."

Dominique was embarrassed by her sister's abject defensiveness. She looked up at the naked lightbulb that provided the only illumination in the hall. A few steps away was her dingy little room. Her home. Hunger was a daily burden. And, most of all, loneliness was chiseling away at her. Who was she to judge her sister?

"If you still love him," Dominique said raggedly, "then that's all that matters." She sighed. "Anyhow, don't worry. It'll all work out with Mother."

"I suppose." Danielle sounded hopeless.

"Well . . ." Dominique didn't know what more to say. "I'll see you tomorrow."

"Uh . . . Dominique," Danielle sounded uneasy.

"Yes?"

"Ronald's furious over this. Maybe it would be better if we skipped this week."

Dominique's heart plummeted. She wanted desperately to see her sister. And then there was the meal. If she didn't eat at Danielle's, she wouldn't eat at all. But she couldn't force herself on Ronald. She couldn't force Danielle to defy him.

"That's no problem, Danielle," she said in a cold, even voice. "I'll see you . . . another time."

"Thanks for understanding." Danielle sounded guilty. "I love you."

"Good-bye," Dominique replied.

Dominique didn't move from her spot for several minutes. It was hard for her to fathom the changes that were crashing down on her. Her own circumstances were difficult enough, but she had been pre-pared for some hardship when she left Anton. Now, though, she had to worry about Solange. Her stomach knotted as she envisioned her mother's flight from Egypt. Suppose she were stopped at customs again? Now that the French were at war with Egypt, Solange would never escape! She could be beaten or, worse, arrested.

Dominique knew she would not stop fretting until Solange was safe in the United States. But then what? The proud matriarch would have to deal with a resentful son-in-law. How would she accept the change in circumstances? Or would Ron be kinder to Solange than he had been to Dominique? Maybe. After all, Solange was not running away from a husband. Dominique tried to reassure herself that Ron would reconcile himself to Solange's presence in his household. After all, what alternative did Solange have? She would have no money, no one else to turn to.

Dominique sighed and folded her arms across her chest as though huddling against the cold. Her reflections brought her back to the harsh reality of her own situation. She had no job, but worse, she had no food.

The gold watch that had been her grandmother's gleamed mellow and rich in the dim light. Dominique knew she couldn't put off pawn-ing it any longer. She thought about the shop on the corner that she passed each day. It closed at eight o'clock. She could still make it.

Dominique gathered her purse, then pushed herself to her feet. With a firm pull, she cinched the belt of her raincoat. For a second, she hesitated at the top of the stairs. Then she squared her shoulders and limped down the stairs to the pawnshop.

ᦉ ᦉ ᦉ

Saks said no to Dominique. No positions available at all.

But it was only ten-thirty and Dominique had several more stores on her list. She'd spent hours at the library on Saturday researching the list. Her goal had first been to discover which stores sponsored the most events. That done, she had looked up articles about each retailer.

Finally, she had used one of the publicly available typewriters to redo her résumé so that it reflected her background in organizing events.

Now Dominique stood on the sidewalk gazing at Saks' inviting display of fur coats and tried to decide where to go next. It was cold and sunny, with the nip of winter in the air. Dominique shivered in her raincoat and stared longingly at the furs.

She moved out of the shade of Saks' awning and crossed the street to the broad sidewalk in front of St. Patrick's cathedral. Sun flooded the busy thoroughfare, warming Dominique. Her walk slowed as she watched the tourists sitting on the stairs, maps spread on their laps. She thought with amusement that a few weeks before, she, too would have been unable to find her way around New York. Now she knew it intimately, thanks to her job search.

All at once, she was filled with hope. She didn't know why. Maybe it was the bright sun. Or maybe it was that her foot felt so much better after the weekend's rest. Maybe it was the busy, diverse crowd pushing her along. But, suddenly, Dominique felt like part of the vibrant life of the city. She smiled and nodded at the pretzel vendor on the corner. Near him, a man in a business suit lovingly smeared bright yellow mustard on a pretzel. Dominique could almost taste the tang of mustard and salt, the warm dough, crusty on the outside, chewy on the inside. Her stomach growled and she put her hand self-consciously on it. If she bought a pretzel now, she would have to forgo lunch. She turned her head away and quickened her step so that she would not be tempted.

She hurried up Fifth Avenue, passing a montage of bright displays. Then she stopped in front of the venerable Tiffany's — the second store on her list. For a moment, she gazed in the windows, admiring the beautiful diamond necklace in one, the silver place settings in another, the fine crystal in a third. Then, gathering her courage, she took a deep breath and pushed through the revolving doors.

Dominique's interview at Tiffany's was more encouraging than at Saks. The personnel director was familiar with the American College in Cairo, and praised it. He had been stationed in North Africa during World War II and was suitably impressed with Dominique's job experience as secretary to Group Captain Hampton. He would keep her application on file, he promised. But, regretfully, there were no openings at the moment. However, would Dominique care to go to lunch? He was attractive, and Dominique was hungry, but she took one look at the gold ring on his left hand and said no.

Bergdorf-Goodman's personnel director looked over her résumé carefully. "You have a good background," he told Dominique. Her heart soared with optimism as he telephoned the director of publicity to ask if he would see Dominique. But when she presented her ideas to the second man, he told her they were too extravagant. Dominique wanted to argue, to remind him that they were just broad concepts, not final plans, that she could work within any guidelines he set. But she could tell from his closed expression that arguing would be futile.

That left six names on Dominique's list. It was almost four o'clock and she estimated she had time for only one more try that day. Orman's was the closest, so she chose it. As she made her way through the late afternoon crowd on the street, she tried to remember everything she'd learned through her research.

Only five years old, Orman's wasn't like any store in New York, or anywhere else for that matter. Out to make a splash in the world of retailing, it contained a couture department as exclusive as Bergdorf's and a furniture department as fine as Lord & Taylor's. The square footage was almost the same as Macy's, but with a less crowded feeling. It had more salespeople than any other store, larger dressing rooms, and more custom services. Yet Orman's was anything but stodgy. The philosophy was that shopping should be fun, an event. To this end, there were daily makeup demonstrations, food samplings, and fashion shows. In addition, Orman's had initiated a system that *Retailing Today* predicted would become the norm for high-toned department stores. Clothes and other merchandise were not grouped by function as in other department stores, but rather arranged in small, exclusive boutiques, many devoted to one designer. In fact, Orman's was always the first to launch new trends, to try new kinds of publicity, to experiment with the psychology of decor.

Dominique had visited Orman's before, and she liked it, but she had always viewed it through the eyes of the customer. Now, as she stepped through the main doors into the sweetly scented cosmetics department, she tried to observe as much as she could about the store's clientele, displays, and general image.

Orman's had none of the museumlike quality of Saks, but it nevertheless exuded an air of opulence. There were mirrors everywhere, reflecting imaginative displays of accessories and cosmetics. Mannequins were adorned with items from several different departments to create fanciful vignettes. But most appealing was the sense of life that pervaded the atmosphere. Salespeople smiled and moved busily about. Models glided down the aisles sporting the latest fashions and handing out small samples of perfume. Orman's bewitched Dominique with its air of adventure, discovery, and possibility.

Standing in the black marble entrance, Dominique felt a surge of optimism. She was sure that she was right for Orman's. She made her way past the mirrored pillars of the scarf and handbag department until she found the elevator. An attendant in a navy blue uniform with gold epaulets held open the doors as Dominique entered, then closed them behind her.

Dominique's first stop when she exited was the ladies' room. Standing in front of the full length mirror, she pivoted from side to side, checking for hanging threads. She decided her peach wool suit looked immaculate but dull, with its rounded collar and straight lines. Not nearly as snappy as the Orman's image. She withdrew the silk scarf she had tucked into the sleeve of the raincoat and draped it around the collar of the suit. That was better. The apricot-colored print brought out the auburn in her hair. A touch of lipstick and she was ready. Dominique stared into the mirror at her reflection. Her eyes stared back at her, their expression serious. Too serious. She wanted to project confidence and sophistication. She forced a stiff smile. Then she thought about actually getting the job at Orman's and her smile broadened so that dimples appeared at either corner of her mouth. She tilted her chin up, pivoted, and marched to the personnel office.

⟋◦ ⟋◦ ⟋◦

Brash and innovative as Orman's was, the New York store manager, Bruce Fisher, seemed the opposite. He was a soft-spoken man who wore horn-rimmed glasses, discreet gold cuff links, and a conservative suit that looked as if it was tailored on Savile Row. He had an air of wisdom and maturity, though Dominique estimated that he was no more than forty.

As she sat opposite him explaining her ideas, she felt she had discovered a kindred spirit. He seemed to understand just the sort of mood she was trying to create with her concepts. As she spoke, he picked up the thread of her ideas and carried them one step further, mulling aloud how they might work at Orman's.

Filled with enthusiasm, Dominique pulled from her purse some typewritten pages. She unfolded them to reveal diagrams of her ideas — lists and cost estimates as well as logistical details. It had been her first opportunity to show them to anyone, since her other interviewers had not been interested.

Bruce Fisher took the papers from her and studied them seriously. Then his frank gaze met Dominique's. "This is very impressive. Well thought out."

Dominique held her breath. Clearly, Fisher had something to add.

"I can offer you a job today, but not the job you're hoping for."

Dominique almost cried out with relief and joy. Any job would be welcome.

Fisher sat back in his chair and regarded her for a moment. "Everyone here starts at the bottom unless they already have a retailing background. We believe that our employees should be acquainted with many facets of the store before taking on a position of greater responsibility. And" — he paused — "we find that retailing isn't for everyone."

He put down her diagrams and picked up her résumé. "It says here that you have secretarial experience."

Dominique nodded, trying to suppress a small twinge of disappointment. She should be thrilled to be offered any job. And she was! "Yes, sir."

"I have a secretarial opening in my office. You'd be working just down the hall from me with two other ladies who help organize our events. They're both secretaries, but with considerable responsibility. They report directly to me, as you would. Every once in a while, they help out our press secretary, Hank Benson. Mostly if he has a big press mailing. But he's a former reporter and does most of his own typing." Fisher chuckled. "Probably the fastest in the office.

"I pretty much oversee the events. They're very important to Orman's image, especially as we're still such a new store."

Dominique tilted her head thoughtfully as she listened. An article she had read in the *Wall Street Journal* about Orman's came to mind. There had been several paragraphs devoted to Fisher.

For all his seeming gentility, Fisher is cutthroat in his marketing strategies. He doesn't underprice his competition; instead he beats them to market with new, innovative lines. He has successfully built Orman's image with a two-pronged approach. The first is his buying strategy. "I look for what's different, extravagant, whimsical, bold, yet still within the confines of acceptability," Fisher says.

The second element he relies on is publicity. He could easily entrust Orman's public relations to an underling, but it is his pet project. It was he who launched the publicity/special events department and he who realized that it was the key to distinguishing Orman's from all the other up-market department stores in New York. While other stores put on fashion shows and sponsor decorous charity benefits, Fisher fills the society pages with events that range from gala to just plain irreverent, but never stodgy.

Dominique was glad now that she'd taken the time to research the stores to which she had applied. "It seems like you want Orman's to be regarded as more creative than the competition . . . more avant garde," she said.

Fisher smiled his approval. "Right. We want to attract the wealthy customer, but not by offering the same type of merchandise as Bergdorf's or Saks. We're trying to create a demand for younger clothing and furniture. Expand our market."

Dominique sat forward in her chair, thoroughly engrossed in the conversation. "I noticed that you have departments that are trendy and fashionable, but not as expensive. I passed some on the way in."

Fisher gave her a respectful nod. "You're very observant."

Dominique's excitement was almost impossible to contain. She felt as jittery as if she'd drunk ten cups of coffee. "I want very much to work for Orman's," she said. And it was true. She felt more at home here than in any of the stores she'd visited that day.

"Well." Fisher gave her a genial smile. "I think that can be arranged."

૭૭ ૭૭ ૭૭

Dominique was grateful to have found a job before her mother's arrival in New York. As Dominique and the Markses waited at the pier for Solange's ship, she enthusiastically described her first week at Orman's. Ronald congratulated her, his manner warmer than before. Clearly, he no longer worried that she would burden them.

A resounding blast of the ship's horn halted all conversation as Dominique, Danielle, and the rest of the family turned to face the large gray and white vessel. They searched the crowd at the ship's rail for Solange, but didn't see her. Almost thirty minutes passed before the gangplank was lowered and people began to disembark. Still no sign of Solange. Ronald looked at his watch impatiently and pulled his coat tighter.

Danielle said worriedly, "Where can she be?"

Dominique scanned the deck again. "I have no idea."

The line of passengers disembarking grew more straggly and irregular. Soon both the deck and the gangplank were empty except for white-uniformed crew members. Then Dominique saw a cluster of people emerge from the bridge area. A man in a dark uniform and a white hat appeared first. He was followed by a prosperous looking man in a pearl gray suit and a cowboy hat, a man in a dark pin-striped suit, and a woman in a white coat and matching beret.

"There's Mother!" Dominique cried. She waved frantically, trying to catch Solange's attention, but none of the party on the ship looked at those on shore.

Danielle took a few steps forward, then stopped, her eyes riveted to the group. "She looks wonderful!" Danielle exclaimed, her voice incredulous.

Dominique gave her an amused look. "What did you expect?"

Danielle turned bewildered eyes on her sister. "I don't know exactly. She had to leave in such a hurry. They said she couldn't bring anything. I expected her to be depressed or . . . I don't know." She looked back at the ship. "Are those champagne glasses they're holding?"

Dominique laughed out loud. "Looks that way." She turned her attention back to those on the ship. The group was now at the top of the gangplank. The three men leaned toward Solange, as though not to miss a word she said. Solange was laughing, throwing back her head. She turned and looked at the dock.

Danielle and Dominique waved vigorously. Solange flashed a smile and waved back. She started down the gangplank, then turned to say something over her shoulder. Like children following the Pied Piper, the men followed her down the gangplank.

"Girls!" Solange cried in French. She stopped at the bottom of the gangplank and held out her arms. Dominique and Danielle automatically scurried forward into them while Ronald remained behind with his daughters.

Dominique felt herself smothered in soft wool perfumed with Lanvin's My Sin.

"Let me look at you!" Solange said, holding her daughters away from her. She swept them with her gaze. "Hmmm."

Did the little sound have an edge of disapproval? Dominique felt herself growing defensive and tried to stifle the feeling. Her mother had just arrived!

Solange turned to the men waiting patiently behind her and said in French, "These are some of the friends I met on board." The men crowded closer. "This is Captain Charles Montague and Monsieur Buck Wilson" — Solange's pronunciation made it sound as though she were saying "Back We-saw" — "and finally Monsieur Maurice Charpentier. He has been kind enough to act as translator."

Buck Wilson removed his cowboy hat at the sound of his name. "A pleasure to meet you both. You're pretty as your pictures.

"I'm afraid," he continued politely, "that I didn't pick up enough French from your mother to understand everything she says, but I sure enjoyed her company. She made the trip a pleasure for us all." The other two men beamed and nodded in agreement. "And she's a heck of a card player!"

"And," the captain said, taking Solange's hand and bowing over it, "an exquisite dancer."

"It is with regret that we part," said the Frenchman, looking mournful.

Dominique and Danielle didn't know what to say. Solange, however, stepped in with her usual aplomb. "It's sad that shipboard friendships must end, but I'll always remember the wonderful time we had." M. Charpentier rapidly translated her words for the other two men.

They shook their heads in resignation.

Solange smiled and hugged each of them. "Good-bye, my friends. And now" — she took a deep breath and turned toward her daughters — "I'm ready."

Once at the car, Dominique observed without comment the discussion over who should sit where. Solange protested when Danielle indicated she should sit in front, but soon allowed herself to be persuaded. Automatically, she waited for Ronald to open the door for her, but he was preoccupied with the luggage. Instead, Danielle jumped forward and pulled open the door. For a moment, Solange stared in the direction of her son-in-law, then she bent to get in the car. Before the action was completed, she stopped. She turned to Danielle and asked, "Can't you sit in the middle, dear?"

"It would be too crowded. If you don't mind, I'll put Lana in the middle with you and I'll keep Monique."

Solange expressed delight with this arrangement. She reached into her pocketbook and found lemon drops to give the children, then helped Lana into the seat. The little girl held her grandmother's hand and obeyed her as though she had known her all her life.

A few seconds later, Ron got in. "All set?" he asked, a barely concealed edge to his voice. Without waiting for an answer, he started the car. Solange, cooing over her granddaughter, seemed not to notice him. But a few moments later, she turned to Danielle and said, in French, "He's not happy to have me, I gather."

Danielle shifted uncomfortably, but said nothing.

"Of course Americans don't look after their families the way Europeans do," Solange said derisively. She shrugged, then glanced again at the man beside her. "He's changed. He doesn't have that dash anymore. And he's put on weight, hasn't he?" she asked in the same tone.

Danielle sighed, *"Oui, Maman."*

Solange shifted her gaze to Dominique. "You've lost some." She was silent as she assessed her younger daughter. Finally, she announced. "It suits you, I think. You had a tendency to plumpness."

"I was never overweight!" Dominique snapped.

"No . . . ," Solange conceded calmly, "but you had a *tendency* . . ."

Dominique was about to reply sharply when she felt Danielle nudge her. She clamped her mouth shut and stared out the window. Why did her mother always have this effect on her?

"Danielle, you look wonderful," Dominique heard Solange say. "You've grown even prettier than when you were eighteen." Solange sighed and turned to face forward again. "Maybe Dominique will, too."

Dominique swiveled her head to face her mother, her posture one of outrage. She stared at the back of Solange's head, a retort burning on her tongue. Again, Danielle nudged her. Dominique looked at her sister. Danielle smiled sympathetically and murmured in English, "Ignore her."

"What?" Solange asked from the front seat.

"Nothing, Mother," Danielle answered in French. "I was just talking to Monique."

"Oh." Solange turned again toward the back seat. "As soon as we get home, remind me to show you the jewelry I brought from Cairo."

"I thought you couldn't take jewelry," Danielle said.

"I hid it in my brassiere and under my hat. I couldn't get much out because I knew they would search all the trunks." Solange said this so casually that Dominique wondered if the older woman fully grasped the danger she had been in. She shuddered as she remembered the experience with the customs police. After that, how could Solange have been so reckless?

Danielle asked, "Did they let you bring any money?"

"None." She turned and fixed her gaze on Dominique and said seriously, "I wanted to help you, you know. I would have sent money if I could. I was" — she seemed momentarily at a loss for words — "very distressed," she concluded.

Dominique was surprised. "You don't think I was wrong to leave Anton?"

"After all ... no." Solange said thoughtfully. She turned back around as though to end the conversation.

Dominique looked at Danielle. The sisters mirrored each other's expressions of comic disbelief.

After a few moments, Danielle leaned forward in her seat and pointed out the windshield. "Mother, this is Central Park."

"My heavens, but it's huge!" Golden hills and forest stretched into the distance. Walking paths wound charmingly through the vista. "This is lovely!" Solange exclaimed. She tilted her head and looked out the windshield, taking in the skyline. "I've never seen buildings so high in my life!"

"Look! Horsies!" cried Lana, bouncing with excitement.

Solange didn't understand the word, but she looked where Lana was pointing and exclaimed in delight at the horse-drawn buggy. "Just like Egypt!"

Dominique laughed. "That's the first thing I said when I arrived. Probably we're the only two people in the world who think that Cairo and New York are similar."

"It's certainly as crowded. And as noisy," Solange observed. Then a delighted smile lit her features. "Ah, look at the beautiful houses!" she said, pointing at the old Italianate mansions on Fifth Avenue, opposite the park.

"These are mostly clubs and apartments now, Mother. Individual families used to own them though," Danielle said.

Solange fell quiet. After a moment, she sighed heavily. "Things don't always change for the better, do they?"

Dominique's heart went out to her mother. To start over with nothing at age fifty-three! She put a hand on Solange's shoulder. "It's good to see you again," she said softly.

Solange half turned and covered Dominique's hand with her own. "It's good to see you, too, darling." She looked at Danielle. "All of you."

Seconds later, Ronald smoothly pulled the car into the space in front of their building. The doorman hurried out to help them with the bags.

Just as Dominique emerged from the car, another man sauntered up to the group. He wore a cheap business suit and dark glasses. "Dominique Renard?" he said.

Automatically, Dominique answered, "Yes?" She was puzzled by the use of Anton's last name. She used her maiden name now.

He handed her a folded sheath of papers and walked away.

"What the hell . . . ," Ron said. He came from his side of the car to stand protectively beside the women. "What is it?"

Dominique couldn't imagine. Her heart pounding, she unfolded the document and scanned it in silence. Then she threw back her head and burst out laughing.

"What?" Danielle demanded to know.

Dominique waved the papers victoriously above her head. "Sometimes it pays to be poor! Anton must have found out that they took Mother's plantation," she chortled, "because *he's* suing *me* for divorce!"

CHAPTER 7 ୦୦

DOMINIQUE was one of three secretaries in Orman's public relations department, and she had quickly made friends with the other two. Lucinda Marsh was a pretty blonde of twenty-two who had recently graduated from Vassar. She was actually more than a secretary, for her social connections made her a valuable aide to Bruce when he organized store events.

The other secretary, Maude Frazier, was a forty-year-old war widow. The attractive brunette efficiently processed mountains of paper each day. She typed one hundred words a minute, took excellent shorthand, and after two years with Bruce anticipated his needs before he even knew them.

Hank Benson, the store's press secretary, was an affable fellow in his mid-thirties — a string bean of a man with a shock of thick black hair and an easy laugh.

All three welcomed Dominique with genuine pleasure. The women were so sure of their own skills that they felt not in the least threatened by her. Dominique, in turn, was ecstatic to have found friends to stave off her loneliness. On Friday of her second week, the two women invited her to join them for dinner at a nearby restaurant. Afterward, they all went to a movie. Dominique felt that her life was finally falling into place.

Meanwhile, Orman's was preparing for its Christmas gala, where lavish, one-of-a-kind gifts would be auctioned for charity. Many were donated by Orman's, but several corporations and individuals had also contributed. Auction items were so extravagant that talk of them filled the society columns as well as the trade bible, *Women's Wear Daily*. The costliest gift was a trip around the world provided by Pan American Airlines. A close second was the week's stay at the fully-staffed villa of Noel Coward in Jamaica, with transportation provided by Larry Orman's private plane.

Dominique was kept busy translating cables that flew back and forth from Paris and Rome. In addition, she assisted Maude in selecting menus and wines, interviewing caterers, and bargaining for discounts. Bruce, though, would sign the contracts. There was no better negotiator than he.

Orman's interior decorating department was to transform the store's restaurant into a glittering gold, silver, and white fairyland for the evening. Dominique, Maude, and Lucinda had happily agreed to work as hostesses for the event. They exclaimed with delight when they saw the drawings of the gowns they were to wear: pure white velvet, with extravagant, wide skirts.

But one week before the gala on December 20, Lucinda became seriously ill with the flu. "I can't believe this," she rasped over the phone to Dominique. "I've been looking forward to the gala for six months and I won't even be there to make sure the last minute details are taken care of."

"Don't worry," Dominique reassured her. "I'll make sure nothing slips through the cracks. Take good care of yourself and maybe you'll feel well enough to come to the gala." Dominique added that she would stop by Lucinda's that evening with some groceries and chicken soup from the deli.

"No!" Lucinda croaked. "You might get sick, too, and Maude can't possibly handle the gala alone."

"I'm coming and that's that," Dominique declared. "Besides, I have to go to the grocery. My family is coming to dinner this weekend. It'll be the first time they see my new place."

"All the more reason you don't want to get sick. Please don't come. If you do, and you get sick, I'll never forgive myself. Anyhow, I spend most of the time sleeping."

Dominique thought for a moment. "I'll tell you what: I'll bring the package up, ring your doorbell, and go away."

"You don't need to —"

"I *want* to. You're my friend." Dominique liked the sound of the words.

৩৩ ৩৩ ৩৩

Dominique's new apartment, a Greenwich Village efficiency, was larger and far more agreeable than her room at Mrs. Parsons'. It had a kitchenette, a patio garden, and a spacious, old-fashioned bathroom with a claw-footed tub. Like Mrs. Parsons', the room came furnished, though sparsely. There was a plump camelback sofa-bed covered in a cheerful flowered print and, near the kitchenette, a round cherry table and four ladder-back chairs. Two lamps and a coffee table were the only other pieces, but, with careful bargain hunting, Dominique added a few items that made the apartment feel like home. From a Village flea market, she bought a set of four country print cushions, which she placed on the dining chairs. In a neighbor's trash pile, she found a beautiful, but scarred, mahogany end table. She draped it with a simple cloth of white linen trimmed in lace — fifty cents with her Orman's discount. As a final touch, she filled her windowsills with geraniums and the corners of the room with larger plants.

Dominique loved the cozy, residential streets of the Village, in contrast to the more bustling, urban character of the East Side. And she thought her apartment, with its little brick fireplace and generous windows, was welcoming and cheerful.

Solange, however, seemed to disapprove. "I don't know why everyone here lives in one room," she remarked, taking off her hat. As it had been impossible to find parking nearby, the Markses had dropped Solange in front of Dominique's apartment while they attended to the car.

"Because, Mother," Dominique said wryly, "rents are high in New York." Dominique gestured around the room. "Do you like what I've done with it?"

Solange sniffed as she looked around. "Well . . . it seems clean enough."

Dominique felt her irritation rising. Was it impossible for her mother to praise her? She pressed her lips together and frowned.

"Oh, don't look so sour," Solange said casually. "Why don't you get us some drinks?"

"What would you like?" Dominique asked evenly.

"Do you have champagne?"

Dominique almost laughed out loud. "Is that what Danielle serves?" she asked dryly.

"Danielle is one of a family of four. Five, now that I'm with them. They are not in the practice of buying champagne." Solange removed her gloves and coat and looked around for a place to put them.

Dominique went to her and took the garments. As she hung them in her closet, she said over her shoulder, "I have some white wine or some red wine. I have gin and vermouth for martinis and I have scotch. Which would you like?"

"White wine, I suppose." Solange pulled out one of the ladder-back chairs and sat down in it gingerly, as though afraid it would dirty her dress. After a few moments, she asked, "What's that smell?"

"Spaghetti sauce, Mother. One of the few dishes I've mastered."

"Hmmm."

Dominique was saved from trying to interpret the sound by the arrival of the Marks family.

Dominique went to Danielle and hugged her, then Lana and Monique. She wasn't sure how to welcome Ron, so she settled for taking his coat with a smile and a greeting.

"I'm glad you could come." She diplomatically directed her remark to him. "I poured your scotch. It's on the counter."

Ron looked pleased at the attention. "Thanks," he said with a smile. Maybe, Dominique speculated, he had gotten over his annoyance at having Solange with them.

"Mother" — Dominique turned to Solange — "have you learned any English?" She felt bad that she and Danielle would be forced to exclude either Ron or Solange from the conversation, depending on the language they spoke.

"Yes," Solange answered in English. "My name eez Solange Avallon," she said haltingly. "I leev wiz my daughter."

"That's good!" Dominique laughed as she poured the drinks.

Solange struggled on. "I don't speak English."

Danielle put her arm around her mother's shoulders. "She's doing well. She knows even more words than that."

"Do you ever speak in English at home?" Dominique asked, leading the group over to the couch. She didn't sit, but instead went back to the kitchen to make the salad dressing. Lana, now five, followed her, while three year-old Monique played on the floor with a rubber ball.

"They never speak English!" Ron complained. But he said it with wry humor.

"Poor you!" Dominique smiled at her brother-in-law. He smiled back and, for a moment, his eyes held the sparkle of the young soldier Dominique had met a decade ago. With a start, she realized that he was only thirty. Only thirty and yet so changed from the youth she had known! Only thirty and, in the space of a few months, he had had to cope with the loss of his job and the burden of two in-laws.

He waved his hand dismissively. "I've given up trying to figure out anything they say." He shook his head ruefully.

Dominique saw Solange give her son-in-law a baleful look. Solange might not have understood the words, but she clearly understood that reference to her was being made.

Dominique wondered how much longer their uneasy arrangement could endure.

CHAPTER 8 ∽

DOMINIQUE was crimson with rage and shame. In Lucinda's absence, she had been put in charge of several tasks for the gala and already a mistake — a glaring one — had occurred.

"The centerpieces are all wrong!" Dominique cried. "We told the florist not to use any carnations or mums, and no asparagus fern!"

Bruce Fisher's face was calm, but Dominique knew that he couldn't possibly find the centerpieces acceptable. They were downright ordinary!

Maude looked ready to go to war over the mistake. "We've worked with them a hundred times before! What are they trying to pull?"

The gala was that very evening and it was almost noon. How could Dominique possibly solve the problem in so short a time? It didn't matter *how*, she told herself grimly, so long as it was done.

She looked up at Bruce Fisher, angry determination written on her features. "I'll take care of this," she said between clenched teeth.

Her first move was to call the florist. "Lucinda told you what kind of flowers were unacceptable." Dominique tried to keep her voice calm. "Why are all two hundred centerpieces wrong?"

The florist was a New York debutante turned businesswoman. Kiki Van Alt's tone was supercilious. "We've done all of Orman's events for the past two years. They've always been satisfied. Where's Lucinda?"

"Lucinda," Dominique said icily, "is otherwise occupied. What happened?"

"Our supplier ran out of white roses. I could have given you half the centerpieces one way and half the other, but I thought it would be better if they were all the same."

"Why didn't you tell us there was a problem? We might have chosen another kind of flower. But *never* carnations!"

"I should think that Orman's would prefer to rely on the judgment of a professional rather than someone who —"

"Let me stop you right now." Dominique's tone was threatening, and the woman on the other end of the line was silent. "We're wasting time. You have six hours in which to correct the mistake. Do you want to do it or shall I hire someone else?"

Kiki Van Alt indulged herself with airy, mocking laughter. "You can't be serious! Where else do you think you're going to get two hundred centerpieces in six hours?"

"That's not your problem," Dominique shot back. "Your problem is to decide whether you can do the work. Or would you like to come and pick up these centerpieces and absorb their cost yourself?"

Kiki lost her cool. "I'll do no such thing! *Where is Lucinda?*"

Dominique ignored the question. "I need your decision right now. Otherwise, you'll never do another Orman's event. I've already spoken to Mr. Fisher and he's in complete agreement," Dominique concluded bluntly.

"Where am I supposed to find —"

Dominique interrupted. "*That's* your problem. Go down to the wholesale flower district. Other florists. I don't care. We need the centerpieces by six tonight."

"But if I have to buy exotics, it could be more expensive. I can't absorb —"

Dominique interrupted her again. "Consider the alternative, Miss Van Alt. There are many florists in New York who would kill for the Orman's account. Absorbing the cost of the extra trouble you've caused us might be a worthwhile investment."

There was silence on the other end of the line. Dominique didn't try to break it. The next move was Kiki Van Alt's.

Finally, the woman said, "I'll be there in an hour."

Dominique hung up the phone, a victorious smile on her face.

✑ ✑ ✑

"You did good work, ladies." Bruce Fisher surveyed the wreckage of Orman's most successful Christmas gala ever. Tables were covered in dirty linen and wine bottles, the floor was strewn with feathers and glitter and white flowers, but Maude, Dominique, Hank Benson, and Bruce beamed happily at one another.

All the press had been there, even those representing out-of-town media. The room had been packed with society luminaries and celebrities. Almost one million dollars had been raised for charity.

"The centerpieces were perfect, Dominique," Maude commented.

Bruce regarded Dominique with a twinkle in his eye. "I guess you put the fear of God in Kiki Van Alt. Good work!"

Dominique beamed at the compliment. "Did she try to get you to overrule me? She threatened to, you know."

Bruce gave her a sly smile. "Let's just say that I made it clear that you were in charge where that was concerned."

Dominique smiled gratefully at him.

"We also got a lot of compliments on these dresses, Bruce," Maude commented. "I think we should use Susan Swope again."

"She's an up-and-coming designer," Bruce said thoughtfully. "I've been thinking of buying more of her line." Bruce tilted his head and studied Maude. "The dress looks great on you."

Dominique noticed with amusement that Maude blushed at the compliment. Was there something going on between them? Indeed, Maude, usually so businesslike, radiated feminine allure in her white dress. The top layer of her long dark hair was swept back into a pearl clip at the back of her head, while the rest tumbled to her shoulders in thick, glossy waves. Her makeup was skillfully applied to highlight the deep blue of her eyes and the delicate ivory of her skin.

Hank, oblivious to the romantic undercurrents, said, "That was an incredible dinner. Maude, how much did that set us back?"

"You'll be surprised when you hear," Bruce chuckled. "She's a top-notch negotiator."

Maude turned admiring eyes on Bruce. "You're the one who negotiated the final price," she protested modestly.

Bruce beamed at her. "Let's just say it was a great team effort." He looked around the table expansively. "All of you."

There were murmured thanks, a few more comments, then Bruce stood up. "Well," he said, looking at Maude. "I can't let you ladies take the subway alone this time of night."

"Oh, but you both live uptown," Dominique protested. "I live in the Village like Hank." She turned to the amiable press secretary. "Can you drop me?"

"Glad to," Hank said easily.

Bruce turned to Maude, "Well, I guess it's just you and me."

Maude looked directly at him and smiled.

Oh, yes, Dominique thought smugly. There was definitely something going on.

ᕫᕙ ᕫᕙ ᕫᕙ

As January passed into February, the weather in New York grew colder. Dominique couldn't believe how cold — she'd never before experienced such weather. But her job enabled her to buy a heavy coat and she consoled herself with the fact that spring was only a month away.

On Valentine's Day, Lucinda tried to persuade Dominique to go on a blind date.

"He's a classmate of my brother's at Harvard and *very* cute. Why won't you give it a try?"

None of your business, Dominique wanted to cry. She would wait for her divorce to become final before she began dating, *if* she began dating. She wasn't ready to get involved with anyone yet. It wasn't that she didn't meet men — there were plenty at work who were interested. But, in her mind, she compared each one to Stephen, and none tempted her. Aloud, she said, "I want to concentrate on my job."

Lucinda shoved the file cabinet shut in mock anger. "Ooh, you're frustrating. Let your hair down and have some fun! If you won't go out with Porter, then what about the men's department manager? He's always hanging around you."

Dominique gave Lucinda a look of gentle warning. "No. And don't press me any more," she said, not unkindly. "I have work to do." She picked up the phone — an unmistakable signal that the discussion was closed.

"Naturally," Lucinda said flippantly.

But Lucinda's absorption with Dominique was diverted when, a few moments later, Bruce and Maude arrived together.

Fisher had a gleeful twinkle in his eye. "We have an announcement to make." He went to the door of Hank's office. "Hank, could you come out here, please?" The lanky man appeared in the doorway as Bruce returned to his place beside Maude. With an air of occasion, he cleared his throat and said, "Maude and I would like to invite you all to dinner this Saturday evening. It's a very special celebration." Bruce and Maude beamed at each other. "We were married this weekend." He took Maude's arm and drew her to his side. She blushed and grinned at her friends.

"Maude!" Lucinda gasped. "How wonderful! What a surprise! We had no idea, did we?" She turned to Dominique — and caught her exchanging a conspiratorial look with Maude. "You knew!" she laughed. "You're awful! Why didn't you tell me?"

Dominique smiled and shook her head. "I didn't know, but I suspected," she said mischievously.

"And you didn't tell me?"

Bruce nodded approvingly. "Thank you for your discretion." He laughed and gestured toward Lucinda. "Especially with this one around." His tone was affectionate.

"I can keep a secret!" Lucinda pretended to be angry, but she was laughing.

The others hooted at this.

"I can!" Lucinda pushed out her lower lip in a sulk, but she could only hold the position for a second before she started laughing again.

"You can't!" The others cried in unison.

After a few moments, Bruce held up his hand to quiet them. "Anyhow, on to more serious matters. Maude has officially submitted her two weeks' notice."

Everyone groaned in unison.

"Listen, kiddies," Maude said, "I'm tired of commuting every day and Bruce is tired of coming home to an empty house. I want to stay home and take care of my husband." She laced her arms through Bruce's and looked up at him lovingly.

"Besides," Bruce added, "Orman's doesn't allow nepotism." He paused. "So there are going to be a few changes in our procedures."

Everyone immediately quieted. Bruce smiled at their grave expressions. "I think you'll be pleased. It's meant as a reward for all your hard work and successes these last few months." He gave them an appreciative nod before continuing.

"We don't really generate much secretarial work. Dominique and Lucinda spend most of their time on event planning, with secretarial duties only secondary. So I've decided to organize your duties so that the two of you are less involved in paper pushing. We'll hire a top-notch executive secretary to take care of the correspondence that Hank and I generate, as well as the repetitive work associated with our events. Hank will continue to handle press. You'll each continue to handle your own correspondence.

"But rather than divide duties for each event, I'll assign either Dominique or Lucinda to oversee it start to finish. From now on, ladies, your events will be just that. Yours. You will be held responsible for their success or failure. You may call on your colleague for assistance, but you will direct her efforts when the event is yours. And, of course, I will continue to give final approval for all ideas and expenditures.

"Lucinda, I want you to be in charge of the Spring Into Summer event. You helped think of the theme and you've already done the preliminary work. Dominique, you'll have to dream up a way to launch the new French line we'll be introducing in June. It should be right up your alley. Now, these events are only a month apart, so each will have to be distinctive. Dominique, your event is only four months away and we haven't even begun to brainstorm on ideas. You'll have to start planning immediately.

"Any questions?" Bruce concluded.

Dominique was thrilled. Her own event! She would make it the most spectacular party Orman's had ever hosted! She would do something . . . wonderful. She didn't know what yet, but she was determined to justify Bruce's faith in her.

⮂ ⮂ ⮂

Dominique sat in the smoky café near her house and stared out the bay window at the magical winter landscape. A snowstorm the night before had encased the trees in ice crystals that glittered in the sun like thousands of tiny fairy lights. In the park across the street, children romped, ecstatic with the glory of the morning. Dominique watched with amusement as a little boy and girl debated whether their snowman should wear a smile or a frown. They arranged the pebbles one way, then backed up to study the effect, like artists. The girl shook her head and moved forward to try it the other way. After more discussion, they repeated the entire process. Finally, their mother broke the tie and the snowman remained smiling.

Dominique, too, was enthralled with the snow; she had previously seen it only in pictures. She loved the pure fluffy whiteness, and that morning had rushed outside to sweep the powder off her front steps, just for the sheer joy of it. Afterward, she had gathered up her Sunday *Times* and walked to the café, looking forward to the stuffy, comforting warmth of the place.

"More coffee, Dominique?"

Dominique smiled up at the black-clad woman. Nan Patrick was the proprietor of Café Espresso, an artists' gathering place at the end of Dominique's block. "As always." Dominique laughed. Nan served the best espresso in New York, and it pervaded the air with a tempting aroma.

Dominique had become a regular at the café, usually spending an hour or more there with the *New York Times* on Saturday and Sunday mornings. She felt perfectly comfortable sitting alone at her tiny wooden table. Many of the people who wandered in, books or newspapers under their arms, greeted Dominique by name. Often a fellow patron would join her for a few moments, then wander to a table for one, respecting the atmosphere of leisurely privacy that made the café such a comfortable place to while away the morning.

Dominique took a sip of the strong, warming brew, then turned back to the crossword puzzle. She found it sharpened her English skills, though she rarely had the patience to complete it. Today, in particular, she was distracted. She was thrilled with the reorganization that Bruce had announced earlier in the week, but she felt pressured to prove she could handle her own event. So it was frustrating that all the ideas that came to her seemed commonplace.

Dominique put down the paper and stared out the window. What was so unique about the new French line? Well, it was three types of products at once: cosmetics, sportswear, and evening wear. That hadn't been done before. So what? Why did three make it more interesting than one? Dominique thought about it and decided that wasn't the angle to pursue. Instead, she focused on the designer himself. Jean-Claude Berri was a rugged looking thirty-two-year-old whose top model was his twenty-one-year-old wife. Berri had created a sensation in the design world when he had left the house of Christian Dior to launch his own line of young, innovative clothes. His announced goal was to capture the eighteen-to-forty-year-old market by designing bold ready-to-wear and selling it for thirty percent less than his competition. Couture, he said brashly, was for the over-fifty crowd. The fashion press pounced on the story, devoting many pages to photographs of the glamorous couple. Sketches from Berri's spring line, exhibited in Paris the previous fall, filled the trade press.

It had been a coup for Orman's to obtain the exclusive right to market Berri's products in the United States. The June event would introduce the American public to the designer's fall/winter line. Dominique's goal was to create an event that reached a wide public as well as the popular press. She had to make Jean-Claude Berri a household name in the cities where Orman's had branch stores: San Francisco, Los Angeles, Chicago, and New Orleans.

What could she do? Dominique looked around the little café as though she would find a clue there. The brick walls were hung mostly with the original art of patrons, but six framed travel posters behind the bar added to the international flavor of the place.

Dominique focused on the posters. Exotic locales often provided effective themes for events, she knew. One poster was a splashy drawing of extravagantly costumed dancers. The caption underneath, in bright red lettering, read, "Rio de Janeiro." The second poster was a surrealistic photograph of a beautiful blonde sitting at a poolside table with a much older man. They both wore bathing suits and sunglasses, but over the blonde's shoulders was draped an ermine. A surfeit of diamonds glittered at her throat, wrists, ears, and fingers. "Hollywood," read the caption. Dominique almost laughed out loud. She'd never really noticed it before. The next poster depicted an outdoor café overlooking a yacht-filled harbor. On the table in the foreground was a bottle of wine and a vase of daisies. The caption read "Côte d'Azure."

Dominique sighed, struck with a sudden pang of homesickness for the place she had visited every year of her life — until that year. It was a shame New York didn't have more sidewalk cafés. She turned away from the poster and picked up her coffee cup. But just as she was about to drink from it, she stopped. Her head swiveled back to the Riviera poster. It was as if a lightbulb had come on. That was it! What could be more atmospheric — and more inclusive — than a sidewalk café on a fashionable street? She wouldn't just hold her event in Orman's, she would hold it *outside* of Orman's. She would throw open the doors to the store and line the surrounding sidewalks with cute little tables and chairs. People would be able to order French food and wines. She would hire street entertainers like she saw in Paris — acrobats and jugglers and fortune tellers. Musicians would play café music. And while the people were sitting at the little tables enjoying the atmosphere, she would parade Jean-Claude Berri's latest fashions before them.

Then another brainstorm seized her. This wouldn't be an invitation-only event! They would advertise it, publicize it, and draw in the general public. But was a French café on a city street enough to draw in large numbers of shoppers? To attract significant press coverage? There had to be a way to enhance the idea. Dominique thought again of the cafés in Europe. Their festival atmosphere came from the people who crowded around them. Europe had broad sidewalks and plazas just made for people watching. New York sidewalks were narrower, and traffic would distract from Dominique's show. Unless . . . She thought of Europe's most exciting streets and plazas. Many were closed to traffic. Suppose she were able to obtain a permit to block off the streets near Orman's. That would be the perfect solution, she thought excitedly. She had seen such an event in San Francisco once. It had been called a block party.

Dominique imagined the streets around Orman's lined with crepe stands and ice-cream vendors. She envisioned a section devoted to artists with their easels, just as in Paris' Montmarte. She saw little booths resembling the flea market, except that Berri products would be sold. It would be unlike anything that had ever been done before!

Dominique was filled with elation. She pulled a small notepad from her purse and began to scribble. She intended to present Bruce Fisher with a coherent, defensible plan. He would bring up potential problems. She would need answers. As long as she anticipated all the problems that might arise, things would go smoothly. And that wasn't so difficult, was it?

CHAPTER 9 ∽

TIME was whizzing by too quickly, Dominique thought, as she riffled through a pile of papers on her desk. With only four days until her debut event, she had begun to virtually live at Orman's, going home only to shower, change clothes, and snatch a few hours of sleep. Despite that, there remained a plethora of last minute things to be done.

Dominique finally located her checklist with a sigh of relief. She scanned it, a frown on her face. Then a movement in the corner of her eye made her look up.

"Lucinda, thank God, you're back. We need to —"

Lucinda interrupted her. "Dominique?" She was pale, hesitant.

Dominique's stomach knotted. "What's wrong?"

"Berri's evening dresses weren't in the shipment!" Lucinda blurted.

Now it was Dominique's turn to go pale. "What do you mean? His office promised they would be in this one. We have the wire right here!" Dominique pulled a yellow piece of paper from her desk and waved it in front of her.

Lucinda looked pained. "I've been through every crate. I don't know what to do."

Dominique tried to still the panic that was rising in her. Everything was going wrong. She wanted to rush in a thousand different directions. Things she couldn't possibly have foreseen were eating up valuable time. And the clock was ticking! She tried to think of what to do next. "Call Berri's people. Find out exactly who the shipper is and when they picked it up!"

"Right." Lucinda nodded nervously and scurried away.

A man in a blue uniform appeared at the door wheeling a dolly piled high with boxes. "Where d'ya want these?" he asked between puffs of his cigar.

The smell assailed Dominique's nostrils and made her head ache all the more. "What are those?" she asked, approaching the dolly.

The man looked at the clipboard in his hand. "All it says here is 'Samples.'"

"Oh, the gift baskets." To be given away with purchases, they included samples of Berri perfume and cosmetics. Their arrival was the first good news Dominique had received all morning. "Put them in there, please." She gestured toward Hank's office.

The man wheeled in his load and left. A few moments later, a strong smell began to fill the office.

Dominique raised her head and sniffed. Slowly, she stood up and looked around. Perfume. Strong perfume. She jerked open her desk drawer and pulled out her pocket book. The perfume inside was intact. Then she remembered the boxes in Hank's office. "Oh, no!" she cried. She pushed herself away from her desk and ran to the little room near the reception area. The bottom half of one of the cardboard boxes was soaked. Dominique could see the wet spot rising higher as more perfume was absorbed into the thirsty cardboard. "Oh, no!" she repeated. She sank to her knees and pulled the box open. Sure enough, several bottles of perfume lay in shards amidst the stuffing.

"Stay calm," she whispered to herself. "This is not a serious problem."

"What happened?" Hank stood in the doorway, his expression perturbed.

"Don't ask," Dominique replied wearily. "And don't say anything. Just don't."

"But that smell. It's . . . it's suffocating." Hank protested.

Dominique gave him a crooked smile. "Don't let the press hear you say that. I'll call the janitor and have it cleaned up."

Hank studied Dominique for a moment, then said, "Look, *I'll* call the janitor. You just go ahead with your work."

"Thanks," Dominique said gratefully.

"It's okay." He paused. "Say, is everything going all right?"

Dominique gave him a droll look. "Oh, yes, smooth as silk."

ᏭᎷ ᏭᎷ ᏭᎷ

The night of the party, Dominique saw success unfurl before her like a red carpet. From the moment the first curious passersby entered the French café, Dominique knew the evening would be a hit. The café was filled in less than half an hour. By sunset, the blocked-off street in front of Orman's was choked with people. The store was open and sales booming. It was a festival, a fantasyland, *the* place for all Manhattan to be that night. The lights from Orman's made Fifty-seventh Street as bright as day.

Smart young career women came, lured by a Berri dress or a bottle of perfume. And, just as Dominique intended, dwellers of the fashionable neighborhood that surrounded the store were drawn by the noise from the street party.

The store's gold-charge customers were invited to a private cocktail party with Berri himself that preceded the block party. Chic Manhattanites in little black dresses and society doyennes in Chanel suits crowded around the designer and his models, eager to be his first clients in America. Their daughters came, too: chattering debutantes, for once in agreement with their mothers that Berri was *absolutely* the last word. Dominique had expected the rarefied types to leave once the block party began, but only a few did. Instead, the exclusive gathering, well lubricated by French wine, spilled into the street festival when it began an hour later.

Jean-Claude Berri and his beautiful wife were delighted. Photographers dogged their footsteps, blinding them with their flashes. Reporters pounded them with questions. Dominique was stunned to see a crew from a network news show just outside the store's main entrance. And she was even more shocked when Hank and Bruce pushed her forward and introduced her as the creator of the event. Larry Orman personally congratulated her.

"What's your name again?" he yelled over the noise from the crowd.

"Dominique Avallon," she said into his ear.

He pumped her hand and repeated the name, as though committing it to memory. Then he was swallowed by yet another throng of photographers.

"Did I hear correctly? Dominique Avallon?"

Dominique turned in the direction of the man's voice — a voice as deep and smooth as vintage cognac — and found herself looking into a pair of mesmerizing blue eyes. Bedroom eyes, she immediately thought — to her embarrassment.

The man gave her a rakish grin and held out his hand. "Clay Parker."

Why was the name familiar? Dominique extended her hand and watched it disappear into his. A surge of warmth flared between them at the contact. The man was tall, his presence so dominating that Dominique was suddenly heedless of the crowd surrounding them. God, he was handsome! Movie star handsome, with luxuriant chestnut hair and the kind of tanned, chiseled face — almost beautiful in its perfection — that would look breathtaking in film close-ups.

Dominique had almost forgotten what it was like to feel this kind of attraction. It hit her like a lightning bolt, taking her unaware. Her body came alive with energy. It radiated from her, magnetic and utterly compelling.

Clay Parker's eyes gleamed appreciatively. "I would have never guessed that the person responsible for all this" — he made a gesture that took in the entire street scene — "could possibly be so young and —" He didn't falter; rather he stopped deliberately, suggestively. His blue eyes narrowed, focusing tightly on Dominique's face.

Against her will, she blushed. "I headed the project, but a lot of other people were involved, too."

For a moment, Parker's flirtatious demeanor was replaced with one of respect. "Congratulations on a superb job," he said. "I think the Berri line will be a huge success."

Dominique's eyebrows went up in surprise. "You're familiar with it?"

Clay laughed. "My company delivered it here. And I personally escorted the evening gowns that your office was so worried about."

Parker Shipping, Dominique thought. Very impressive.

She put her hands on her hips in mock anger. "You drove us crazy!" she declared.

Clay bowed, a graceful, courtly movement. "My apologies." Upright again, he gave Dominique a sheepish look. "One of our barges ran aground and there was a delay. When I found out how soon you needed the goods, I decided to bring them personally. Larry Orman invited me to the party anyhow, so I just came a couple of days early."

Dominique forgave him instantly. It would have been impossible not to.

Clay responded to the softening of her features with a devilish grin.

He knows how seductive he is, Dominique thought, as his eyes swept over her. A thrilling little frisson pranced up Dominique's spine.

"Your accent," Clay said in a low voice, "drives me crazy."

Dominique laughed, glad she was having the same effect on him that he was on her. For an instant, Stephen flashed in her mind. It had been so different with him. The attraction had evolved over several weeks, and at its base had been mutual respect. With this man, there was instant electricity. Desire, pure and simple.

He gestured toward one of the outdoor cafés. "Listen, why don't you take a break and have a drink with me?"

"Thank you," Dominique smiled. She imagined that it was very difficult to say no to a man with a voice and manner so charming. Where was he from, she wondered? He himself had a mellifluous accent that captivated her.

As soon as they were seated, a waiter materialized at their side.

"Drink?" Clay asked.

Dominique laughed again, with a lovely flash of her dimples. He was making her light-headed. But she had to keep her balance. She had responsibilities. "Just coffee. I need to stay alert."

Clay looked disappointed. "You still have to work?"

Dominique was flattered by his dismay. "Of course. Things can still go wrong."

Clay looked up at the waiter. "Tanqueray martini for me. Up. Olives," he said.

He looked like a martini sort of man, Dominique thought. Languorous, sophisticated, hedonistic. His outrageous good looks were set off by a tan suit of Italian silk. A fine shirt of pale blue cotton made his eyes appear even bluer. A striped silk tie completed a look that was tasteful and discreet. And yet, the startling perfection of his features made him appear almost flamboyant, as though he were the hero of a spy movie.

Dominique couldn't suppress her curiousity about him. "You're not originally from New York, are you?"

He shook his head slowly, still keeping his eyes fixed on her. "No, ma'am," he drawled, "New Orleans." He pronounced it "N'awlins."

So that explained the accent, less extreme than other southerners, but softer than northerners. Dominique dropped her eyes, feeling the need to escape the intensity of his gaze. "That's your headquarters, then. I've seen your company's bills, of course, but they say you have offices in New York, Philadelphia, New Orleans, and Miami."

A look of pride came over Clay's features. "We're pretty big, I suppose. Stay busy."

One of the biggest shipping companies in America, Dominique knew, amused by his understatement.

The waiter brought their drinks and Clay raised his glass to Dominique. "You deserve a toast for putting together such an incredible party. And . . . ," he added with a self-mocking smile, "I'm an expert on parties."

"Oh?" Dominique leaned forward and gazed up at him. She couldn't keep a flirtatious note of interest from her voice. "And why is that?"

"Don't you know that New Orleans is the greatest party city in the entire United States? Our motto is *'Laissez les bons temps rouler.'*"

Dominique smiled. "Let the good times roll. . . . Sounds inviting!"

His voice dropped a register. "I'd like to show it to you sometime."

It sounded like an offhand remark. "That would be nice." Dominique smiled.

He sat up straighter in his chair. "No, I mean really."

Dominique was taken aback. She gave him a questioning look.

"How about tomorrow?" Clay asked.

"Tomorrow!" Dominique gasped and let out a burst of incredulous laughter.

"My company plane's here. We can go down for dinner." He leaned forward, enthusiastic.

Dominique stiffened. Undoubtedly, he was used to girls swooning at the offer of such a glamorous evening. "I don't think so," she said, her voice cool.

Unabashed, Clay went on. "It's perfectly respectable! We'll be in public the entire time. The plane even has two stewards."

Dominique couldn't remain offended, his manner was so guileless. At the same time, she had no intention of getting on a private plane with a stranger, no matter how intriguing he was. She finished the last sip of her coffee and put the cup down with an air of finality. "I'm sorry, I really can't," she said firmly.

He regarded her with an air of mock exasperation. "All right! You win!" He threw up his hands in a gesture of surrender. "How about dinner tomorrow night? Here."

Dominique gave him a severe look. Feeling contrary, she lied, "I'm busy tomorrow night." If he was really interested he'd —

"What about next Saturday?" He pounced on the challenge. There was no doubt he was intrigued by her resistance. "I'll fly up 'specially."

How could Dominique say no?

ঔৎ ঔৎ ঔৎ

Dating Clay was like being back in the halcyon days of Egypt. On Saturday, he took her to dinner at "21," then dancing at the Copacabana.

Since Dominique couldn't justify the extravagance of a new evening gown, she was relieved that Anton had finally sent the clothes she had left in San Francisco. At first, he had refused, but as soon as he had filed for divorce, he had evidently lost all interest in her. Dominique suspected that his eagerness to sever their ties was the result of a new woman in his life. Well, she was welcome to him. Dominique only wished she could warn the poor thing.

For her first date with Clay, Dominique wore a strapless gown of black silk, regretting that she had no real jewelry to set it off. If it wouldn't have meant endless questions, she would have borrowed something from Solange. Still, when Dominique was dressed and ready to go, with her curls gathered up in a frothy hairdo and the sheer black scarf floating over her shoulders, she decided that she looked very good. More than good, she admitted to herself. Her shoulders were glossy and smooth, begging to be caressed. Her cleavage teased invitingly without revealing too much. And her eyes, carefully made up to emphasize their exotic slant and color, illuminated her entire face.

Once at "21," Clay and Dominique were whisked past the crowd at the door to a table in the prestigious front room. As the captain, busboy, and maître d'hôtel hovered attentively around their table, ensuring that everything was to Mr. Parker's liking, the sommelier brought a bottle of Krug 1947 vintage champagne in an ice bucket. Clearly, Clay was a regular patron, and a valued one.

Dominique looked happily around the room. It had been over a year since she'd been in such a rarefied setting. Despite the fact that the restaurant was located in a cozy brownstone with beamed ceilings and varnished wood, it was as unmistakably exclusive as the marble palaces that housed clubs in Egypt or Monte Carlo. At the bar, she recognized several famous faces.

"You've never been here before?" Clay asked.

Dominique turned back to him. She was too sure of herself — and too accustomed to places like "21" — to lie. "No, but I've heard about it," she said, thinking once more how handsome he looked in evening clothes.

"Hmmm. I would have thought that a girl like you would have been everywhere in New York," he teased.

Dominique tilted her head. "A girl like me?"

Clay took a sip of champagne and looked at Dominique over the rim of his glass. "Sophisticated, talented, beautiful, amusing." He paused. "The men up here must be fighting over you." He smiled and put down his glass. "If not, they're crazy."

Dominique raised her eyebrows and gave him an enigmatic smile. Then she changed the subject. "How long will you be in town?" she asked.

Clay gave her his wicked grin. "As long as it takes."

Dominique's heart fluttered. Oh, he was altogether too appealing. Dangerous. "Takes to do what?" she ventured, knowing the answer pertained to her.

"Get you to come to New Orleans."

Dominique laughed. She looked squarely at him, her eyes twinkling. "How long does it usually take?"

Clay blushed, like a child caught with his hand in the cookie jar, but he laughed, too. "No comment," he said. "That's my safest course." As his laughter died away, he cocked his head and studied Dominique. He looked at once puzzled and respectful.

"Maybe we should change the subject." Dominique glossed over the moment with good humor. "Does your family live in New Orleans, too?"

Clay leaned back in his chair and rested his arms on the snowy tablecloth. "Since the 1850s. None of us have ever lived anywhere else."

Dominique sighed. "That's nice. That's the way it was for us in Egypt." She had told him a little about her background in the ride from her apartment — a ride that took place in a shining, black Cadillac limousine.

"How'd you end up in the United States?" he asked.

Dominique stiffened. She knew she was in treacherous waters. She didn't want to lie, but she had no intention of divulging her history to someone she barely knew. Not even her friends at work knew about Anton. "The French are no longer welcome in Egypt," she said carefully, "and my sister was here."

Eager to turn the conversation back to Clay, Dominique asked, "Do you have brothers or sisters?"

Clay shook his head. "I'm an only child."

Dominique wondered how old he was. He seemed young to be the head of his own company. Perhaps it was his father's. She tried to think of a subtle way to find out. "And how long has Parker Shipping existed?"

Clay chuckled. "As long as there have been Parkers in Louisiana."

"Oh, so your father must still be active in the firm." Clay didn't look older than thirty, so the father probably wasn't more than sixty.

A shadow passed over Clay's features, then just as quickly disappeared. He forced a smile. "He's president of the company. They'll probably have to carry him out on a stretcher." He raised his hand and a waiter instantly appeared with long, leather-bound menus. A wine list, also thickly bound, was placed at Clay's elbow.

Dominique sensed she had probed a touchy subject. Tactfully, she opened the menu. "Well," she said, "what do you recommend?"

"The Dover sole is good. So's the rack of lamb. Or we could split the Chateaubriand for two."

"Is medium rare all right?" Dominique asked.

"Just the way I like it," Clay said cheerfully.

After dinner, they entered the limousine for the short ride to the Copacabana. In the nightclub, Latin music pulsed, vibrating through the floor. Dominique's eyes were immediately drawn to the orchestra — handsome men in flowing shirts with ruffled sleeves. At the microphone, the lead singer was belting out a lively tune in Spanish. Dominique was dying to join the sleek couples on the dance floor — it had been so long!

Clay seemed to sense her mood, for no sooner were they seated at their table for two overlooking the dance floor — another bottle of champagne at their side — than he invited her to dance. As Clay led Dominique around the semicircular tier to the red-carpeted main stairs, she gazed at the other colorful patrons. The crowd was more diverse than any Dominique had seen in Egypt. There, Parisian chic had been the standard for women, no matter what their nationality. But in New York, there was more glitz. Many of the women wore long white gloves with diamond bracelets over them. One exotic brunette held a red lacquered cigarette holder which her escort, a much younger man, lit with a gold lighter. The women wore more makeup and jewels than their European counterparts, and their dresses were adorned with more frills, sequins, and feathers. It made for a lively, interesting scene, Dominique decided, though she would never have dressed that way herself.

As Clay took her in his arms, he remarked, "You have the tiniest waist I've ever seen. My hand almost spans it."

Dominique smiled up at him. She knew his admiration wasn't feigned. The way he treated her, the things he said, made her feel genuinely beautiful. She had so long shied away from romantic attachments that the feelings he aroused made her light-headed — like smoking a cigarette or taking a drink after a long abstinence. She melted into his arms, matching her steps perfectly to his.

As it turned out, Clay was an expert dancer. "My mother tortured me with four years of cotillion," he laughed. "Every afternoon, from the time I was ten till I was fourteen. Of course, just about the time it ended, I really started getting interested in girls." He rolled his eyes. "If only she'd waited, I would have been a willing victim."

"I have no complaints," Dominique bantered. "I think your mother did just the right thing."

They danced five tunes, then Clay pled exhaustion and they went back to their table. Dominique noted that, once again, they occupied the club's prime spot. "You must spend a lot of time in New York," she remarked.

"My father likes to keep me busy," Clay said lightly. "Sends me from one branch to another." Before he even completed the sentence, he turned to summon the waiter.

Dominique's earlier intuition seemed confirmed. There was definite strain between father and son. Well, she could sympathize, given her relationship with Solange. She made sure to avoid the subject for the rest of the evening.

At three-thirty in the morning, Clay and Dominique left the Copa. Dominique's feet were sore from dancing, but she was wide awake. When Clay suggested that they stop for breakfast on the way home, Dominique saw no reason to say no.

There were many other people in evening clothes in the coffee shop across from the St. Regis Hotel. Early breakfast, Clay told her, was a tradition among New York revelers. They had an authentic American meal of bacon, scrambled eggs, hashed browns, toast, and coffee. And they talked about everything from classical music to the Louisiana bayou.

It was dawn when the limousine finally drew up in front of Dominique's apartment. Clay walked her to her door, admiring the rural silence of her street. "You don't find that very often in New York," he commented.

"It's nice, isn't it?" Dominique sighed. "It won't stay that way. Things get noisier after the sun comes up."

As they reached her door, Clay turned Dominique toward him. "I'm not going to ask permission," he murmured as he drew close.

"I wouldn't expect that from *you*," Dominique smiled. Then she went into his arms, willingly succumbing to his kiss.

掙掙 掙掙 掙掙

What finally convinced Dominique to go to New Orleans with Clay wasn't the dinner at the Stork Club, nor the helicopter tour of Manhattan. Not the roses he sent each week, nor the giant bottle of Chanel No. 5 he bought to celebrate their two-week anniversary. None of his extravagant gestures charmed her as much as the luncheon date at the relatively modest Taft Hotel. For it was that flight of fancy that made her fall in love with him.

"You have to take two hours for lunch today," he insisted good-naturedly when he phoned her on the Monday a little more than three weeks after their first meeting.

"I can't." Dominique laughed indulgently. She was constantly surprised — and flattered — at how often he arranged to be in New York. They had gone out ten days out of the last fourteen. On the days they didn't see each other, he took quick trips home or to branch offices. Whenever he was in town, though, he picked her up after work in the limousine. Sometimes he would drop her at her apartment so she could change for one of their elegant dinners, but other times they would simply take a walk, then stop at a neighborhood restaurant for a light meal. Dominique never offered to cook for him, however. She only knew how to make a few basic things, none of them particularly well, and she had noticed that Clay was exacting about cuisine.

But of all the times they'd been together, he'd never proposed lunch until now. "You have to come," he said. "I'm begging you. If you don't say yes, I'll go directly to Bruce Fisher. And you're much too discreet to want me to do that. So say yes."

Dominique was secretly delighted. Whereas she had resented Anton's imperious tone from the first, she found Clay's use of it endearing, since he tempered it with charming zeal. "Well . . . all right." Dominique feigned reluctance, though she knew she wasn't really fooling Clay.

At noon, when the limousine passed through the raffish neighborhood of Times Square and stopped in front of the Taft Hotel, Dominique thought it must be a mistake. The place was pleasant, but it didn't strike her as the sort of exclusive spot that Clay normally frequented. But when they entered the Grill Room, she discovered the reason for his insistence.

Couples were whirling about a large, colorfully lit dance floor to the live music of the Victor Lopez Orchestra.

Dominique clapped her hands together in astonishment. "Dancing? At lunch?"

Clay gave her such a gleeful look that Dominique's heart swelled with love. As the feeling hit her, she was momentarily hypnotized. Lost in a trance, she followed Clay through the restaurant to their table. How in the world had she allowed this to happen?

When they were seated, he leaned close to her and said, "Now then, isn't this romantic? Aren't you glad you came?"

Dominique looked at his beaming face. "Yes," she admitted, her face lighting with a smile, "yes, I am!"

Clay gave her a look of comic smugness. "And isn't it fun?" His delight was contagious.

"Very," she said merrily.

"Well," he said, taking her hand. "If you came to New Orleans with me, we'd have even more fun. Come on, Dominique." He fixed her with an exaggeratedly pleading stare. "I want to show you off to my friends and I want to show off my home city to you."

Dominique's pulse raced. Under his comic pleading, Clay sounded serious. For the first time, it occurred to Dominique that his intentions might be more than simply hedonistic. He was the kind of man girls were warned about — who gave every appearance of being a playboy. The kind of man who could never be caught. He would show you the time of your life, then he would break your heart. But now, suddenly, Clay seemed sincere. How Dominique wanted it to be so! She had loved only one man in her life, a man she could never have. Here, though, was a man she *could* have. And everything she had seen so far made her want him.

Nevertheless, she had to be wary, she reminded herself. She had suffered two devastating experiences in the short space of a year. She had to keep a steady hold on her emotions. He mustn't know his effect on her. How many other women had he captivated? And did they ultimately make him feel trapped? Bored?

Dominique looked at Clay thoughtfully. But if she went to New Orleans just for the day, what harm could it do? "How long would we be gone?" she asked.

Clay looked like he would jump for joy. "The plane's fast, one of the new jets. If we leave early Saturday morning, I'll have you back by Sunday morning. I don't usually get you home until dawn anyhow."

Dominique couldn't help noticing his use of the word "usually." It made her feel they were a couple. But an instinct of caution made her say, "Usually? We've only been out a handful of times."

"Hmmm." Clay pretended to reflect. "You're right. Then let's say I'd like it to *become* usual."

Dominique's heart did a cartwheel, but she smiled calmly. "I can't go next Saturday, I've invited my family to dinner."

"Why don't you invite me, too, so I can meet them?" Clay asked breezily.

Dominique inwardly cringed. All it would take was one of Solange's critical remarks to taint the rosy glow of Dominique's relationship with Clay. "Not this time," she said, avoiding his eyes. "But we can go the Saturday after next," she said hastily.

Clay frowned. "That's the week after July fourth. We always have a big family reunion then. And I'll be expected to do my duty." He didn't sound too happy, but then his voice brightened. "What about the week after?"

"Wonderful," Dominique said. She couldn't wait!

"I have to find a project to keep me busy in New York until then . . . I can't stay apart from you that long," Clay said huskily.

Things were moving too fast, Dominique thought. He was saying all the right things and her resistance was slipping. He was handsome and eligible and probably had a hundred women after him. Maybe she was just one of many.

But Dominique's logic didn't stand a chance against Clay's allure.

ᕤ ᕤ ᕤ

Sultry was the only word for New Orleans. One either fought the tropical atmosphere or surrendered to it. New Orleanians had long ago decided that surrender was sweeter. Lulled by the pervasive warmth, they moved slowly, strolled, lingered, lazed. Sweating was for outsiders.

Dominique emerged from the plane and was engulfed in a weighty cloak of humidity. She hadn't experienced such implacable heat since she'd left Egypt, and she suddenly realized how much she'd missed it. She felt herself being seduced by it, and she, too, surrendered.

A white Lincoln convertible waited for them near the plane. The top was down and Dominique knew that riding in it would destroy her hairdo, but she didn't care. The hard-driving tension of New York slipped away, to be replaced by southern laissez-faire.

Dominique and Clay walked slowly to the car and got in. They pulled away and the breeze, still hot, caressed her face. She closed her eyes, reveling in the feeling, then rested her right elbow on the door and gathered her hair at the base of her neck so it wouldn't blow in her face. She was glad Clay had warned her to dress lightly. The simple pink sundress with matching jacket was perfect for this weather.

"Let's get some lunch, then I'll show you the town," Clay said.

Dominique smiled and nodded in agreement, not bothering to open her eyes.

It took about twenty minutes to reach downtown.

"This is Canal Street," Clay said. "One of the main arteries."

Dominique opened her eyes and saw a wide avenue lined with palm trees, just like in Egypt. She sat up and looked around, recharged by excitement.

Clay made a left turn and they entered a narrow cobbled street flanked by townhouses. "The French Quarter," he said, slowing the car to a crawl so that Dominique could look around. "It's the oldest part of town. And" — he turned and gave her a wink — "most of the good restaurants are here!"

The buildings were the most romantic she had ever seen — of dusky, faded brick or deep, earthy stucco. They gracefully wore the patina of age, like proud grande dames with intriguing histories. Many were adorned with exquisite iron balconies cast in intricate patterns of winding vines, more Spanish than French in style. And there was greenery everywhere. Plants cascaded over balconies, flowers tumbled out of urns and window boxes, potted trees furnished shade and privacy. There was an impression of overwhelming, almost suffocating, fecundity. Dominique could practically smell the plants growing, as if in a greenhouse.

In contrast, the street was hushed, almost lifeless. Long wooden shutters, crooked on their hinges, were pulled shut. Only a few people were on the street, and their footsteps echoed through the narrow passageways.

Most of the buildings, Dominique noticed, housed little shops on the ground floor — dark, secret-looking places, half hidden in the shade. Many had dusty front windows crammed full of exotic wares that Dominique couldn't quite identify. Occasionally, a shop door would be propped open and Dominique would try to see inside. But she could spy only a vague glitter in the dim light and the shadow of ceiling fans moving in a languorous rhythm.

A sign affixed to one building caught Dominique's eye. Gold lettering on black metal announced, "Voodoo, Charms, Black and White Magic."

"What in the world?" Dominique asked.

Clay followed her gaze and laughed. "Shops like that are mostly for tourists now, but voodoo is still practiced here. It's a religion. The New Orleans version is sort of a mixture of Catholicism and magic, but it originated in the Caribbean. They use all kinds of charms and dolls and symbols."

Dominique shivered. There was something mysteriously fascinating about that. About the whole place.

Clay turned onto Bourbon Street and pulled the car into a spot along the curb. "You're in for an authentic New Orleans experience," he said. "Galatoire's. It's an institution."

They got out and began to walk. As they rounded a corner, the quiet street sprang to life. A line of well-dressed people, perhaps thirty of them, stood laughing and talking outside the door of a restaurant. The women wore dramatic hats, white gloves, and pearls, and the men sported cream, tan, or seersucker business suits. None of them seemed bothered by the heat; they looked as though they were enjoying themselves.

"What are all these people doing?" Dominique asked.

"Waiting for a table," Clay said casually.

Dominique expected him, as usual, to lead her past the queue into the building, but instead, he went to the end of the line.

Dominique's eyes widened. "We don't have reservations?"

Clay smiled down at her. "Galatoire's doesn't take them. Never has. And they don't play favorites, even if you come here every day of your life. Most of these people are regulars. Sometimes they come for lunch and don't leave until ten o'clock at night."

Dominique was consumed with curiosity. What kind of place could possibly merit such loyalty? A half hour later, she found out.

They stepped into a long, mirrored room with the decibel level of Grand Central Station. Tables were crammed together, privacy out of the question. On the contrary, conversations spanned several tables as though everyone had been invited to one huge party. Businessmen traveled around the room, greeting their cronies. Waiters rushed to and fro, shouting to one another over the heads of diners. Women issued cries of delight and leapt to their feet to kiss the cheeks of new arrivals.

Dominique's head was spinning. Clay had to stop every few feet to shake hands as they made their way to their table, a tiny space for two directly under the bank of mirrors.

As they sat down, he apologized for not introducing her. "It's kind of noisy right now. We'll wait until everyone's eaten and the tourists have left. It'll be a little quieter then. Meantime, how about a Ramos gin fizz?" Clay asked.

Dominique's eyes sparkled. "It sounds good. I've never heard of it."

Clay's eyebrows shot up. "No? Well, this you've got to try." He raised a hand and held up two fingers. A waiter with a handlebar mustache and a long white apron nodded as he sped by.

Dominique was anxious to wash her hands and refresh her makeup after the long wait outside, so she asked Clay where the rest room was.

"Through the kitchen and up the stairs," he replied.

"The kitchen?" Had she heard right?

Clay pointed at the swinging doors in back of the room just as a waiter came barreling out. "Make sure no one's coming before you try to go through," he warned with a grin.

The Ramos gin fizzes were delicious, frothy concoctions of cream, gin, sugar, egg white, and a touch of orange flower water. "One of our official drinks," Clay said. "It's mandatory to have at least two before lunch," he said with mock seriousness.

It was another hour before the waiter plopped down a plate over-loaded with sticks of fried eggplant. With it was a saucer containing a powdery white substance. "What's that?" Dominique asked.

"Powdered sugar," Clay said, picking up a stick and dipping it in.

Dominique shrugged skeptically but did the same. "Delicious!" she exclaimed.

Clay laughed. "Don't look so surprised. Have I ever steered you wrong?"

Dominique pretended to think about it. "No," she finally admitted.

The lunch courses flowed at a leisurely pace. There was a spicy Creole bouillabaisse which they had with crisp white wine. Afterward, Clay suggested they "visit a little." He took her hand and headed to a table of eight men at the back of the room. They were business associates, he explained, but also friends. Dominique wondered if he introduced all his girlfriends, or was it possible that she was special?

The men complimented Clay on his good taste and teasingly asked Dominique what she was doing with a rascal like him.

Dominique laughed. "He's holding me hostage."

The men guffawed appreciatively. One slapped Clay on the back and said, "Well, I guess you're smarter than you look, boy."

"Mr. Parker," yelled a waiter from across the room, "your food's waiting!" He stood holding steaming plates of crawfish sautéed with green onions.

Dominique turned, astonished but amused. She'd never seen such a place. It was raucous and brash and unpolished and clubbish. She loved it.

They emerged from Galatoire's at four o'clock, and this time Domi-nique said good-bye to as many people as Clay. She felt as though she'd made a roomful of friends.

As they stepped outside, she blinked at the bright sunlight, stunned once more by the blanketing humidity.

"C'mon," said Clay, "let's take a ride and cool off. I'll show you where I want to live someday." He removed his jacket and slung it over his shoulder.

As they walked to the car, Dominique suddenly became aware of the change in the street's atmosphere from earlier that day. People walked two by two and stopped to peer into shops. Music drifted from doorways: jazz, classical, show tunes. Shutters and windows were flung open, and transparent curtains wafted out on the evening breeze. People sat on their balconies. Passing beneath them, Dominique could hear the murmur of their conversations and the tinkle of ice in glasses. New Orleans had come alive. The mood was no longer haunting and nostalgic. Rather there was an air of celebratory expectation. Like Italy after siesta time. The feel of the city was so European that it made Dominique homesick.

I could live here, she thought.

Clay took a different route out of the French Quarter, passing by a row of prosperous-looking antique shops on the Rue Royale. He turned back onto Canal Street, then left. Soon they were keeping pace with a lime-colored streetcar as they made their way up a broad avenue divided by a wide strip of plantings.

"This is my favorite place in New Orleans," Clay said in a dreamy voice. "St. Charles Avenue. It's the main street in the Garden District."

"These trees, they're so huge!" Dominique looked up in wonder at the green canopy that spanned the broad avenue.

Clay nodded in approval at her praise. "Live oaks," he explained.

"Spectacular!" Dominique breathed.

"How about these houses? Big enough for you?"

Mansions in a variety of styles — from neoclassical to Spanish — were widely spaced along sweeping lawns of rich, blue-green grass. There were pink stucco mansions with red tile roofs, brick ones with huge white pillars, white wooden ones with ornate terraces and verandahs. Dominique had never seen such a hodgepodge of styles. But it all worked beautifully together. It was one of the most inviting places she had ever seen.

"This is where I grew up, right here in the District. When I'm head of the company, I want to move back here, buy one of these big places on St. Charles." Clay sounded determined.

This was the first time Dominique had seen any evidence of financial limitations. She had thought Clay independently wealthy.

Clay turned his mouth into a rueful half-smile. "My father doesn't believe in making things too easy for me. I'm supposed to work my way up in the company like everyone else."

Dominique gathered that he also received a salary like everyone else, rather than a blank check, as she had originally assumed. "Seems like good training," she ventured.

Clay kept his eyes fixed on the road. "That's the idea," he said. "Except there's something wrong when —" He stopped short and gave Dominique a furtive look. Then he turned back to the road. "Sorry," he said, "don't mean to sound bitter."

Dominique's heart went out to him. "I understand," she reassured him. "Sometimes I feel unfairly treated by my mother."

Their eyes connected. The communication, the mutual sympathy was unmistakable.

Clay sighed. "At least you don't have to work for her."

Dominique gave him a look of commiseration. "When will your father retire?"

Clay snorted. "Not until he thinks I'm old enough to handle the company. I'm twenty-nine now, so I estimate another twenty years, at least," he said sarcastically.

Dominique laughed softly. She reached out and squeezed his arm.

Clay turned at her touch. The look he gave her was so needy, so grateful, that she caught her breath. Suddenly, he pulled the car to the curb and turned off the engine. With an urgency she had never seen him exhibit, he pulled her to him, kissing her fervently, devouring her.

Dominique's heart hammered. She sank into his arms, meeting his passion. Like a dream, she was aware of the tree swaying overhead, the dappled sun on her face, the perfume of magnolia and jasmine. But mostly she was aware of the overwhelming need that telegraphed itself in his kiss. And her need was as great.

A streetcar clattered by and its bell pierced the air. Dominique and Clay drew apart, startled. Breathlessly, they gazed at each other.

Dominique, confused, drew back.

Clay's eyes burned into her, his usual smooth nonchalance gone. He opened his mouth to speak, then closed it, his expression all at once grim.

"What is it, Clay?" she asked, alarmed at the rapid change.

"Don't go back!" he appealed to her.

Dominique made a noise of disbelief. What exactly was he proposing?

He rubbed her hands in an agitated fashion. "Marry me instead."

"Marry you!" Dominique might have anticipated a declaration of love, an act of seduction, but not this! Butterflies whirred in her stomach. She had a wild impulse to say yes. To forget objections and constraints, like any other girl her age, and simply give herself to this man who had galloped into her life like Prince Charming.

"You look like you can't make up your mind." Clay fixed her with an intense stare. "Don't think about it. Come with me, now. We'll get a ring. We'll elope, unless" — he paused and looked at her from under his lashes — "you want a big wedding. Either way, it doesn't matter. We'll be happy, you'll see!"

"But we've only known each other a month, Clay!" The objection sounded hollow, even to her.

"I don't care," he insisted. "You're not like any other girl I've ever known. Down here, they're all a bunch of daddy's girls, spoiled rotten. You're different. You don't let anyone tell you what to do. You take care of yourself just fine. But you still make me feel like I'm the most important man in the world to you. You're always on my side. The way you look at me —" He stopped.

Dominique could see that he was revealing something profound and unspoken. A need for her strength and support.

But suddenly, Clay took hold of his emotions. His intensity gave way to a sexy grin. He leaned toward her, his manner once more polished. "You have to admit, darlin', we've got the chemistry."

Dominique smiled tremulously. One minute he was a supplicant — needing her. The next, he was a man of the world, a suave charmer. Dominique loved both sides, his power and his vulnerability. She looked at Clay with a grave expression. "What will your parents say about you running off and marrying a stranger?"

Defiance fired Clay's eyes. "Dammit, I don't care! I'm tired of doing everything just to please my father. He's run my —" Clay stopped and took a deep breath. After a second, he regained his self-possession. "He won't disown me. I'm his only heir and he's said a million times that he doesn't want the business to go outside the family."

He changed tacks. "It's clear you come from a fine family. . . . Besides, you're French, and in New Orleans that's like aristocracy. Father spent two years in college over there just so he could pick up the language! *His* father told him it would be useful when he took over the business." He shook his head and gritted his teeth and said, "So he'd better not have any criticism."

Dominique was silent. His family life was more disturbing than she had realized. And yet, surely, there must be love between father and son or they wouldn't be working together. "What about your mother?" she asked. Why did he never mention her?

Clay shrugged and gave a half-smile. "She's okay. Follows my father's lead."

None of it sounded terribly reassuring, but Dominique had learned long ago to get along without parental approval. Furthermore, she had enough self-esteem to believe Clay when he told her that his parents would be pleased once they met her. Something else was troubling her far more.

"Clay," Dominique said, haltingly, "there are things about . . . my past that you should know. I'm afraid . . . they may change your opinion of me." Then she added, "And your parents won't be pleased."

Clay gave her an understanding smile and whispered, "What could be so bad?"

Dominique took a deep breath. "There's no way to make this easier. . . ." She looked straight at him and put her hand on his arm. "Clay, I'm divorced."

Clay looked as though he'd been socked. The air went out of his lungs in a gasp. For a long moment, he said nothing. He simply stared at Dominique, his face growing paler with each second that passed. "That's . . . a . . . a . . . shock," he stammered.

"I know," Dominique said, chilled by his reaction. She was frightened as she saw happiness slipping out of her grasp. For a second, she wished she had kept her counsel. But, no, she couldn't do that. He *had* to be told.

"Tell me about it," he commanded, looking squarely at her.

Where to begin? With Stephen? No. No one had the right to know that. No one. Then how to explain her crazy marriage? She thought back to the weeks preceding it. There had been the threat of war. The disaster in the customs house. But the reasons really didn't matter, he would either accept the news or not. Accept *her* or not.

She pressed her tongue to the roof of her mouth, trying to find moisture. She wished she could have a sip of water. She wished her confession were already over and that she didn't have to think about it anymore. She gathered her thoughts and began, her voice deceptively calm. "There was a man who wanted to marry me. Our families pushed us together. . . . That's the way it is in the Middle East." She told Clay of the anti-European atmosphere in Egypt. Of the incident with the customs police.

Clay's face went from stubborn disbelief to empathy as her story unfolded.

"But why did you leave him?" he asked.

"It was a mistake from the start. He didn't really love me. He only wanted my family's money. And I" — she cast down her eyes in shame — "didn't love him," she murmured. "After I left, he sued me for desertion."

"Where is this guy now?" Clay asked, his expression worried.

"San Francisco. Why?"

"Do you think he'll ever try to contact you?"

"Once he found out we lost everything in the war, he had no more use for me," she said bitingly.

Clay averted his eyes. He seemed to study the cars as they made their way up St. Charles Street.

What was Clay thinking? Dominique wondered. She fidgeted with the handle of her purse as she anxiously watched his profile.

"Dominique" — Clay turned back and scrutinized her — "who else knows about this?"

"Well . . . my family, of course."

"No one at Orman's?"

"Of course not!"

Clay nodded. He sank into a brooding silence that Dominique was hesitant to break. After several moments, he said wistfully, "I thought I'd be the first for you."

Dominique met his gaze evenly. "I'm sorry," she said. She drew herself up. "But it's important for you to make a decision based on the truth. If you want to take back your proposal, I'll understand." Oh, but she would be devastated!

There seemed to be nothing more to say. Once more a pall fell over them.

Clay rubbed his temple with his index finger and seemed to consider a moment.

Dominique couldn't stand the suspense. It was shocking to realize how important he had become to her. He had filled her life, he had given back her youth, he had wiped away the hurt and disillusionment of her failed marriage.

Clay abruptly reached for her hand and pulled her close to him.

Then he caressed her cheek. "Thank you for telling me those things. I know it was hard for you."

Dominique was overwhelmed with emotion, but she continued to look squarely at him. "I couldn't keep them from you . . . now."

"Dominique," Clay said, gently brushing her forehead with his lips, "you're no different than you were an hour ago. I haven't changed my mind."

Dominique's heart soared. She had given Clay news that might have caused another man to condemn her, but Clay still wanted her. He still loved her! She had trusted him and he had rewarded her trust. She felt heady with renewed faith and optimism. She smiled up at him, her eyes shining.

Clay continued. "I want to forget about what you told me. And, if you don't mind, I'd like to keep it between us."

Dominique's smile faded. "I have no desire to tell anyone else," she said quietly.

"Then" — he turned and started the engine — "let's get married."

CHAPTER 10 ∾

IT WAS late Sunday evening when Dominique and Clay returned to New York. The past twenty-four hours had passed in a magical blur, and Dominique tried to recapture the images as they drove from the airport. The flight to Maryland, where they were able to marry in the middle of the night and without a waiting period — Clay once more arranging things seamlessly. The drive in the rented convertible to Washington, D.C. Top down, warm breeze blowing, stars shining in the onyx sky. The surprise of the grandly lit Memorial Bridge and the Lincoln Memorial itself, as uplifting as a Greek temple gleaming silver in the night. The White House, its fountain scattering mirrored rays. And, just across the park, the Hay-Adams Hotel, where a beautiful suite awaited the newlyweds. Their first night together.

Dominique inhaled deeply and closed her eyes. She reached across the soft leather of the seat to find Clay's hand and twined her fingers in his, recalling their more intimate encounter. The thought of Clay's body, tall and bronze and even more magnificent naked than dressed, made her shiver. He had engulfed her petite form, surrounded her with his protection and warmth and ardor. And how he had aroused her! She had almost forgotten that such feelings were possible. There had been none of the bittersweetness of her coupling with Stephen. On the contrary, the knowledge that Clay was *her* husband, *all hers*, added a new dimension to her excitement.

The first time they made love was swift and eager, the joining of two young people venting their desire. There had been little foreplay and Dominique hadn't missed it.

The second time, toward dawn, had been more leisurely. Clay had moved with hypnotic deliberation, knowing exactly where to touch, how to arouse: the soft skin on the insides of her arms and thighs, the back of her neck, the soles of her feet. His strokes were fluid, almost silky, as he trailed his hand from her nipples to her waist, then lower. Dominique was hardly aware of their bodies shifting, of Clay entering her. It all seemed to glide, flow, come together like the crescendo of a masterfully composed symphony. What moved Dominique most were his words of endearment — words that made her feel bound to him — truly married. Whereas Stephen had been reticent, Clay's emotions overflowed. And Dominique, naturally discreet like Stephen, was freed by Clay. Again and again, she told him of her love, and he never tired of hearing it. "Do you love me?" he would ask. And she would tell him so once more, for she never tired of saying it. Not once did she have second thoughts about her rushed marriage. Clay was the kind of man women fantasized about. This, the kind of marriage she had always hoped to have. The bad experience of Dominique's first marriage seemed a hazy nightmare.

Clay's brandied drawl broke into her reverie. "Happy?" he asked.

Dominique gave her husband a smile of elation, her expression transmitting all that was necessary.

Clay looked satisfied. "Wait till you see our place at the Waldorf Towers. It's really something."

Dominique gave him a look of inquiry. "I thought we'd go back to my place. I've paid until the end of the month."

Clay waved his hand in a nonchalant gesture of dismissal. "Believe me, you'll like the company apartment *much* better."

Dominique was suddenly self-conscious as she thought of the contrast between her modest apartment and the kind of living quarters to which Clay was accustomed. Of course, he would prefer the Waldorf. Once upon a time, a simple little place like hers would have seemed totally foreign to her. Well, Clay had had much the same upbringing — with none of the hardship. She would have to reaccustom herself to his way of thinking, she realized. Still, her apartment *was* cheerful and cozy — she'd been happy there. Dominique wasn't sorry that she appreciated things on a more humble scale now.

"Anyhow," Clay continued, "we'll only be here two weeks." He smiled at Dominique. "Just enough to plan the perfect honeymoon."

At Clay's reference to two weeks, Dominique thought of Orman's. She felt guilty about the prospect of only giving them two weeks notice, but she reminded herself that Maude had done no more following her sudden marriage to Bruce Fisher. In any event, Dominique was lucky that Clay had respected her wish to serve out the notice period. Many husbands, she knew, would have insisted that their wives leave immediately.

❧ ❧ ❧

The next evening, Dominique returned to the apartment at the Waldorf bursting with jubilation. She couldn't wait to share her news with Clay! It was too good to be true! She fumbled with the long brass key, then, finally, threw open the apartment door. For a moment she hesitated in the foyer, a gleaming oval of parquet and Grecian columns. Then she heard sounds coming from the living room.

"Clay!" she called. She hurried into the formal salon draped with yellow and celadon silk.

Her breath caught as her husband turned to face her. He was so handsome! He stood before a brass bar cart, a martini shaker in his hand. She saw his expression brighten as his eyes found hers. He put down the shaker and fixed his attention entirely on Dominique, a smile expanding across his face.

She hurried across the Aubusson rug to his side. "You'll never guess what happened today!" she said excitedly.

Clay put his index finger to his chin and jokingly furrowed his brow. "Hmmm. . . . A talent agent spotted you walking down Fifth Avenue and said, 'You're the most beautiful woman I've ever seen. Come to Hollywood and I'll make you a star!'"

Dominique crossed her arms in mock exasperation. "Almost! Guess again." She laughed at the silliness of their game.

Clay's eyes sparkled. "We're going to have a baby!"

"Too soon to tell." Dominique's tone was lighthearted, but she most definitely was not ready for pregnancy. Her diaphragm was the first thing she'd retrieved from her apartment the day before.

Dominique stood on tiptoe for a kiss. She wanted to tell Clay her news, but wanted even more to kiss him. Closing her eyes, she savored his nearness — the fresh starch of his shirt, the aroma of his cologne. She buried her fingers in his hair and pulled him to her. Her nerves tingled as their embrace grew more fervent. The urge to sink down on the couch and make love with him was strong. For a moment, she forgot her news. But when he reached for the buttons on her suit, she stopped him with her hand.

"Wait!" she said breathlessly. "I have something to tell you."

"It can wait," Clay murmured, reaching once more for the buttons.

Dominique stepped back. "No, really . . . ," she said gently.

Annoyance flitted across Clay's face. Then he composed his features into a look of expectation.

Dominique smiled. "I told Bruce about us today —"

Clay nodded, a little impatiently. "That was the plan."

" — and that we'd be moving to New Orleans. . . ."

"Ye-e-es." Clay's tone prodded her to continue.

Dominique drew herself up. "Well," she said proudly, "he says I'm too valuable to let go."

Clay looked blankly at her. "I'm not sure I understand," he said in an unreadable monotone.

Dominique couldn't help laughing. "He offered me a job in the New Orleans store!" she crowed, throwing up her hands in victory. "A better job than I have now. They don't even have an event department per se, and he wants me to start one! Can you believe it?" she gushed. "Of course, I'll get a raise, even though the cost of living in New Orleans is less. And I'll have my own office and a title. He says he wants to start an event planning department in all the branches. Sales really jump after each event."

Clay stared at Dominique, his expression neutral. Then, abruptly, he turned his back to her and went to the bar cart. He poured the martini into two glasses and took a sip before he turned and offered her the other glass. "Sit down, please," he said sharply.

Dominique's smile faded as she automatically took the proffered drink. She tilted her head and studied her husband's face with a questioning expression, but he avoided her eyes as he sat on the ivory brocade sofa.

Dominique sat beside him, nervous tension twisting her stomach. She took a sip of her drink and grimaced. It tasted metallic, unwelcoming. She put it down on the coffee table.

Clay said quietly, "You sound as though you've already told Bruce yes."

Dominique looked at him incredulously. "I'd be crazy not to! It's a wonderful opportunity."

"Did it ever occur to you to discuss it with me first?"

No, it hadn't. When was the last time she'd consulted anyone about a decision? Everyone she had counted on had, in some way, disappointed her. Perhaps she had once expected too much, but she now expected nothing. She'd been through too much alone. But how could she say such a thing to Clay? He was her husband. Not a husband like Anton, but one who loved her. She had been thoughtless, she realized, not to at least talk over the decision with him. It wasn't unreasonable of him to expect that.

Dominique took his hands in hers. "Clay, I'm so sorry," she said fervently. "I've always been independent. And now that I've been living on my own, well . . . can you understand why I didn't think about asking you?"

Clay looked a little mollified, but his tone was sulky when he said, "Women down home don't work after they're married, Dominique. Not if they don't need to. To be blunt, the ones who work before they're married are just looking for husbands."

Dominique smiled. "It's not so different up here, Clay. I mean, there are a few career women at Orman's, but most quit when they get married." She paused, thinking for a moment about her life in Cairo. *Never* would a married European woman have worked. And the rare Arab wife who worked either served as a domestic or helped her husband in a small business. And yet, Dominique had grown used to working. She liked the sense of accomplishment it gave her. She couldn't imagine the kind of leisured existence for which she had been raised.

When she had a child, that would be another story. She didn't want to make the same mistakes as Solange, and one of the prime ones, she believed, had been Solange's reliance on Nanny to raise her children. It had created an emotional distance that Dominique was determined not to suffer when she became a mother. But that was a long way in the future.

Dominique gave her husband a look of appeal. "Clay, I love my job. And when Bruce offered me the position in New Orleans, it seemed so exciting that I didn't think." She looked up at him appealingly. "There's no reason not to take it, is there? I promise to quit if I get pregnant." Which she wouldn't any time soon, she added silently.

Clay pulled his hands from hers and stood up. He walked to the bar cart and refilled his glass.

Dominique watched him anxiously. He remained with his back to her, taking what seemed like a long time to garnish his drink, stir it, taste it. Dominique wished he would turn around, say something. What would she do if he opposed her working? Would she defy his wishes? The thought was distressing. Dominique couldn't imagine a conflict of that magnitude so early in the marriage. But what an opportunity Bruce was offering! Her own event department. The liberty to let her imagination run wild, to conquer a new market. It would be fun and, at the same time, challenging. She *couldn't* give up a chance like that. She had to make Clay understand.

All at once, a new idea occurred to Dominique. "Clay!" her voice rang with enthusiasm. "If I took this job, we'd be able to afford that house in the Garden District!"

Clay swung around to face her, his face a study in irritation. "You're missing the point!" he said. "If you work, everyone will think I can't provide for us."

Dominique stood up and came toward him. "Not if we present it right . . . " She refused to let him quash her excitement. "I'm just being transferred down from New York. It's not like I married you, then found a job. Besides, it's obvious that my job is fun. I imagine a lot of women will be jealous of me!" She put her hand on his arm for emphasis, willing him to see things her way.

Clay met her gaze unsmilingly, but he didn't contradict her.

She could convince him! "Think of it," she said in a dreamy voice. "You told me this weekend that it would be at least a couple of years before we could afford a place in the Garden District. This way, we wouldn't have to wait."

For a second, Clay seemed to catch her enthusiasm. His face brightened at her words. Then his mood changed. He averted his gaze to a point over Dominique's shoulder and his face turned grim. "I can just imagine what Father'll say about it if I let you work." He rubbed his hand over his chin. "I'm still trying to think of a way to tell him I'm married."

Dominique's eyes widened in alarm. "You have to tell him right away! What if he were to find out from someone else?"

Clay shook his head. "I know, I know. That would be bad."

Dominique's temper flared. Clay's father sounded like a tyrant! Couldn't Clay do anything without being criticized? Well, she'd be damned if she'd live her life to please her father-in-law! Clay had to stand up to him. Tell him he'd married. As for Dominique's work, that was none of her father-in-law's business. Why was Clay so apprehensive? But as soon as the question occurred to her, the answer followed. Money, of course. It always came down to that. Well, all the more reason for Dominique to work. At least they wouldn't depend on Clay's father for their entire livelihood.

Dominique tilted her chin up and said, "As far is work is concerned, Clay, I'm not sure it's a question of 'letting' me do anything. I mean, we're both adults, aren't we? Just tell your father that I *want* to work. If he thinks the worse of you for it, so what? He's not going to fire you. Besides," she took a step toward him and put her hands on his chest. She looked up at him, her face full of love. "*I* think you're wonderful. And no matter what your father believes, I'll *always* think you're wonderful."

She shrugged and assumed an expression of deliberate nonchalance. "You know, sometimes parents just won't *let* you please them. Who knows why?" She sighed. "You have to learn to accept it." She wrapped her arms around Clay's waist. "And then someone comes along who loves you and has faith in you and recognizes how wonderful you are." Dominique laid her head against her husband's chest and pressed herself against him. "And suddenly you realize that your parents don't have as much power over you as you thought." She lifted her head and looked up at him.

Clay stared down at her, absorbed by what she was saying.

Dominique smiled softly. "And even though you still love them, they can't hurt you like they once could."

Two nights later, Dominique had to again confront the problem of parents, only this time, she had to contend with Solange. It was all very well to assure Clay that parental approval wasn't necessary, but it certainly made life more pleasant, Dominique acknowledged to herself. Would Solange like Clay? She hadn't been thrilled that he was American, but she hadn't protested as much as Dominique had expected, perhaps because of the disaster with Anton.

Solange's main concern was Clay's lack of personal wealth. "You say he hasn't any money of his own?"

"He has to work for a living, Mother, like almost everyone in America. But he'll inherit his father's business one day."

"Hmmm." Solange's tone implied that anything could happen.

On the plus side, Dominique knew that Solange would be susceptible to Clay's good manners and looks. She tried to reassure herself with that thought as she walked through the apartment, checking nervously to see that everything was in place. Of course, it was — the hotel staff saw to that. The table in front of the living room windows was beautifully laid for five. Wine was cooling in the ice bucket. Fresh roses in the foyer gave off a delicate perfume.

Dominique turned to the long mirror that graced the entrance and smoothed her navy silk sheath. She knew that its sophisticated lines made her look older than her twenty-two years — twenty-three in less than a month — and she was glad of it. Solange sometimes had difficulty treating Dominique like a responsible adult.

The trill of the doorbell startled Dominique. She glanced worriedly at her watch. Only five-thirty! Solange and Danielle weren't due for another half hour; Ron and Clay not until six-thirty, for they were coming straight from their respective offices.

Dominique smiled at her attack of nerves. Of course, it had to be one of the hotel staff, for who else could have passed the reception desk unannounced? She crossed the gleaming floor and opened the door. A tall, distinguished-looking white-haired man filled the space. Instinctively, Dominique took a step back.

As the man moved past her and into the foyer, Dominique stood frozen with her hand on the doorknob, vacillating between incredulity and outrage. The man, exuding glossy arrogance, pivoted to face her and said, "Clay Parker." His deep voice seemed to echo through the high-ceilinged foyer.

Dominique, still holding the door open, said coldly, "I'm sorry. He's not in at the moment."

The man's thin lips twitched. "You don't understand." He paused. "*I'm* Clay Parker."

Dominique's grip on the doorknob tightened. Sweat prickled at her underarms. For a moment, she was speechless. The man swept her with a regard of steely assessment.

Dominique's spine stiffened. She looked her father-in-law directly in the eye and held out her hand. "How do you do?" she said with deliberate politeness. "I'm Dominique Parker."

For a second, he hesitated. Then his calculating gaze was replaced by a wide, practiced smile. With forced bonhomie, he took her hand and said, "Delighted."

Dominique closed her fingers around his with a firm grip. He released her hand first. Dominique turned and closed the apartment door. She took a deep breath, then faced her father-in-law. Best to be direct, she decided. "I assume you've heard the news," she said.

Parker's smile collapsed. For only a second, he looked grim. Then he compressed his lips and turned them up at the corners in the sort of bland nonexpression seen in expert poker players. "I don't think we should discuss this standing here in the hallway, do you?" he said softly. He touched Dominique's elbow briefly, then let his hand fall to his side. "I believe they keep a stock of my favorite bourbon on hand."

Point taken, Dominique thought. Again, she decided to meet his thrusts head-on. "If you'd prefer to have the apartment to yourself, sir, Clay and I can easily go back to my place," she said smoothly. "We're leaving next week for our honeymoon, anyhow."

Parker raised his hands in a gesture of protest. "I wouldn't think of inconveniencing you young people," he said heartily.

When they reached the living room, Parker went immediately to the bar cart and fixed his drink. "Get something for you?" he asked Dominique, a pair of tongs poised above the ice bucket.

Dominique smiled and sat down on the sofa. "No, thank you." She watched him carefully as he turned back to the cart. Like Clay, he had a presence that filled the room. But unlike Clay, his power had nothing to do with looks and everything to do with authority. From his Roman nose to his self-assured stride, Clay Parker III bespoke majestic, resolute autocracy.

"Now then." He turned and came toward Dominique. "We can have a little talk."

"That would be delightful," Dominique said with studied innocence. She crossed her legs and saw Parker's eyes flicker toward them.

He cleared his throat and quickly looked away as he sank into one of the large armchairs that flanked the sofa.

Dominique dropped her eyelids so he would not see her knowing glance. In that moment, she became absolutely convinced that he was regularly unfaithful to his wife. Probably the sort of man who considered it his *droit de seigneur* to have one or more mistresses. Without looking at him, she uncrossed her legs and pulled her skirt down over her knees. Then she raised her eyes to Parker's.

He took a long swallow of his drink. "Well, Miss Avallon," he drawled, "this is all rather sudden, isn't it?" He smiled once more, as though to say, Don't take this personally.

Dominique nodded in acknowledgment. "Very."

Parker flicked some imaginary lint from his navy pin-striped slacks. He shook his head and clicked his tongue. "Young love," he said in a falsely indulgent tone.

"Yes," Dominique said. Impossible to keep the warmth from her voice when she thought of Clay. "We are very much in love."

Parker smiled and fixed Dominique with a shrewd gaze. "Any particular reason for haste here?"

Well, at least he didn't look at my stomach, Dominique thought wryly. "Just as you said, Mr. Parker, 'young love.'" Her voice was equable. She didn't want to lose control by responding to his implication with defensiveness.

Parker shifted in his chair and gave her a skeptical look.

Dominique raised one eyebrow. "Of course, you'll have to wait nine months to discover if I'm telling the truth."

Parker gave a bark of surprised laughter. "Not afraid of anything, are you, Miss Avallon?"

"It's Mrs. Parker now," Dominique said firmly. "But you may call me Dominique."

Parker rubbed his hand over his chin in a gesture Dominique had seen Clay make when he was pondering something.

Dominique sat perfectly still, hands crossed on her lap. She was determined not to fidget, but it was an effort to look serenely back at Parker and wait for him to speak.

Finally he said in a gruff voice, "You're not what I expected. Clay told me you came from a fine family, but, frankly, I didn't quite believe him."

"You expected a chorus girl?" Dominique quipped, amused by Parker's admission.

This time, his laugh was genuinely sunny. "Maybe!"

Dominique laughed with him. She began to relax a little. She had a feeling that she had scored a point. Not a complete victory — that would take more time — but at least a partial one. Then she turned serious. "I don't think you give Clay enough credit. He's intelligent, hard-working . . . you should be very proud of him. Why don't you trust his judgment?"

Parker's brow darkened. "I don't believe in speaking ill of a man to his wife, and this man happens to be my son. But I'll tell you this and that'll be all: he may be almost thirty, but he still has some growing up to do."

Dominique didn't want to argue with him, but she inwardly shrugged off his observation. That's what every parent says, she thought.

She was about to invite him to stay for dinner when the doorbell rang.

"That's my mother and sister," Dominique said, getting up. "I've invited them to dinner to introduce them to Clay. I hope you'll stay, too."

Parker stood up and smoothed his tie. "I'd be delighted," he said with a smile.

Dominique hurried into the foyer and threw open the door. "Maman! Danielle!" She kissed them and ushered them in. She whispered in French, throwing a significant look in the direction of the living room, "Clay's father is here."

"You didn't expect him?" Danielle asked with a look of commiseration.

Dominique shook her head. "But it's all right," she murmured.

Solange gave her a disdainful look. "All right?" she said. "Of course it is! What did you expect?" She paused in front of the mirror and smoothed her dress — plain black silk, but adorned with a scarf of leopard-printed chiffon that streamed behind her when she moved. Anchoring the scarf was a stunning Cartier brooch, one of the pieces smuggled out of Egypt. It was shaped like a leopard with spots of diamond and sapphire. Solange looked stylish and . . . formidable.

Dominique felt a thrill of pride as she thought of the impact Solange would make on Clay's father. "Shall we?" she asked, gesturing toward the other room. She laced one arm through Solange's, the other through Danielle's. For a moment, she studied the three of them in the mirror. She registered Solange's aristocratic handsomeness and Danielle's dark, classic beauty. And she recognized the intensity of her own allure. They made an impressive trio, she decided happily. She turned away and led her mother and sister into the living room.

With her instinctive flair for drama, Solange paused when she spotted Clay's father. She released Dominique's arm and took one step forward. Then she lifted her hand in front of her like a queen waiting for homage. "Ah . . . ," she purred. Her eyes were directly on Parker, though she addressed Dominique in French. "If my son-in-law is only half as handsome as his father, then you're a very lucky girl!"

Parker's eyes gleamed appreciatively. He gave a courtly bow and said in perfect French of his own, *"Merci bien, Madame!* I was just thinking that my son is the lucky one. But it seems that I've out-maneuvered him. Since he doesn't speak French and I do, I'll have you to myself this evening."

∾ ∾ ∾

The flight to Switzerland was blessed escape to Dominique. Though the marriage seemed to have won the approval of the in-laws, she was relieved to find herself alone with Clay, away from parental scrutiny.

They flew first to Geneva, but instead of staying in the cosmopolitan city, they rented a car and made the scenic ninety-minute drive to the medieval village of Morat. Half-timbered houses, gardens spilling over with vivid flowers, idyllic lakes — that was Morat. The gingerbread inn where they stayed was the image of whimsical charm. The bedroom was a quaint octagonal shape, its walls draped with cheerfully sprigged material. The balcony overlooked a scene from an Impressionist painting: weeping willows, swans, and a flower-bordered lawn sloping to the edge of tranquil, blue water.

Clay leaned on the rail and turned Dominique toward him. "Happy?" he asked softly.

Dominique looked up at her husband. The blue of the sky was reflected in his eyes, the wind ruffled his hair. And he belonged to her! They belonged to each other. She put her arms around him and pulled him close.

Clay lowered his mouth to hers, then lifted her into his arms.

Dominique shrieked with surprised laughter. "What are you doing?"

"What every groom is supposed to do. Carrying you over the threshold." He grinned. "In case you haven't noticed, I like doing that." Clay carried her inside and playfully threw her on the bed. Dominique giggled as she sank into the feather mattress. Then Clay slid onto the cover beside her and, with a lazy, sensuous smile, unbuttoned her shirt. Dominique shivered with pleasure as she anticipated the warmth of his touch. It was lovely to be stroked and admired — so different from Anton. She put her arms around Clay and ran her fingernails over his back. She knew he loved that. Immediately, Clay hardened and, urgent now, he slid her panties down until he was kneeling at her feet. Too impatient to undress fully, Clay slid on top of her and Dominique, as hungry as he, wound her legs around Clay and drew him into her. Together, they began to move in a driving rhythm.

"I love you, Dominique," Clay said breathlessly.

Dominique closed her eyes and abandoned herself to the warmth and security of his love.

◌◌ ◌◌ ◌◌

Their week in Morat was idyllic. They rowed on the lake and visited tiny, walled villages, hiked in the mountains, and ate fondue in outdoor cafés. Often, they had to stop their car to let a herd of plump cows pass in front of them. The farmers hailed the strangers with a friendly wave.

The temperature never rose above eighty degrees and the nights were cool enough to justify lighting the fire in their suite. Dominique never wanted to leave.

But when Dominique saw their next destination, it took her breath away. Clay drove her through the French countryside to the bucolic region that bordered the Dordogne River. It was a land of rolling meadows and sharp, craggy cliffs. And around each bend of the road was a castle loftily perched at the crest of a hill. Many had been transformed into small hotels, and it was in these that Clay chose to stay. And so they meandered through the region of prosperous farms, fields of golden sunflowers, and romantic water mills. Particularly fascinating to Dominique were the ancient villages built into the sides of mountains so that the houses became part of the sheer rock face.

It was as they were exploring one of these, Rocamadour, that Clay and Dominique had their first lovers' quarrel. Rocamadour was built on a vertical plane, with a church of pilgrimage at the top of a cliff, the residential area a few hundred feet below. Probably — Dominique realized later — they wouldn't have argued at all if they hadn't been hot, tired, and hungry from a day spent traversing the stairs that acted as the town's main thoroughfare.

By the time they had finished sightseeing, it was three o'clock, well past time for lunch. They agreed to skip the meal and dine a bit earlier than usual. Before they left Rocamadour, however, they went back to the main street to pick up some souvenirs they'd admired. Dominique and Clay had already discussed what they wanted, so when they entered the first shop, she rapidly asked the salesperson in French for the hand-painted cream and sugar set displayed in the window.

Dominique didn't notice Clay's silence until they paid for their purchase and exited the store. She was chattering about the beauty of the pottery when she noticed that Clay was not responding.

"What's wrong?" she asked.

Clay looked away. Dominique put her hand on his arm. "What is it?"

Clay fixed her with an angry glare. "You don't have to rattle off your French every time we want something. Some of these people just might speak English. You should give me a chance to try."

Dominique knitted her brow. "I don't understand. Why?"

Clay tightened his lips angrily and again looked away. That annoyed Dominique and she decided not to probe further. If he wanted to sulk over an imagined slight, she wasn't going to wheedle him back into good humor.

Clearly outraged by her silence, Clay swung his head aggressively back to her. "It makes me look stupid to have my wife do all the talking!" he burst out.

Dominique made a sound of exasperation. "It's obvious we're tourists and that you don't speak the language. I'm sure they realize that it's easier to let me talk."

"Well, it may be easier but I don't like it," Clay said emphatically.

Dominique stopped and folded her arms across her chest. "Then what do you propose?" she asked sarcastically. "That I stand by like an idiot while you struggle to make yourself understood? Is that what last night was about? You didn't want to ask me to translate the menu, so you ordered something without knowing what it was?" Dominique thought about the incident, and a bubble of amusement broke through her irritation. She started to smile as she remembered the disgust on Clay's face when the waiter planted a slab of tripe in front of him.

Dominique looked up at Clay with affection. "You know," she began indulgently, "your face last night was so fun—"

In the middle of her sentence, Clay turned his back and walked away.

Dominique stood motionless, dumbfounded. She couldn't believe that Clay was reacting so disproportionately to a humorous mishap. Well, she certainly wasn't going to cater to him! She would stay where she was until he returned to look for her.

She coolly watched his back disappear through the crowd on the street. Then she wandered over to a nearby shop window and stared blankly at the objects within. She wasn't really seeing them; she was thinking about Clay's extraordinary reaction. He had never behaved so rudely.

A voice directly behind her startled her. "I'm leaving now. Are you coming?" Clay asked frostily.

Dominique wheeled about to face him. His words were ungracious, but at least he'd returned quickly. She would meet him halfway. "Thank you for coming back," she said softly. She reached for his arm, but he jerked away from her touch.

"Let's go," he said in a monotone. Again, he turned away and began to walk.

It crossed Dominique's mind to once more remain where she was. But the stupid fight had gone on long enough! Angry at Clay for prolonging it, but anxious for peace, she stalked after him.

When they reached the car, he strode ahead and opened Dominique's side, but instead of waiting for her to get in, he left the door ajar and went to his own side.

Surely he'll say something when we're inside, Dominique thought. If he doesn't, I will.

When they had driven for five minutes in silence, Dominique ventured, "Fascinating town, wasn't it?"

Clay didn't answer. Instead, he turned on the radio. Fast French chatter. News — incomprehensible to Clay.

Dominique forged ahead with determination. "They say in the guidebook that penitents used to climb up the stairs to the church on their knees. Can you imagine that?"

Clay turned up the volume of the radio until it was blaring.

Dominique whipped her head around to face him. "Stop it!" she cried. She leaned over and snapped off the radio. "I can't believe you're behaving this way over something so trivial!"

Clay said nothing. He stared fixedly ahead. They drove all the way to the hotel in hostile silence.

This is such a shame, Dominique thought as they entered the gravel drive that led to the enchanting little castle. She wanted to exclaim at the scene, to share her pleasure with Clay, for it was almost painfully beautiful: in the foreground, a garden of pink, yellow, and red flowers were set in geometric beds; behind the hotel, the silky Dordogne River wended its way through overhanging trees.

Clay brought the car to an abrupt halt and got out. He walked into the hotel without a glance at Dominique.

Was he going to spend the rest of the day in silence? Dominique couldn't bear the thought. The disagreement had ruined the entire afternoon! On the other hand, Clay was the one behaving like a boor. Dominique wasn't going to apologize. She had tried to talk to him, but he was determined to be angry.

When Dominique reached the room — where Clay was lying on the bed apparently absorbed in a book — she went directly into the bathroom, took a shower, and dressed for dinner. She emerged forty minutes later to find Clay still on the bed.

Dominique put a hand on her hip. "Do you intend to have dinner?"

Clay slowly put his book face down on his chest. He turned his head to Dominique. "Yes," he said sharply.

"Well," she answered in the same tone, "you don't need to worry. I won't translate for you. In fact, I won't say a word. I'll just point to what I want."

"I understand that there are times when you need to translate," Clay said testily. "But some of the people speak English; that's the point I was trying to make." He swung his legs over the side of the bed and got up quickly, as though to forestall further discussion. "I'm going to take a shower. I'll be ready in a few minutes." His tone was almost normal now.

Dominique, eager to resume good relations, decided not to argue his point. She gave him a look of appeal. "The menu looks awfully good," she said tentatively.

Clay nodded — cool, but no longer adversarial. "I'm looking forward to it," he conceded.

By the time they went to dinner, the argument was behind them.

The remaining weeks of their honeymoon passed too quickly for Dominique. From the Dordogne region they drove to the French Riviera, staying in the posh yachting haven of Saint-Jean-Cap-Ferrat. Their room overlooked the lively harbor and, beyond it, the royal blue Mediterranean.

Each morning, Clay and Dominique drove a few miles to the bustling farm market in the pedestrian area of Nice. There they bought the ingredients for a picnic lunch. One stall sold nothing but goat cheese, another a cornucopia of tropical fruit. But the one Dominique and Clay found most tantalizing specialized in olives — dozens of varieties, colors, sizes, and preparations.

Clay had to stifle laughter when the saleswoman asked them, in passable English, the purpose of their olive purchase. "Salad, aperitif, sauce, or tapenade?"

"Oh, just a picnic," they responded, far more casually than the saleswoman would have wished.

"And what wine with your picnic?"

Dominique and Clay looked blankly at each other. "White, I suppose," Dominique finally said.

The woman sniffed at Dominique's lack of specificity. "White" told her almost nothing, but she saw it was futile to pursue that particular line of questioning. "What will you have for lunch? Possibly a baguette with prosciutto and cheese?"

Dominique seized on that. "Exactly!" she lied. They hadn't yet bought their sandwich ingredients.

"Ah, then . . ." The woman reached for a little white box and filled it half full with green olives bathed in fresh oregano and vinaigrette. From another section of her stall, she selected some wrinkled black olives in a red sauce.

"Thank you, madame," Dominique said sheepishly.

She and Clay scurried away, giggling like truants who had just escaped an adult.

ꙮ ꙮ ꙮ

The couple's first days back in New Orleans were almost as enchanted. Though it was September, the only sign of waning summer was the early twilight. And it was in this fragrant, still twilight that they loved to wander and search for just the perfect house in which to begin their life together.

Dominique was in no hurry. She was perfectly content with Clay's uptown apartment, but he was eager to move to the Garden District. So each day they went with a real estate agent to examine properties. Most were too expensive for them; the ones they could afford were at the edges of the Garden District, and thus unsatisfactory to Clay.

"It's a great home for a couple just starting out," the agent would insist. She was a motherly sort of woman, who freely offered advice to counter Clay's objections. But Clay wouldn't listen.

Often, they would pass the type of house Clay had in mind and he would order the agent to stop.

"You'd probably need a little help from your father on that one," she'd say. She knew of Clay's family, of course.

Clay would shake his head. "Let's keep looking." They had arranged an extra week of vacation before resuming work so Clay could devote himself full time to the search.

At the end of the day, they'd dismiss the agent and, at a quiet, easy pace, explore the Garden District on their own. They would drive in Clay's convertible along St. Charles Avenue — already darker and cooler than the side streets, thanks to the overhanging canopy of live oaks — then park and walk for hours. They loved to look into the floor-to-ceiling windows of the grand houses, lit from within to reveal intriguing glimpses of their occupants' lives.

"That's the kind of library to have!" Dominique exclaimed on one of their forays. "Nothing on the walls except books."

Clay agreed. "My Father has one like that. There's a ladder attached to the shelves and it slides around the room so you can reach everything." He looked down at her and squeezed her hand. "But you'll see for yourself this weekend."

Dominique was looking forward to their dinner at his parents' home just a few blocks away. She was very curious about her mother-in-law, whom she'd yet to meet. In addition, the rest of the family would be there and Dominique hoped she'd make friends with some of them. Clay said he had several cousins their age.

Dominique had already made a few friends in New Orleans simply by walking through the Garden District with Clay. Almost every night, the couple would encounter people enjoying the breeze on their wide, galleried porches. And since Clay had grown up in the neighborhood, he knew a number of them.

"C'mon up and have a drink — give us a chance to meet your bride," they'd say, and Clay never refused. They would open creaking gates and mount the wooden stairs. They would be offered mint juleps or gin fizzes as they settled into a porch swing or glider. The fans overhead would thump softly, keeping the mosquitoes at bay. And the voices would float lazily through the thick, balmy air. Even the silences were pleasant — they'd just sit and listen to the hypnotic music of the crickets. Crickets, tinkling ice, languorous voices. That was the southern way. Always time to stop and chat with neighbors, to sit and enjoy company.

To Dominique, all this seemed natural. The fast, impersonal pace of New York and San Francisco, the long work days and early-to-bed mentality, had been new to her. She fit in with Clay's friends as she had nowhere else in America. Many of them spoke French, thanks to their antecedents. And, as Clay had predicted, her nationality was regarded as a charming attribute. No one had trouble understanding her; no one even questioned her foreignness.

By the end of her first month there, Dominique already considered New Orleans home.

CHAPTER 11 ∽

DOMINIQUE fairly leapt off the St. Charles streetcar, in a hurry to get home. She hoped Clay was there — she couldn't wait to tell him her news. Only one year at Orman's New Orleans branch and she was already winning accolades for pulling off the biggest coup in its short history. Clay would be so proud of her!

She crossed St. Charles and entered the quiet side street that led home, four blocks away. The first few houses she passed were grand mansions set well back from the road. As she progressed, though, the neighborhood changed. Mansions gave way to smaller, albeit charming, houses. No more antebellum pillars or Italianate villas, no Tudor fantasies or Georgian palaces. The houses were pure New Orleans, with deep porches, two-story galleries, and long windows with real shutters that were pulled closed during storms. Unlike the pristine, formal landscapes of St. Charles Avenue, the lawns here were often punctuated by tricycles, scooters, or roller skates.

After only ten months in the new house, Clay was eager to move out — or move "up," as he and the realtor termed it — but Dominique loved the down-to-earth character of her block. She often mused that she and Clay had had almost opposite reactions to their privileged childhoods. Dominique enjoyed luxury, but in ways that made a difference to her personal comfort: fine wine, good food, linen sheets, or well-made shoes. She liked pretty things, but they didn't have to be grand. Clay, on the other hand, would not consider himself a success until he lived on the same scale as his parents.

Now that Dominique had seen the home of the elder Parkers, she couldn't agree. It was exquisite, but almost like a museum in its perfection. She was determined that if she and Clay moved to St. Charles Avenue, their house would have a more human decor.

As always, her heart lifted at the sight of her own welcoming front porch twined with morning glory vines. Dominique and Clay had repainted the house pure white with glossy black shutters. And at either side of the front door was a waist-high planter of ivy and fragrant petunias.

Dominique entered the foyer, sniffing appreciatively the clean scent of furniture wax and fresh cut flowers. For the hundredth time, she acknowledged that Clay had been right to insist on the daily housekeeper. Lucy, an attractive, middle-aged woman with smiling features, arrived each weekday morning at nine to clean house and prepare dinner.

Dominique chuckled when she remembered that she had tried to dissuade Clay from hiring the woman. "I've become used to fending for myself," she had insisted.

Clay had looked at her skeptically. "You've already admitted you can't cook."

"I'm learning," Dominique had said defensively.

Clay had taken her in his arms. "Look, everyone here has help, not just the very wealthy. It's like what you told me about Egypt. It would look odd if we didn't have someone. Besides, you'll be gone all day and won't have time to see to the house, much less to prepare the kind of dinner I like. Do this for me," he'd coaxed.

Now Dominique was glad she'd given in. Clay hated arriving home and finding Dominique still out. But the problem would have been compounded if he'd had to wait while Dominique threw together an inexpert dinner. With Lucy, things ran smoothly.

"Clay!" she called, as she spotted his hat on the hall table. "Lucy!"

Lucy appeared in the doorway, drying her hands on a towel. "Good evening, Mrs. Parker," she said with a smile. "Mr. Parker's on the back patio enjoying his martini."

Dominique put down her purse and hat beside Clay's and smoothed her hair in the mirror above the table. "Thanks, Lucy," she said breathlessly. Then she hurried through the house to the kitchen. The old, wood-framed screen door squeaked as Dominique pushed it open to go out on the patio.

Clay turned at the sound. When he saw her, he stood up.

"Congratulate me!" Dominique said cheerfully, letting the door fall shut behind her.

Clay smiled indulgently. He put down his drink and came toward her. "What for?" he asked as he bent to kiss her.

"Mark Patout has agreed to host Orman's charity gala! The one we're putting on for the cancer society."

Clay smiled cautiously. "Mark Patout, the representative?"

Dominique proudly recited what she had learned about the man. "One of the founding families of Louisiana. Old French aristocracy. And a member of the Louisiana House of Representatives."

"Sounds like you did your homework," Clay teased. He turned and went back to his chair. He pulled the empty chair beside him closer — a gesture of invitation.

Dominique kept talking as she sat down. "It was so strange how it happened. I was reading an article in *Life* about the country's one hundred up-and-coming young politicians. I wasn't even paying attention to where he was from, I just noticed that his last name was French. Anyhow, when I saw he was from here, I decided to call him about the gala." Dominique laughed victoriously. "And it was a good thing I didn't ask anyone's opinion first, because they told me later that he never does this sort of thing. It's just that the charity is for cancer and his mother died of cancer, so he feels very strongly about it. At least that's what his secretary said. I didn't talk to him personally. But she called me back right away and she said he'd definitely do it!" Dominique gave a contented sigh and relaxed into her chair. But a second later, she eagerly perched at the edge of her seat. "Tomorrow, I'll send one of the secretaries to the library to find every article there is about him. I really don't know anything more than the little paragraph I read in *Life*. I'm sure there's all sorts of useful information."

Clay took a sip of his drink and gave Dominique a brief smile. "Sounds good, hon."

Dominique was about to remark that Clay didn't seem very impressed, when his face underwent a transformation. He turned to Dominique and narrowed his eyes. "You know" — he paused, looking contemplative — "Patout could do us a lot of good in the legislature. There's a tax matter . . ." Clay's eyes glazed over as he became lost in thought.

"Clay!" Dominique was half amused, half annoyed. "I'm trying to involve him in our charity, not a tax matter for Parker Shipping!"

Clay's eyes snapped back to Dominique. "Hey, what's good for the company is good for you and me, too."

"I know," Dominique admitted grudgingly, "but this is my first big gala for the store and I want Patout to concentrate on *it*. . . ." She paused. "You can understand that, can't you?" she asked in a reasonable tone.

For a moment, Clay seemed about to argue, then he picked up his drink and finished it in one swallow.

Dominique followed his movements warily. She began to feel resentful, but before she could voice her sentiments, Clay abruptly backed down.

"Look, I don't want to horn in on your project. I know that's the most important thing. I'm just saying that it would be good to cultivate a friendship with Patout. Like that article said, he's going places."

Dominique smiled. "I thought you already knew everyone in New Orleans."

"Know *of*," Clay corrected her. "I've met Patout just a few times. He's not in New Orleans all that much. He has an apartment in Baton Rouge near the capitol, but his real home is a plantation about twenty-five miles out into the country. Whole family lives there — old-style, close-knit bunch."

Dominique raised her eyebrows. "I'm beginning to see I was very lucky to get him for my event."

Clay gave her a significant look. "Can you also see why I don't want this opportunity to slip away? If you could befriend him, and we could have dinner with him a few times . . . develop some social ties . . . that would be more valuable to me than a hundred meetings in his office. And it would give me a real edge at work. You understand?"

Dominique nodded. She couldn't fail to be sympathetic with Clay's ambition to prove himself at Parker Shipping. And, of course, she wanted to help her husband. His point was really quite reasonable. "But, Clay, I think you're getting a little ahead of events. I'll probably be dealing with his wife —"

"He's not married," Clay interrupted, clearly eager to dispense with one of her objections.

Dominique gave him a tolerant look. "His secretary then. I don't know how personally involved he wants to get. Besides" — she smiled mischievously — "he may not like me at all!"

෨ ෨ ෨

Over the next week, Dominique was in daily communication with Patout's secretary and, through her, secured his approval for the party theme: "Carnevale in Venice," a masked ball.

"Everyone loves Mardi Gras," the woman commented, "and this gives them a chance to celebrate it twice in one year!"

And to Dominique's amazed delight, Patout had agreed to meet personally with her about the guest list.

"He'll do anything he can to help," said his secretary.

But before the meeting, Dominique wanted to know as much as possible about Mark Patout. With that in mind, she had brought home a manila folder of articles about him. Clay was in Houston on a business trip, so she could take a tray to the study and curl up for the evening.

When she arrived home, Dominique was pleased to see that Lucy had lit a fire in the study. It was only October, and not cold enough to warrant one, but Dominique enjoyed them and Lucy knew it. Dominique settled cozily on the down-filled couch that faced the fireplace and opened the folder on Mark Patout. The first item was his official biography, which his secretary had sent. But it was brief, not nearly as interesting as the newspaper clippings her department's secretary had found.

The more Dominique read, the more she became fascinated with the history of the Patout family. The first Patout in Louisiana had been a former officer in the French army by the name of Alexandre Patout. In the 1700s, he had bought a twenty-thousand-acre tract of land along the Mississippi River from the Houmas Indians. There he had built a home and established a sugarcane plantation. Dominique flipped through the file until she found a photograph of Belle Terre. It was a two-story Greek Revival mansion wrapped on all four sides by a columned porch and balcony overhead. She saw from the article that the original farmhouse had been torn down by Alexandre's son, Alphonse, and the present structure built in 1840. Dominique was simultaneously amused and shocked to read that in 1845, Alphonse had lost ten thousand acres in a poker game. It was in 1856 that the first Patout entered politics. Every succeeding generation of the family seemed to have had at least one member serving in the state legislature or the U.S. Congress.

Dominique noted with interest that Mark Patout was the youngest man elected to the Louisiana House of Representatives in the twentieth century. He had won his seat at age twenty-five and was now only twenty-nine. She searched through the file for photographs of him and found three old ones. There was a sprawling family portrait taken when he was only fifteen. Dominique counted the number of children in the photograph. Seven! Patout's head was partially concealed by that of his mother, standing in front of him. She was a delicate-looking woman with soulful eyes and softly waving hair. The next article in the file was an announcement of Marie-Ange Patout's death in 1955. It was on the front page of the *Times-Picayune*, as befitted a member of one of Louisiana's first families. The caption under the photo said, "Mourners at the funeral of Marie-Ange Patout. From left: Christine, Blake, and Mark Patout accept the condolences of family friend Wilson Beaubien." Patout faced the camera, but was largely obscured by the comforting arm of his friend.

The last few clippings discussed Mark's political career. One of the articles noted that he had attended a northern law school, Yale. That was unusual for Louisiana men, Dominique knew. Students who wanted the cachet of an out-of-state degree usually chose a southern university — Vanderbilt or Rice.

Dominique came to the announcement of Mark's election to the legislature four years earlier. It contained a profile shot of him shaking the hand of the Speaker of the Louisiana House. The photograph was so grainy that it was hard to distinguish Patout's features. The next article came not from the *New Orleans Times-Picayune*, but from the *Washington Post*. As in the *Life* article Dominique had found, Patout was named as one of the up-and-coming young politicians around the nation. He was noted, the article said, for accepting no political contributions whatever. There was a rather cynical quote from a fellow legislator: "It's easy to make honorable gestures when you've got enough money. Most of us, though, haven't got a rich daddy to pay for our campaigns."

Dominique closed the folder and stared into the fire. She wondered if Mark Patout were indeed nothing more than a spoiled young man. Would he be impossible to work with? Demanding? Dominique sighed. It really didn't matter. A man of his prominence would serve as a major draw.

ᢒᡉ ᢒᡉ ᢒᡉ

Dominique liked the quiet of her office when everyone was at lunch. It was a good time to think over her plans for the gala and weigh decisions. After checking to ensure that there was no one around, she leaned back in her chair and propped her feet on the extra chair opposite. Then she slipped her heels out of her black suede pumps. The sun shone through the window behind her, making her feel warm and just a little lazy. She bent forward to remove her jacket. Rolled up the cuffs of her shirt. That was better. With a sigh, she closed her eyes.

Dominique had already made rapid progress on the gala since Patout had approved the theme two weeks before. She'd contacted caterers and printers, costume companies and decorators, and had a fairly good conception of how the event would operate. But there were still some major items to consider. Which caterer to use? Orman's had always gone with old-line Champs Elysée Catering, but Dominique had received a bid from a creative new firm. It was significantly cheaper than Champs Elysée and, equally important, their proposed menu had more interesting selections. But what if something went wrong? The rest of the staff at Orman's was comfortable with the old firm. Perhaps she should stick with it and concentrate on other facets of the gala.

The sound of someone clearing his throat startled Dominique. She instantly dropped her feet to the floor and swiveled toward the door. A pair of jolly green eyes framed by windblown salt-and-pepper hair connected with hers. A split-second impression flashed through her mind: boundless charm. The man gave Dominique a delighted, lopsided grin, like a young boy who has just discovered a shiny, red bicycle on Christmas morning.

Flustered, Dominique asked haltingly, "May I . . . help you?" He had probably thought she was napping!

"I believe," the man replied, "that we have an appointment."

Dominique felt a sick thud in her stomach. She had forgotten an appointment? Though the man looked young — no more than his mid-thirties — he was clearly someone important, someone she ought to have remembered. His clothes, from the fine leather of his shoes to the expert tailoring of his navy blazer, told her that. And yet, despite his rich clothes, Dominique had the impression he didn't take himself too seriously. His blazer was unbuttoned, his burgundy silk tie was askew, and his wavy hair curled just slightly at his collar. If she had forgotten an appointment, she had a feeling this man would forgive her.

Faced with his smile, she couldn't help but smile back — it was irresistible! She knew she should be serious and apologetic, but the man evoked a lighthearted response in her.

"I'm terribly sorry! I'm glad I didn't go to lunch or I wouldn't have even been here!" Dominique stood up and shuffled the papers on her desk until she located her appointment book. She leaned over her calendar and studied the little white square for October 12. Blank. She looked up at the man — and caught him studying her figure. When he realized that she had caught him, he gave her a grin that seemed to say, "You can't possibly blame me!"

She laughed, absolutely positive that the grin managed to get him out of most scrapes. "I'm sorry," she said, pushing herself fully upright. "I've been doubly neglectful. I don't have anyone marked down for an appointment. Um . . . you are . . . ?"

He walked toward her, hand outstretched. "Mark Patout."

Dominique stiffened with tension. Mark Patout! She stared at the outstretched hand. Then, realizing that she was being rude, she abruptly leaned across her desk and shook it. "I'm so sorry, sir. This is unforgivable. . . . I know your time is valuable and I —" Dominique stopped in mid-sentence, suddenly remembering something. She looked back down at her calendar. "Oh, no!" she moaned. "I'm afraid I made a terrible mistake. I had you down for *next* Tuesday."

Patout laughed easily. "You did?" He pulled out a small leather appointment book from his jacket and studied it. "You're absolutely right!" His tone was so pleased that Dominique couldn't suppress a smile. "I must have turned to the wrong page. My fault." He casually let the book fall shut and put it back in his pocket. "Oh well, can I buy you lunch? I haven't had any and I'm starving."

Dominique had had only an apple at her desk. Besides, she couldn't very well refuse the host of Orman's gala. "That . . . that would be nice," she said tentatively. She reminded herself that she had no reason to feel uncomfortable now that they'd discovered that the mistake had been his. She took her pocketbook out of her desk drawer and slung her jacket over her arm. "I'm ready," she said.

"How about Café Tartuffe?" Mark asked. With a gesture of his hand, he indicated she should precede him out the door.

Dominique's brow furrowed as she tried to remember if she'd been there. "I don't think I know it," she said as she pressed the elevator button.

"No!" he said with mock incredulity. "Then you haven't really eaten in New Orleans!"

When they emerged from Orman's, Dominique found she didn't need her jacket after all, for the day had turned warm.

"Would you like me to hold that for you?" Patout asked.

"Oh . . . thank you, that's all right." Dominique was a little surprised at the small gallantry. It seemed somehow . . . personal.

They strolled a few blocks to a little restaurant holding no more than a dozen tables. Each one was whimsically covered in a tablecloth bearing a different flower-print pattern. Dominique had never before seen anything like it, and she smiled in delight.

When they were seated, Mark said, "Would you like a drink?"

Dominique held up her hands in a sign of refusal. "I can't possibly or I'll fall asleep after lunch."

"Me, too." He smiled broadly as though it were a miraculous coincidence.

He made her feel so at ease! It was as though they had known each other before. As he looked at the menu, Dominique furtively studied him. He was really one of the most charismatic men she'd ever met. Not because of his looks — his features were pleasant rather than sensational. His eyes were spring green and surrounded by tiny laugh lines. His lean, narrow face bore the tan of a sportsman and his nose, typically Gallic, had a rough bump near the bridge that indicated a schoolyard injury. But Dominique's eyes kept coming back to his mouth. The perpetual laughter she saw there was the source of his appeal. In repose, his lips curved up, as though anticipating a joke. And when he actually smiled, a long dimple formed on the right side of his face. Dominique couldn't imagine that mouth ever turned down in anger. She wondered what had given Patout such a sunny outlook. He seemed totally at ease with himself and the world. She thought of the old French expression *"bien dans sa peau"* — comfortable in his own skin.

"Have you decided what you want?" Patout asked, looking up from his menu.

Dominique flushed. She hadn't even looked at the menu. "Um . . . whatever you're having," she said feebly. Then, trying to justify herself, she added, "I've never been here before, so I don't know what's good."

"I'm having the veal Oscar and a salad," Patout said.

"That sounds good," Dominique said.

After they ordered, Mark leaned toward her and launched a barrage of questions. He seemed impatient to learn as much as he could about Dominique. He was particularly interested in Egypt and her life there before she left.

"How did you learn English so well?" he asked.

Dominique hesitated, and for the first time there was an awkward pause in their conversation. She kept her eyes down as she responded. "In school. But it improved a lot when I worked for the Royal Air Force."

Patout studied her for a moment, as though sensing there was more to the story.

Dominique twisted her napkin in her lap and tried to think of a new topic.

The waiter broke the silence by bringing their salads. When he left, he seemed to take the sudden pall with him. Patout and Dominique lifted their forks and hungrily began to eat.

"Wonderful dressing," she remarked.

Patout lifted his head and smiled. "Best in town. Simple, but good. By the way, how do you —"

Dominique interrupted with a laugh. "We've talked enough about me! Why don't we talk about you? How did you get into politics?"

Patout gave her a crooked grin. "Family business. That and sugar-cane."

"And I suppose that your ambition is to one day be president?" Dominique said flippantly.

Mark leaned forward and lowered his voice. "My ambition is to clean up Louisiana politics," he said with a significant look. "To the extent anyone can," he added in a cynical tone.

Dominique gave him a knowing look. "I haven't been here long, but your politicians seem very open about corruption."

Mark snorted and shook his head. "It amazes me. And I don't want you to think I'm holier-than-thou. The Patout family has had its share of rogues in the legislature."

The waiter arrived to take their empty salad plates.

Dominique folded her hands under her chin and rested her elbows on the table. "So what made you decide to be different?"

Mark picked up his spoon and began to trace lines on the tablecloth. Then he looked directly at Dominique. "Have you seen much of this state?"

Dominique shrugged. "Not really."

"It's poor. Lots of services needed. And I don't like seeing money going into the wrong pockets." He smiled self-consciously. "I don't mean to sound preachy, but it irks me." He sighed and put down the spoon. "I may be fighting an uphill battle. Too many people have been on the take for too long."

Dominique nodded understandingly.

Mark continued. "They say to me, 'Look, Patout, you're set for life. Who are you to interfere when I try to do the same for myself?' But, of course, they're doing it at the expense of other people. A lot of the old timers laugh at me. They think I'm young and idealistic. They say I'll get over the 'reform bug' as they call it."

Dominique laughed. "Do you think you will?"

Mark shook his head. "No. I'll just bide my time until I get more seniority, maybe a powerful committee chairmanship. Until then, I have to settle for a few small victories." He turned up his palms in resignation. "That's the way the game's played."

The waiter placed their veal Oscars before them. Dominique picked up her fork and knife. When she looked up, Patout was watching her expectantly.

"I'm waiting for the verdict," he said, gesturing at her veal.

Dominique took a bite, feeling sinful for having ordered such a heavy lunch. "Mmm, wonderful!" she said.

They enjoyed their meal in silence for a few moments, then Dominique said, "I must tell you that we are *very* grateful you agreed to host our gala."

For the first time, Dominique saw a shadow fall over Patout's features. "My mother died of cancer." He paused as though reliving the memory. After a moment, he continued. "Her suffering at the end was . . ." His eyes clouded with grief.

Dominique had the urge to put a comforting hand on his, but she held herself in check. After all, she hardly knew him. Her expression serious, she said, "I think working on the gala will be of comfort. It will raise a lot of money for cancer research."

"That's what I'm hoping," Patout said seriously. He took a bite of his veal. "I'm looking forward to working with you," he said. Then, with more energy, "What do I do first?"

"We need to devise a list of people you believe will contribute something beyond the cost of the ticket. We have an extensive list already, of course. You'll need to go through it and see whom you feel comfortable contacting. There are other volunteers like you on the gala committee, so you won't be alone with that task. And, of course, my husband knows quite a number of potential contributors himself."

Patout, who had been about to take a bite of his veal, slowly put his fork down. His lids dropped over his eyes. When he raised them, the twinkle was gone. He gave Dominique a half smile and said in a subdued voice, "Your husband's from here?"

Dominique couldn't fail to register the change in Patout. She could see him withdrawing. And the effect on her was as though someone had snatched a warm jacket from her shoulders and shoved her into the cold. The feeling was peculiar and disturbing. And it made her ashamed, as though she were being disloyal to Clay.

Dominique forced a smile. "Clay Parker of Parker Shipping. We were married a little over a year ago."

Patout smiled weakly, "Oh . . . newlyweds . . ."

Dominique thought of Clay. She had a sudden memory of being wrapped in his arms on the balcony in Switzerland. She remembered the romance of the moment, the sweet, unadulterated joy of it. She relaxed, and her smile broadened. "Yes, . . . it was rather a . . . whirl-wind romance. We just . . . fell in love so suddenly."

Patout nodded. "I know what you mean," he said.

⟨∿ ⟨∿ ⟨∿

I'm going to marry her.

That was the thought that crossed Mark Patout's mind the moment he saw Dominique Parker. The idea startled him. He'd never had such an outlandishly romantic impulse. But when he walked into her office and saw her there, eyes closed, shapely legs stretched out, the thought surged unbidden through his mind.

What was it about her? He couldn't say. She was by no means the most beautiful woman he'd ever seen. But she had a magical effect on him!

The sun streaming in her window had cast a halo around her. Like a spotlight on a dark stage, it drew the eye — everything else in the room seemed invisible. Her hair had been a little mussed, as though she'd walked through a crisp breeze, and the effect had been friendly and sexy all at once. Her head had been thrown back and her eyes closed. In his imagination, it was a pose of welcoming expectancy; as though she were waiting for someone — for him — to embrace her. The happy yellow of her silk blouse had fallen in soft drapes around her lush breasts. He had followed her curvaceous lines down to her slim ankles and her daintily arched feet, which — he noticed with amusement — were more out of her shoes than in them. Then his eyes had traveled back up to her face. Her features were strong, with unmistakable dignity. He could tell that she would be intelligent and charming. He had met beautiful women who, when they'd opened their mouths, had disappointed him to the extent that he no longer found them attractive. Sometimes it was their accents, coarse or grating, sometimes it was what they said. But he knew that nothing of the sort would happen with Dominique Parker.

And from the moment those remarkable golden eyes had met his, they'd clicked. It had been undeniable, the magnetic hum between them. When he'd asked her to lunch, there'd been no contrived vacillation. She'd simply said yes. It had been difficult to restrain himself from taking her hand as they walked to the restaurant. He knew what it would feel like. Soft and warm and giving. He had instead contented himself with politely guiding her by the elbow through the door. But even that ever-so-small, ever-so-conventional contact had sent a radiant heat through him. It was more than desire: it was instinctive recognition. She was meant for him and no one else.

Then she had given him the shattering news. She was already married. It had knocked the wind out of him, just as when he'd been a little boy and fallen out of the live oak tree behind the plantation house. Sitting across the table from her, surrounded by people, he had had to fight to conceal his dismay. How could she be married! He wanted to deny it. To insist that there must be some mistake. They belonged together! She had felt it, too, hadn't she? Or had it just been his imagination? She had said that she and her husband were in love. . . .

⑥ ⑥ ⑥

Dominique hung up her coat and went to the side table in the foyer. She sifted through the mail lying there with vague interest until she spotted Danielle's familiar handwriting. It was the same French schoolgirl's script that she used. With happy anticipation, Dominique picked up the letter and walked into the study.

She delayed the pleasure of opening the letter until she had settled on her usual spot on the couch.

October 8, 1958

Dear Dominique,

The plans for your gala sound so glamorous! I wish we could accept your invitation, but Ron says the drive is too long and he doesn't want to spend money on a gown for me. Please send photos of you and Clay at the gala. I know you won't believe this, but Mother is very proud of you and her new son-in-law and loves showing off your photos. You should hear how she goes on about Clay. Ron finds it difficult to endure at times, I'm afraid. But we all think you're very lucky to have found a kind, handsome man — and from a good family, as Mother says! You must pinch yourself sometimes to make sure you're not dreaming, especially after that horrible Anton. Personally, I think it's remarkable that Clay hasn't insisted you stop working. Not many husbands are so agreeable.

Everyone here is fine. Lana loves school. She drew the enclosed picture for you. Monique has turned beautiful. She is Mother's pet. Mother claims that a modeling agent stopped her and asked if we would consider allowing Monique to pose for advertisements. I told her not to talk to strangers! But you know how Mother is. Even though she hardly speaks English, she makes friends wherever she goes. It's funny, but she seems to live much as she did in Egypt. Twice a week, she plays canasta with some of the neighborhood women and — you'll laugh at this — every Friday night, she plays poker with their husbands. She's the only woman in their group and I think she loves it that way. If she weren't such good friends with the wives, I'm sure there'd be all kinds of jealousy. Aside from that, she enjoys looking after the girls. Ironic, isn't it, considering that she never had time for us!

Ron has finally agreed to get a house. I've convinced him that the girls should each have their own rooms and Mother, too. Everything is going well for him at the agency. He's even been approached by two other men about starting an agency of their own. Ron is hesitating. He's been with McCallister, Dewey for such a short while and he's grateful to them. I'm sure you remember how worried he was when he was out of work. But I told him that he should consider the move. He'd be his own boss that way.

Also, the advertising business is such that he could be fired tomorrow if he made one mistake. I don't believe in one-way loyalty! You have to look out for yourself.

By the way, I've enclosed a bank signature card that I'd like you to sign and send back to me. I've opened an account in both our names. That way, if anything ever happens between me and Ron, the money will be secure.

Please write soon. Mother says she will write you back next week.

                                                            Love,
                                                            Danielle

∾ ∾ ∾

Dominique leaned back in her chair and cradled the phone with her shoulder as she spoke to Mark. She was smiling broadly, and that fact was clearly transmitted in her voice. "The cancer group says they've never had so many large donations *before* one of their events. I said it was all due to you."

Mark felt a thrill of pleasure at the warmth of her tone. He knew it was wrong, but he couldn't help it — didn't even bother trying to fight it. After all, hadn't he carefully refrained from contriving ways to see her? And hadn't he kept his notes to her cordial and businesslike? He had not tried to pursue her in any way. So what harm was there in a little mild flirtation? He wasn't strong enough to resist that small gratification.

"This project interests me —" Mark paused, then added, perhaps more caressingly than he should have, "*Very much.*"

Dominique kept her tone light, deliberately misunderstanding his suggestion. "And you're doing a lot of good. I think this event will be the most successful of Orman's galas." Then, in a more serious tone, she said, "Your name has brought in a lot of people who in the past have looked down their noses at our events."

"So what's left to do?"

"Insofar as the logistical details are concerned, nothing. But there are a few people on the list you gave us who should be buying tables and who haven't."

"Hmmm, do you want to" — he hesitated. He wanted so much to see her again. Just to see her, that was all. But to do so was asking for trouble, he knew that. Still, the words came out of his mouth — "discuss it over lunch?"

Dominique was tempted, but she immediately dismissed the idea. She enjoyed Mark's company immensely, but she knew that he was dangerously attracted to her. If she weren't married, she knew that she, too, would be attracted to Mark. However, she was married. Very happily married. She didn't want to lead Mark to believe that there could be anything more than friendship between them.

"I don't need that much of your time," Dominique said easily. "I can send the list over. When you get it, we can discuss it on the phone."

Mark's sunny smile faded. "But I thought we had to go over the seating arrangements. We can't do that over the phone." Even as he argued, he realized the wisdom of her decision. Why was he investing emotion in a woman he couldn't have?

"We still have three weeks to go. And it's a little premature, since not all the tickets have been sold," Dominique said gently. She couldn't help but be flattered by Mark's attention. He was one of the most eligible bachelors in New Orleans. He could have his pick of New Orleans women, yet he was clearly infatuated with her. She didn't encourage it, but it *was* flattering and it made her like him even more.

Dominique heard the disappointment in Mark's voice as he replied, "Oh . . . yes, I suppose so. . . ."

It made her feel sorry, but she knew that she was doing the right thing. "I'll just messenger this list to you," Dominique continued. "Can you follow up this week?"

Mark forced himself to adopt a cheery air. "Anything for you! I'll get back to you with the results by Thanksgiving."

"That's already next week, don't forget." Her voice sounded a note of anxiety.

Mark smiled. He knew she had the party under control. He had gained tremendous respect for her almost military efficiency — a result of her work with the RAF? She thought of every detail and followed up to make sure things were done correctly. Had he not felt about her as he did, he would have offered her a job. She was turning out to be even more than he had imagined on the day he had met her.

He should end the conversation, he told himself; they had no more business to discuss, but he didn't want to let her go. So he asked, "Will you see your mother at Thanksgiving?" His eyes went automatically to the photograph of his own mother on his desk. He pulled the worn frame toward him and lovingly ran his thumb over the picture.

"No, just Clay's family. Mother's talking about coming down next year. What about you?"

"I'm going to the country." Mark had a fantasy of Dominique sitting at the long table in Belle Terre's dining room, one of his nieces or nephews on her lap. He knew she would fit in with his family, knew they would love her. "Everyone'll be there," he continued. "It always seems like about a hundred people!" He thought wistfully how much his mother's presence would be missed. He remembered the last Thanksgiving she'd been alive, her bravery in maintaining a cheerful demeanor as she lay dying of cancer. She had hidden her pain for the sake of her family, had never complained. Only in the last week of her life had she allowed herself the oblivion of morphine. Before that, she had chosen to remain alert, her senses fully attuned to the world around her.

"I'm still alive, aren't I?" she'd told the family. "I want to feel it. I want to see it. I have little enough time left and there's so much I want to say to you all. . . ."

In the last week, when the pain grew unbearable, Mark had cried, "Mama, please, I can't stand to see you suffering like this. I can't stand to see you in pain."

She had looked up at him with her bright, strong eyes and said, "I thank God for the pain, Mark. If it weren't for the pain, I wouldn't be ready to die." Then she had asked for the priest. And the morphine.

Now, as Mark listened to Dominique with half an ear, he wondered what his mother would have advised. And, with a sinking heart, he admitted the truth to himself. Marie-Ange Patout had instilled in her children a strong moral code. Adultery was wrong. Mark had never had an affair with a married woman and, though most men he knew cheated on their wives, he had always vowed that when he finally married, he would remain faithful. He had had many love affairs — the frivolous sort enjoyed by young, eligible bachelors. But he had never met anyone to whom he wished to remain faithful. Until Dominique.

With a pang, he imagined cuddling with her in front of a fire on Thanksgiving. "Are you cooking the turkey?" he joked, knowing that she hardly cooked at all.

Dominique threw back her head and laughed. "You know I'm not."

Dominique wasn't sure how it had happened, but during the course of their monthlong acquaintance, they had learned a great deal about each other, though they had never again met in person. Their phone conversations often lasted an hour and went off on obscure tangents. It was wonderful to feel so comfortable with a new friend. Dominique told herself that she would be happy when Mark finally found a woman to love. When that day came, they could allow their friendship to blossom uninhibited by his suppressed desire (she always thought of it as only his). Then she wouldn't have to be afraid to see him.

Her laugh lifted Mark's heart. "You'll never be a real New Orleanian until you learn a little about cooking."

"Well, as the fellow in the art gallery said, 'I may not know much, but I know what I like.'"

I do, too, Mark thought sadly.

CHAPTER 12 ∾

DOMINIQUE was happy at Orman's. Though she had been on good terms with virtually every staff person in the New York store, the pace had been so frenetic that she had only had time to cultivate friendships with those in her department. Not so in New Orleans. Almost every day, groups of workers went to lunch together, and Dominique was always invited. The staff mixed freely, regardless of rank, because most of the people knew one another from childhood. The "salesgirls" were as likely as not to be related to the store manager through an intertwining, highly complex family tree. The switchboard operator was a debutante who had decided to work "just for fun," as she said. "I wanted to take a year off before I started at Tulane," she explained. "I'm tired of all those books!"

By the end of Dominique's first week at Orman's, she and Clay were receiving invitations to the homes of Dominique's co-workers. "You're Clay Parker's new bride? Why, I've known Clay since our daddies took us hunting for the first time!" said the store's operations manager. By the end of the first year, Dominique and Clay had been invited to the shoe department manager's wedding, plus a christening and a housewarming. In return, the Parkers began to host dinner parties of their own, inviting friends from the store and from Clay's circle.

But Thanksgiving in New Orleans was family time. Parker cousins from as far away as California came "home" for the gathering at Clay's parents'. Dominique liked the hubbub of the reunions and enjoyed many of the cousins, nieces, and nephews. Clay's parents, however, were a different story. Her in-laws welcomed her warmly enough, but she wasn't sure she really liked them. Clay's mother was a vague, rather silly woman, who appeared more suited to the century before. She deferred to her husband in all matters, professing ignorance of anything other than child rearing or home decorating. When the entire clan was present, she devoted most of her attention to her young grandnieces and nephews, leaving adult conversation to others. And when Clay's father criticized Clay — as he inevitably did — Lenore Parker assumed a pained expression, but she never came to her son's defense, never interfered. Dominique found it difficult to forgive her that.

She found it even more difficult to endure the tension between her father-in-law and Clay. Parker treated his son as though Clay were still a youth, incapable of mature reasoning. Though they rarely strayed from the topic of business, and Clay was well informed, Clay Senior reacted to most of his son's ideas with disdain, even if he later implemented them. This Thanksgiving, it had been no different.

"Father, I've been thinking . . . maybe we should open an office in the Port of Philadelphia. Latin American exporters seem to be using it more and more. The access to market is almost as good as the Port of New York, but labor's cheaper and the fees —"

"That's ridiculous!" Clay Senior had barked. "New York will always be the preeminent port in the Northeast."

Clay had flushed and looked down, fuming but silent.

"Don't worry," Dominique had murmured consolingly as they made their way to the dining room. "He'll change his mind." That was the pattern.

"Yeah, but he'll never admit the idea was mine," Clay had muttered with disgust.

And he was right. Parker seemed conditioned to respond negatively to Clay. Dominique believed it was his way of controlling him, keeping him off-balance and undermining his confidence. If she came to her husband's defense, Clay Senior ignored her, as if she had not spoken. It was identical to the manner in which he treated Lenore; Dominique wondered if he was even aware of it.

But what disturbed Dominique most about these interactions was Clay's uncharacteristic passivity. Away from his father, Clay projected confidence that bordered on arrogance. But with Clay Senior, he was a defeated little boy.

Dominique was relieved to spend the Saturday after the holiday home alone with Clay. It was a luxuriously lazy day of reading by the fire and napping.

"We didn't do one productive thing today," Dominique teased as she slipped out of her dress and into her nightgown.

Clay pushed back the covers of the bed and got in. "That's what holidays are supposed to be," he said with a chuckle. "Now come to bed," he added suggestively.

Dominique laughed. "Just a second," she replied. Then she went into the bathroom to wash her face and put in her diaphragm. She was just opening the cabinet when Clay called to her.

"Dominique!" She could hear his raised voice in the bathroom.

Dominique poked her head around the corner.

"Come to bed, honey." His voice was husky as he pulled back the covers and plumped her pillow.

Dominique smiled. "I will. I just have to put in my diaphragm."

Clay stretched one hand toward her and smiled persuasively. "Come on! Forget it this time. You just finished your period. You won't get pregnant. And besides, even if you do, so what?"

Dominique felt a mixture of amusement and irritation. This had become a regular game between them. Clay would try to stop her from interrupting their lovemaking to insert her diaphragm. And Dominique wasn't always able to exercise the self-discipline necessary to fight him. But now she said patiently, "This will only take a minute."

Clay got out of the bed and came toward Dominique. He wrapped his arms around her and gave her a long kiss. "Come to bed," he whispered. He ran his hands over the thin silk of her nightgown and cupped her buttocks.

She felt his erection through the flimsy cloth. The warm pressure against her stomach aroused her. "Just a second," she murmured as she tried halfheartedly to push him away.

Clay nudged down the straps of her nightgown and lowered his head to her neck. He softly nibbled a trail to her breasts, his hand following the same path. Dominique's nipples rose with excitement. Clay eased his hand down and gathered her nightgown, slowly raising the hem. When the material was bunched at Dominique's waist, Clay slid his fingers between her legs. He massaged her expertly until she felt her resistance slip away. Then he led her to the bed and eased her onto it. Before she could object, he slipped between her legs. Dominique wrapped herself around him and moved in the familiar rhythm of their coupling. As always, their lovemaking brought her a wonderful feeling of contentment. It was how married people ought to feel about each other, Dominique thought, comforting and pleasant. She closed her eyes and sighed.

ᖆ ᖆ ᖆ

Dominique's stomach churned with anticipation as she slipped the midnight-blue velvet gown over her hips and pulled the strapless bodice into place. "Clay!" she called, "would you please fasten this for me?"

Clay emerged from the bathroom, splendid in his evening clothes. Dominique couldn't help but smile. And, seeing the warmth on her face, Clay smiled, too.

"You'll be the most gorgeous woman at your gala," he said softly.

Clay was even more complimentary when they arrived at Orman's. Valets in black-and-white harlequin costumes waited to open car doors. A similarly patterned carnival tent covered the walkway to the store entrance. Hundreds of tiny lights illuminated the black interior, creating an atmosphere of nocturnal promise.

Inside, Dominique had ordered midnight-blue draperies hung tent-like from the ceilings with silver stars and moons spotlighted from below. The store's various departments had been transformed with theatrical facades into a fantasy world that evoked Venice's mysterious streets. Terra-cotta pots filled with flowers were everywhere, just as in the streets of Venice. But the coup was the water-filled "canal" with its ersatz gondolas (papier mâché extensions and hatches on canoes) and its very real miniature bridges obtained from a landscaping company. The canal had been rented from a firm that designed amusement park rides and was actually a waterproof shell filled with water. The canal wove through the first floor's widely spaced display cases. The entire effect was decadent, but extravagantly festive, exactly like Venice.

Clay stood just inside the entrance and did a three-hundred-sixty degree turn, his lips parted in awe. "Unbelievable! You did all this?"

Dominique beamed under his approval. "You know I did!"

Clay once more surveyed the room.

Dominique was bursting with pride. "Go up to the mezzanine before everyone gets here. You can look down and see everything!"

Clay took her hand and grinned. "Let's go!"

"I'd love to, but there are a million things I need to check," Dominique said apologetically.

Clay looked up at the mezzanine. "Oh . . . sure." His voice was subdued.

Feeling a little guilty, Dominique pecked him on the cheek and disappeared in the direction of the elevator. She wanted to find the store manager, and she suspected he would be on the top floor, overseeing the caterers.

When she emerged from the elevator, she looked around for the rotund figure of Turner Coltrane, smiling as she thought of the little man. His cherubic face and slow drawl hid an incisive business mind. With an air of jovial congeniality, he ran the three-year-old store so that it far outstripped more established competitors. He was always open to new ideas and had welcomed Dominique, immediately recognizing the advantages an event planner could bring to the store.

At the moment, however, Turner was nowhere in sight, so Dominique pressed the elevator button and asked the attendant to take her back to ground level.

An hour later, after a check of the entire store, and warm reassurances from Turner Coltrane, Dominique was back on the mezzanine. She found Clay leaning on the rail, a glass of champagne in his hand.

"Everything okay?" he asked, his face brightening at the sight of her.

"Fine," she said with a sigh of relief. She looked anxiously at the bank of brass doors that marked the store's main entrance. Guests would begin to arrive at any moment, and Dominique had carefully instructed the costumed hostesses on how to receive them. Coats were to be speedily checked, champagne and hors d'oeuvres immediately offered, and the crowd directed away from the entrance and into the store, where the orchestra had begun to warm up.

First in a trickle, then in a riotous throng, the crowd began to arrive. As Dominique and Clay watched from the mezzanine, each guest stopped short to exclaim on the decor. Even from a distance, Dominique could hear their cries of delight.

"This is just how I pictured it," she confessed to Clay. "Look at those costumes! Everyone's gotten into the spirit of Carnevale!"

On cue, a bevy of wildly dressed women tumbled through the door. There were hoopskirts and capes, feathers and glitter, lace and lamé.

There were wide picture hats and foot-high wigs. Their escorts, just behind them, were as lavishly outfitted as courtiers in the time of Louis XIV. Many, in fact, wore satin breeches and brocade jackets reminiscent of earlier centuries. But most impressive were the elaborate masks. Intricately handcrafted confections sporting grotesque leers, Pinocchio noses, or delicate cat's eyes trimmed in rhinestones.

No sooner had the first guests moved on than the second group appeared, this one dressed in long dominoes of satin and velvet. Behind them was a quartet in black tie and ball gowns, carrying exquisite masks.

Dominique and Clay had chosen this more simple dress, as Dominique hadn't wished to hamper her movements with an elaborate costume. Instead, she carried a silver mask decorated on either side with ice-blue plumes, and Clay held a black-and-gold mask on the end of a wand. The masks, like those of many of the guests below, were family heirlooms, lovingly brought out each year at Mardi Gras, then carefully packed away in tissue when the celebration was over.

A waiter passed by with a tray of champagne, which Dominique declined. "I still have to work," she reminded Clay.

"I don't!" he said firmly. He put down his empty glass and reached for a full one. "Cheers," he said, and took a long swallow. "I know you're busy, so I'll see you later."

Dominique watched fondly as he plunged into the festivities, calling down to friends on the level below.

The volume of noise was high — and rising with each new arrival. People were mixing freely and, in true New Orleans form, consuming huge amounts of liquor. Groups of men were clustered around each of the room's four bars, smoking and laughing. Already a thin blue haze floated near the ceiling.

It occurred to Dominique that she should order the fans turned up higher. She went to the house phone on the wall near the elevator and called the custodian standing by for just such eventualities. A few seconds later, she returned to the rail, scanning for trouble. She was pleased to see that the "canal" was an unqualified success. People were queued on the bridges for rides in the little gondolas — delighted by the novelty.

"Could I persuade you to take a ride with me?" A deep voice behind Dominique interrupted her thoughts.

She knew without turning that it was Mark. Suddenly she was excruciatingly aware of her bare shoulders, her plunging bodice. At once, Dominique stifled the thought. She turned and held out her hand with a smile. "I'm afraid I'm on duty this evening. But you should definitely try it and tell me how it is." She gave him a warm look. "How are you?"

He took her hand without replying. His eyes held hers and she sensed that he wanted to say something far more intimate than he should. She eased her hand from his. The impression of his fingers left a warm feeling on her skin, like a footprint in the sand.

She said lightly, "It seems as though it's going to be a successful evening."

Mark smiled, a wide, dancing smile that charmed Dominique. He gestured at the canal below. "I'm truly amazed by all this. I've never seen anything like it. I know you told me about it, but I never had a clear picture of what it would look like. Everyone's going to be talking about it tomorrow!"

"I have to earn my keep." It was disturbing when he looked at her that way. He meant nothing to her, of course. He was no more than a friend. Still, his unfettered admiration was . . . somehow unsettling.

Mark's expression changed. Now he cocked his head with curiosity. "How much do events like these really do for sales?"

"That's a good question." Dominique was relieved to be talking business. She placed one hand on the banister and shifted her weight to the opposite foot — a pose that indicated she was prepared to chat a while. "Quite a large effect, actually. Not only in sales immediately following the event, but in overall trends for the store. Orman's is still fairly new. We're trying to create a certain image, and events like these help. They also ingratiate us with the community. This is the first time we've attracted so many prominent New Orleanians," she said, giving Mark a grateful smile. "Thanks to you."

Mark smiled back. He loved to watch her eyes as she spoke. When she talked about her work, he could see her enthusiasm and vigor. That was how he felt about his work, too, and he liked to think they had traits in common. "The success of this event has more to do with you than me." Mark touched her arm lightly when he said the word "you." He wanted an excuse to touch her, to move closer to her. The momentary contact left a tingle at the tip of his finger.

Dominique unconsciously put her hand over the spot where he had touched her. She rubbed it softly as she spoke. "I think a lot of the success is due to community enthusiasm. New Orleanians love attending these things. A lot of New Yorkers have a more jaded attitude."

Mark looked around the room, then turned back to Dominique with a smile. "I can't imagine anyone being too jaded to appreciate this. It's incredible!"

They had somehow shifted positions and were now standing side by side overlooking the ground floor. Dominique's bare arm almost touched the dark wool of Mark's dinner jacket. Occasionally, when she gestured, she felt the cloth brushing her arm, the heat rising from his body. Subtly, she inched away, then pushed off from the rail and pivoted to face him. He mirrored her movement. Dominique noticed a bit of lint on his lapel and had the urge to pluck it off. She knew it would please him if she did. She was a person who used her hands when she spoke and often reached out to touch the person to whom she was speaking. But she was very careful not to touch Mark. She left the lint where it was. Looking up at him, she asked, "Did you come alone?"

"No," he said. He gave a cursory glance around the mezzanine, then turned back to Dominique. "My date's around here somewhere. Do you know Nina Rivers?"

Dominique felt a thrill of curiosity. It was the first time Mark had ever mentioned a woman. "Her father owns Rivers Oil, doesn't he? I think he bought a table."

Mark nodded. "I actually know him better than I know her," he explained unnecessarily. "But it's not much fun to come to these things alone." He wanted her to know it was nothing serious . . . but why? What was the use?

Dominique lowered her eyelids and made a moue with her lips. "Shouldn't you try to find her?"

Mark shrugged. "She knows everybody here. She doesn't need me to have a good time." He paused, wondering if he sounded boorish. He didn't want Dominique to think that of him. He flushed and went on, more uncertainly. "I mean . . . I'll find her before we go in to dinner, but she has a lot of friends she wants to say hello to."

Dominique saw his embarrassment and thought it adorable. He really was such a nice person! She smiled reassuringly.

"Dominique." Mark didn't know why he had spoken her name. He had just wanted to say it. But he had to get hold of himself. It was ridiculous the effect she had on him. He had to keep reminding himself that she was married. Happily married.

"Mark, what is it? You have such a peculiar look." Instinctively, Dominique put a hand on his forearm. Mark covered her hand with his, and she immediately pulled back, as if she had been burned. Then she was ashamed of herself. Why should she jerk away as though he were poisonous?

Unspoken words hung in the air. Mark gave her a weak half-smile and said, "Nothing's wrong." He paused. "I hope you'll save a dance for me after dinner." He was surprised that he sounded normal, friendly.

"It's the least she can do!" Clay's hearty voice broke the spell.

Mark looked up, as startled as a burglar caught breaking into a safe.

Dominique took a step away from him. She looked from Clay to Mark and back again. Then she reached for her husband's arm with a welcoming smile.

Clay put out his hand and gave Mark a broad grin. "Clay Parker," he said. "We've met a couple of times over at the capitol. Dominique's told me about your work on the gala. Mighty generous of you to have given so much of your time."

Mark responded with equal bonhomie. "I'm ashamed to say I foisted most of the work off on Dominique. But I think it was a wise move. It looks like it's going to be a big success." Mark was an inch or so shorter than Clay, and Dominique saw him straighten his spine and square his shoulders.

Clay casually draped his arm around Dominique. "All that talent and looks, too," he remarked. He had a spot of bright color on each cheek and his drawl was more pronounced than usual. Though he was by no means slurring his words, Dominique could tell that he had drunk quite a bit. She was acutely aware of Mark's scrutiny of her husband and she suddenly felt embarrassed for Clay, though she knew it was ridiculous to think that someone would look down on him for a slight overindulgence. In New Orleans, a man was admired for being able to hold his liquor, but if he lost control once in a while no one thought the worse of him. Clay was nowhere near that point, so Dominique couldn't understand why she felt him to be at a disadvantage with Mark. But the impression aroused a protective loyalty in her.

"Clay's been very understanding about the time I've had to devote to this project," Dominique said, keeping her eyes fixed on her husband.

Mark smiled politely. "Well, I'd better not take up any more of it. I'm sure you have plenty to do. And I need to go and find Miss Rivers." He gave Dominique a little bow, then put out his hand to Clay. "Pleasure seeing you again, Clay."

Clay's expression was ingratiating. "Hope to see you soon." He gave Mark a hearty handshake.

The couple watched Mark disappear into the crowd. As soon as he was gone, Clay turned to his wife. "You haven't forgotten about inviting him to dinner, have you?"

Dominique raised one shoulder and let it drop. "The opportunity didn't come up," she replied, not meeting Clay's eyes. She knew very well that Mark would accept her dinner invitation.

"We shouldn't let this chance slip by," Clay reminded Dominique. "In a couple of weeks, he'll have forgotten who you are." His voice rose decisively. "I'm going to ask him myself. After dinner, when everyone's relaxing." He paused for a moment, lost in thought. Then his face brightened. "Maybe I should invite Nina Rivers with him! Her father's oil company uses Seaward Shipping instead of us." Clay was already envisioning a lucrative new client and a helpful new friend in the legislature.

Dominique tried to think of a diplomatic way to discourage him from issuing the invitations. But before she could speak, Clay let out a low whistle and said, "Boy, that Patout sure is a lucky fellow!"

Dominique followed his gaze. Across the room, Mark stood with a statuesque blonde of the same aristocratic style as actress Grace Kelly. Dominique had once or twice seen Nina Rivers' photo in the society page, but she'd never seen the woman in person. She was exquisite. Unconsciously, Dominique shook her head. If she told Clay about Mark's crush on her, he would accuse her of being delusional!

CHAPTER 13 ∾

THE WEEK after Christmas, Clay surprised Dominique with a four-day trip to New York. They spent one evening with Dominique's former co-workers, Bruce, Maude, Lucinda, and Lucinda's new fiancé, a polished Wall Street investment banker. The remaining time was devoted to family. Clay insisted on taking his nieces, Lana and Monique, to FAO Schwarz and spoiling them with new toys. For Solange and Danielle, there were huge bottles of French perfume, and for Ron, who had recently discovered an obsession with golf, a sleek new driver.

"We'll be paying these bills for months!" Dominique gently scolded.

He shrugged off her caution. "It'll be okay."

It was impossible not to be warmed by Clay's extravagance; it touched her that he wanted so much for her family to like him.

Then, in April, shattering news threw Clay's own family into disarray.

The phone call came near dawn when Dominique was home alone, Clay on a business trip to Los Angeles. She barely recognized the broken voice on the other end as that of Lenore Parker, her mother-in-law.

"Dominique, I'm at the hospital. It's Clay. . . ."

Dominique jolted upright in bed, uncomprehending. "Clay!" she cried. "What's wrong with him?" Why would Lenore be calling her about Clay?

"Oh, God!" Lenore sobbed. "I mean Clay's daddy. He's . . . he's had a heart attack. He" — the woman choked on her words — "he didn't make it!" No sooner had she uttered the phrase than she broke down completely. "I don't know what to do next! Clay has to come right away!" More sobbing.

Dominique, numb, tried to murmur some words of comfort. "I'll call him at his hotel. He has the company plane. He can leave right away."

A lost wail from Lenore. "But what am I supposed to do? I'm all alone. Clay's daddy always took care of everything. . . ."

Dominique tried to clear her thoughts. In a decisive voice, she said, "I'll come right away. I'll call Aunt Ellen and Aunt Anne." Lenore's sister and sister-in-law. She raised her voice to be heard over the sobbing. "Don't worry, Lenore, I'll be there in a few minutes and I'll take care of everything."

Luckily, Dominique reached Clay at once. He reacted to the news with silence. Dominique assumed he was too stunned to speak. Then, all at once, his voice came over the line, steady and crisp. "I'll leave now. Tell Mother I'll handle everything."

For the next week, Dominique barely saw Clay. He was embroiled in a plethora of morbid details, on the phone constantly — to the funeral home, the office, the Parker Shipping branches. He reassured clients, scheduled a meeting of the company's top officers, and contacted Parker relatives throughout the country. He was head of the family now — that was clear.

The day after the funeral, Clay returned late from "a meeting with the attorney," as he casually labeled it to Dominique. When she met him in the foyer, she was distressed to see the gravity of his expression. Had he suffered yet another blow? She went toward him, prepared to offer sympathy.

She reached for his hat. "Here, let me take those for you."

As Clay handed it to her, his eyes met Dominique's for the first time.

For a moment she hesitated, struck by what she saw. There was a secret excitement in him, a flame of . . . something she couldn't identify.

Clay abruptly averted his eyes.

Troubled, Dominique turned and put his hat in the closet. Clay was keeping something from her. She closed the door and turned back to him, a question in her eyes.

Clay rubbed his hands over his face in a gesture of weariness.

"Tired?" Dominique asked, reaching up and rubbing the back of his neck.

"Yeah," he sighed. He met her gaze again.

"You have news?" Dominique asked, once more troubled by the fire that seemed inconsistent with the fatigued droop of his mouth.

Clay took Dominique's elbow. "Let's go into the study. We need to talk."

"All right," Dominique said, apprehensive.

But they had taken only a few steps when Clay stopped short. He turned Dominique toward him and put his hands on her shoulders. "Babe . . . ," he whispered as he shook his head in wonder, "the business is finally mine. We're filthy rich now." His gaze became dreamy and unfocused. "Everything's going to be different."

Clay was true to his word. Things began to change immediately. In typical patriarchal fashion, Clay's father had left almost $2 million in stocks, cash, and bonds, as well as Parker Shipping, in Clay's hands. Lenore Parker was provided with more than enough money to maintain her lifestyle, but the bank was assigned to execute the trust. Clay chafed at that — even from the grave, his father had found a way to strike a blow to his confidence. But the excitement of the inheritance soon overcame his hurt. Clay had an agenda he was eager to implement.

His first move was to put the house on the market and start looking for a new one on St. Charles. Dominique was stunned by the swiftness of his action, but she didn't have the heart to discourage him in a project he had spoken of with longing since she'd known him. What was the point in delaying? She had always known this was his intention. Still, when the time came to move from their quaint little house to the kingly antebellum mansion on St. Charles, Dominique was struck with an attack of nostalgia. They had been so happy in their first home.

Clay, on the other hand, couldn't stop marveling at the new place.

"Now *this* is an entrance!" he crowed as they drove up the bricked semicircle to the front steps. Dominique looked at the fountain in the middle of the broad green half-moon that comprised the front yard, at the six massive white pillars that guarded the portico, and she had to agree. It *was* impressive! The facade, with its expansive southern grandeur, was even more imposing than her childhood home. She couldn't help but catch Clay's excitement.

Inside, an echoing foyer of black-and-white marble reminded her of a European castle. A double staircase with bronze Art Nouveau banisters cascaded gracefully down either side of the broad room, continuing the semicircular theme. In the center hung a crystal chandelier — large but delicate.

"Baccarat," Clay said, following Dominique's gaze.

"So you've mentioned," she said dryly. A hundred times, she thought with silent amusement. Aloud, she said, "This place is awfully big for just the two of us."

Clay took her in his arms. "Then let's have kids," he said with a grin. He hugged her, and his expression grew earnest. "You don't have to work — we can afford anything we want. We'll hire a live-in couple to help Lucy. You won't have to do a thing."

"But I want to work! I've already told you I'll resign when I get pregnant. But I'm only twenty-four. There's still plenty of time for children," she said casually.

Clay fixed her with a somber look. "We need to start thinking seriously about starting a family. I want a son to take over my business."

Dominique laughed. *My* business. Since his father's death, Clay was sometimes impossibly self-important. Well, it *was* his business now, and Dominique couldn't blame him for caring about it. The self-importance would fade, she was certain. It probably came from trying to grapple with all the new responsibilities that had fallen to him. Responsibilities that he handled with remarkable competence, she reminded herself. Still, her natural reaction to pompousness — in anyone — was to laugh at it. "Clay, you're only thirty-one and you're already thinking about heirs!"

Clay abruptly released Dominique and looked away, his brows coming together in irritation. "I should think," he said severely, "you'd understand my concern, considering how suddenly Father died."

Dominique was taken aback. "Don't speak to me as though I were an idiot," she snapped. "I understand your concern. I just don't think the situation as urgent as you do."

They glared at each other in angry silence.

Finally Clay made a noise of exasperation and averted his eyes. "Look, I've been waiting a long time for this day." He turned back to Dominique with a stony gaze. "Don't ruin it for me."

ᘒ ᘒ ᘒ

The death of Clay's father was followed a few months later by an event almost as unexpected.

It was late September and Dominique could smell a hurricane coming. As she rode the streetcar home from work, she kept checking the sky with a worried expression. Dark, greenish clouds hung low over the trees. The air was thick, almost suffocating. Dominique was anxious to get home. Louisiana's wild storms petrified her — she'd never seen anything like them, coming as she did from a desert climate. Even in a normal thunderstorm, the trees bent so threateningly low that it seemed they would surely crash down on her. And the wind howled — gratingly, continuously — causing all sorts of strange rattles and creaks, so that Dominique felt it was invading even the safety of the house's interior.

She heaved a sigh of relief when she reached her front door just as the first fat drops of rain began to splatter down. At least she hadn't gotten wet. She entered the house quickly and locked the door behind her.

"Good afternoon, Mrs. Parker," said the new live-in housekeeper. Clay had hired Myrna and Bill Jefferson, a middle-aged couple, shortly after the move. Bill saw to the grounds and Myrna cleaned house. Lucy had remained as cook.

"Awful day, isn't it?" Dominique shuddered as she handed her raincoat to Myrna. Then she went to the mail waiting on the marble-topped table in the foyer. A letter from Danielle or Maude would be a welcome distraction. She picked up the mail and started to sift through it. Good! A letter from Solange. The electric bill, the phone bill. Then came a thick, creamy envelope, addressed in beautiful calligraphy. Her interest piqued, Dominique picked up the envelope and slid her index finger under the flap. The paper was so thick and stiff that it cut her.

"Ouch!" she cried, letting the envelope fall on the table. Reflexively, she brought her finger to her mouth, but the unpleasant taste of blood made her grimace. She dropped her hand and looked at her finger. A thin, red line bubbled from beneath the cut. Bringing the finger back to her mouth, she picked up the envelope. A spot of blood marred the pristine surface, and Dominique stared at it accusingly. Then, holding her cut finger away from the paper, she pulled out the contents.

Mr. and Mrs. Franklin Carlisle Rivers
request the honour of your presence
at the marriage of their daughter
Nina Merrill
to
The Honorable Mark Patout
on Saturday, the first of October
Nineteen hundred and fifty-nine
at twelve o'clock noon
Willow Gardens Plantation
Destrehan, Louisiana

Dominique stared at the card in disbelief. Why, Mark and Nina had come to dinner just a month before, and there had been no sign that they were even in love, much less engaged. Dominique tried to picture the couple as she had last seen them. True, Nina possessively watched Mark's every move. When Mark left the room, Nina's eyes followed him. When he spoke, her eyes were trained on his face. All of which made Mark's offhand manner toward the blond woman all the more noticeable. He was unfailingly polite, attentive even, but he didn't look at her like a man in love. Dominique knew, because . . . a quick thought flashed through her consciousness — and was immediately suppressed. Guiltily, Dominique tried to fill her mind with chatter.

I'm pleased for Mark. It's time he married. Nina's the perfect wife for a politician. Beautiful, intelligent, photogenic, well connected. Just because she acts cold doesn't mean that she really is. Probably she's different when she's alone with Mark. After all, I'm sure she loves him. She'll try to make him happy.

And Dominique wanted Mark to be happy. She forced a smile. It was *wonderful* that Mark was getting married. Her smile faded, to be replaced by a look of concern. If her happiness for him was less than wholehearted, she told herself, it was only because she wasn't overly fond of Nina. Of course, that was all.

CHAPTER 14 ∽

"CLAY really is the perfect husband," Solange told Dominique. It was the third time since Solange's arrival the day before that Dominique had heard that.

"I'm glad you like him, Mother," Dominique said patiently. She *was* glad that her mother liked her husband, but there was an unspoken implication in the lavish compliments that bothered Dominique. As though Solange couldn't believe Dominique had captured such a man.

Or was she, Dominique, just being overly sensitive? She bit her tongue and reminded herself of her resolution to make this visit peaceful. After all, it had been over a year since she'd seen her mother, and then only for a day or two during the Christmas visit to New York.

Solange turned another page in the album. She stopped at a photo of Clay on the beach in Nice. "So handsome!" Solange said admiringly. She dropped her voice as though divulging a secret. "Much handsomer than your sister's husband."

"Mother, it isn't a contest," Dominique said mildly. She was careful to maintain a tone of affectionate amusement. She had taken a two-week vacation to spend time with her mother. It would be a long, tiresome visit if she reacted to every little irritation. Still, there was no denying that they got on each other's nerves.

In contrast, Clay and Solange seemed to get along perfectly. From the moment the Parkers picked up Solange at the train station, Dominique had almost felt like a fifth wheel. Clay flattered Solange extravagantly, and she bloomed under his compliments.

But Clay wasn't with the two women on this drizzly January morning.

"I didn't say it was a contest!" Solange retorted, not bothering to temper her own voice. "Can't I be happy that you've done so well for yourself?" She swept her arm through the air in a gesture that took in the room. Like the rest of the house, it was beautifully decorated with antiques and fine art. Warming the atmosphere were bouquets of fresh flowers and amusing knickknacks Dominique picked up in the dusty little shops of the French Quarter.

"I'm sorry, Mother," Dominique said. "I'm glad you're pleased." She felt ashamed. After all, Solange had *praised* Clay. It was just that Dominique had become peeved in advance of her mother's visit by imagining the types of slights Solange would inflict — the backhanded compliments, the niggling criticisms, the constant comparisons to Danielle.

Solange turned the upper half of her body and studied her daughter. "Well, aren't you pleased, too?"

"Of course I am!"

Solange sniffed and turned back to the album. "You should be. After all, you were a penniless divorcée when Clay met you. A lot of men of his background wouldn't have married you. I'm sure he had many lovely young women to choose from."

Dominique was stung. Her first impulse was to say something rude in return. But she knew she was jumpy, ready to react angrily to a wrong word from her mother. So she made an extra effort to control herself. Dominique wanted to show Solange that she was above losing her temper now. She was a married woman. An adult. She fixed her eyes on the pages of the album, determined not to betray her feelings.

When she received no response, Solange went on with her lecture. "You should remember how lucky you are. And you should stay home and take care of him instead of running to that store every day. It's time you settled down and had children, anyhow." She gave her daughter a head-to-toe perusal.

It was as though Solange had pushed a button that said "Blast off!" Dominique's self-control was shattered as, with brutal accuracy, Solange hit on the only real trouble spot in the Parkers' marriage.

Dominique sprang to her feet, causing the photo album to slam shut on Solange's lap. She stood above her mother, hands on her hips, her face scarlet with anger. "You haven't even been here a day and already you're criticizing me!" she fumed.

Solange threw up her hands in exasperation. "Oh! You're like a child! One can't say anything to you! I'm simply trying to warn you that you have a very handsome husband and you should be careful."

"Mother, do you think Clay is going to leave me because I work?" Dominique demanded. "Wasn't I working when he fell in love with me?"

Solange drew herself up and crossed her arms over her chest. "That was different. You didn't have a wealthy husband to support you," she said coldly. "This . . . this *insistence* on working is certain to alienate him! No man wants a woman like that!"

The glacial quality of Solange's tone fueled Dominique's lifelong resentment. She felt like a pressure cooker about to burst. "Just because you've never found anything to love in me, don't assume that others haven't!" she hurled.

Solange looked stunned by Dominique's vehemence. Her eyebrows shot up into two arcs, then dropped into the V of a scowl.

Dominique saw the outrage in her mother's face and burst forth with a torrent of words before Solange had a chance to interrupt. Her head shot forward, the veins in her neck throbbing. "It's true! All my life you've told me how much better Danielle was, how much prettier. You've never supported anything I wanted to do!" Dominique wanted nothing more than to hear her mother deny the accusations. She wanted to be told that she had misunderstood everything. That Solange loved her as much as she loved Danielle. That she really did think Dominique as pretty and smart as her sister.

Solange leapt to her feet, letting the photo album crash to the ground. Her lips were drawn back from her teeth in an expression of unadulterated rage. She pointed an index finger at her daughter and shook it with each syllable that she spoke. "I always treated you equally! I never gave her anything I didn't give you. You had *everything* when you were growing up!"

"I'm not talking about *things*," Dominique said, as though Solange were unspeakably stupid. She turned her face away from her mother. She had something more to say, but the words stuck in her gut. They were the crux of the matter. Yet to accuse her mother was to admit her own shame. Without even realizing it, Dominique dropped the volume of her voice. Her mouth quivered uncontrollably as she spoke. "You never loved me as much as Danielle." There. She had finally said it. Finally brought the taboo subject to light. It had been festering since earliest childhood. The knowledge that she was not as well loved as her sister, that she wasn't as good.

Solange glared silently at her daughter. The only emotion visible in her face was anger. Dominique had hoped to see more. Love, penitence, understanding. Something to show that she had reached Solange. But she saw only anger.

"It's true, isn't it?" Dominique asked, her voice bitter.

Solange turned her back to her daughter. She folded her arms around herself; her back hunched forward. It was a curiously vulnerable pose, one very unlike Solange. For a moment Dominique thought her mother might cry. But then Solange turned her head so that her profile was visible to Dominique. Her eyes were dry, her voice harsh as she said, "It's terrible that you would say such things to me."

"What about me!" Dominique hated the sound of her voice, of the words. Hated the pleading motion she made with her hands. It was all so childish, so ignoble! But she couldn't stop herself. "What about how you've hurt me?"

Solange whirled about to face Dominique. "What have I done that was so terrible? Name one thing!" Her tone was challenging.

Dominique saw with despair that Solange wasn't even trying to see her point of view. Instead, she was trying to defend herself. Dominique let out a long, shaky sigh. She put one hand on the mantel and rested her forehead against it. She was too drained for anger. She had said all she could, but she still hadn't gotten through to Solange.

Then she remembered an incident from her childhood. Slowly she raised her head and released the mantel. She stepped toward Solange, her expression imploring her to understand. "Do you remember when the three of us were in France on the train from Nice to Paris? It was right after the war, the year before Danielle was married."

Solange nodded uneasily, as though she knew she would dislike what she was about to hear.

"The lady sitting near us said how pretty I was. I was only twelve, but it was the year you let me grow my hair long and she said she liked the color. Do you remember what you said to her?" Dominique's voice was shaking.

"I don't even know what you're talking about!" Solange snapped.

But Dominique could tell Solange was lying. She continued as though she hadn't heard her. "You said, 'Dominique? Pretty? No, her nose is too long! Danielle is the beauty of the family.'" Dominique perfectly mimicked Solange's breezy manner as she relived the memory. When she finished, she leaned forward from the waist, her hands at shoulder level punctuating each phrase. "How could you say that, Mother? How could you humiliate me that way? Didn't you ever stop to think how it made me feel?" Dominique shook her head in incredulous outrage. "The woman knew. She looked at you like you were a monster —"

Solange stamped her foot. "She did no such thing! You're just overly sensitive and you twist everything —"

"Mother!" Dominique yelled, startling Solange into silence. She took a step toward the older woman. Something in the intensity of her gaze caused Solange to step backward. Dominique stepped forward again, forcing Solange to look directly into her eyes. "Don't you see? You made that woman pity me! She felt so sorry for me that she said to you . . ." Dominique forced herself to exhale slowly. The lump in her throat subsided a little and she continued. "The lady said, 'I think you're wrong. Your younger daughter's features are more unusual, it's true, but also more expressive. I think *she* will be the beauty.' Mother, why couldn't you just let one person think I was better than Danielle? Why did you have to contradict her?"

The blood drained from Solange's face. She looked so shaken that Dominique was suddenly afraid for her. "I'm . . ." Solange bowed her head. "I'm sorry, Dominique. I never meant to hurt you. . . . I just didn't think." She raised her eyes to her daughter's and took a step toward her. "The two of you were so different. Danielle was obedient and affectionate. She adored me. But you . . ." Solange turned her head so that Dominique was again looking at her profile. "It was almost as though you were Nanny's child, not mine," she said quietly. Her eyes came back to her daughter. They were soft, full of emotion. "It's not that I didn't love you. You argued constantly with me. You did as you wished and didn't seem to care if it made me angry." Solange paused. Her gaze shifted to a point behind Dominique. "Do you remember when you were little and you broke the lock on the sideboard where I had hidden the cookies for my canasta group?"

Dominique was surprised to find herself smiling tearfully at the memory. "I remember."

Solange shook her head slowly from side to side. "You used a nail file to get it open, and you left those gouges in the wood."

Dominique met her mother's eyes. She used the back of her hand to wipe her tears and her nose.

"Stop that!" Solange commanded. She reached into her pocket and pulled out a clean handkerchief. "Here, use this."

Dominique took the little square of cloth. "Thank you," she said softly. She blew her nose.

"That was a very valuable antique, you know," Solange said. Her voice grew more animated. "I was furious!"

"I remember," Dominique said ruefully. "You spanked me and sent me to bed without supper." She gave a tremulous laugh at the memory.

"But you didn't seem to care. That's what was so maddening!" Solange wore a scolding expression, but the younger woman knew she meant it in humor.

Dominique grinned. "I didn't care because I was sick from the cookies."

Solange returned her smile. "That was the sort of thing that only you would do. Danielle would have never —" She stopped short and looked cautiously at her daughter.

"It's all right." Dominique gave her mother a reassuring nod. "I know what you mean."

"It's not that I didn't love you." Solange's voice was insistent. "But Danielle was easier for me to understand." She tapped her index finger against her chin. "We're more alike."

Dominique nodded slowly. "I know."

Solange gave her daughter an uncharacteristically sheepish look. "I'll try not to nag you so much. I know it annoys you, and I always vow to keep silent, but when I see you doing something that isn't best for you, I can't help saying something."

Dominique sighed and reached for her mother's hands. "And I'll try to be more tolerant," she said warmly. "I know you mean well."

"Well," Solange said in a heartier tone of voice, "I'm glad we've resolved this."

Dominique squeezed her mother's hands. It was as though a huge burden had been lifted. It was a relief to give voice to the anger, envy, and frustration she had carried with her her entire life. And she understood a little — though not entirely — why Solange felt closer to Danielle. It still hurt to know that it was the case, but it was better than thinking that her mother simply didn't love her. Dominique wondered if she and Solange would ever truly feel comfortable with each other — ever truly be friends. Even now it didn't quite seem possible. But at least they had talked. Dominique knew that there remained more to be said. She would have liked to talk for hours, days, about all their misunderstandings. Yet Solange wasn't ready to say more. She was anxious to gloss over the hard feelings, to call the problem solved and move on.

ᮧ ᮧ ᮧ

Dominique knew Clay wanted to make Solange's last night with them special when he suggested dinner at the Pontchartrain Hotel's Caribbean Room. It was not the spot for a casual, drop-in sort of dinner, and Clay had taken Dominique there only twice before: on their first anniversary and on the day they had moved into their grand new home on St. Charles Avenue.

Throughout Solange's two-week visit, Clay's manner toward her had continued to be as solicitous as on the first day. Now, as they were led to their table, he gave her his arm, leaving Dominique to follow a few steps behind. He held out Solange's chair as the waiter held Dominique's.

When they were seated, Clay ordered a bottle of champagne, then turned to Solange to discuss the menu with her. Clay had learned a smattering of French — hardly enough to string together a sentence — and Solange spoke only broken English, but with Dominique's help, they made themselves understood to each other.

When the champagne came, Clay raised his glass and proposed a toast. "To family," he said as he tipped his head in Solange's direction. She smiled warmly at her son-in-law and the three of them clinked their glasses together and took a sip of champagne.

"Soon I hope we'll have an even bigger family to celebrate," he said, looking pointedly at Dominique. For Solange's benefit, he cradled his arms as though they contained a baby.

Solange's eyes widened and she looked questioningly at Dominique.

Dominique shot Clay a warning look that said "Don't start," then, with some embarrassment, admitted to her mother, "He's talking about having a baby."

Solange turned to her daughter with an "I told you so" look. "Why you no want baby?" she asked in English, her tone accusatory. For two weeks she hadn't revived the subject, but she clearly thought Clay's comment gave her license to do so now.

Dominique was irritated no end. Given their recent argument, Solange had to know she was treading on sensitive ground. Dominique was tempted to retort that it was none of Solange's business. But, of course, that would have started a row. Instead, she glared at her mother and allowed a lengthy silence to develop, hoping it would make the same point. Out of the corner of her eye, she saw that Clay had turned to look at her. His hands were folded in front of him and his eyebrows were raised in an exaggerated pose of expectancy.

Solange didn't seem in the least bothered by her daughter's glare. She met Dominique's gaze and held it, as though she were prepared to wait in silence as long as necessary for an answer.

Dominique thought back to their fight two weeks before. As cathartic as it had seemed at the time, it hadn't altered Solange's behavior for more than a day or two. Nor Dominique's, for that matter. Oh, there had been moments of companionability — more than ever before — but all too often, the women had fallen into their old pattern of interaction: an endless cycle of criticism, irritation, eruption, and finally a return to civility without any resolution of the issue that had caused the discord. Dominique didn't feel like going through it all again on their last night together. So, to keep the peace, she decided to answer her mother.

"I want children, but later," she said emphatically.

"Later!" Solange mocked. "You see, it's just as I told you," she said in rapid French. "He doesn't want you to be a career woman. He wants you to be a wife and mother — as you should!" She waved a hand in Clay's direction as she concluded, leaving no question that she was speaking of him.

To Dominique's immense annoyance, Clay was nodding, as though he understood every word. Clearly, he understood the gist of what was being said.

Dominique stood up. "I'm going to the powder room," she said stonily, "and when I return I don't want to discuss this anymore." She gave Clay a pointed look, then turned to her mother with the same expression.

Dominique saw a flash in Solange's eyes, as though she intended to argue further. Then the older woman blinked and let out a puff of exasperation. She sat back in her seat and held her hands in front of her, flipping her wrists dismissively. "Enough!" she said. "I don't want to ruin this nice evening your husband has planned by arguing about your stubbornness."

She always has to have the last word! Dominique thought, biting back an angry reply.

But as it turned out, Clay had the last word. Three weeks after dinner at the Pontchartrain, Dominique learned she was pregnant.

CHAPTER 15 ∽

DOMINIQUE squinted against the sun to peer anxiously at her daughter and niece. Fourth-grader Lana was fussing over the toddler, pretending to be her mother. She lifted twenty-month-old Gabrielle from the pram, cradled her in her arms, then sank to the dewy lawn of Audubon Park. Her younger sister, Monique, looked on with obvious envy. She, too, longed to play "Mommy," but was too small to lift Gabrielle.

Dominique wanted to indulge her nieces — they so rarely visited — but she couldn't help tracking every move with her eyes.

Danielle followed her sister's gaze and smiled. "Don't worry. Lana used to be like that with Monique. She's good with little ones."

"They're sweet!" Dominique smiled and shook her head in wonder. Still, she kept her eyes trained on her child. She knew she was overly cautious with Gabrielle, but the birth had been difficult and, after her second miscarriage the month before, Dominique's doctor had discouraged her from having more children. Though the Parkers wanted at least one more child, the fact that it might not be possible made Gabrielle even more precious to Dominique.

In seconds, the restless Gabrielle wriggled free of Lana and began to waddle across the grass.

Dominique and Danielle laughed as the two older girls scrambled after her. When they caught her, each cousin protectively took one of her hands, then led her toward a bed of irises.

Audubon Park, a pleasant stroll from Dominique's house, was a sprawling expanse of green on St. Charles Avenue, across from Loyola University. Each day it was filled with students, promenaders, and mothers with young children. But the park was so big that it never seemed crowded.

"Don't pick any flowers!" Danielle warned. She tilted her head back and inhaled contentedly. "What a glorious day! In New York, it's still cold and raining. You can't even tell it's spring. It's so good to get away for a few days." She looked at Dominique and smiled. "And, of course, Ron's in heaven as long as he can play golf. It was nice of Clay to arrange things at your club."

"Our pleasure. . . ." Dominique stretched her arms across the back of the bench, closed her eyes, and lifted her face to the sun. "This is so relaxing." Her smile became a laugh. "I thought I knew what exhaustion was when I was working, but it's nothing compared to looking after a baby!"

Danielle gave her a sardonic look. "I suppose Clay's as much help as Ron?"

Dominique snorted. "None, in other words. And, of course, he travels so much now. . . ."

The sisters mirrored each other's shrugs of resignation.

Danielle turned sideways on the bench so that she was facing her sister. "Do you miss work?"

Dominique averted her eyes. To admit that she did might sound as though she didn't love Gabrielle as much as she ought, and that wasn't the case at all. She loved her more than anyone on earth. But Dominique did miss the excitement of work, though she was strongly committed to staying home with Gabrielle.

She skillfully sidestepped the question. "I've just been elected chairman of the Heart Fund ball. That will keep me so busy I won't have time to miss work. Besides, it's nice to do something for charity." As Dominique uttered the words, she realized they were absolutely true, and the thought cheered her. Still, there was something about earning a living that was gratifying.

As though reading her mind, Danielle said, "I hope you started your own savings account while you were working." She gave Dominique an accusatory look, clearly guessing the answer.

"Why should I?" Dominique asked impatiently.

"No woman" — Danielle wagged her index finger from side to side — "should rely entirely on her husband for financial security."

Dominique pressed her tongue against the roof of her mouth and made a sound of dismissal. "Believe me, whatever I want, Clay gives me."

Danielle narrowed her eyes. "Then he should open a bank account in your name so you can put aside a little money each week."

"Clay would think I didn't trust him!" Dominique argued.

For a moment, Danielle studied Dominique as though she were a specimen under a microscope. "Have you forgotten what it was like when you left Anton? I would have thought that you would never want to depend on anyone again. At least, that's what you said at the time."

Dominique waved her hand in front of her face as though she were swiping at a gnat. "All that is behind me now. I love Clay!" She turned and looked at the little girls. "We have Gabrielle. A life together. Besides," she pointed out, "a bank account doesn't mean independence. You've been saving for years and you still depend on Ron!"

Danielle squared her shoulders. "But I won't always."

Dominique was growing weary of the conversation. She found it disturbing. It made her think about issues she preferred to bury. She didn't want to remember the lowest point of her life. She didn't want to base her actions on that awful experience. It was easier and more pleasant not to worry about the future. Still, the idea of a bank account wasn't such a bad one. She wondered what Clay's reaction would be. "Well" — Dominique's tone signaled an end to the conversation — "I'll think about it." With a pointed look at Danielle, she added, "I'm sure Clay won't mind."

Danielle lowered her eyes and nodded, but her doubt was evident.

Dominique ignored it and turned to check on the children. She smiled at the sight of them, then closed her eyes and let the sun warm her face.

"Dominique?"

Dominique opened her eyes and looked at her sister. "Yes?"

"I have almost five thousand dollars of my own now."

"You're kidding! How?"

Danielle grinned. "I've been buying stocks."

Dominique laughed incredulously. "But how do you know what to buy?"

Danielle's eyes sparkled. "I go to the library once a week and read all the *Wall Street Journals*. Plus I make sure to read the *Times* every day from start to finish."

"That's wonderful!" Dominique squeezed her sister's hand.

Danielle glanced over at the children, who were happily playing some distance away. Her voice turned furtive. "Sometimes I think that when the girls are grown, I'll leave Ron."

Dominique stared at her. It took a moment for the words to register. "But you've been together fifteen years! I thought you loved him!"

Danielle sighed. "I don't know anymore.... We don't talk. He works so hard and he's almost never home. And . . . in a way I can't blame him. He never wants to be unemployed again and his business is so competitive. But it seems like he never does anything with us anymore. Even when we take a little vacation, he's on the phone to the office five times a day!" She paused, her expression brooding. "Sometimes I think only the girls keep us together."

Dominique studied her sister. "You don't think he's having an affair, do you?" she ventured, her voice dropping to a whisper.

"Never!" Danielle answered immediately. She was silent a moment. "I know he loves me." She gave Dominique a winsome smile. "And he's probably too overworked to even think of it."

Dominique was glad to see Danielle's conviction on that point, at least. Ron was an enigma to her, almost impossible to read. He had none of Clay's gregariousness — not anymore. Nevertheless, Ron had a way of focusing on Danielle, of listening closely to what she said, that had long ago convinced Dominique of his love for his wife.

"He's working for you and the girls," Dominique pointed out.

Danielle considered this. "But what good does it do if you never enjoy the rest of your life?" She shrugged. "I don't know. . . . I suppose it's the nature of his business, but it makes me feel . . . detached from him."

Dominique nodded, thinking this over. "But people don't divorce for reasons like that. It's such a drastic move." She looked at the children. "The girls would be devastated." She shook her head vehemently. "As long as neither one of you is in love with someone else, you can work it out. Besides, if you left him, what would you do? You'd have to work."

Danielle's shoulders slumped. "I know." She absently plucked at her skirt, looking defeated. Then she sat forward on the bench, her legs crossed, her chin propped on her elbow in a reflective pose. "I wish I'd waited to get married. Maybe gone to college like you. To tell the truth, I'm not interested in the kinds of jobs I'm qualified for."

Dominique leaned forward so that her head was on the same level as her sister's. She sensed that Danielle wasn't looking for advice, but rather an outlet for her frustration. She put her arm around her and they leaned against each other companionably.

Danielle stared straight ahead. "Ron and I argue a lot," she confessed, then fell silent for a moment. "Of course, it doesn't help to have Mother there. They're like oil and water."

"I thought you liked having her to baby-sit."

Danielle rolled her eyes. "Ron would rather pay a baby-sitter. He says she puts on airs. I try to tell him that's the way she's always been. Thank God, she goes out a couple of evenings a week. Her cards, you know. Otherwise, I'm not sure she and Ron could stand each other."

Dominique thought about the problem for a few minutes. Suddenly she sat up and grabbed her sister's arm. "Danielle!"

Danielle sat up, too, and stared at Dominique. "What?"

"Why shouldn't Mother come to live with us part of the time? Clay's crazy about her and it would give you and Ron time to yourselves."

Danielle looked bewildered. "But you and Mother don't . . ." She let her sentence fade, though her meaning was unmistakable.

Dominique grimaced. "I know what you mean, but" — she paused — "after the last visit, things seemed a little better. Anyhow, if having her around is jeopardizing your marriage, we should at least try this." Dominique nodded encouragingly. "Clay and I have so much room, I probably wouldn't even notice she was around after a while. And she'll make friends. You know how she is."

Danielle raised her eyebrows and turned down her mouth in an expression that meant "Possibly."

Dominique tilted her head and smiled. "What do you have to lose?"

Danielle gave her a droll look. "I'm worried about what *you* have to lose."

Dominique shrugged. "We can see how she likes it. She'll have another grandchild to occupy her. It can't be *that* bad."

The sisters stared at each other, then burst out laughing. Dominique said, "Okay, maybe it could be, but we'll never know until we try."

"Well, if you don't mind. . . ." Danielle was smiling now, as though a weight had been lifted.

Dominique put out her hand. "Then it's a deal." Danielle shook it. Suddenly, Dominique's smile faded. "The only thing is . . ."

"What?" Danielle's look of alarm was a reflection of Dominique's tone.

Dominique pointed at her sister and said, "*You* tell her."

掓 掓 掓

Life was different with Solange around. There was the downside: the small irritations, the extra responsibility, and the diminished privacy. But over the course of Solange's first year with them, Dominique discovered many advantages. Solange was delighted to look after her granddaughter and would each morning take Gabrielle to the park for several hours. Most of the time, Dominique went with them. But if she had an errand to run, Solange's presence allowed her the free time and she enjoyed it. Dominique had never liked to leave Gabrielle in the care of household help or baby-sitters, but the child's own grandmother was a different matter. And Clay was pleased that they could go out in the evenings whenever they chose.

They entertained more, too. Solange loved parties and was eager to meet new people. After Dominique introduced her to her circle, Solange began receiving invitations of her own. If they were for daytime events, she insisted on taking the streetcar. "I can fend for myself," she told Dominique. "Why should I inconvenience you when the stop is one block away?" Solange liked being able to move about with more independence than in New York, where the dirty subways frightened her.

Best of all, Solange and Dominique enjoyed a more peaceable relationship than in the past, though they still had flare-ups. Together they joined the New Orleans French club, a group of women who lunched together once a month for the purpose of practicing their French. There Solange met several women who enjoyed canasta, and they organized weekly card games. She was named to the club's party committee and transformed the events from sedate monthly teas to long, liquid afternoons in one of New Orleans' splendid restaurants. Attendance went up dramatically and the women went home happy. The next year, Solange was elected president.

As Dominique predicted, Clay and Solange got along like best friends. There were five bedrooms in the Parkers' house and, rather than simply assign one to Solange, Clay insisted she pick her own and decorate it to her taste. Clay warned the decorator not to discuss prices with his mother-in-law; he would take care of everything.

Clay had always been generous, and since his father's death, spendthrift to the point of extravagance. He wanted a superlative lifestyle. His home had to be the most grand; Dominique, the best-dressed woman in New Orleans. Clay insisted that she buy a new gown for each party they attended. And birthdays, holidays, and anniversaries were celebrated with lavish gifts: a sable coat, a mink stole, a new car, a diamond necklace.

Dominique sometimes worried about Clay's spending. She didn't need so many things, she protested. Last year's gowns were perfectly fine.

"Look, we've got the money. Why not enjoy it?" he insisted.

When Solange moved in, Clay seemed pleased to have the opportunity to exercise his largesse on yet another family member. Dominique couldn't fail to be touched, especially as his hospitality helped to smooth her own relationship with her mother.

She was pleased to assure Danielle that things were going well.

February 7, 1964

Dear Danielle,

Thanks for your last letter. Stop worrying. I know Mother hasn't been to see you in over a year but, just as I predicted, Clay is perfectly content for her to live here permanently. If it gets too hot for her in August, she may want to go up to your place for a visit. Last summer, I think the humidity was too much for her. Your new beach cottage sounds wonderful and I know it will be cooler than New Orleans! If Clay can get away from the office, maybe we'll take you up on your invitation, too. But I don't think that's likely. His schedule is more demanding than ever. He's opening a new office in Seattle, so he's out of town on business even more than before — at least twice a month.

How are Ron and the girls? I've enclosed a little thank you note to Monique for the last drawing she sent me. She's remarkably talented. I'm sure she's the best in her class. Mother is so proud of her. She shows the drawing to everyone.

You'll laugh when you hear that Clay suggested we send Gabrielle to art classes after he saw Monique's picture. Can you believe it? She's not quite four, after all. Everything's a competition to him, I'm afraid. Maybe men are just like that. Our next door neighbor, Lance, made his seven-year-old son go duck hunting with him. And, in case you don't know, duck hunting means sitting in a cold, wet marsh for hours, waiting for the poor beasts. Anyhow, the son caught a chill and wanted to go home. So Lance gave him a shot of bourbon and told him to be a man. The little boy fell asleep, and when he woke up he vomited all over Lance's knapsack. I told Lance it served him right. And of course, his wife, Betty Ann — she's the tiny redhead you met at that dinner party we had when you were here — agreed with me. She was furious about it. But Lance wasn't in the least sorry. At least Clay wants Gabrielle to draw, not hunt.

Speaking of differences between women and men, I picked up that Betty Friedan book you told me about, The Feminine Mystique. *Some of my friends here have heard of it, but they think women like her too extreme to take seriously. As for me, I agree that being a wife and mother may not provide total fulfillment for some women, but if I had a choice between my life or one of a single career woman, I'd choose the course I've taken. Maybe some women can do both well, but since none of my friends work, I can't say I've seen proof. How about you?*

By the way, you can stop nagging me about that bank account business. I finally asked Clay if he would mind my having my own savings account. He didn't even look up from the newspaper. Just reached into his pocket and pulled out his checkbook. All he said was "Suit yourself." Of course, I feel ridiculous now for even bringing it up. It seems insulting to Clay and I don't think I'm going to do it. I know you're just thinking of my good, and I appreciate it, but what's right for you may not be right for me.

Well, that's all for now. Kisses to everyone.

Love,
Dominique

∾ ∾ ∾

Dominique opened the French doors of her bedroom and stepped onto the balcony that overlooked St. Charles Avenue. It was just growing dark and the sky was a velvety blue, the moon already high and full — a Mardi Gras moon.

Dominique paced back and forth across the wooden floor, all the while looking down the boulevard for Clay's black Cadillac. Her bead-encrusted sari — she was costumed as an Indian princess — jingled with each step. Impatiently, she leaned over the balcony railing and strained to see past the live oaks and magnolias that obscured her view of the street. No sign of Clay.

Exasperated, she went inside to her dressing area. Why did Clay insist on accepting dinner invitations if he was going to be late? Only that afternoon, he had returned from a trip to Houston, but instead of coming home, he had gone to the office. Tonight, of all nights — the Saturday before Mardi Gras.

A fever pitch of excitement was firing the city. The festivities had begun, and Clay and Dominique, like their friends, would spend the next four days at an unending string of parties. Even now, each time a streetcar rattled by, Dominique could see that it was packed with revelers. They hung out the open windows, letting loose rebel yells. Cars careened by, their occupants heedlessly tossing out empty liquor bottles — there were no prohibitions against drinking and driving in New Orleans. And in the French Quarter, a writhing mass of humanity made the narrow thoroughfares impassable. The weather was unseasonably hot; liquor and crowds made it hotter. Men stripped off their shirts and threw them into the air with abandon. And, occasionally, women did the same.

The parties Dominique and Clay would attend were more rarefied. There would be lavish costumes adorned with heirloom jewels, bacchanalian feasts in the most splendid of private homes and the most exclusive of hotel ballrooms. There would be very little sleep, plenty of champagne, and so much dancing that Dominique knew she would be sore for days afterward.

Tonight, she and Clay had been invited to a sit-down dinner for twenty-four at the home of a neighbor. Afterward, the guests would join a much larger gathering at the Pontchartrain Hotel. Elite though the party was, the guests had paid to attend — all for charity, of course. Dominique, working with two other prominent New Orleans women, had helped organize the event. Such was Dominique's reputation that she had been responsible for the sale of at least fifty tickets.

Dominique no longer felt nervous before her events — they had become second nature. Now the excitement came at the beginning, as she tried to devise a party theme, then turn the vision into reality. Once the planning was done, Dominique knew things would run smoothly.

Still, she wished Clay would hurry. He had known about the Houston trip *before* they had received the dinner invitation. Why hadn't he just let her send their regrets? They could have gone to the party afterward with time to spare. But, of course, she knew the answer. Clay thought every social contact might turn into a business opportunity. He had doubled Parker Shipping's revenues, but he didn't seem satisfied. Dominique thought he behaved as though his dead father were looking over his shoulder, as though Clay still had something to prove.

She sighed and leaned close to the mirror to check her makeup. Then she saw headlights. Dominique abandoned her reflection and hurried downstairs, primed to scold Clay. But as soon as she saw her husband, Dominique's annoyance disappeared. He emerged from the car holding a huge stuffed giraffe with a green bow around its neck.

On cue, Gabrielle came clattering down the stairs. "Daddy!" she cried.

Clay never came home from a trip empty-handed, and the little girl each time drove herself into a fever of excitement as she anticipated her surprise. But most of all, it seemed to Dominique, Gabrielle was glad to see her father. She leapt into his arms, planting a dozen noisy kisses on his cheeks before she turned her attention to the giraffe.

Dominique smiled and went to them. She reached up and pecked Clay on the lips. "Good trip?" she asked, wrapping one arm around her husband, one around her daughter.

"Fine," Clay answered, gently disentangling himself from Gabrielle and setting her on the floor. "Do you remember giraffes from the zoo?" he asked the little girl.

She was four years old, precocious, and always eager to demonstrate her knowledge. "Of course!" she said, in a good imitation of a slightly miffed adult.

Clay laughed at her tone.

Then she became a little girl again and hugged the giraffe's neck. "I'm going to name him . . ." Gabrielle reflected for a moment. "Peanuts, 'cause his spots look like that!"

"Good name, sweetheart!" Dominique said. "We'll have to play with Peanuts tomorrow. But right now, Daddy has to get ready to go out. Why don't you go back to Grand-mère's room and show her your new friend?"

Fifteen minutes later, Clay and Dominique were speeding toward the dinner party. Dominique's resentment was forgotten as she saw that they would arrive only a few minutes after the appointed time.

Clay, too, seemed in an exuberant mood. "Dominique, something's come up that I think you should get involved in," he said in a cheerful tone.

Dominique kept the smile fixed on her face, but inwardly she groaned. How much more could she possibly handle? She was the program chairwoman for the cancer ball, director of volunteers for the cerebral palsy foundation, a member of the French club — and full-time mother to Gabrielle. Nevertheless, she didn't want to dampen the festive mood, so she invited Clay to continue.

"You remember that Mark Patout's running for the Senate, don't you?"

Dominique's stiff smile relaxed into one of genuine feeling as she thought of Mark. Over the years, she had invited him and Nina to dinner several times at Clay's urging. They accepted almost always, but it was clear that Clay would never attain his goal of becoming a close friend of Mark's. Even Clay admitted it, though neither husband nor wife delved into the reasons why. What's more, Nina had only once returned the invitations. Even on that lone occasion, the Parkers had not been invited to the Patout home, but to a large dinner Nina and Mark were hosting in a restaurant. Despite that, Clay considered the couple a stellar addition to any dinner party — especially since Mark had been elected to Congress. Clay encouraged Dominique to invite them again and again. Recently, though, Mark had been occupied with his bid for the U.S. Senate, a perfect excuse for Dominique to stop issuing invitations.

"Of course I remember that Mark's running for the Senate," she answered Clay in a tone of amusement. News about the political race was splashed across the front page of the *Times-Picayune* every day.

"Well, it looks like he'll win. Now's the time to volunteer for the campaign," Clay remarked with gusto, as though hoping to transmit his enthusiasm to Dominique.

Dominique tightened her grip on her purse and stared at her husband in astonishment. "I don't know anything about campaigns!"

Clay laughed and dismissively waved his hand. "You don't need to know anything. All you do is go there and do what they tell you."

Dominique cocked her head. "What do you mean?" she asked doubtfully.

Clay shrugged. "Stuff envelopes, make phone calls, clerical stuff." He kept his eyes fixed on the road. "It's important for us to participate in this," he said. He turned and gave Dominique a pointed look. "It would seem strange if we didn't."

Dominique nodded. She followed Clay's logic and she thought Mark would make a wonderful senator, but she didn't relish the idea of doing dull, repetitive clerical work or, worse yet, making phone calls to strangers to try to drum up support. Her volunteer work was always of a supervisory nature, never a clerical one. Why, then, was Clay assuming that they'd only want her for secretarial work?

"What if . . ." Dominique began haltingly. She was like a bather dipping a toe in the sea, not sure of the water temperature. "What if they found something more interesting for me to do? They must need events organized or —"

Clay interrupted. "They'd never turn that over to you," he said with a regretful shake of his head. "Let me explain how these things work. Housewives like you volunteer all the time for campaigns, and the campaign staff tells you what to do." He paused. "They've got political professionals for the glamour jobs. The people who organize these events know who the important players are, not just here in New Orleans, but all over the state, and even the country. They don't try to make these things flashy or interesting in and of themselves. The purpose is to showcase the candidate."

"It sounds a bit different than what I do with the charities," Dominique admitted.

Clay patted her knee. "You're the best at that, I know. But you're right about this being different. I'm afraid you'll be at the bottom of the totem pole at the campaign, but it'll be worthwhile for us. And I know you support Mark."

Dominique looked out the window and considered saying no. The work sounded dreary and she was so busy! Out of the corner of her eye, she could see Clay, his gaze trained on her. She turned and gave him a look of appeal. "Clay, I'm not sure I have time —"

Clay's lips tightened. "This is more important than those charities," he said harshly.

"But, Clay, I have obligations. I can't just —"

He didn't let her finish her sentence. "They're not paying you, are they?"

Dominique looked at him in astonishment. Clay had always praised her charity work, avowing that the prominence and respect she earned reflected well on him. How could he suddenly brush it off? Stung, Dominique said, "That doesn't mean I should leave in the middle of a project!"

Clay regarded her in sulky silence. Then, all at once, his expression grew appealing. His voice became low and persuasive. "I'm sorry, babe. I know your work is important. But couldn't you get one of the other women to help? I mean, you don't have to step down entirely. All I'm asking is that you give Patout maybe three days a week."

Clay's eyes, as much as his words, softened Dominique.

As though sensing her weakness, Clay pressed on. "I know it's a lot to ask, but . . ."

But, Dominique concluded silently, he really didn't ask her for much. All at once, she was ashamed that she had hesitated to grant his simple request. After all, it would only be for a few months.

Nevertheless, something stopped her from immediately agreeing. Mark had once been extremely attracted to her, she remembered. Would her constant presence now be a strain? She smiled as she realized the absurdity of the notion. Impossible! He was married to a stunning woman. He had probably gotten over Dominique long ago.

ᕲ ᕲ ᕲ

Mark almost didn't realize that it was Dominique — *Dominique* — typing at one of the crowded office's twelve desks. She was obscured by the clutter of cardboard boxes, posters, and desks piled high with paper. Then he stopped in his tracks and did a double take, not quite believing his eyes. That thick, wavy, auburn hair couldn't possibly belong to anyone else.

"That's our new volunteer," his office manager, Sally Devereaux, whispered to him. "Dominique Parker."

Mark stared at the familiar figure. She was wearing a yellow blouse, just as at their first meeting. It was a color he associated with only her, for every other woman he knew claimed to look terrible in it. But Dominique looked splendid.

"I know . . . ," he murmured to Sally. Then, aware of the curious gaze of the office manager, he continued more energetically, "I haven't seen her in months, but I actually know her quite well. Her husband mentioned that she might sign up. I'll go say hello."

Sally looked down at a clipboard she was carrying. "Don't forget, you have an appointment uptown in twenty minutes."

Mark nodded and held up his hand, signaling his assistant to be patient. Then he strode over to Dominique.

She looked up and saw Mark coming toward her, a generous smile on his face. He looked wonderful — more weathered, more becomingly gray; more . . . *adult*. For a moment she reeled at the sheer charisma that flowed from him. She had forgotten the impact of his presence. Now it hit her full force and she gave him a responding smile.

He watched her face undergo a transformation. Her eyes went from serious to sparkling. Her full lips parted in a brilliant smile. Her body straightened and her skin — her marvelous golden skin — came alive with a pink blush.

Without fully realizing what was happening, Mark felt the old emotions stir. Dominique's effect on him was beyond his control. His hand was extended, ready for a handshake, but he instead found himself wrapping her in his arms. He felt the warmth of her body against his. He smelled her light perfume with its hint of gardenia. And everything was as it had been before. He couldn't escape it.

Reluctantly, he withdrew his arms and released her. She was commenting on something in her captivating accent, but it was difficult for him to focus. A hot flush rose in him. He stared at her and tried to regain control of his emotions. He took a step back. He didn't want to feel the heat from her body anymore, nor to smell her perfume. Deliberately, he thought of Nina. Nina, whose icy demeanor was in such contrast to Dominique's radiant warmth. Whose admiration for Mark's position had turned to resentment of the time it required. And here was Dominique, ready to support him.

". . . doing so well in the polls. They say your chances are very good."

He caught the end of her sentence and smiled automatically. "Yes. I think folks are ready for a change." He forced himself to concentrate on the fact that she was a wife and mother. Definitely unavailable. "How's the baby?" he asked.

"Not a baby anymore," Dominique laughed. "I feel that if I spend an hour away from her, I miss a whole stage in her development."

Sally Devereaux sidled up to them and elaborately looked at her watch. Mark laughed. "I think I'm being ordered out of here." He took a step back. "I'll see you later." He tried to sound casual.

"I'll be here!" Dominique said, her voice lively. It was so nice to see Mark again! She had almost forgotten how easy it was to be around him. She never had to measure her words or account for his moods. Around him, she felt unconditionally accepted. For a moment, she reveled guiltlessly in the good feeling he gave her. Then she thought of Clay. Well, of course, it was easy to view Mark as flawlessly charming when she didn't have to live with him, she reminded herself. He could probably be as much of a bear as her own husband, once you got to know him. She had to be careful not to idealize Mark. After all, he was an extremely desirable man. It would be very easy to develop a crush on him. And that was a folly she wouldn't allow.

ᏯᎣ ᏯᎣ ᏯᎣ

When Dominique arrived at the office two days later, it was in turmoil. Aides were scurrying about with frantic expressions and Sally was shouting into the telephone, trying to locate Mark. Dominique wasn't sure what to do next. Cautiously, she picked her way across the office, trying to avoid the staffers that darted back and forth. She collided with one just in front of the desk of Mark's press secretary, Bruno Cartier. The other woman mumbled, "Excuse me," and skittered away.

Dominique heard Bruno say, "There's a reporter nosing around about farm workers' rights. We hear he's got pictures of some shacks over at Whispering Cypress plantation. No running water. Open sewers. That kind of thing. That's only a few miles from the Patouts'. Anyway, he's latched onto the fact that the Patouts have a cane plantation and he wants access to the property! He wants to bring a photographer," he finished ominously.

Bruno was silent as the person on the other end spoke, then he pressed the phone to his chest and yelled to Sally, "When's he coming in?"

"Not till afternoon. He's got a meeting with —"

Bruno didn't wait for her to finish. He went back to his conversation. Dominique hurried to her desk, thinking about what she had heard. She didn't know anything about the issue, but it distressed her to think of people living in the conditions Bruno had described in such an offhand fashion. She wondered if Mark's own workers lived that way. She knew he was wealthy, as was the owner of Whispering Cypress. It didn't seem too much to provide decent standards of living for people who worked the plantation. Dominique sighed. She didn't like to think of Mark as the kind of person who would exploit others. She expected more of him.

Dominique was startled from her thoughts by Sally's voice. "My God!" she heard the office manager exclaim. "The reporter has sent over some of the photographs for our comment. Look at these!" she said with disgust, slapping them on Bruno's desk. Bruno picked up the first one and grimaced. Then he slowly studied the remainder. Dominique could tell that he was deeply disturbed by what he saw. When he was finished, he laid them gently on his desk. He looked reflective for a moment, then he said, "Powerful stuff." He shook his head. "I hope there's nothing like this at Mark's place."

"What are you going to do?" Sally asked.

Bruno rubbed the bridge of his nose and turned down his mouth. "We'll just have to wait to see what Mark says when he gets in."

Dominique was burning with curiosity, but she knew it would be inappropriate to ask for a look at the photographs.

Later, though, when Bruno went to lunch, Dominique wandered to his desk and placed a letter she had typed for him in his "in" box. At the same time, she leaned over to look at the photo lying on the blotter.

She almost gagged when she saw it. Her eyes clamped shut in horror. She gripped the edges of Bruno's desk and braced herself to look again. Slowly she opened her eyes and stared, transfixed. The photo was of two girls, one white, one black. Both children's bodies were covered in filth. The white one's hair hung in long, limp strings to her hips. They were standing ankle deep in mud — at least Dominique hoped it was mud — and they were naked. But they were about eleven years of age — too old to be naked. They stood in front of a tar-paper shack that leaned precariously to one side. The two windows had no panes, nor screens. The door was a burlap flap.

Most shocking, however, were the open sores on the black child's face, flies crawling along their edges. The white child held something in her hand that she was putting in her mouth — perhaps a slice of bread. It was also covered in mud. Slung across each girl's shoulders was a burlap sack filled with cane.

Stunned, Dominique straightened — and found herself face to face with Mark. He could tell that she was deeply shocked. Her face was pale and she didn't even say hello. She took a step backward and stared at him.

"I understand there are some photographs I need to see," he said quietly.

Dominique looked at the pile on Bruno's desk. She stood mutely as Mark picked them up. The room fell silent as the staff waited for his reaction.

"Oh, God!" He gasped and averted his eyes. Then he slumped into Bruno's chair and for a moment sat frozen in that position. Finally, gathering his fortitude, he lifted the pictures. With rapt concentration, he lengthily studied each one. When he was finished, he placed them face down on Bruno's desk and rose.

"That," Mark said, pointing at the photos, "is not to be tolerated. No one should have to live like that. No one." His voice was intense, vehement.

Sally approached him cautiously. "Well, but . . . at Whispering Cypress . . . "

Mark turned menacing eyes on her. Dominique knew he wasn't angry at his office manager, but he appeared unspeakably angry at the conditions he had just seen.

At that moment, Bruno came back, carrying the sandwich he would eat at his desk. He strode up to Mark, but stopped short when he saw the older man's expression. "You . . . you're back," Bruno said lamely.

Mark's eyes burned. "I understand that the reporter who took those wants my comment."

Bruno shifted uneasily. Like everyone else in the room, he knew Mark to be easygoing and good-natured. He had never before seen him so enraged. "Actually . . ." He hesitated. ". . . It's worse. The guy wants to take pictures at your place." Bruno hung his head and mumbled, "If it's anything like that . . ." He gestured at the photos, but didn't complete his sentence.

Mark grew paler still. One by one, he gave each person in the room a glacial, speculative stare. There was not a sound. It was as though everyone were holding their breath. Finally, Mark spoke. "How could any of you work for me if you thought I would treat my employees like that!" he spat.

No one said a word. A few hung their heads.

Mark continued to stare at them. Then he focused on Bruno. "Tell that reporter he's welcome to drop in anytime at Belle Terre. He can visit the school we have there, or the infirmary. He can have lunch in the snack bar, which you can tell him is owned by a former farm-worker. And he's welcome to look in the houses, as long as the people who live in them say it's all right. Tell him that the easiest way to get there is to ride on our bus. It stops every day in New Orleans and Baton Rouge.

"As for my comment on those photos, tell him this: I knew that workers in Louisiana weren't universally well treated, but I had no idea that living conditions like these still existed. Not all plantation owners clear the kind of profit that enables them to provide as well for their workers as we do for ours. We've been lucky. But there's *no* excuse for the conditions shown in those photos. Tell him that I thank him for bringing them to my attention and that my immediate priority in Congress will be to persuade my colleagues to enact laws to outlaw conditions like these. *Before* the election. That's all." Mark glared once more at the assembly, then turned and stalked into his office, closing the door firmly behind him.

Dominique felt a thrill of admiration for Mark. Her estimation of him soared. She was so proud of him. She suddenly wanted with all her heart to help him win his Senate race.

⁊ ⁊ ⁊

Dominique settled into a routine of working at the campaign every Monday, Wednesday, and Friday. Her initial schedule had called for her to arrive at eleven and depart at four. But the paid staff were so impressed with Dominique's office skills that she was always in de-mand. As a result, she found herself coming in earlier and leaving later with each visit. It felt good to be part of the close-knit campaign team. She enjoyed the camaraderie and the frenetic energy. The one rule she set down for herself was to leave no later than five-thirty in order to be home when Clay arrived at six-thirty.

Dominique had barely seen her old friend Mark since she'd begun working for him. He was in Washington a lot and, when he returned on the Thursday evenings, he often went straight to the state capital, Baton Rouge. His schedule was packed with events the campaign manager thought worthwhile, from interviews to Kiwanis dinners. But his presence was always felt.

"Mark wants . . ." Sally would begin almost every sentence with those words.

"Mark says . . . ," Bruno would announce.

"Mark called . . ."

Mark had never struck Dominique as self-centered, so it was odd to see that he was in fact the sun around which the lives of the rest of the staff — his satellites — revolved. His word was law. His wants were anticipated. He was treated with slavish deference.

As Dominique grew accustomed to the office, she found that the new volunteers gravitated to her with their questions. She never made them feel stupid or slow. She was brusque, but not short-tempered like Bruno or Sally. She got a lot done and, at the end of each day, left with a feeling of accomplishment.

"I don't know how we ever survived without you," Sally admitted one day as she handed Dominique revisions for a press release.

Sally rarely stood still, so when she leaned against Dominique's desk and crossed her arms as though she had more to say, Dominique stopped typing and looked up inquiringly.

"I didn't know you were an event planner," Sally said in a tone that was mockingly accusatory, as though she were chiding Dominique for withholding vital information.

"Well, . . . I thought volunteers mainly did clerical work. . . ." She remembered Clay's words.

Sally pushed her glasses up on her nose with her index finger. "That all depends on the size of the campaign staff." She sighed. "Ours is pretty stretched."

Dominique leaned forward and rested her elbows on her desk in a relaxed pose. "Can I do more to help?"

Sally shifted and scrunched up her face as though she had something difficult to say. "Since you ask, . . . as a matter of fact . . ." She hesitated. "You know about the dinner he's having next month for his top advisers, don't you?"

"Yes." It was to be small. Only about fifty people. Anyone could handle a dinner like that, Dominique thought. It didn't really fall into the realm of event planning.

"And you know that we have to start putting together the primary-night party?"

Dominique sat up with a look of alarm. "But that's only six weeks away! You haven't done that yet?"

Sally, shamefaced, shook her head. "We haven't had the time to focus on it."

Dominique was speechless.

"Anyhow, Mark thought you might be able to help. We want you to become part of the paid staff." Sally was gushing as though she were afraid that if she stopped, Dominique would have a chance to refuse. "If you could work full time we'd be thrilled, but I don't know how Mr. Parker would feel about that. So many husbands won't let their wives —"

Dominique held up her hands in a signal for Sally to stop. "Wait a minute! You're overwhelming me!" Dominique laughed. "This is completely unexpected."

Sally smiled self-consciously. "That's because Bruno and I had no idea of your background until Mark told us."

Dominique wondered what he had said. In the beginning, Bruno and Sally had barely spoken to her, not because they were hostile but because they were busy. More recently, they had taken to shoveling all their clerical work on her. But they had never sought her opinion or input. Now all the brusqueness was gone from Sally's manner. Dominique was smart enough to know that the office manager's new demeanor was attributable directly to Mark, and she was tremendously flattered. She looked down and with one hand lightly poked the keys of the typewriter in an absentminded way.

The idea of working full time was appealing. Very appealing. The office was stimulating and her colleagues fun. On the other hand, she didn't like to leave Gabrielle so much. Solange had her own life and it wasn't fair to ask her to give it up so that she could keep constant watch over the little girl. Finally, there was Clay to consider. He was already complaining about how exhausted Dominique seemed at the end of each day. She had twice in the past three weeks asked him to turn down dinner invitations that he considered important. In addition, she had had to give up most of her charity work. She was still chairwoman of the Heart Fund ball, and tried to perform her duties on her free days or on weekends. But it was hard. There just wasn't enough time. She was glad the ball was only two weeks away.

Dominique looked helplessly at the office manager. "Look, Sally, I'm honored that you and Mark would trust me with such important projects and I'd truly like to take the job, but I can't."

Sally's mouth turned down in disappointment. Dominique watched the other woman try to control her urge to argue. Feeling as though she owed her more of an explanation, Dominique said, "Gabrielle is still so young and . . ." She turned her palms up.

Sally peered at Dominique and waited for her to continue. But Dominique remained silent, her expression helpless.

Sally sighed. "That's bad news. I guess I'll have to try to pull things together myself. . . ." She was clearly distressed.

Dominique touched her hand reassuringly. "You don't need to hire me if you want me to organize those events. We can turn over my typing to another volunteer and I can start concentrating on events, but I'll have to report to someone on the regular staff who will ultimately be responsible. Emergencies always come up before these things and I can't always be there to deal with them." Dominique pulled a pencil from behind her ear and picked up a notepad. "I'll also need a couple of volunteers to help with some of the logistics. We need to get started right away." Dominique began to make notes, her thought processes already moving in their familiar organizational patterns.

Sally, suddenly in the position of taking orders instead of giving them, waited quietly for Dominique to finish outlining the next steps she would take.

Dominique looked up at her and said crisply, "Don't worry. I'll have this organized in no time. I can make calls from home, too." She watched the young woman's expression change from anxiety to relief.

໑໑ ໑໑ ໑໑

Clay would be proud of her, Dominique thought, as she mixed a pitcher of lemonade. Proud that Mark Patout held Dominique in such high regard that he was willing to entrust her with the organization of his campaign's most important gatherings.

She glanced at her watch, impatient for her husband to come home so she could share her news. This was the kind of regard he had been seeking when he had asked her to volunteer for Mark's campaign.

Dominique poured herself a glass of lemonade and settled on a lounge chair overlooking the lush back garden — a subtropical Eden created by New Orleans' top landscape designer. She shaded her eyes with her hand and peered up at the second story of the house, wondering if Solange and Gabrielle were still napping. She knew she should wake Gabrielle or the little girl wouldn't be sleepy at night, but she wanted some time alone with Clay.

She stared dreamily at the swaying banana trees until she heard Clay's car pull into the driveway, then she put down her glass and went to the front door.

Dominique smiled as she watched Clay gather his briefcase and jacket from the back seat. His sleeves were rolled up to reveal his strong forearms and his hair was tousled from driving with the window open. He was still as handsome as a matinee idol, she thought. It had been some time since she had truly studied him as a woman meeting him for the first time might.

Dominique descended their front steps to greet him. "Hi, darling!" she said, her voice gay.

Clay's face lit at the sight of her waiting for him. "Hi!" he said. He pulled her into his arms and gave her a long kiss.

He hadn't done that in months, she realized. They were like an old married couple, taking each other for granted. She needed to focus more on him, she told herself as they walked arm in arm into the house. He traveled so much and it seemed something was always distracting her — either Gabrielle or Solange or her volunteer work. She was suddenly glad she had turned down the full-time job at the campaign.

She grinned up at Clay. "I have drinks ready on the terrace," she murmured.

He smiled appreciatively as he slung his jacket over the banister and put down his briefcase. The maid appeared from the kitchen and greeted him, then took his jacket upstairs.

Hand in hand, Clay and Dominique went outside. She poured his martini, handed it to him, then refilled her lemonade glass.

He clinked his glass against hers. "Cheers," he said, pulling off his tie with the other hand. He collapsed onto one of the lounge chairs with a grunt of satisfaction. "Where are the girls?" he asked.

Dominique settled into the chair next to his. "Napping," she said, her voice tender. She turned and rested her weight on one hip so that she was facing him. "How was your day?"

Clay sighed and took a sip of his martini. "Tiring."

"Well mine was exciting!" Dominique said, unable to suppress happy laughter.

Clay stopped the glass midway to his mouth and raised his eyebrows.

"Today the office manager invited me to join the paid staff," Dominique announced, proudly lifting her chin.

Clay didn't react immediately. He lowered his eyelids and nonchalantly took a sip of his drink. Finally, he murmured, "I guess they always need good secretaries."

Dominique's eyes twinkled. "They don't want me as a secretary." She waited for him to ask the implied question. To her disappointment, he said nothing. He was teasing her! Well, Dominique would play along — prolong the mystery. She got up to refill her lemonade glass. Patiently, she watched the pale yellow liquid tumble into her glass, then she turned to face Clay. Now she was enjoying herself. "Well!" she said in a voice of mock frustration, "don't you want to know what they want me for?"

Clay gave her a superior look. "Since you're dying to tell me . . ."

Dominique could tell he wanted to know, even if he wouldn't admit it. She placed the glass on the bar cart and put her hands on her hips in a victorious pose. "They want me for event planning!"

Clay's face was transformed. His brows came together, his expression severe. "What did you tell them?" His voice was sharp.

"Clay!" Dominique stamped her foot playfully, still smiling. "Aren't you even impressed that Mark thinks so highly of me?"

Clay expelled a short, mirthless laugh. "Yeah, if I wanted to be married to a career girl, but I don't! Besides," he jerked his head at the second story. "Have you forgotten Gabrielle? You've always criticized your mother for letting your Nanny raise you. You've always said you weren't going to be like that. If —"

"Just a minute!" Dominique interrupted indignantly. She marched toward Clay until she was standing directly in front of his chair. "You haven't bothered to ask what I told them!" She had been floating on air all day; now Clay had completely deflated her. It was almost as though he was purposely trying to make her feel bad.

Clay took a deep breath, as if he were trying to control his temper. "I assume that you'll put your family first," he said. His voice was cold and cutting, each word crisply set apart from the next. He stood up so that he was towering over Dominique. He looked down at her, his expression self-righteous. "I assume that you told them no."

Why should he take such a hateful tone? Dominique wondered resentfully. It was both patronizing and autocratic. Why should he take her happy news and turn it into a quarrel? She tightened her hands into fists until her nails cut into her palms. "If that's what you *assume*," Dominique hissed, "then why are you so angry?"

CHAPTER 16 ∾

"WE WON'T be seeing much of Mark anymore," Dominique whispered as she and Clay watched him on the podium. They sat at a round table for ten, two of many campaign workers, friends, and fellow politicians there to witness the next step of Mark's political career.

As soon as Mark finished speaking, the crowded ballroom erupted in applause, confetti, and festive music. How different from the scene earlier in the day, when Mark had quietly thanked his office staff for their efforts. To each individual, Mark had personally presented an engraved silver pen. Dominique had thought it a handsome gesture, and so had the others.

Even tonight, Mark seemed the most subdued person in the exuberant crowd. Aside from Nina. Nina briefly rose to his side, issued a restrained smile and wave, then settled once more into her seat, her expression distant.

Clay stood up. "Let's go congratulate him."

Dominique kept a tight hold of Clay's arm, lest she lose him in the throng. On the way to the podium, she introduced him to everyone she knew. And she was proud to see the women's eyes flicker with surprise when they met him. People's husbands didn't usually look this good! she could see them thinking.

Dominique, too, was the subject of much appreciation, but of a different sort.

"I don't know what we're going to do without you!" was the constant refrain from her co-workers.

When Dominique introduced Sally Devereaux to Clay, the office manager told him, "Your wife was indispensable. I've never seen anyone accomplish so much so efficiently."

After Sally moved on, Clay turned to Dominique and said, "They really counted on you around that place, didn't they?"

Dominique's answering smile was effervescent. "You sound surprised. I think you forgot how good I was at my job."

Clay gave her a sheepish look. "I guess so." He heaved a huge, comic sigh. "But all I can say is, I'll be glad to get my wife back."

She stood on tiptoe and kissed Clay lightly on the mouth. "I'll be glad to take a little rest," she admitted. She grinned mischievously. "But, you know, they wanted me to stay on. Work in his office here."

Clay hesitated a fraction of a second, then he laughed and slung his arm around Dominique's shoulder. He pulled her close and said, "No more! I'm kidnapping you! It's my only chance." He paused. "In fact," his expression grew playful, "as soon as we say hello to Mark, let's get out of here. I'd like some time alone with you, for once!"

BOOK TWO

CHAPTER 17 ∽

"I'D LIKE some time alone with you this evening." Clay was calling Dominique from the office, and his tone was serious. Then, more lightly, he said, "Let's have dinner at Commander's, just the two of us."

"But your mother's here and we have to pack for the trip. We won't have time in the morning. The plane leaves at seven-fifty."

Clay laughed easily, dismissing Dominique's objections. "Have Lucy put together a nice dinner for the girls." The "girls" meant Solange, Gabrielle, and Lenore, Clay's mother. "They won't even care that we're gone."

"Clay" — Dominique scolded him affectionately — "you shouldn't call grown women 'girls.' It's not very respectful."

"You women's libbers are so militant!" Clay teased.

Dominique was vaguely irritated, but let the comment slide. She was certainly no militant "women's libber." The phrase made her picture a bra-burning radical wearing granny glasses. Nevertheless, she had discovered feminist views with which she agreed, like equal pay for equal work. Clay either mocked her or grew annoyed when she voiced support for such issues. "Men should get paid more because they have families to support!" he'd once declared. Dominique had protested, "When I worked, I needed to!" Clay had smiled victoriously. "Only before we married. Afterward, you were just working because you felt like it. You can't compare that to a man who's supporting

a wife and kids." The debate had continued for some time, with neither side conceding. Since then, Dominique avoided the subject unless she felt energetic enough to argue.

Clay's voice, distracted, broke into Dominique's thoughts. "Look,
babe, I have to go. Be out front at seven. I'll drive by and get you."

After Dominique hung up, she rejoined Solange and Lenore at the
inlaid gaming table. She had never particularly liked cards, but canasta
was more fun with three players, so, to be polite, she occasionally
played with the older women.

No sooner had she taken her seat and told them of Clay's plans for
the evening than eleven-year-old Gabrielle dashed into the room.

"Bye, everyone!" she said breathlessly. She wore a pair of dunga-
rees, a gingham shirt, and sneakers. Under her arm she carried a skate-
board.

Dominique put down her cards and half stood. "Just a minute!"
Her tone was commanding, but the love she felt for her daughter came
through. When Dominique looked at Gabrielle, her face automatically softened.

The girl stopped and turned to her mother, her short curls bouncing
with the sudden movement. Her face was alive with gamine charm,
her uptilted eyes two blue-green sparkles of light.

"Where are you rushing off to?" Dominique asked with mock se-
verity, sitting back down.

Gabrielle avoided her mother's eyes. She glanced first at her grandmother Parker, then at Solange, both of whom sat at the card table
with Dominique. "Susie's house," she answered guiltily.

"Have you cleaned up your room and laid out the clothes you want
to take?" Dominique persisted.

Gabrielle widened her eyes. "Al-mo-ost." In a singsong fashion, she
made the word three syllables, inserting a pleading note into the last
one.

Solange and Lenore exchanged glances. The two women got along
well. Ever since the death of her husband, Lenore had become a frequent visitor to Clay and Dominique's home. Solange understood
most of what Lenore said to her and Lenore pretended to understand
all of Solange's broken English. Unlike her husband, Lenore had
never learned French.

Both women adored Gabrielle, and they gave the exchange between her and Dominique all the attention of a championship tennis
match.

Now Dominique looked at her wristwatch, then back up at her daughter. "You don't have time to go to Susie's today, but you'll see her first thing in the morning. So go back upstairs and do what I said."

Gabrielle cast down her eyes. "Oh-ka-ay," she said with melodramatic resignation.

Dominique flashed her an amused look. "You're a ham!" she said.

The girl's woeful expression turned into a giggle as she turned and ran from the room.

Lenore raised her eyebrows. "Her room looks like a cyclone hit it," she said primly. "Why doesn't Myrna help her?"

Dominique fought the impatience that rose in her. Lenore behaved as though any flaw of Gabrielle's was surely someone else's fault. And she was the same about Clay.

"Because we want Gabrielle to learn responsibility. She's discovered how much fun it is to have a social life and she's a little distracted, but she should still pick up after herself." Dominique's tone was mild. She would have to spend the next week with her mother-in-law. Clay had arranged for the five of them — plus Gabrielle's friend Susie — to pass the winter school break in St. John, one of the U.S. Virgin Islands. The holidays were difficult for Lenore since the death of Clay's father. For the past decade, she had left on the day after Christmas to visit her widowed sister, Ellen, in Palm Springs. Now Ellen was dead, and Lenore seemed fractious and lost.

Dominique felt sorry for her. Trying to divert the conversation to a cheery subject, she asked, "Are you both finished packing?"

Lenore spoke first. "Almost. Though I don't know what we're going to find in some foreign place that we can't find here." She gestured at their surroundings.

"The water eez beautiful. You weel like," Solange assured Lenore, with a pat on the hand. This would be her third trip to St. John with the Parkers. Clay liked to rent a villa there and Solange enjoyed her little private pavilion, which connected to the main house via a flower-edged walkway. This year, however, they would stay at a resort, for "their" villa had been unavailable.

"I know Clay means well," Lenore continued in a worried tone, "but it's a terrible waste of money."

"He wanted very much to please you," Dominique said, prickly in defense of her husband. "I'm sure you'll enjoy it."

"I don't know," Lenore said skeptically. "All those foreigners . . . "

Dominique stared at her. Lenore was xenophobic in the extreme and, in remarking on it, she seemed to forget that Dominique and Solange were of foreign origin, too. Dominique tried not to take the complaint personally. "St. John is a U.S. Virgin Island."

"You know what I mean!" Lenore said in a pained voice.

Dominique looked down at her cards. "I have to leave after this hand. I need to dress for dinner." She looked at Solange. "Would you like Lucy to make you lasagna?"

Solange nodded absentmindedly. Her attention was focused on her cards. She put down two nines to form a canasta, then gathered it into a pile. She expertly tapped the cards with one hand to make the edges even, then put them beside her other canastas. She casually tossed an extra nine onto the discard pile.

Lenore wrinkled her brow and drew a card. "You'll remind Clay to get the extra suitcase from the attic for me, won't you?" she asked Dominique. She threw down a six.

"Of course," Dominique assured her. "We'll be home early, I'm sure."

"It seems odd to go out the night before a big trip," Lenore said plaintively.

Dominique sighed and picked up the discard pile, then spent a few seconds arranging the new cards in her hands. She swiftly formed two canastas, put the rest of her cards down, and got up. "I'm out," she yawned.

"She always wins," Lenore said to Solange.

Solange nodded and laughed.

Dominique went upstairs to shower and change. When she had finished, she slipped into a chic amber suit, checking her reflection in the mirror. She nodded approvingly, pleased that she was still a size six. Her eyes traveled up to her face and she wondered if she should put on a little makeup. Clay said he preferred a bare face — the natural look that was all the rage. Dominique thought the natural look was better on young girls than on women of thirty-seven. It looked incongruous with the elegant suit. She decided to compromise: a light coat of lipstick and some rouge, but no eye makeup — well, maybe just a touch of mascara.

Dominique smiled as she thought of Clay. It was nice that he had suggested taking her out to dinner. He must have known that it would be a strain for her to spend her vacation with his mother, her mother, and the two girls. He could be so thoughtful.

Dominique twisted the lipstick cylinder and put the wand to her lips. Afterward, she studied the effect. Good, she concluded. It seemed to brighten the color of her eyes and hair. She tilted her head and tried to view herself objectively. Thanks to the humid climate of New Orleans, she displayed no more than a few tiny lines around the eyes. And her sharp, strong features looked more at home on the face of a woman in her thirties than one in her twenties. She could probably pass for thirty-three, she decided. Maybe even thirty-two — no, that was pushing it. Thirty-three, then.

She thought of Clay. He looked much younger than his forty-three years, especially since he had taken up an exercise regimen. Two nights a week, he played squash, and every morning he did sit-ups and push-ups. He had dropped ten pounds, and all their friends commented that he looked like he had dropped five years, too. And there was another side effect: Clay was more interested in sex than he had been in some time. It wasn't that their sex life had ever been in danger of fading away — not by any means — but it had become a hurried thing, squeezed in between their social obligations. That is, until Clay had begun to get back into shape. Dominique smiled. She was glad there was new life in their marriage. She hadn't realized how much she was missing until it had been resurrected.

As Dominique passed Gabrielle's room on the way downstairs, she paused, then lightly tapped the door with her fingernails.

"Who's calling?" Gabrielle's teasing voice, muffled, came through the door.

Dominique laughed. "Mrs. Pistachio," she said, reviving their old game. As a little girl, Gabrielle had become infatuated with certain words, wanting to adopt them as her name.

The door swung open. Gabrielle stood there holding a pair of shorts. "I can't decide whether to take these white ones or the ones made out of jeans material."

"They're both nice," Dominique said, amused at her daughter's newfound vanity. She was growing up!

"I just wanted a kiss goodnight," Dominique said. "You might not be up when we get home."

"Okay. The stuff I want to take is over there." She pointed at a beanbag chair in the corner of the room. Gabrielle had recently asked if she could pick out her own furniture. The pink and white decor of her childhood was too "babyish," she maintained. Now there was new, modern furniture and psychedelic carpeting. The walls were covered with posters, including one from the 1968 musical *Hair*. Clay and Dominique had bitten their tongues, assuring themselves that it was good she was showing initiative.

Dominique looked doubtfully at the pile of clothes on the chair. "That's a lot! I think your father may have to get your blue suitcase down from the attic."

A look of alarm came over Gabrielle's face. "No, don't ask him!" she said quickly. "He'll get all mad. . . ."

"Don't be silly, sweetheart," Dominique countered. "He won't."

Gabrielle hesitated. "Well, . . . don't ask him anyway."

Dominique put her hand under Gabrielle's chin and looked into her eyes. "Gabrielle, your father loves you very much. He'd do anything for you."

"Then why is he always trying to make me different?" Gabrielle burst out. "He wants me to like the stuff he likes and to do everything his way! And he's never happy. If I get five A's and a B on my report card, he wants to know why I got the B." Fear flashed across Gabrielle's face. "Mom" — she hesitated — "I may get a C in math."

So that's what was bothering her. Dominique's eyebrows shot up. Gabrielle had never received such a low grade. "Why?" she asked.

"I can't do fractions!" Gabrielle moaned. She went to the long desk/bookshelf combination that dominated one wall, sat down, and picked up a pencil. Nervously, she twirled it on the desk. "Mom . . . do you have to show Dad my report card?"

Dominique felt her heart melt in sympathy. She remembered the feeling she had had — still sometimes had — of never being able to please Solange. She realized that Clay imposed the same sort of expectations on Gabrielle.

Despite her sympathy, however, Dominique and Clay had agreed to always present a united front to Gabrielle in terms of discipline and expectations. "Gabrielle, your father has to see your report card." Dominique's voice was kind but firm. "In any event, he knows it's due. He'll ask about it."

Gabrielle's expression was worried. "What do you think he'll do when he sees the C? Will he make me go to summer school?" Gabrielle had been invited by Susie's family to accompany them on a camping trip that summer. She had whooped with joy when Clay had given her permission to go.

Dominique sat on the edge of the bed so that her eyes were level with Gabrielle's. "Darling, you may not be learning what you need to."

"But why do I need math in real life?"

Dominique smiled. "You know better than that." She paused. "Besides, you're always saying you want to be a vet. If you want to do something like that, you need to learn math *and* science."

"Then I'll be a movie star," Gabrielle said ruefully.

Dominique couldn't help laughing. "You're too young to know exactly what you want to do, but it's important to learn math now, so you'll understand it when you get to junior high." Her expression became grave. "You know that, don't you?"

"Mom, I'll try to do better, but I'll die if I don't get to go with Susie this summer!"

Dominique leaned forward and put a steadying hand on Gabrielle's leg. "I'll talk to your father about the trip. I'm sure we can think of a way to get your grades up without canceling it."

Gabrielle brow fretted with doubt. "Okay, . . . let's hope so."

☙ ☙ ☙

"Did you get reservations at Commander's Palace?" Dominique asked Clay in happy anticipation as she slid into his Cadillac. The scent of new leather was still strong: Clay never kept his cars more than two years.

Clay smiled. "Sure did."

"Wonderful!" Dominique said. The hundred-year-old restaurant was one of the most popular spots in town; noisy and festive.

She gave her husband a sidelong glance, recalling her thoughts earlier in the evening. "You look handsome," she told him softly. She wondered if he would want to make love later. She hoped so.

Clay briefly looked away from the road, then back again. "You look great, too," he said heartily. Then, he turned and gazed at her more lingeringly. "I love you, Dominique," he said seriously.

Dominique's heart melted. "I love you, too, darling." She touched his arm, then snuggled into her seat with a sense of well-being.

Once at Commander's, they were led to a small crimson dining room furnished with tufted Victorian chairs.

"Cocktail?" Clay asked Dominique.

Dominique patted her stomach. "No, thanks." She was determined to keep her figure, especially now that Clay looked so fit.

"C'mon, I don't want to drink alone." Clay smiled persuasively. "How about a Ramos gin fizz?"

Dominique dimpled. "I guess it won't hurt just this once."

Clay grinned and nodded his approval.

A few moments later, the drinks were in front of them.

Clay held up his glass. "Cheers." He took a sip without waiting for Dominique's response.

Dominique savored the scent of orange blossoms as she brought the frothy white cocktail to her lips. "Mmmm, I haven't had anything this good since we took that trip to San Francisco."

"Speaking of trips," Clay said, "are we all packed?"

"Almost," Dominique said with an air of accomplishment. "Lenore needs the extra suitcase from the attic, and I'll have to check on Gabrielle when we get home."

The waiter brought their menus. As Dominique started to open hers, Clay said, "I'd like to talk to you for a moment before we order."

Dominique looked up at him, curious. She closed her menu and laid it down.

"Dominique . . . ," he uttered, then stopped. He pulled at his collar as though his tie were too tight.

Dominique's puzzled look turned to one of exasperation. Was he going to tell her that he couldn't make the trip after all? Over the years, he had canceled so many family trips! There was always a business emergency. "Is it work?" Dominique asked, her jaw tightening with annoyance.

"Dominique" — Clay's eyes locked onto hers — "after the trip, I'm moving out of the house."

Dominique held her breath and remained completely immobile. The room was so noisy! Clamorous. She couldn't have heard correctly. Clay's voice was incomprehensible — the drone of an overhead plane. His face was spinning into a blur. Spinning while little black spots burst in front of her eyes.

"Dominique! Listen to me!"

Clay's voice pierced the fog. His face came into focus. Dominique stared at him, her mouth half open, her breath coming in short gasps. Soon she would wake up from this nightmare. She sometimes had vivid — terribly vivid — nightmares.

"I don't understand. . . ." Dominique's voice echoed in her own ears. It sounded hollow.

Clay's face took on a familiar expression of irritation. He turned his eyes away from her and put his thumb to his mouth, biting hard on the nail.

Dominique sat rigid, unable to do anything but stare. Unable to move the conversation forward. Because she had misunderstood. There had been a mistake.

Clay shifted in his seat and inhaled deeply, then he brought his eyes back to Dominique's. His gaze was intense, demanding her attention. "Dominique, I need some time to myself. I need to get away. I've got some thinking to do. You have to understand." His voice was firm, deliberate.

Dominique seized on one of his phrases. "You need to go away for a while?" Her heart was thudding, thudding against her ribs like a kettle drum pounding inside her. The feeling threatened to overwhelm her. She wondered if she was having a heart attack. Her whole body hurt — a pain that had no center. It simply engulfed her.

Clay leaned into the table as though proximity would impart understanding. "Dominique, I'll always love you, and I intend to make sure you're provided for. You don't have anything to worry about."

Nothing to worry about? Her world was falling apart. It was disintegrating. She wanted to fight, to hold it together with sheer physical will, yet she felt powerless.

"Why?" she whimpered.

Clay's eyelids came down. "I just need time to myself." He shook his head. "I feel trapped."

Comprehension began to dawn on Dominique. A sickening image filled her mind. "Are you having an affair?" she blurted.

Clay looked furtively around the room. "Keep it down, will you?" he said between clenched teeth.

"Are you?" Dominique's voice was strident.

"No!" Clay whispered insistently.

The nerves in Dominique's face jumped. Her lips trembled. She felt as though her whole face would start twitching uncontrollably in another second. "Then why?" It came out as a sob. She hadn't meant to cry, but there were tears spilling down her face.

Clay hastily reached into his breast pocket and pulled out a handkerchief. He shoved it across the table to her. "Why don't you go to the ladies' room and get hold of yourself." His voice was rough, impatient, as though her reaction were inappropriate.

Ignoring the handkerchief and his command, she asked again, "Why?" She shook her head as she spoke, still not believing that she had correctly understood. "You said you loved me. You tell me every day. . . ."

Clay cradled his forehead in one hand and took a deep breath. Then he dropped his arm to the table with a thud that shook the silverware.

Out of the corner of her eye, Dominique saw the waiter approach and Clay wave him away. She picked up the handkerchief and dabbed at her eyes, then crumpled the fine linen into a tight ball and raised her eyes to Clay's.

"You said you loved me," she repeated. Her voice, still choked with tears, was accusatory.

"I do." Clay defended his betrayal. "I just . . ." He looked at the ceiling.

Dominique watched him intently, breathlessly waiting for him to continue. Waiting for him to offer her hope. Waiting for him to present an argument that she could counter with logic.

But when he finally met her eyes, she saw nothing there but sympathy. And when she looked at his mouth, it was tight with irritation.

Dominique's face broke into a hot sweat. The room tilted crazily. She felt rubbery, about to collapse. She clutched the corners of the table hard — so hard that her knuckles turned white with the effort. She watched them protruding in a neat row that made her think of gravestones. Then, suddenly, she knew she had to escape. She jerked her chair backward and stood up. Grabbing her bag, she ran from the room. She scurried down the stairs as though she were fleeing an assassin. She bumped into a waiter and heard a crash, but kept running. People turned to stare. A face appeared in front of her, the mouth an O of surprise. Hands clutched at her, trying to stop her. Still she ran.

She burst out of the double doors that marked the restaurant's entry. The Cadillac was there, right in front. Clay always tipped generously for just that privilege. She searched frantically in her purse for the extra key. She felt the cold metal and wrapped her palm around it as though it offered salvation.

Then she was in the car, the warm leather offering familiar comfort.

She turned the key and stepped on the gas. She drove, much too fast, through the narrow streets of the Garden District. She drove and drove, her mind too numb with shock to reason properly. Uptown, then downtown. As long as she kept driving, she didn't have to confront the reality of what Clay had told her. She saw neighborhoods she'd never before seen. She got lost often, but kept driving until she found herself on familiar streets. Finally, when she noticed that she was almost out of gas, she turned toward home.

Clay was waiting for her in bed. She stopped on the threshold, stunned by the sight of him in so ordinary a situation. He threw back the sheets. "I was just about to call the police," he said in an aggrieved voice. "I was worried sick!"

Her heart pounded with hope. He cared! He had changed his mind! Why else would he be in their bed?

"Clay," she sighed with relief.

"Get to bed," he ordered. "We have to catch an early flight tomorrow."

Dominique went limp with relief. "We're still going then?"

"Of course!" Clay said in an annoyed tone. He turned away from her and got back into the bed. "I wouldn't disappoint everyone by canceling. And I'd appreciate it if you'd keep things to yourself until afterward. I don't want to ruin Mother's vacation."

"Mother's vacation?" Dominique repeated stupidly, her blood rising. Who gave a damn about that!

"There's plenty of time to tell her when we get back," Clay said with finality. He picked up a magazine from his nightstand.

The breath went out of Dominique. She fixed Clay with an incredulous stare. "You expect me to go on this trip and behave as though nothing has happened?" Her voice was shrill.

Clay looked at her coldly and replied in a low voice, "First of all, don't shout. You'll wake the whole house. Second, I don't see any option." He paused and looked thoughtful, as though trying to muster his most persuasive argument. "You don't want to ruin Gabrielle's holiday, do you?"

Gabrielle mustn't know! She would be shattered. And there would be the humiliation of explaining to Susie and her parents. It was unthinkable to back out now! But to go on the trip with Clay, to share his bed as though nothing were amiss, that seemed equally abhorrent. How was she supposed to behave with him? How was she supposed to undress in front of him? Sleep in the same bed? Unless . . . unless there was still some hope of changing his mind. Maybe what was bothering him had nothing to do with her really. Maybe it was something at work or maybe he was simply depressed. A change of scene might do him good, make him see things through new eyes. Dominique's heart beat faster at the thought. It was possible that he would change his mind. After all, a man didn't just walk away from his family without a second thought.

Dominique was beyond pride — all she could think of was how to hold Clay. If she was loving and gay, if he had a wonderful time, wasn't it possible that he would want to stay? That he would realize that he was making a terrible mistake? Suddenly, Dominique felt giddy with hope. She would be extra nice to her mother-in-law. She would make sure that everyone got along. She would see that things went smoothly. She wouldn't nag or complain. She would do all that Clay asked. Anything to make him change his mind.

CHAPTER 18 ෴

DOMINIQUE shook the sand out of her espadrilles and set them neatly on the tile patio, then opened the French door and entered the hotel room. It was decorated in soothing tones of peach and sea blue, so airy that it remained cool even in the heat of midday. Despite her troubles, Dominique couldn't help but feel a sense of sheer physical well-being. It seemed as though she were suspended in an unreal place and time where everything was perfect. The sun was turning her a lovely bronze. She enjoyed long walks each day on the pristine white sand, and swims in an ocean as clear and warm as a swimming pool. When she avoided thinking about the future, she was almost happy.

Clay seemed happy, too. He was solicitous of everyone's enjoyment. He generously handed out quarters to Gabrielle and Susie so that they could buy Cokes. He hired a driver to take Solange and Lenore sightseeing. He carefully arranged the beach umbrella over Dominique each morning before he departed for the tennis court. At noon, he reappeared showered and changed to take everyone to lunch, then spent the rest of the day with his family.

Dominique slid out of her bathing suit and headed to the shower. She was to meet Clay at half past noon for lunch — her first lunch alone with him since their arrival seven days before. The mothers and the girls had wanted one last shopping excursion to the neighboring island of St. Thomas before they had to depart.

Dominique sighed as she thought of going home. Back to reality. Then what? She couldn't believe that Clay would move out. He had seemed so content in the past week. Dominique had carefully refrained from asking about his plans. A superstitious part of her believed that if she didn't speak of his leaving, he wouldn't. And it seemed to be working. Not once had Clay discussed the subject. Maybe he had changed his mind. Maybe his announcement prior to their vacation had been an effort to jolt Dominique into . . . into what? Being more attentive? She furrowed her brow as she considered this. It was true that her volunteer work sometimes cut into their free time. Did he resent that? Did he want her to be more seductive? Sex was more frequent lately, but it was the comfortable, unsurprising sex of a long-married couple. Until this week.

Dominique turned on the shower and let the water cool her sun-heated skin. She soaped herself absentmindedly as she thought of the past few days. Clay had been . . . different. She had expected him to be distant and impatient. She had expected their time alone to be stilted and uncomfortable. She had not expected him to touch her. Instead he made love to her almost every day. She had struggled with herself over whether to refuse him. Why should she permit him relations that he said he no longer wanted? And yet . . . what better way to bring him closer, to show her love? Each touch of his hand on her body seemed to reaffirm that they belonged to each other. Each shuddering sigh from him, each emptying of his seed into her, made Dominique feel she had a claim on him.

Knowing that she might lose Clay, Dominique looked at him with new eyes. Suddenly he seemed more desirable than he had since their courtship. He didn't share many thoughts with Dominique, and that elusiveness added perversely to his attraction.

Despite Dominique's suppressed anger and hurt, their lovemaking was more intense and creative than it had ever been. Clay touched her in new ways.

Now, as Dominique rubbed herself dry with a fluffy white bath towel, she blushed to remember their lovemaking in the torpor of the previous afternoon. The sun had filtered through the slats in the windows as the overhead fan cooled their bodies. They had been salty from the ocean. Without bothering to shower, they had tumbled on the bed, Clay hard even before he removed his bathing suit. He had kissed her breasts as he always did, then, to her surprise, had moved his head lower and lower until his mouth was at the very center of her.

Dominique had been shocked at first. What had come over him? Why was he only now doing something he had not even done in the happy first days of their marriage? At first, she was terribly self-conscious. Would he enjoy it? Should she stop him? But with an expertise Dominique would not have thought he possessed, he lulled her into acceptance, then excitement. She abandoned herself to him, throwing her head back on the cool pillow and accepting his offering. Why not? She wanted it. She wanted to take it from him. She wanted him to exert himself solely for her pleasure. He owed her that.

She let him melt into her. Let him tantalize her, bring her to the brink of orgasm, then retreat to delay the final moment. Never had he shown such finesse, such sensitivity for what she was feeling. Never had his timing been so perfect. Finally, when she thought she could bear the suspense no longer, when she was drowning in sensation, he brought her to a climax more resonant than she had ever experienced.

"Clay!" she gasped.

It took a long time for the tingling waves of pleasure to recede. When they did, Dominique was limp, drained of energy. She lay with her eyes closed. Clay, his head on the pillow next to hers, gently caressed her. Guilty for her selfish pleasure, Dominique pulled Clay closer, a signal that he should move on top of her, though she would have been as content to simply go to sleep. But Clay was moving inside her, no longer able to wait. Dominique wrapped her arms around her husband, overcome with bittersweet emotion. It wasn't possible that he could make love to her this way if he intended to leave. It was clear that he loved her, wasn't it?

As Dominique remembered the moment, she realized she was crying. She, who cried so rarely, had cried often in the past week. Impatiently, she turned on the water in the wash basin and splashed her face. She had to meet Clay in half an hour, but it would be better if she went to the lobby now. It wasn't good for her to be alone in the room.

She wended her way down a flagstone path through tropical foliage to the main building — or "great house," as it was called in colonial tradition. Dominique knew there were many other guests at the hotel, but the only sounds she heard were the gentle rolling of the surf and the clicking of palm fronds as the breeze passed by. They were peaceful sounds and they acted as a balm to Dominique's troubled emotions.

An entirely different mood was evoked by the great house. The lobby, open to the breeze on two sides, was furnished in the English style, with heavy mahogany furniture. Even the two telephone booths, which stood at the far end of the room near the entrance to the restaurant, were mahogany paneled enclosures. Usually there were several men waiting in line to use them, for the guest rooms had no telephones.

Dominique glanced at her wristwatch. Still twenty minutes until Clay was due. She glanced around at the various furniture groupings in the room, deciding where to sit. Most were for six or eight guests and were already occupied. Only the plump chintz sofa near the phone booth was meant for two.

The sleeve and brass buttons of a navy blazer emerged from one of the booths, whose occupant had left the mahogany door open. However, no other anxious businessmen hovered nearby waiting for a chance to call their offices, so Dominique wandered over to the little sofa and sat down.

"I know it's a bad connection." The voice, muffled and distorted by the mahogany walls, was barely intelligible. "I'll try to talk louder, but this phone booth is stifling and I don't want to shut the door."

Dominique discreetly ignored the conversation. She leaned forward and picked up a magazine from the coffee table. It was one of those expensive English journals with thick, glossy pages and vivid photographs of country manors.

"I miss you, too, darling. I've been going crazy. I can't wait to get back!" The disembodied voice floated out to Dominique.

She put down the magazine. With a quizzical expression, she looked at the phone booth. A cold jab of fear: Was that Clay? Hard to tell through the partition. Maybe she was imagining the resemblance. She hesitated. Should she look? If it wasn't Clay, she would be terribly embarrassed. She stood. Indecisive, she stared at the mahogany wall of the phone booth. What if she just wandered by and pretended she was going to the next booth? She started to move forward, then she heard the voice again.

"Of course we don't! The room has two beds. I told you, all that's over between us! I only went through with this because I didn't want to disappoint my mother and Gabrielle. As soon as we get home, I'm moving in with you."

Dominique was rooted to the spot, stupefied. She turned a sickly pale yellow. Cold sweat erupted on her face, but she felt unbearably, suffocatingly hot. She took two jerky steps. Blindly, she reached forward. The cool mahogany was under her fingers. She braced her palms against the wall for support and leaned against it, willing herself to take a breath.

"I love you, too," she heard Clay say tenderly. So tenderly. Just as he had once spoken to her.

Suddenly she had a vision of Clay above her the night before in bed, gazing at her with lust and, yes, love. She felt a spasm in her stomach, then the taste of bile in her throat. She had to find the powder room or she would humiliate herself right in the lobby. She shoved herself away from the phone booth and spun. With a resounding bang and a scrape of wood, she collided with the coffee table. Her shin screaming with pain, she lurched past it and scurried down the hall. Frantically, she shoved the bathroom door open. Then she collapsed on the floor in front of the toilet and spewed the contents of her stomach into the bowl. Gasped. And then vomited again.

When the spasms subsided, Dominique shakily pushed herself to her feet, flushed the toilet and — clutching the sink for support — dropped the lid and sat down. She leaned forward, her elbows on her knees, her head in her hands. She felt faint, completely without volition or control. A great, shuddering sob exploded inside her and she moaned, "Oh, God!" Her agony was so great that it seemed dying would be better. It was like a living creature slamming upward into her chest, encompassing every negative emotion: betrayal, anger, hatred, fear, and despair.

Clay's lies! He had sworn that he wasn't having an affair. Over and over. Dominique thought of him in bed with another woman. Who was she? That he could touch another woman as he had his own wife — murmur the same endearments, perform the same acts — sickened Dominique. She thought of what he'd done the previous evening. Something he'd never done before. The other woman's style of lovemaking! And he had tried his new technique on his wife! How could he! How could he!

The contents of Dominique's stomach surged upward again and she was barely able to get her head over the sink in time. She clung to the cool white basin for support, sure that her trembling legs would give way if she let go. Yet she wanted nothing more than to return to her room and scrub her body under the shower. Scrub away the filth of the other woman. He had made love to that stranger, then he had come home and made love to her! The idea was revolting. Why hadn't he simply left Dominique alone? But Dominique knew the answer. The affair had given him new sexual energy. He had been more stimulated than ever. He had derived a secret thrill from making love to two women. He had never felt more virile, Dominique was certain. He had taken up exercise and bought new clothes to make himself yet more desirable.

And Dominique had succumbed. Knowing that he planned to leave her, she had still let him make love to her! The degradation!

Yellow liquid spurted up from Dominique's stomach and she heaved helplessly over the sink, tears stinging her eyes. There was nothing left in her stomach, yet her body continued to be wracked by uncontrollable spasms.

She had to get to bed — couldn't remain upright. She didn't have the strength. She fumbled for the tap and turned it on, splashed cool water on her face. She let the water run until the yellow bile had vanished down the drain.

Dominique lifted her head and looked in the mirror. She wiped away a bead of yellow from the corner of her mouth. Her eyes were hollow, her face pale and worn-looking. She turned away and grasped the doorknob, then hesitated. If only she could simply stay in the little powder room and never have to face reality. Once outside, she would have to deal with her life — an unbearable thought.

Ever so slowly, she turned the knob and opened the door. Directly opposite her stood Clay. He wore a stricken expression. His tan had drained away.

"You overheard. . . ." His voice was resigned.

Dominique stared at him, hating the sight of his handsome face. She wanted to hurl herself at him and tear at his skin. She wanted to pummel him with her fists until she had no energy left. She wanted to humiliate him as he had humiliated her. And yet she felt too weak to make a move. Too weak even to speak.

Clay took a step toward her, concern on his face. He reached for her arm, but Dominique recoiled.

"Get away! You make me sick!" she hissed. From somewhere inside her, she found the strength to walk past him, through the lobby, and back to their room.

ல ல ல

Their last night in St. John was hell. Dominique pled illness and stayed in the room, forcing Clay to host dinner. When he returned, he found Dominique in bed. A pillow and blanket, obviously meant for him, rested on the sofa.

Dominique hadn't spoken since their encounter outside the bathroom. But now she pushed herself up to a sitting position and asked, "Who is she?"

Clay walked toward the bed and prepared to sit down.

"Don't sit there!" Dominique's voice slashed through the air.

Clay, looking startled, straightened. He faced Dominique.

"Who is she?" she repeated coldly.

"Marie Annis," Clay said flatly.

"The decorator?" Dominique asked incredulously.

Clay nodded, a single crisp motion of his head.

"The one who wears all the makeup?"

"She's very stylish," Clay said defensively. "She has to be in her job."

Dominique threw back the covers and sprang out of bed. She pushed past Clay, then, when she reached the space beyond the foot of the bed, whirled to face him. She pointed an accusing finger at him. "She's young enough to be your daughter! How old is she? Twenty-five? twenty-six?" Dominique had an image of the slender young brunette. She was undeniably chic, in a steely, New York sort of way. She wore her hair in a severely cut, shiny dark pageboy. Her makeup was always precisely applied in strong, dark colors. She had a slender, tall, well-proportioned figure, which she showed off in clothes that were ultrafashionable, yet a little too sexy to be entirely businesslike.

Clay, obviously stung, answered, "She's twenty-eight and she loves me!" He jammed his fists into his pockets and stuck his jaw out defiantly.

Dominique slammed her palm to her chest. "What about me? *I* love you! What about Gabrielle and the rest of the family?"

A look of impatience crossed Clay's features and he turned his head away. "It's not the same. . . . Marie's given me back . . . passion. She's made me —"

Dominique interrupted, her voice scornful. "She's made you feel young! That's all! It's nice having a twenty-five-year-old pet idolize you. It makes you forget —"

"She's twenty-eight!" Clay cried. "And it has nothing to do with age. I love her! She's the person I've been looking for all my life."

Dominique marched toward Clay until she was standing directly before him. "I thought," she spat, "that you stopped looking when you married me."

Clay curled his lip with annoyance. "Don't be so literal!" Now it was his turn to stride past Dominique. She pivoted to follow his progress. He went to the armoire and withdrew the bottle of port that the hotel supplied to its guests. With a harsh clank, he slopped some of the deep ruby liquid into a glass and took a long swallow.

"Clay!" Dominique's voice was demanding.

He turned to face her.

"This woman is everything you've always made fun of. She's cold and always overdressed and over made up. I don't understand."

Clay's eyes softened in an expression of pity. "I know you don't," he said softly.

The pity was too much for Dominique to bear! That was worse than anger, worse than defiance. Pity! "Clay!" she cried. "This can't be anything more than a passing thing." Her voice betrayed her desperation. Men had affairs. She hadn't thought Clay would do it, but he had. Still, it was impossible that he would leave her for that woman.

Clay drained his glass, then refilled it. He brought it to Dominique and handed it to her. She shoved his arm away, not caring that the liquid sloshed onto the tiles.

Clay looked surprised by the violence of her gesture. Abruptly, he sat down on the edge of the bed, his shoulders wearily slumped. He looked down at his glass, then drained the liquid that remained there.

Clay's passive attitude infuriated Dominique. She wanted his involvement. She wanted him to look at her. To explain. She raised her voice bitterly. "What could you possibly have in common with her?"

His head remained down as he replied, "Our ambition, our outlook on life. We have . . ." Now his eyes sought Dominique's and begged her for understanding. "The passion between us is magical."

Dominique felt her stomach lurch in disgust, humiliation, betrayal. She had to get hold of herself or she would be sick again. She swallowed and said with stiff dignity, "We've never had a problem in that area." She dared him to deny it.

Clay stood up and began pacing. "It's not the same," he murmured. He stopped near the armoire, turned, and looked at Dominique standing at the bedside.

Dominique didn't want to know more. Couldn't ask. It was too savagely hurtful. Instead she focused on another point. "Is she going to give up her work for you?" she asked sarcastically, her voice trembling.

Clay made a noise of exasperation. "Of course not. She has a career!"

Dominique's mouth dropped open. For a moment, it was impossible to formulate a coherent thought. Then she burst out, "You didn't want *me* to work!"

As though explaining things to a child, Clay replied evenly, "Marie and I have an equal relationship. I don't tell her what to do. She's too independent for that."

Dominique gasped and crossed the floor until she was standing directly in front of Clay. "You bastard! How can you say that to me?" Her voice rose to a shrill pitch. Her arms slashed downward to punctuate each word. "After your father died, you plagued me about working! You wanted me at home. What's so different now?"

"Marie and I don't have a child for one thing!" Clay riposted, his voice also rising. He looked at the glass in his hand and went back to the armoire to refill it. He took another long swallow, then began to speak more calmly. "She's a very creative person. To deprive her of work would be to deprive her of the very force that makes her what she is. You never had her creativity. You were simply working until you had a child."

"That's a lie!" Dominique shot back. How could he distort their common history that way? She had been as creative an event planner as Orman's had ever had. And since then, her reputation had grown. Just because she didn't get paid, Clay didn't value it? How had her skill been so downgraded in his eyes? Dominique wanted to argue, but she was choked by emotion. Clay thought so little of her that he couldn't even acknowledge her talent! And since when had that been a criterion for Clay's admiration? He didn't want a "career girl." Or so he had always professed.

"Look," Clay said gently. He took a step toward Dominique, but didn't touch her. "There's really nothing to argue about. We've just grown apart."

"Grown apart?" Dominique shrieked. "We planned our lives together! Since I got pregnant and quit work, when have we disagreed?" She threw up her hands in a wild gesture of bewilderment. "You were happy with our entertaining, my volunteer work." Dominique counted off the list on her fingers. "I supported the expansion of your business, even when it meant you had to travel so much —" She stopped short. It suddenly struck her that Clay's numerous business trips might have been fabricated. Boiling rage welled up in her.

Before she could hurl the accusation at him, Clay cried, "Don't you see?" He put down his glass and spread his hands in a gesture of appeal. "Marie has her own life, independent of mine. And I need a woman like that." He put one hand to his throat, the other he balled into a fist. "If I stay with you, I'll feel ... I don't know ... stifled."

"Stifled!" Dominique mocked bitterly. She put her fists on her hips. "By your own family? When have I ever questioned you or tried to prevent you from doing something you wanted?"

"It's not you!" Clay backpedaled, and his voice became soothing. "I just need —"

Dominique couldn't listen. "*You need!* I'm sick of hearing about what you need!" She put her hands on her hips. "What about your family? What we need?"

Clay turned away and resumed his pacing. "You'll be provided for," he said stiffly.

"Oh, I know that!" Dominique said in a threatening tone. "But I'm not talking about money." Now her tone grew insistent. "I'm talking about the fact that you have a daughter who needs you. And a mother. And I'm ..." Dominique's voice broke. She couldn't continue. She loved Clay. He and Gabrielle were the focus of her life. Dominique couldn't imagine her life without him. "I need you, too, Clay!" she cried.

Clay came toward her and wrapped her in his arms. Dominique knew she should push him away, but she hadn't the strength. She put her head on his shoulder and wept. It was so comforting to be held by him. How many times had she cried like this against his shoulder? There had been the miscarriages. The car accident that had resulted in a broken leg for Gabrielle. The time Solange had been in the hospital with pneumonia and the doctors had thought she might die. Clay had been there to comfort Dominique every time. Now he was the cause of her heartbreak, yet it was difficult not to seek him out for comfort. He was her husband, her ally, her friend.

Clay caressed her hair and murmured soothing words. She wrapped her arms around his waist. Why couldn't they simply stay this way forever? How could he be so tender and caring if he didn't love her anymore?

Clay rubbed her back, then raised his hand so that he was gently massaging her neck. That always made her relax. Released the tension from her stiff muscles. Clay cradled the back of her head with his fingers, all the while rubbing her scalp in a comforting way. Dominique let her head relax against his fingers. She hadn't had any of the port, but her emotions were so intense that she felt almost drunk.

Clay slipped his hands under the straps of Dominique's nightgown so that they fell from her shoulders to her upper arms. He massaged her shoulders. He slid his hands slowly up and down her arms. The straps of Dominique's nightgown fell further. With a barely perceptible movement, Clay slid the straps all the way down. The bodice of the nightgown clung to Dominique's breasts. Clay slid his hand around Dominique's waist, up over her shoulders, and pushed down the stiff material of Dominique's bodice until it was barely held aloft by her erect nipples.

Dominique sighed. She felt drugged. Engulfed in an unreal world. A buried part of her consciousness cried out for her to put a stop to Clay's seductive stroking, but she didn't want to listen to reality. She wanted to be held in the arms of her loving husband and to believe that all would be right. Clay gently eased his index fingers into the space created by the gaping bodice and pushed the material down. Dominique stood with her full breasts exposed, the breeze from the overhead fan teasing her nipples deliciously. Clay lowered his head to Dominique's breasts and ran his tongue over them. Then down the center line of her torso, pulling the nightgown down as he sank to his knees.

For a brief moment, Dominique was aware of the irony that Clay should find her desirable even as he claimed not to want her. But it was only a brief moment. She was lost in sensation. Clay gave one final tug and the nightgown fell in a puddle at Dominique's ankles. He stroked her calves, the backs of her knees, and her thighs. His fingers ran teasingly up her leg, making her grow moist with desire. He teased the opening between her legs, then, for the second time in their lives together, Clay moved his mouth to the same place.

Dominique started as his tongue touched her. Suddenly, reality came crashing in. He was doing to her something he had learned with that whore! He was performing the most private act possible, only he hadn't kept it private, he had squandered it on another woman. Had done it first to her!

Dominique shoved Clay's head away and took a step backward. "Don't! Don't make love to me while you think of *her*!"

Clay, still on his knees, looked up at Dominique with a stunned expression. "But it's not like that!" he protested. "You're two different people. I still care for you!"

"Care for me!" she said scornfully. "If you cared you wouldn't be leaving!" She bent down and snatched her nightgown from the floor. She covered herself, first with the nightgown, then with the stolid terry cloth robe that lay at the foot of the bed. She wanted to hide her body. She was filled with shame and self-hatred at her malleability in Clay's hands. She had been so weak. How could she have degraded herself that way? Her face turned crimson as she thought of her passion. How eager she had been to please Clay, to be close to him. She was like a dog, she thought to herself. A stupid, ever-loyal, panting dog! She wanted to throw herself face down on the bed and scream into the pillow. But her dignity was already in ruins. She wouldn't add to the destruction.

She stood before Clay and said fiercely, "Don't touch me again!"

Slowly, Clay rose to his feet. His face wore an expression of bewilderment, as though Dominique's mood had changed too fast for him to comprehend.

"I'm going to bed," Dominique snapped. "You sleep on the couch."

"But that's silly —" Clay began.

Dominique glared at him, her eyes blazing.

"All right," he murmured.

Dominique clicked off the light before he was halfway across the room. In the darkness, she turned her face into the pillow. Buried in the cool, white softness, she cried silently to herself.

CHAPTER 19 ∽

DOMINIQUE sat huddled in the bed and stared at the gaping door of Clay's closet. He'd been in too much of a hurry to close it on the way out. Marie had been waiting in the car.

How dare he bring her here! Dominique tortured herself with the thought. Marie, in Clay's Cadillac, in Dominique's place beside him. Clay couldn't have considered the effect of such an action on his wife's feelings. He couldn't have been so deliberately cruel. Could he?

Yet he had been cruel. Cruel in his haste to leave the home he had so coveted once. Cruel in the certainty that his life with Dominique was over.

Dominique shuddered as she thought of her entreaties to him, in spite of his stubbornly closed demeanor.

"Clay," Dominique's voice pleaded for a breakthrough, "what about Gabrielle?"

Clay, a self-righteous expression on his face, replied, "She's handling this fine."

"You think because she didn't cry and carry on that she's handling it well?" Dominique's voice rose in outrage. "How can you lie to yourself that way?" Clay turned his back on her and went to the bureau drawer, pulling out handfuls of socks and underwear. He carried the clothes to the suitcase and dropped them in, not bothering to tidy them. Dominique's voice grew more strident. "Gabrielle may not show it, but she's completely bewildered. She has no idea how to cope!"

Clay paused in his packing and met Dominique's gaze. "*Gabrielle* will be fine," he said pointedly.

"Then why hasn't she come out of her room all day?" Dominique challenged him, her face hot and red with emotion.

"I *told* you," Clay said tightly, "she'll get over it."

Clay's deliberate calm sickened Dominique. She wanted him to show emotion. Wanted to find words to hurt him. To bring him alive. "You know nothing about your daughter!" She pointed an accusing finger at him. His face stiffened, and Dominique could tell that he was trying to restrain himself from responding. He didn't want the involvement. That enraged her further. "You've been so busy travel-ing and . . . and . . ." — she sputtered for a moment, trying to think of the most insulting phrase she could — "and having your sordid little affair, that you haven't even bothered with your own daughter!"

Clay's eyes snapped with anger. He took a step toward Dominique. "My daughter loves me. And she knows I love her!"

Dominique felt as though the top of her head would blow off from the pressure of her mounting emotion. Don't be so sure! she wanted to counter. But she held back. Gabrielle was sacrosanct. Dominique refused to use her as a weapon in her quarrel.

Instead, she changed tacks. "Have you thought about what our friends are going to say?" she asked in a venomous tone. "Have you thought about how people are going to laugh behind your back for making a fool of yourself with a woman half your age?"

For the first time, Dominique saw that she had stung Clay. Bright spots of color appeared on his tan cheeks. "Marie and I are a perfectly appropriate couple," he said huffily. "No one has ever —" Clay stopped, realizing that he'd given away too much.

Dominique blinked as the full import of his words sank in. Her voice sank to a dangerous growl. "You've told other people about this."

Clay dropped his eyes. "Just one or two." He sidled away from Do-minique as though trying to escape a tiger's cage without arousing the occupant's attention.

"Who?" Dominique hurled at him. She took several steps forward until she stood directly in front of him. "You've humiliated me like this? You've let other people gossip about this and feel sorry for me behind my back?" Her stomach burned painfully as she realized the extent of the betrayal that had been visited on her. Not only her hus-band, but her friends. Why had they conspired with him? Didn't they care about her?

For a moment, Clay didn't answer. He stood still and gazed down at the top of Dominique's head, careful not to meet her eyes.

"Who?" Her voice rose and cracked.

"Only Lucas and Henry!" Clay shot back, his voice defensive. His golfing chums, both vice presidents at Parker Shipping. Their wives were Dominique's friends. Henry's wife, Celeste, belonged to the French club and often came to the house.

Dominique's glare bored into Clay until he was forced to meet it. "Celeste and Linda know about this?" she asked dangerously. "You introduced them to your *whore?*"

"Don't be naive!" Clay said scornfully. "You think those guys aren't doing the same thing? You think they'd let their wives know about it?"

Dominique was aghast at her own blindness, the blindness of her friends. She lifted her hands to her face, but no tears came. Her despair, her sense of loss, went beyond tears. She wished she could block out what was happening. She felt as though she were headed for a raging waterfall in a barrel and could do nothing to stop certain disaster. Helplessly, hopelessly, she dropped her hands. Clay stood silently before her. He stared at her without emotion. Dominique was reminded of the flat, black eyes of a shark she had once seen at an aquarium — two eerie pools of emptiness. Where was Clay, her husband, behind those stranger's eyes? Was he so focused on his love affair, that he had no emotion for anyone else?

She took a deep, trembling breath and said, "Why is it so necessary that you move in with her? Why can't you just do what your friends are doing?" Her voice broke, but she forged ahead with the shameful words. "Why can't we make some" — she turned away, unable to look in his eyes — "accommodation?"

Clay shrugged, seemingly unmoved by his wife's despair. "Because she's the woman I love."

That had been hours ago, Dominique wasn't sure how many. How long had she sat huddled, trembling in her bed? She blinked in the dim light and tried to focus on her watch. It was almost five and already growing dark. A violent wind outside, a winter storm, slammed a loose shutter against the house. Dominique cringed miserably.

She knew she should call Gabrielle and Solange in to her — explain things more clearly, talk about the future. But she hadn't the will. She had kept the news from them for the past four days, ever since their return from St. John. After all, there had still been the chance that Clay would change his mind. There had still been the hope.

What could they possibly be thinking now, her mother and daughter? Clay said that Gabrielle was "handling it well." As for Solange, Dominique had had to suffer the ignominy of hearing her own pleadings repeated by her mother as Clay marched down the hall with his suitcase. Clay hadn't raised his voice to Solange. Dominique had heard little, but the portion of the conversation that had taken place directly outside her bedroom door had been enough to reveal that Clay still bore a deep affection for his mother-in-law. He was more tolerant of her appeals than of Dominique's! But as the voices drifted away, Dominique knew her mother was fighting a battle already lost. Then the slamming of the front door, the crunch of tires on gravel. Silence.

Dominique became aware of a pressure on her bladder. She unfolded her stiff limbs and made her way shakily to the bathroom. Her muscles felt rubbery, of uncertain strength. When she emerged, she went back to the bed and sprawled on it face down. She lay still, collapsed, her mind a blank. The room darkened, but she made no move to turn on the light. She wished she could escape into sleep, but it seemed impossible that she would ever find the peace to sleep again.

A soft knocking at the door entered her consciousness. She didn't answer, didn't want to see anyone. Dominique buried her head in her arms.

"Dominique?" It was Solange's voice, muffled by the thick wood of the door.

Dominique opened her mouth to reply, but no sound came out. She gave up and closed her eyes.

The knocking resumed. "Dominique?"

Dominique turned on her side. She drew her legs up in the fetal position and pulled the pillow over her head.

Then her mother was beside her, her hand on her arm. "Dominique, get up. We have to talk."

"I can't," Dominique whispered hoarsely.

"Dominique, what's wrong between you and Clay?" Solange's voice was urgent and her hand insistently tapped Dominique's arm to punctuate her words.

Dominique pulled her arm away and flipped in the bed, so that her back was to her mother. "I . . . I can't talk now." The words came out with difficulty, and when Dominique was finished she was short of breath.

Solange stroked her daughter's arm more gently than before. "My poor girl," she said, her voice soft. "It's just a caprice of his. It happens to men. He'll get over it," she said with conviction.

"He wants to marry her," Dominique said dully into the pillow.

Solange made a sound of surprise. "That doesn't seem possible. Why, when we were in St. John he was very attentive toward you. He must love you still."

Dominique thought of how she herself had been deceived by Clay. So, he had deceived Solange, too. Everyone. When had he stopped loving her? Dominique wondered. How many times had he made love to her since?

At the thought of it, Dominique's teeth began to chatter. "He doesn't love me!" she cried bitterly.

"But your marriage was good!" Solange protested. "What happened?"

"Why do you ask me that?" Dominique said in a tortured voice.

"There must have been some sign that things weren't right!" Solange pounded the mattress with her fist for emphasis. "There must be something you can do, even now!"

Dominique jerked into a kneeling position facing her mother. Solange's attempts to reason enraged her. There was nothing logical about what was happening! "This has nothing to do with me, Mother! He's decided he wants someone younger. He fell in love. If you could have seen his face" — she choked on the words — "you would know that he feels nothing for me anymore. Nothing!"

Solange recoiled at the rawness of her daughter's emotions. "Calm down, Dominique," she said in the tone of one talking to an unbalanced person. "I didn't say you had done anything wrong. I'm just wondering how something like this could have happened without your having any hint of it. Men often go through a stage where they seek out a younger woman for" — Solange blushed — "reassurance. They think they're growing older, and a younger woman makes them feel important and virile. But things like this rarely happen without reason. There must have been some sign that —"

"I can't believe you!" Dominique cried, slapping her thighs in outrage. "Clay walks out and you try to blame me!" She jabbed her finger at her own chest. "What do you know about things like this? Father died when I was nine — he didn't have time to grow tired of you!" Dominique's voice rose to a hysterical pitch. "What difference does it make why Clay left? He doesn't want to come back! He wants a divorce!" Dominique clamped her hands over her ears, trying to block out further conversation. "I don't understand why you're bothering me with these ridiculous questions!"

Solange's careful self-control snapped under her daughter's assault. "I'm not blaming you!" she shouted back. "I just thought that there might be a chance to get him back. That if you knew why he —"

Dominique could stand it no longer. "I don't know!" she yelled. "I don't know! I don't know!" She sank back onto her pillow and covered her eyes with her arm.

Solange made no reply. She simply stared at her in shock.

After a few moments of silence, Dominique said wearily, "Mother, please go away. I'm tired."

Dominique didn't open her eyes, but she heard the mattress creak and felt the weight equalize as Solange got up.

"May I" — Solange hesitated — "may I bring you something? A glass of sherry? something to eat?"

"I'd just like to be left alone."

Dominique heard her mother take a deep breath as though preparing to say more. She uttered only one word. "Gabrielle?"

Dominique dropped her arm and stared at her mother.

Solange continued. "Do you want me to —"

Dominique interrupted. "No!" she said sharply. "I'll talk to her myself. I'll get up." She struggled to her elbows.

Solange leaned toward her, her face full of concern. "You're too emotional just now," she said in a soothing tone. "Wouldn't it be better if you waited until tomorrow?"

"And leave my daughter alone all night wondering what happened? I can't do that!" Dominique declared. "She needs to talk to me. She'll have questions."

"Clay told —"

"Clay!" Dominique expelled the word as though it were a piece of spoiled meat. "Who knows what he told her!"

"He said" — Solange hesitated, as though measuring the effect of her words on Dominique — "he said that you had mutually agreed to divorce."

Dominique's lips tightened into a thin line of anger. "Did he?"

"You mustn't turn the child against her father!" Solange said the words in a rush, as though afraid she would be interrupted.

Dominique looked up at her mother, her expression icy. "How can you think I'd do such a thing?"

Solange replied defensively, "You're very hurt. It would be understandable —"

"I would never hurt Gabrielle," Dominique said vehemently. She gave Solange an accusatory glare and pushed herself off the bed. Then she went into the bathroom and slammed the door behind her.

∽ ∽ ∽

Gabrielle, only Gabrielle, kept Dominique going. In the two weeks since Clay had left, Dominique found herself unable to rise from bed until noon. She would toss on a bathrobe, then go downstairs for an inadequate, hastily bolted meal of sweets from the freezer. All she craved were sweets: frozen cheesecakes, cookies, and chocolates. She had never been one to binge, but now she stole items up to her room to wolf down in solitary misery. She didn't care that the food wasn't healthy, nor that she was rapidly gaining weight. The sweets provided comfort.

After eating, Dominique would go back to bed until it was almost time for Gabrielle to come home from school. Then she would shower and dress to await her arrival. It was important to keep up appearances for Gabrielle. For the same reason, she would descend each evening for dinner with her mother and daughter. The evening meal had become a desultory affair with little conversation, despite the fact that Dominique roused herself to ask Gabrielle questions about school. But she accepted the monosyllabic answers typical of youngsters without further probing, though she had never done so before. In the end, Dominique would leave most of the food on her plate and retire to her room with packages of sweets.

Then, one afternoon, as Dominique was zipping up her dress, she heard the crunch of tires in the driveway. With an inexplicable feeling of alarm, she rushed to the window to see who it was. An unfamiliar sports car shimmered white in the February sun. Before Dominique had time to wonder who it belonged to, she saw Gabrielle emerge, wave good-bye to the occupant, then jog up the stairs to the house.

Dominique slipped on her shoes and hurried down the hall to meet her. Her daughter was too young for drives with boys, and Dominique intended to tell her so in no uncertain terms. She mustn't allow Gabrielle to take advantage of the fact that her father was no longer a force of discipline in the house.

"Gabrielle!" Dominique called out sharply.

Gabrielle stopped at the foot of the stairs and looked up at her mother with a guilty expression.

Dominique marched down the stairs with more energy than she had shown since Clay's departure and came face to face with her daughter. "Who was that who dropped you off?" she demanded.

Gabrielle looked surprised. "Didn't you know? It was Daddy."

Now it was Dominique's turn to look astonished. "Your father? Where's his car?"

Gabrielle said breezily, "He got rid of the Cadillac." Her expression brightened with admiration. "That was an Alfa Romeo!" She gave her mother a sidelong glance and asked tentatively, "Isn't it neat-looking?"

"It's a little young for your father," Dominique sniffed.

Gabrielle shook her head in denial. "All the girls at school thought he was so handsome in it! Like Paul Newman or something!"

Dominique suddenly became conscious of her dowdy dress — one of the few roomy enough to accommodate her weight gain.

"Why did your father pick you up?" Dominique asked in an even tone.

Gabrielle looked down. "He just wanted to talk," she said.

"That was nice." Dominique forced herself to say it without irony.

"He . . . " Gabrielle looked at her mother, apprehension written on her face.

Dominique crossed her arms, unaware that she was making the protective gesture. "Yes?"

"He wants me to spend the weekend with him."

Dominique nodded. "That's a good idea." She was relieved that Clay was keeping up contact with Gabrielle.

"Well, it's just that . . . " Gabrielle kicked at the newel post with her sneakered toe.

"Stop that," Dominique said, enervated, "and tell me what's on your mind."

Gabrielle blurted out, "He has a new friend and she'll be there!"

Dominique took a deep breath and suppressed an expression of disgust. "I know about her." She had prepared herself for this and had vowed to accept it with good grace. Dominique remembered losing her own father at a young age, and it had hurt. It had to be even worse for Gabrielle, who was an only child, and whose father had left of his own free will. Dominique had no intention of saying anything to alienate Clay and Gabrielle.

"It'll be weird with her there," Gabrielle confessed.

Dominique reached forward and stroked her daughter's cheek. "I know," she sighed, "but it looks like she's going to be your father's new wife, and you'll have to meet her sometime." Dominique fought to smother the panic that welled up in her at the thought of the impending divorce.

Gabrielle studied her mother for a moment without speaking, then took a step forward and wrapped her arms around Dominique.

Dominique grasped her daughter tightly. It felt good to be touched again.

∾ ∾ ∾

Dominique paced anxiously in the living room as she waited for Gabrielle to arrive home from her weekend with Clay. She was sure that her daughter would want to talk — pour out grievances, confess to feelings of homesickness. It couldn't have been easy, Dominique thought sympathetically, trying to behave nicely toward the woman who would marry her father. She wondered if Gabrielle would guess that Marie had, in fact, been responsible for the breakup of their family.

Dominique had reached that peculiar stage of denial that allows wronged women to forgive the man his transgressions while holding the other woman responsible. Never mind that Dominique had exchanged marriage vows with Clay, had lived with him and supported him in his endeavors for fourteen years. It was easier to blame the other woman. Easier to believe that one's own judgment hadn't been wrong after all, that one's husband was still basically a good man. He had simply been tempted beyond endurance.

Dominique cocked her head as she heard the car. She wanted to run to the window and look out, but didn't for fear that Clay would see her. A moment later, Gabrielle burst into the house.

"Mom!" she called from the front hall.

"In here!" Dominique called back, hurrying to the foyer. She halted in astonishment when she saw Gabrielle. "You've cut your hair!" she exclaimed.

Gabrielle self-consciously raised a hand to her chestnut curls. "Do you like it?"

It was a sleek, short cut, far too sophisticated for the child. And there was something else different about her daughter. Dominique took a few steps forward and peered warily at Gabrielle's face. "Are you wearing makeup?" she cried.

Gabrielle rolled her eyes. "Mom, I asked you about my hair."

"Your hair looks very nice, but are you wearing makeup?" Dominique insisted. She approached her daughter and carefully studied her face. There was no doubt about it! She was wearing mascara, blusher, and pink lipstick.

"You know you're not allowed!" Dominique said menacingly.

"Dad said I could," Gabrielle said smugly. "Marie said that you need makeup with a short cut. Anyway, I'm old enough. Susie's only twelve and she — "

"I don't care what your friends do!" Dominique interrupted sharply. "When you're sixteen, you can do as you like, but not until then!"

"But that's years away!" Gabrielle moaned.

"Go and wash your face," Dominique snapped. "I don't know what your father was thinking of. He doesn't like makeup, and he's the one who felt most strongly about you not wearing it until —" Dominique stopped abruptly. A sudden vision of Marie Annis came to her. Marie Annis, with her perfectly penciled lip-liner and her dramatically made-up eyes. How could Clay allow himself to be so influenced by her! How could he so casually abandon the rules by which he and Dominique had agreed to raise Gabrielle?

"I don't know what the big deal is anyway," Gabrielle said sulkily.

"Get upstairs and wash your face!" Dominique commanded harshly.

Gabrielle's eyes widened with alarm. Keeping her gaze trained on her mother, she began to back up the stairs. Then, suddenly, her eyes filled with tears. "You're mean!" she cried. "I hate you!" Then she whirled and scurried away.

When she was out of sight, Dominique sagged against the newel post. Her outrage gave way to remorse. It hadn't been the child's fault, after all. It had been Clay's . . . and Marie's. How, in just one weekend, had Marie won over Gabrielle? For clearly she had done just that. Gabrielle's face lit up when she mentioned the young woman's name. Dominique sank to the bottom stair and buried her head in her hands.

But the worst was yet to come.

ᡃᠥ ᡃᠥ ᡃᠥ

A few weeks later, Clay called her, his tone cordial, as though there had never been trouble between them. He spent several minutes on pleasantries before he got down to business.

"Say, Dominique. Don't you think that house is too big for you?" He adopted a sympathetic tone.

Dominique bit back a retort. It wouldn't do to anger him now. With a start, Dominique realized that she relied entirely on him for financial support. Her position suddenly seemed precarious. "We're fine," Dominique said flatly. He had promised to continue supporting them. She would hold him to it.

"You wouldn't feel more comfortable in a smaller place?" His tone was wheedling.

Dominique's reply was firm and swift. "Gabrielle's life has been disrupted enough. I won't have any more changes."

Clay was silent for a moment. Finally, in a voice of deliberate patience, he said, "Neither of us wants to upset Gabrielle, but she seemed to be adjusting well when we had her last weekend." He added as an afterthought, "Marie made a tremendous effort with her, and I think it paid off."

"Good for Marie," Dominique said dryly. Then she softened. "I'm glad Gabrielle seemed happy at your place. I was a little worried —"

Clay cut her off with a short laugh. "You always worry too much!"

Again, Dominique bit back a retort. "Was there something else you wanted to discuss, Clay?" she asked coldly.

The warmth left Clay's voice. "Have you chosen a lawyer?" he asked abruptly.

The question caught Dominique off guard. A chill of fear went through her. She hadn't hired a lawyer, for to do so would be to finally admit that there was no hope of saving her marriage.

"Have . . . have you?" she asked haltingly.

"Larry Beausoleil," Clay answered.

The name meant nothing to Dominique.

Clay continued. "I want to hammer out a separation agreement, then get the ball rolling on the divorce. I need to know my financial position."

"I'm not sure I understand. You said nothing would change for me." And why should it? Clay had always spent money extravagantly. The company had seemingly provided an endless source of it.

Clay made a sound of impatience. "You're always so literal. Naturally, I don't want to disrupt your life, but I can't afford to support you in the same way!" He paused. When he spoke again, his tone was confidential, as though sharing a secret with a sympathetic friend. "The business is going through a rough patch."

Dominique was aghast. "This is the first I've heard of it!" she shot back.

"I didn't want to worry you." Clay's voice was low and soothing. "But . . . maybe you'd better get rid of the help. And you ought to think about going back to work."

"Work!" Dominique exclaimed. "You never wanted me to work! You wanted me here for Gabrielle! It's been years since I had a job. Who would hire me now?"

"Gabrielle will start junior high this fall," Clay argued. "She's almost a teenager. She can fend for herself for a couple of hours each day. Besides, she has Solange."

"You know Solange goes to Danielle's beach place every summer. It's too hot for her here!"

Clay's voice rose. "It won't kill Gabrielle to be alone."

Dominique's voice rose, too. She was at the edge of panic. "You can't just change your mind about this! Tell me to fire the Jeffersons and Lucy. Sell the house. You made certain promises to me!"

"I'm sorry," Clay shouted, "but the situation has changed! Now, get yourself a lawyer and let's get this settled so we can both get on with our lives."

Dominique heard a loud click, then the dial tone. She stared at the phone with disbelief. Clay had never before hung up on her. She didn't recognize him anymore.

⊕ ⊕ ⊕

"How could you let this happen?" Danielle asked her sister for the third time.

"If you're going to ask me the same question over and over, there's no point in my paying for this call. I can't afford it anymore," Dominique added sourly.

"I'm sorry, I know. Look, hang up and I'll call you back."

"No!" Dominique said emphatically. "That wasn't why I said that. I just mean —"

"All right, all right," Danielle said soothingly. "So you'll have your half of the proceeds from the sale of the house and furniture and things."

"What little there'll be . . ." Dominique felt hot and cold spasms of anxiety rise in her as she discussed her financial situation. It was worse, far worse, than she had ever imagined it would be.

"But a house that size surely is worth plenty!" Danielle said with conviction.

"It would be, except that Clay took out a second mortgage to put in the pool and the pool house. And you know you never get back what you put into a pool."

"I don't know . . . ," Danielle said vaguely. "No one in my neighborhood has one." Danielle lived in a solidly upper-middle-class suburb of New York. The kind of neighborhood in which the houses were mostly alike, the cars high-priced, the shrubbery well trimmed. However, its residents were not so spendthrift as to indulge in their own swimming pools. They simply went to the nearby country club. "But with inflation like it is right now, surely the value of your property has gone up since you bought it?"

"Yes, but the interest rate on the second mortgage is astronomical! Besides, these old places in the Garden District are hard to sell. There aren't many people who can afford them." With a touch of dark humor, Dominique added, "Though I'll bet Clay's lawyer will make enough off this transaction to buy two mansions!"

Whereas the name Larry Beausoleil had meant nothing to Dominique the month before, she had quickly learned that he was the most feared divorce attorney in the state. His specialty was extracting wealthy men from their marriages with minimal damage to their bank accounts. His fees, of course, were hefty. Dominique had gone for aid to the attorney who had represented Clay and her in the settlement of their home. An old friend of Clay's, he had refused to take the case. He had given her the name of an acquaintance who specialized in divorce.

As though reading her thoughts, Danielle asked, "Is your lawyer any good?"

Dominique sighed heavily. "I don't know how to judge. Okay, I suppose."

"Why don't you find one of those killer types?"

Dominique shrugged, though her sister couldn't see the gesture. "I don't want to hurt Clay. I just want things to turn out fairly."

Danielle made a sound of frustration. *"You don't want to hurt Clay!* After what he's done to you? If Ron ever tried anything like that, I'd crucify him." Danielle uttered the phrase with zest, as though daring her husband to try it.

"Well, that's not my style," Dominique said defensively. "I don't want us to be enemies. It wouldn't be good for Gabrielle."

"But Clay's not showing the same consideration. You're letting him take advantage of your concern for Gabrielle! Why are you letting him move this quickly? Why have you agreed to sell the house?"

"He says he can't afford it!" Dominique said heatedly. "What am I supposed to do? Sit here and wait for the bank to kick me out?"

"What if you found a job?"

"Do you think I haven't tried?" Dominique said with frustration. "I haven't worked in years."

"You have, too! Only you did it for charity. Those events you planned were wonderful. Why can't you find a real job doing that?"

"I'm trying!" Dominique cried. "I've been to all the hotels I usually work with for the charities and none of them need someone like me. They don't do enough big events to justify a planner — not when every big group in town has someone like me doing the job for free." She took a deep breath, trying to stifle her tears. She hated this feeling of impotence! "Orman's still has the woman who took my place and she's doing a great job. The only other big department store in New Orleans is family-owned. They're old-fashioned and stodgy and they don't see the need for an event planner." Dominique took a deep, shaky breath, then continued. "The fact is, I can't afford to take the kind of entry-level position that's available, and no one wants a middle-aged person for those anyway. They want a young girl with lots of energy and no children."

"You're still young! You're only thirty-seven," Danielle insisted. Then, without thinking, she blurted out, "If you just drop a few pounds and put on some makeup, you won't *look* middle-aged."

The criticism stung. "Has mother been talking to you about that?"
"She's *worried*."

"Well, I am, too, and I don't need her criticism or yours!" Dominique's voice cracked on the last word. She felt as though *she* were cracking. Each day brought new misery, new struggle. She couldn't remember the last time she had laughed or even genuinely smiled. She didn't socialize anymore — couldn't bear to face her friends. Even her own family was too much to cope with: their bewilderment, their subtle criticism, their false cheerfulness, and, worst of all, their hope that somehow things would come right. That Clay would change his mind. It was as though they expected her to *do* something about him, even though she knew there was nothing to be done. In any event, she had lost her capacity for action. She was overwhelmed with the difficulty of day-to-day living. The loneliness, the fear of the future, the need to keep up appearances for Gabrielle. The difficulty of fighting Clay even as she tried to ensure that his relations with Gabrielle remain unclouded by the dispute. It was all too much. Too much.

ᙆᎧ ᙆᎧ ᙆᎧ

Dominique peeked out from behind the living room curtain as Clay struggled to cram Gabrielle's luggage into his Alfa Romeo. The girl had announced a month before that Marie was treating them to a trip to Europe. Gabrielle's camping trip with her friend Susie had been cast aside in favor of the glamour and excitement offered by the excursion with her new friend. And her new father.

For Clay was like a new man where Gabrielle was concerned. Gone was the perfectionist who had demanded straight A's. This was a new, easygoing Clay. One who wanted to be a hero to his daughter. And he was rendered yet more glamorous by his beautiful young girlfriend and all the other sporty, young accouterments of his new life — the supposed difficulties of Parker Shipping notwithstanding.

"I know it seems like he's living well, Dominique, but, believe me, we can't touch any of it," her lawyer assured her. "It all belongs to the corporation. Or to his girlfriend."

Dominique bitterly gazed at the shiny car full of shopping bags and dry cleaning — the cargo of people preparing for a long trip. A festive spirit surrounded Clay and Gabrielle — a spirit from which Dominique was excluded.

She turned away from the window and winced as she surveyed the cardboard boxes that filled the living room. Unlike Gabrielle, Dominique was not setting out on a happy voyage. In two weeks, she was to move from the Garden District to a little house in a neighborhood that the rental ad had optimistically described as "transitional."

For the hundredth time, Dominique wondered if she had too easily given in to Clay's pressure to reach a quick financial settlement. They were to sign the papers when he returned from Europe. Her lawyer said she had no choice. She felt trapped, worried that she would do no better in court, worried that she would have to pay hefty legal fees. Now, as she mentally tallied her expenses for the next month, it seemed that the amount to which she had agreed was ridiculously low. She would, of course, receive a lump sum from the sale of the house, but it was not a large amount. She had resolved to set it aside for emergencies. She would try to live off Clay's payments and her small salary as a part-time secretary at a bank until she found more lucrative work.

Dominique sighed heavily and moved into the kitchen. At least she wouldn't have to worry about supporting Gabrielle and Solange for the next month, she told herself. A frown of concern crinkled Dominique's brow as she thought of her mother. She hoped that Ronald wasn't making her feel unwelcome in New York. Dominique shook her head. It didn't do any good to worry about that. Danielle would look after Solange.

She squinted at the clock above the sink. Almost eight and she hadn't had any dinner. Of course, with Lucy gone — she could no longer afford her or the Jeffersons — dinners were not a meal she looked forward to. Nonetheless, she knew she should prepare herself a balanced meal. Too often of late, she relied on frozen dinners.

Dominique opened the refrigerator door and scanned the shelves. A loaf of bread, orange juice, some cheeses and sandwich meats, seven eggs, and a leftover macaroni casserole. She opened the freezer. A blast of cold air struck her in the face. Dominique's eyes immediately went to the Sara Lee pound cake. Then the half-gallon of coffee ice cream. There was also a hefty slice of cheesecake that a neighbor had given her. Beside the desserts was a stack of frozen TV dinners. Dominique wrinkled her nose as she viewed the labels: "Savory Salisbury Steak," "Turkey Tetrazzini Delight," "Crispy Fish 'n Chips." She was sick of them all.

Leaving the freezer door ajar, Dominique dutifully lowered her head to the vegetable bin. The idea of going to the trouble to make a salad was defeating.

Dominique closed the refrigerator door and straightened. She might as well eat the cheesecake. Cheese was healthy, it had plenty of protein, and the cake was the only thing she really wanted. She put the entire slab on a plate, grabbed a fork, and went upstairs to her bedroom — her refuge from the echoing silence of the rest of the house.

Dominique ate until she felt ill. Then she ate some more. She ate until long after the waistband of her skirt had begun to pinch. She stood up, removed her skirt, then plopped back down on the bed and picked up the plate again. Only a few forkfuls left — a shame to waste it. Stuffed though she was, Dominique ate until not a crumb remained. When she finished, she got up to take the plate downstairs. No matter how depressed she was, how devoid of energy, Dominique couldn't tolerate dirty dishes in her room. As she passed the full length mirror on the closet door, she caught a glimpse of herself and quickly looked away.

Downstairs, Dominique cleaned up and hurried back to her room. She settled in an armchair and tried to read, but as dusk turned to dark, she became increasingly aware of her isolation. The phone was silent. Gabrielle's friends knew she was gone. Solange and Danielle had called the day before. The women always exchanged calls on Fridays. That meant Dominique had to wait almost a week until it was her turn to call. If she called before then, she would undoubtedly alarm her mother and sister. Dominique thought about calling a friend. But who? It was Saturday night. Her friends would all have social events planned. Social events from which she, as an extra woman, was now almost always excluded.

What Dominique really wanted was to speak to Gabrielle. But she hated to phone Clay's house. Anyhow, Gabrielle had left only a little while ago. It would seem strange if Dominique called.

Longing for the sound of a human voice, Dominique sat on the bed and clicked on the television. She flipped the channels. Two situation comedies and two police shows. Without real interest, Dominique settled on a police show. She fluffed up the pillows behind her and tried to concentrate.

An advertisement interrupted the show and Dominique's mind

wandered. She thought again of her daughter. By this time tomorrow, Gabrielle would be in Paris — she had been bubbling over with excitement at the prospect. And, even in her bitterness, Dominique couldn't help being happy for her, happy that her relationship with Clay seemed easier now.

She was startled from her reflections by the jingle of the evening news. The program had just ended. Dominique shifted uncomfortably in the bed. She had been sitting in the same position, lost in thought, for over an hour. It was ten-thirty and she was already sleepy. In the first weeks after Clay left, Dominique had been unable to sleep well. Now she slept profoundly and awoke reluctantly with a thick, hazy fog clouding her consciousness. Sleep was Dominique's escape from her loneliness, her desolation, her fear. When she first awakened each day, she was unaware of her new circumstances, then she would turn and see the empty space beside her.

During the years of her marriage with Clay, she had been a happy person, grateful for her lot. She wasn't happy anymore.

Dominique rose and went into the bathroom to brush her teeth. She carefully avoided her reflection in the mirror. It would be too disturbing. She would see the bags under her eyes, the jiggly flesh of her upper arms. Better not to look.

The next day, Sunday, Dominique hoped Gabrielle would call before her plane left. They hadn't arranged for a call, but Dominique couldn't help wishing her daughter would think of her anyhow. She knew they were scheduled to leave at five p.m., so she didn't stir from the house all day for fear of missing the call. At six o'clock, Dominique had to admit to herself that the call wasn't coming. The air of expectancy that had carried her through the day ebbed away. It was replaced by a dull ache in her heart. She felt as though her connections with the world were slipping away.

Who truly cared about her? Gabrielle didn't seem to need her anymore. Solange had Danielle, whom she preferred anyhow. Since Clay had left, the relationship between Dominique and her mother, always difficult, had deteriorated. It was just as well Solange had gone to New York for the summer.

But now, alone in her big house with no obligations, Dominique didn't know what to do next. For so many years, her activities had centered around her family. Suddenly, no one was making demands on her, but she didn't feel liberated; she felt purposeless.

I should probably do some more packing, she thought. Dreary, dreary packing. On Wednesday, one of the local auction houses would come to give her an estimate of what she could get for her antiques — Clay's antiques really. One of the few advantages she'd won in the settlement. Only there wasn't room in the new house for most of them. That was all right — she could use the money.

Dominique told herself she should clean out the drawers. That would give her something to do. And she should study the Sunday classified ads. She had to be more aggressive about finding a full-time job. Yet, somehow, she couldn't muster the energy to spend her free time going on job interviews. She wasn't up to the task of selling herself to prospective employers.

She sat in her kitchen and watched the shadows grow longer in the garden outside. It was a lovely, romantic evening. The petunias gave forth a sweet aroma that wafted in through the screened windows. Dominique got up and went outside. The slate of the terrace, shaded by a giant live oak, was cool, though the air was still hot. Dominique looked at the swimming pool that Clay had so desired. She walked to its edge, noting that, in just two days, many leaves and petals had fallen into the water. Gabrielle had cleaned it on Friday before her departure. It was amazing how quickly things deteriorated if they weren't given attention. Dominique knew she ought to clean the pool, but she didn't care.

She sighed and walked to one of the nearby lounge chairs. The beauty of the evening, of the setting, made her think of a similar court-yard that she and Clay had visited on their honeymoon. It had been in a restaurant in the walled city of Eze. As they approached the town, the setting sun had turned the buildings a glowing amber. The entire city had appeared as an enchanted citadel high atop the Côte d'Azure. Clay had stopped the car to savor the view, his arm around Domi-nique, her head on his shoulder. Thinking of it, Dominique was filled with terrible longing, terrible regret.

When had things begun to go wrong in her life? Had she missed a clue that she should have seen? Had she, as Solange intimated, been partly responsible for Clay's betrayal? And what of Gabrielle? Why was she so fascinated by the woman who had supplanted her own mother in her father's life? What was lacking in Dominique to cause her hus-band and her child to turn to Marie?

Dominique shook her head to clear it. Stop brooding, she told herself. You've faced hard times before and you've overcome them. Yes, she argued, but this is different. I was younger. Now I have to start over after eleven years of not working. I'm competing for jobs with girls of twenty!

Dominique couldn't even face the thought of what it would be like to date again. She wasn't interested. She'd had three serious relationships and all had ended in disaster. What was wrong with her?

Dominique slumped in the chair, her arms crossed, hugging herself. Her chin dropped to her chest. She knew her thoughts were making her unbearably depressed, yet she couldn't stop herself from dwelling on them. She was sinking in a quicksand of defeat, powerless to break free. What was the use of struggling? No matter what she did, she ended up in the same place. It was like a nightmare in which she tried to run only to find that her legs wouldn't carry her forward.

As night fell, mosquitoes began to bite her, leaving red welts on her skin. Halfheartedly, she brushed away the creatures, too despondent to move into the house. She realized that she could sit all night by the pool and no one would care. No one would worry or insist that she come in. No one would even know. Even if she died, no one would know.

The thought struck Dominique like a blow. She raised her hand to her cheek and cradled it in the sort of comforting gesture she would have wished to receive — if another person had been there. But no one was.

Dominique clamped her eyes shut and dropped her head back against the cushion of the chair. She turned her face to the sky and the warm night breeze. A dry sob rose in her. From the bottom of her stomach it came up, gathering force as it passed through her diaphragm, through her throat. The cry resounded in the stillness. Even to Dominique's ears, it sounded inhuman. Then came the tears. Choking her, catching in her throat. Dominique heaved and shook with them. They ran unchecked down her face. Oh, she hurt! Her heart pushed against her ribs — a hard, stabbing beat. Maybe it would kill her, she thought wildly. If she died, she would finally escape the hurt — and self-hatred — that had tormented her since Clay had told her that he loved another woman. In her mind, distorted by agony, Dominique began to consider what it would be like to die.

It would be sweet oblivion. It would be like sleep. She would be rid of her problems. She would be rid of that horrible fog that hung over her like a cloud of doom. A strange longing pulled at Dominique. She gazed at the water, so calming, so still. It would be warm and comforting. It would enfold her in benign silence. She found herself mentally drifting to the dark, quiet place. How easy it would be to go there!

Then her thoughts began to wander in a more pernicious direction. A perverse, vengeful side of her, a side she had not known existed, considered with grim satisfaction the guilt she would leave behind. Clay would be sorry. He would have it on his conscience. He would have to live with it. Dominique wondered how deeply it would affect him. Gabrielle would surely blame him. Would it ruin his love for Marie? Would he realize that he had made a terrible mistake, that he had loved Dominique all along?

Solange would be sorry, too. Sorry she had found fault with Dominique. Sorry she had never shown her the same affection she had shown Danielle. Dominique's mouth turned down and her lips trembled. Why had Solange continued to regard Clay as a friend? Why did she find it so hard to blame him and so easy to blame Dominique?

And what about Gabrielle? She would find out that Marie was no substitute for her own mother. She would realize how much Dominique meant to her. She would be shattered, for Dominique knew that, despite her recent infatuation with Marie, Gabrielle loved her more than anyone else.

Then the horror of Dominique's ruminations hit her. She clutched her hands to her chest and drew in her breath sharply. How could she have allowed her thoughts to take her to such depths? Self-loathing filled her. That she should consider hurting her own child, the person she loved most in the world, was evil! How could she have considered leaving her that way!

Dominique sprang to her feet as though she were about to flee. But she didn't move from the spot. She began to shiver and wrapped her arms around herself. She hung her head in shame. How could she have allowed her self-pity to eclipse her will to live? Gabrielle had never needed her more than she did now, whether the girl knew it or not.

Dominique raised her head sharply, as though someone had called her name. She stared at the glassy surface of the pool. Now her problem seemed clear to her. Since Clay had said he was leaving, she had become like a child, without will or initiative. She had blindly relied on Clay and repeatedly given in to him. Where was her defiance, her backbone? She had spent the last few weeks questioning her judgment, reliving perceived mistakes, worrying about who was to blame. No more!

Dominique clenched her fists as she felt a surge of energy course through her. She was tired of being Clay's victim. It was time to regain control. She didn't need him! In her life, she had gone through worse, much worse, than this divorce. She had to move on, create a new life for herself. One that depended on no man — no one but herself. But that didn't mean she was willing to give up what was due her from her years with Clay. She would fight for it!

Dominique stared at the dark pool in front of her. Suddenly she — who was not much of a swimmer — felt an overwhelming impulse to plunge in. She stripped out of her clothes. The feeling of the night air on her skin was liberating. What difference did it make that she had grown plump? That her breasts weren't as high as they had once been? There was no one around to criticize. No one to make hurtful remarks. With a feeling of exultation, she raised her arms above her head and dove in.

CHAPTER 20 ∽

DOMINIQUE was like a convalescent who had been bedridden for a long time: shaky but eager to resume living.

Her first call was to the only divorced friend she had — a fellow committeewoman who, Dominique had noticed, lived as well as she had before her husband had married his secretary. The sleek brunette, it was said, had already found a new beau: her ex-husband's accountant.

"Lilah," Dominique asked, after exchanging pleasantries, "do you mind telling me the name of your divorce lawyer?"

The other woman expelled a throaty chortle. "Larry Beausoleil, love. Who else?"

Dominique's heart sank. "Oh," she said in a gloomy voice, "that's Clay's attorney."

"Hmmm . . . I know only one other person as good. But she's a woman. Do you have a problem with that?"

A woman lawyer? Dominique knew there were a few — a very few — in New Orleans, but it hadn't occurred to her to hire one. "She's supposed to be good?"

Her friend laughed. "You're still buried in the fifties, love. It's a new era. Believe me, she's the best. Probably because all the men underestimate her."

For the first time in days, Dominique laughed. Lilah was right. She needed to change with the times! Come to think of it, she liked the idea of having a woman, rather than a man, speak for her.

Patricia Masterson turned out to be all that Lilah had promised, though not what Dominique had expected. The attorney's office was located in an elegantly restored French Quarter townhouse. To be admitted, Dominique pressed a buzzer on a brick wall next to an elaborate wrought iron gate. An intercom hidden in wisteria vines crackled to life. A second later, the gate clicked. Dominique pushed it open and stepped into a courtyard shaded by yet more wisteria vines. It was like entering a cool refuge.

As directed, she stopped in front of a set of double doors painted glossy black, where a young, neatly dressed woman with a friendly face was waiting to greet her. The woman led her into a reception area furnished in a harmonious mixture of European antiques; it had a spare, almost Oriental aspect emphasized by several exquisite Japanese prints.

With a loud rattle, the receptionist opened an old-fashioned brass elevator door. "Miss Masterson's on the top floor," she said with a smile.

When the elevator doors reopened, Dominique found herself facing a more serious-looking older woman behind a carved rosewood desk.

The woman immediately stood. "Mrs. Parker, Miss Masterson is expecting you." Behind her, an open door revealed a bright, airy space. Dominique saw a bank of long windows and an expanse of rich, Oriental carpeting. Then Patricia Masterson stepped to the threshold.

The attorney, though clearly in her forties, had the statuesque, fluffy appearance of a former beauty queen. Her shoulder-length, ash blond hair was stylishly set. Her makeup was understated but expertly applied to enhance her high cheekbones and wide blue eyes. The skirt of her pink wool suit was by no means a fashionable mini, but it was above the knee. However, all impressions of demure frivolity disappeared when Dominique met the woman's gaze. It was powerful, measured, and determined.

"Mrs. Parker," she said in a throaty southern drawl. Not a New Orleans accent, but something more pronounced, Georgia or Alabama. The kind of honeysuckle purr that made men melt. With a confident glide that bespoke expensive private schools, Masterson walked into the hall and extended her hand.

Dominique liked her firm grip, and met it with one of her own. She accepted the offer of coffee and was led into the attorney's office. Masterson graciously indicated a down-filled sofa, then went to her desk to fetch a yellow legal pad.

"Now," she said, settling on the cushions a few feet away from Dominique, "tell me everything you can about the circumstances leading up to your separation."

At the end of Dominique's story, which took twenty minutes to relate, Masterson shook her head, her expression thoughtful. She leaned forward, lifted the top of an inlaid box on the coffee table, and drew out a cigarette. As she lit it with a gold lighter, her long, manicured nails flashed. She inhaled, then slowly let the smoke drift out her nose. Finally she fixed Dominique with an even gaze. "How much we can obtain will depend on whether your husband transferred his — and your — personal assets to his business." She sighed. "Unfortunately, his are family assets. If he were a doctor, and you'd helped put him through medical school, we'd have a stronger case. But he inherited his money. It'll be difficult to argue that you contributed to his earnings, and that's what judges are looking for." She rested her cigarette in a crystal ashtray, then turned to face Dominique squarely. "Of course, you'll sue him for desertion, and it's clear he's committing adultery." She shrugged. "But times are changing. Those used to be grounds enough to force a man to pay through the nose. Now" — she turned her palms up — "it depends on the judge. And, if your husband has managed to make it look as though he has no personal assets, the judge's outrage won't matter." She picked up her cigarette again, took a puff, then put it out in the ashtray.

Dominique clenched her fists, trying to control her alarm. "But what about our daughter and my mother? I have to support them!"

Masterson gave her a sympathetic look. "The fact that you have a daughter helps, of course. We'll get you fair child support." She looked down at the notepad in her lap. "This offer of your husband's is ridiculous and I intend to tell Larry Beausoleil just that." She paused. "But as for your mother, I'm afraid that it will appear to the judge that your husband has been very generous in supporting her all these years. Besides, you mentioned a sister in New York? Your mother lives there part time?"

Dominique nodded. It was hard not to feel downcast, but she liked Masterson for being frank.

Masterson said in a comforting voice, "Try not to worry. At least, you came to me before you signed this outrageous agreement." She smiled to soften her words. Then her regard turned serious. "I've been in the same situation as you. That's why I decided to become an attorney," she said grimly. "We'll start investigating Mr. Parker's financial situation immediately. Who knows? He may have left some loose ends lying about."

"Let's hope so," Dominique said ruefully. She stood up. Despite the depressing picture Masterson had painted, Dominique felt better for having taken positive action. She felt better still when Masterson proposed a fee structure based on the settlement. She wouldn't have to start paying until the case had been resolved.

Masterson rode in the elevator with Dominique to the ground floor. Before the door opened, she put a hand on Dominique's arm and said gently, "I know all this is difficult, and I'll do the best I can, but if your husband's been smart, I may not be able to do much better than your previous attorney." She paused. "Have you thought of returning to work?"

"Of course!" Dominique said. "But my field is rather limited. I was an event planner for Orman's once, but they already have someone —"

Masterson nodded. "I know of your work. I was at the last Heart Fund ball." She smiled. "Very impressive." She squeezed Dominique's arm reassuringly. "I'm sure that with talent like yours, you'll eventually find something good."

Dominique studied Masterson. It didn't seem possible that this accomplished, supremely confident woman had ever been deserted and tricked by her husband. That it could happen to Masterson made Dominique feel less ineffectual. And it gave her hope for the future. She felt buoyed as she emerged into the June sunlight. It was a glorious day, with a touch of unseasonable coolness in the breeze. The Quarter was quiet, with the curious, spent languor of a summer morning. She turned the corner and found herself in Jackson Square. Artists at their easels were lined in front of the imposing facade of St. Louis Cathedral. Street musicians, their instrument cases open at their feet for donations, staked out the four corners of the well-manicured park. Dominique smiled at the convergence of lively tunes, pausing a moment to enjoy the atmosphere. She drifted toward one of the long pedestrian arcades that flanked the park, its cool shade surrounding her like a cocoon. A little farther, the smell of freshly baked beignets from the French Market across the road beckoned her. She could almost taste the hot, fried dough smothered in confectioner's sugar, and her mouth watered. She thought about crossing the street and buying a small bag of the delicious treats, but the French Market was always so crowded; there would surely be a line. Maybe she would just have an ice cream. At the corner was an old-fashioned soda shop, and Dominique hurried toward it. On each side of the door was a mirrored panel bearing an etched impression of the store's name. As Dominique pulled open the door, she caught a glimpse of herself in the mirror and stopped short, hardly believing her eyes. Could that plump form really be hers? She had always been so petite, so slender. How had she let this happen? Her stomach was a round bulb stretching the front of her black dress. It sickened her to see it. Dominique stepped back in alarm and released the door. She wouldn't go in! She would go straight home. And when she got there, she would throw out all the junk food. What had she let Clay do to her? She shook her head vehemently. Only what she had permitted him. Unconsciously, she raised her chin and tightened her jaw with determination. Then she turned away from the shop and headed for home.

Two hours later, after eating a tuna fish salad for lunch, Dominique sat down at the desk in her study and began to go over the résumé she had put together for her new job quest. As she scanned it, she realized that her approach had been all wrong. She had listed her jobs and education, but not her most recent accomplishments in the event planning field. Why not take the same approach she'd used in New York fifteen years before? Her volunteer work was as meritorious as any for which she'd been paid, just as her background at the time had enabled her to enter event planning in the first place.

She decided to make a draft, which she would type later on Gabrielle's typewriter. Enthusiastically, Dominique began to describe some of the events she had organized. She devoted considerable space to her work on behalf of Mark Patout — it would look impressive to have been associated with a U.S. Senator.

Dominique smiled as she thought of him. For a moment, she paused in her writing, her pen tapping thoughtfully against her pursed lips. How long had it been since she'd spoken to Mark? Only a few times since his divorce from Nina. Clay and Dominique had hosted a dinner in his honor two years before, but Mark had been so surrounded by others that Dominique had barely had the chance to say hello. Most of Mark's time was spent in Washington now. That had been the case ever since he'd been elected to Congress.

Still, Dominique was certain that if she needed a letter of reference, he would be happy to provide it. She could attach it to her résumé so that, right away, people could see that she was well connected. Good connections were a prime asset in the event planning field. Of course, as Clay's wife, she had once had them.

Her brow furrowed as she considered the drastic change in her situation. Since the separation, she'd received only a fraction of the invitations she used to. And they had all been for daytime events, never dinner parties. As for her connections in the volunteer field, she had been too devastated to participate in any of the functions that had taken place since the new year. Why, she had been downright reclusive. There had been days at a time when she had let the phone ring and ring unanswered.

Now Dominique needed her old connections, and she knew she would not find them intact. According to Gabrielle, "Daddy" had "parties all the time."

"Really, who came?" Dominique would be compelled to ask.

"All the people who used to come here," Gabrielle said brightly. In her innocence, she was glad of the chance to see them again.

The thought that Marie was accepted everywhere enraged Dominique, but she struggled to suppress the feeling. She needed her energy for the work before her.

Dominique poised her pen above the notepad. What other assets could she include in her résumé? It would be good if she could get a letter of reference from someone at Orman's. The former store manager, Turner Coltrane, had long ago left for a job with Neiman Marcus in Dallas. Perhaps she could contact him there. And what about her old mentor, Bruce? He was now president of the entire Orman's chain. Surely, he would write a letter of reference. She had kept in touch with him and Maude over the years, exchanging greeting cards and family pictures. And, when Clay had left her, she'd written to them, somehow needing that link with happier times.

Feeling cheery at the prospect of talking to her old friend, Dominique picked up the phone and dialed Orman's number in New York. She spoke to a secretary, and seconds later Bruce's urbane voice, comfortingly familiar, greeted her. "Dominique! What a wonderful surprise!"

"Bruce, it's so good to talk to you again." They exchanged pleasantries for a few moments, then Dominique lowered her voice, suddenly serious. "I've appreciated Maude's letters these past few months. They helped me feel . . . less alone."

"Oh, Dominique, . . . we're so sorry. We wanted to call, but we weren't sure you were up to talking. Maude said —"

Dominique cut him short, but her tone was affectionate. "Sometimes it's easier to put your feelings down on paper. I wasn't ready to talk. . . ." Dominique's voice tapered off.

"I understand," Bruce said gently.

"But I'm better now, Bruce, truly." There was a sprightliness in her voice that lent credence to her claim. She leaned back in her chair, settling in for a long chat.

"Why don't you come up for a visit? We'd love to see you."

Dominique laughed. "Not yet! I'm busy looking for a job." She made an effort to keep her tone jolly. "I'm reduced to living in reduced circumstances."

Bruce's voice turned grave. "Dominique, you know that Maude and I can always give you a loan. I hope you wouldn't hesitate to ask."

Dominique couldn't reply immediately, she was so touched. What good friends they were! She had been feeling so alone, yet she *did* have resources; there *were* people who cared about her. "Oh, Bruce," she said softly, "you don't know how much that means to me, but I'll be fine as soon as I find full-time work."

"You're ready to go back to full time?" Bruce said thoughtfully.

"I haven't much choice." Dominique's tone was dry.

"Hmmm. . . . I didn't realize . . . ," Bruce murmured.

"Anyhow, will you write a letter of recommendation that I can attach to my résumé. I'll try to get one from Mark Patout, also. I think it will set my résumé apart from the rest," Dominique said energetically.

"Have you taken leave of your senses?" Bruce chuckled.

Dominique paused, taken aback. "I beg your pardon?"

"Résumés, letters, job applications? That's nonsense! You've got skills that are very much in demand nowadays. It'll be a cinch to find you a job."

"It hasn't been a cinch so far," Dominique said ruefully.

"Where have you looked?" Bruce sounded skeptical.

"Orman's for one —"

Bruce sighed. "I wish we could do something for you down there, but we're very happy with the person we have in your old slot."

"I know," Dominique said warmly. "She's great! I'm pleased she's done well."

There was a moment of silence. Then Bruce said, "You wouldn't be interested in coming back to New York, would you?"

Dominique hesitated. Move from New Orleans? She hadn't even considered it, yet, in some ways, it made perfect sense. Opportunities in another city would be limitless, since she wouldn't have to deal with people who'd known Clay Parker since childhood. In addition, a bigger city would have more businesses that could use her skills. And above all, there was Gabrielle to consider. She would be changing schools anyhow, since she was entering junior high. But New York? "I think it would be too drastic a change for Gabrielle," she told Bruce. "Besides" — she wrinkled her nose — "it's the most expensive city in the country."

There were a few moments of silence as they ruminated over this. Bruce was the first to speak. "Dominique. . . ." He hesitated. "What about Washington?"

"D.C.?" Dominique's voice quickened. She had always loved the city. It reminded her of Paris, with its flower-laden parks and broad avenues.

"Yes. A friend of mine, Grace Filmore, started a wedding planning business there a few years ago. Then she branched out. She does a lot of work with embassies, museums, lobbyists — that type of thing. Anyway, she called me a couple of weeks ago to ask if I could recommend someone for a vacancy in her office." He chuckled. "She knows we train the best here at Orman's. But, at the time, I couldn't think of anyone. I didn't know you were looking." He paused. "Apparently, the demand for her service is growing almost faster than she can keep up. Especially since most women in Washington have full-time jobs."

"They do?" Dominique asked.

Bruce laughed at her tone. "The winds of change may not have blown into New Orleans yet, but they will soon enough. The Old South is dying. You should see our Atlanta store. Half my top executives are women!"

"Really?" Dominique asked with interest. Of course Atlanta wasn't considered the South in the traditional sense. It was known as a mecca for northerners. Still, Bruce was making her aware of fascinating new possibilities. "You must have a lot of turnover. I mean, once the women get married and have children —"

"No, no!" Bruce interrupted good-naturedly. "They often work until the day they give birth, and then they're back in a couple of months."

Dominique sniffed disapprovingly. "So the child hardly sees its mother. That's not progress. When I was young, every upper-class European woman let servants raise the children. Still do, for all I know," Dominique added darkly, remembering her own childhood.

"You think a woman needs to give up her own aspirations for the sake of her children?" Bruce's challenge was issued in a thoughtful tone.

"Isn't bringing up your children ambition enough?" Dominique countered.

"Sure, but it wasn't for you."

Dominique bridled. "What do you mean? I quit my job before Gabrielle was even born!"

"You quit getting *paid*, but it wasn't long before you were doing the same thing for charity." Bruce had a calm, professorial way of making a point that soothed Dominique's ruffled feathers.

"Yes . . . but I didn't have to be at an office every day. I spent most of my time with Gabrielle," she said emphatically.

"But if the mother's happier working, maybe it's best for the whole family. Especially since a lot of fathers are helping more than they used to." Bruce paused. "You know, the choices you and Clay made may not be for everyone. The point is, the women I know are glad to have more choices than they had even five years ago. Besides" — again he hesitated — "you're going to be a working mother, too," he said gently.

Dominique was startled to think of herself that way. "You're right!" she admitted. She wrapped the phone cord around her finger as she mulled over Bruce's words. She sighed. "I don't regret the time I spent at home with Gabrielle, but I'd be in a better financial situation now if I'd continued to work." She paused. "I was brought up to believe that women didn't do that after they married. It was a big concession on Clay's part, I remember. And when we didn't need my income anymore, he wanted me to quit immediately. I wasn't ready to stop until Gabrielle, but then there was never any question," she concluded quietly. How would Gabrielle adjust to Dominique working? Would she be resentful? Lonely?

She must have betrayed her concern, because Bruce said, "It's lucky your mother lives with you. That way, Gabrielle won't come home to an empty house."

"At any rate," Dominique said in a resigned voice, "I have no choice. We'll have to get used to it."

"You'll do fine," Bruce reassured her.

Dominique thought of the misfortunes that had rocked her life. First in Egypt. Then her nightmarish union with Anton. The time of loneliness and despair in New York. And now . . . this. But she had weathered it. She had weathered it all! A surge of optimism fired her spirit.

"You'll call your friend today?" she asked eagerly.

Bruce chuckled. "As soon as we hang up."

"And you think she'll consider me?"

"You're exactly what she's looking for. Besides, to someone like Grace, a friend's recommendation means a lot more than an impressive résumé. But don't worry," Bruce said reassuringly, "you have both."

⧞   ⧞   ⧞

Dominique's first trip to Washington with Gabrielle began in disaster. As the realtor showed them one blank high-rise after another, Gabrielle's expression grew increasingly fearful and rebellious.

Finally, when they stopped for the day and mother and daughter were back in the hotel, Gabrielle broke down, sobbing. "Why do we have to move from our house? I hate it here. Why do we have to leave New Orleans?"

Dominique soothed her as best she could. "Honey, my new job is here." She was filled with distress, but it was mixed with a sense of urgency. "I begin August first. We have to find something and get settled before then."

"I don't like big apartment buildings! The halls are dark and creepy! They smell like carpet. Why can't we have a house like before?"

Because your father is a bastard, Dominique felt like saying. As Patricia Masterson had suspected, Clay had moved his assets to the business so Dominique couldn't touch them. But Masterson's threat to subpoena all Clay's financial records for the past three years — business and personal — had resulted in a settlement that provided good child support and reasonable alimony. And, to Clay's credit, he had insisted that Gabrielle attend Washington's best private school.

"It's time to start thinking about college," he'd intoned.

Patricia Masterson later told Dominique in private, "Clay's Achilles' heel is his ostentation. He wants to be able to say he's providing the best for his daughter, whatever that is. It's going to be very important to him that she go to a good university, that it doesn't look like he abandoned her." She paused and gave Dominique a shrewd look. "You just want to make sure that Gabrielle does what's best for *her*, not what Clay thinks is best. All he's interested in is brand names."

Dominique had protested. "Not just that! He truly loves Gabrielle."

Patricia Masterson had given her a dubious look, but she hadn't argued.

Now, as Dominique sat in the hotel room trying to comfort Gabrielle, she reflected on Patricia Masterson's words. Dominique wondered what Clay's reaction would be if he could see how unhappy Gabrielle was about moving. Did he care about the upheaval he'd caused in Gabrielle's life? Did he feel guilty that his own home, his own style of living, was so much more grand than his daughter's?

Oh, what was the use of such thoughts? Dominique wondered in frustration. She had no intention of asking Clay for more help. Her life — and Gabrielle's — was in her own hands now.

The next morning, Dominique picked up the classified section with renewed determination. And then she saw it: "Charm galore in exclusive Georgetown. 3 BR/1½ BA apt. in former carriage house. Sep. ent./FP/no pets."

Dominique dashed to the phone and dialed the number. Thirty minutes later, she and Gabrielle were in a taxi bumping over a shady, cobblestoned street. Flanking the narrow lane were discreet townhouses maintained in spit-and-polish style — shining brass knockers and freshly painted trim.

The driver stopped in front of the imposing red brick facade of a Georgian-style townhouse. The residence was the largest on the block, its expanse proclaiming its superiority over the quaint, narrow townhouses more typical of Georgetown. Long Palladian windows shut out the world with heavy draperies. A high brick wall, almost buried in climbing yellow roses, led from the side of the house to a point halfway down the block, where it intersected with a separate residence of mellow beige stucco.

Dominique and Gabrielle emerged from the cab and stepped onto a brick sidewalk set in a herringbone pattern. The walkway was old and, in spots, covered in fuzzy green moss. Two massive sycamore trees, only a few feet from the front of the house, shaded both the porticoed entrance and the street. Though the day was hot and humid, the narrowness of the street and the canopy of mature trees made it seem cooler.

Dominique glanced at her watch and saw that they were early. She turned and gave Gabrielle a reassuring smile, then took her arm. "Let's look around a little." The neighborhood was wrapped in Sunday morning tranquility, and there was no one about to observe them. They stood at the curb and scanned the block, first in one direction, then the other.

The homes were attached in one continuous row — very few had side gardens or alleys. Yet each facade was different, lending an air of eclectic quaintness to the whole. There were bay windows and turrets; houses of wood, stone, or brick; tiny front gardens or none at all. And everywhere there were flowers and trees. Not the exotic hodgepodge found in New Orleans, but regimented, European-style plantings.

"Mom!" Gabrielle called. She scampered to the brick wall of "their" house, and buried her face in the yellow roses. "Come smell these." She closed her eyes in appreciation.

Dominique smiled and went to join her. This was the happiest Gabrielle had looked since their arrival in Washington. When Dominique reached her daughter's side, she leaned close and sniffed the sweet aroma. "Wonderful," she murmured.

The thud of a car door closing made Dominique turn. A cheerful-looking woman of about sixty was heading in their direction.

"Mrs. Parker?" the woman asked as she approached with a smile.

Dominique shook her hand, then introduced Gabrielle.

They exchanged a few pleasantries, then the realtor pulled out a ring of keys and led them to a thick wooden door buried in the brick wall. Its hinges, old-fashioned iron ones, squeaked as the woman pushed it open.

Dominique and Gabrielle stepped onto a crooked stone path, stopped, and smiled at each other. In front of them stood a tiny elves' cottage of aged red brick. Two bay windows were hooded by copper roofs washed with a green patina. Ivy wound its way up the chimney.

The realtor turned to face them. "I should tell you that apartments in Georgetown are *very* small. But this one's a bargain. It just came on the market. The couple who owns it winters in Barbados and they want someone around the place. So they turned the carriage house

into an apartment. It used to be the wife's studio, I think." She lowered her voice confidentially. "They don't really need the money, so
they're not asking as much as they could. In exchange, though, you'd
have to pick up their mail and forward it to them while they're gone.
That's about it." Her voice returned to normal and she smiled.
"They're just looking for nice, stable tenants."

The woman stepped behind them and locked the wooden gate,
then led them through the shady garden to the front door. Despite
her warnings, Dominique wasn't prepared for the small size of the
house. The living room couldn't have been more than twelve feet
wide, Dominique was certain, and it also had to serve as a dining room.
But its uneven wooden floors shone with fresh wax and its built-in
bookcases created attractive alcoves on either side of the fireplace.
Dominique smiled to herself as she realized that the table and chairs
from her old dining room wouldn't even fit through the door. It was a
good thing she had sold them.

"Kitchen's this way," said the realtor, holding open a slatted
wooden door.

Dominique and Gabrielle simultaneously exclaimed in pleasure as
they stepped into the cheery little space. It sparkled with newly in-
stalled white appliances. On the rear wall were two sash windows and
a back door opening onto a small herb garden.

"It reminds me of my old place in Greenwich Village," Dominique
told Gabrielle wistfully.

"I love it!" Gabrielle whispered back. "And we're just a couple of
blocks from Wisconsin Avenue." One of Georgetown's two main commercial thoroughfares, Wisconsin Avenue was an enticing potpourri of
brightly painted boutiques, flower stands, restaurants, and bars. It was
Washington's "fun" district, crowded with pedestrians from ten in the
morning to the small hours of the night.

Dominique put a calming hand on Gabrielle's shoulder. "Let's see
upstairs first."

The realtor led the way up a narrow flight of wooden stairs. Two
small bedrooms at the front of the house had dormered windows, but
were painted bright white, making them appear larger. A bathroom,
with barely enough room for a stall shower, toilet, and sink — all
new — hid behind a narrow door in the hall. The master bedroom, in
the back of the house, had an original beamed ceiling and its own
minuscule half bath. From any of the four windows along the back

wall, it would have been possible to climb out onto the limbs of a huge old willow oak.

"I'm afraid there's no central air," the realtor said apologetically, "but there are window units."

Gabrielle tugged at her mother's sleeve. "Let's take it!" she whispered excitedly.

Dominique hesitated. The rent was more than she would have expected for such a small place, but it *was* unique. She looked around the little room, already envisioning how nice her white cotton and lace bedspread would look there. And she'd hang window boxes, fill them with flowers. Dominique turned to the realtor. "We'll take it!"

CHAPTER 21 ∾

DOMINIQUE pushed forward from the waist, her hands stretched toward her knees, her face scrunched into a grimace. "Twenty!" she gasped. "That's enough!" She lay back on the rug and swiped at her face with the sleeve of her sweatshirt.

"Mom," Gabrielle said with an air of superiority, "that's not enough." She released Dominique's ankles and stood up. She crossed the tiny living room and went into the kitchen. Dominique heard the sound of a cabinet opening, then closing, the rush of the faucet. A few seconds later, Gabrielle reappeared, a glass of water in her hand. She took a sip, then handed it to her mother. "You should do another twenty in a couple of minutes," she said firmly.

Dominique looked at her daughter's slim figure, then down at her own lumpy form. "Easier said than done," she remarked wryly. She turned over onto her stomach, her arms and legs splayed out in exhaustion. "What an awful way to spend our first weekend in Washington! We should be out exploring — the Smithsonian or something."

Suddenly Gabrielle was a little girl again. Her face lit with enthusiasm and she clapped her hands together. "Yeah, and can we see a movie after?"

Dominique looked over her shoulder at her daughter. "What movie?"

Gabrielle's eyes sparkled with mischief. "*Klute*?" she asked, flinching comically.

Dominique rolled her eyes and pushed herself back into a supine position. She folded her arms behind her head as a pillow. "You know better than that!"

"Aw, Mom!" Gabrielle moaned. "I'm old enough."

Dominique laughed at her daughter's maudlin show of disappointment. "No! Besides, we still have to unpack." She looked around at the cardboard boxes stacked against the walls. Their new place was small, and the boxes made it appear positively cramped. Especially when compared to the baronial home they had left behind in New Orleans. Dominique wondered what Solange's reaction would be when she arrived from New York the following week. The older woman had exclaimed over the photographs of the cottage, but would the size come as a shock when she experienced it in person? "We should get these boxes unpacked before Grand-mère comes," Dominique said. "And, don't forget, I start my job on Monday, so it has to be done this weekend."

"Are you scared about your new job?"

Dominique looked up at Gabrielle's worried face, thankful that her daughter was there. How alone she would have felt without her! And Dominique knew they would both be glad when Solange arrived. They needed a sense of family, now more than ever. "Why should I be scared?" Dominique said in a soothing voice. "I know what I'm doing and, besides, Grace Filmore is a very nice lady." Dominique drew her limbs in and prepared to stand up.

Gabrielle looked back at her mother, her gaze speculative. "The exercise is helping, you know," she offered.

Dominique, kneeling, looked down at herself. "You see a difference?"

Gabrielle nodded. "Yeah." The syllable ended with an uplift of surprise. "Yeah, I do." Gabrielle folded her legs under her and sank to the floor. "Ready for another twenty?"

"No!" Dominique protested. "Come on, let's go out!" She pushed one foot under her and made as though to rise.

Gabrielle gave her a reproachful look. "After you've finished your sit-ups," she insisted. She tugged on the front of her mother's sweatshirt.

"Oh, all right!" Dominique conceded grumpily. She let her body fall backward, then heaved herself up and began to count.

CHAPTER 22 ∾

DOMINIQUE hurried through the sleek lobby of the office building until she reached the bank of brass-fronted elevators. As soon as she pressed "up," she heard a chime, and a set of double doors slid open. Two men wearing pin-striped suits and holding briefcases emerged. With a thrill of anticipation, Dominique took their place. It was fun to be working again! To be on her way to "the office."

She pressed the button for the tenth floor and stepped to the back of the elevator. As the doors were about to close, she heard high heels beating a tattoo across the polished granite floor. A glossy brown hand with long, shining red nails thrust through the opening and determinedly shoved the doors apart.

Into the car stepped one of the most stunning women Dominique had ever seen. She was perhaps six feet tall, with a close-cropped black Afro and impossibly high cheekbones. Even more dramatic was the vivid red mididress, slit to the thigh.

Fashion model, Dominique thought immediately.

"I'm sorry!" the young woman opposite her said. She was breathing hard from her run. "I'm late." She glanced at her watch. "Not really late. It's only nine, but I would have been if I hadn't caught this elevator." She gave Dominique a friendly glance with her long-lashed black eyes. They were heavily made up à la Cleopatra but, on her, anything less would have been out of place. The look worked sensationally.

Dominique smiled. "What floor would you like?"

The woman turned to the panel of buttons. "You've already pushed it. Are you going to Capital Events?"

Dominique let out a startled laugh. "How did you know?"

"Mrs. Filmore announced it at the staff meeting on Friday. So I guess you're Dominique Parker." She held out one of her perfectly manicured hands and said, "I'm Felice Michaels, the receptionist."

Dominique shook her hand and said, "Pleased to meet you."

The elevator came to a halt and the doors opened with a subdued *whoosh*.

"Follow me!" said the woman with a bright smile. "It's right here." She stopped in front of a set of double glass doors opposite the elevators. Inside the office, the lights were on. "Uh-oh," she said softly, "Dragon Lady's here."

Dominique raised her eyebrows in surprise. "Mrs. Filmore?" The woman was one of the most refined and pleasant people Dominique had ever met.

Felice expelled a whispered giggle. "Of course not! She's an angel! But she only comes in about once a week." She pushed open the door and leaned against it so Dominique could pass through. "You know, for important presentations, that sort of thing." She paused and cast a secretive glance down the hall. "Sylvia Brussels pretty much runs the show." She lowered her voice even more, and spoke in a manner both urgent and conspiratorial. "You should report to her right away."

Felice let the door fall closed behind Dominique, then hurried to the reception desk. It was an antique Regency writing table of a quality rarely found in offices. Dominique looked around at the rest of the furniture. All of it was fine, the sort one might expect to see in an embassy. But the muted cream and peach color scheme, and the pastoral landscapes on the walls, softened the elitist effect. Though it transmitted an aura of distinct success, the reception area was welcoming.

Dominique had never before visited the office. Mrs. Filmore had instead invited her to lunch — "to give us a chance to get acquainted in a more relaxed setting" — treating her more like a social acquaintance than a prospective employee. "Your résumé is impressive and, of course, I hold Bruce's opinion in the highest regard. You're probably just what the firm needs. We have some very competent people, but I've been looking for someone with your social background. Someone who understands protocol and dinner service à la Russe, if you see what I mean." Dominique saw. She told Mrs. Filmore about some of her recent projects. In the end, Mrs. Filmore said uncertainly, "You seem overqualified for the opening we have, but we could certainly use you." Then she had smiled reassuringly. "And we reward good work with promotions."

Dominique had leapt at the offer, and Mrs. Filmore had visibly relaxed. "Enough business! You're from New Orleans? You must know Loulou de la Houssaye. Really? Her place in Cap-Ferrat? August 1970? Why, we must have missed each other by just days!"

In that glow of acceptance, Dominique would have felt boorish to press for details of her employment. The salary mentioned was adequate and her title would be that of project assistant. Only once had Grace Filmore uttered the name of Sylvia Brussels. "It's a shame she's out of town. She runs the office on a day-to-day basis and you'll be reporting to her, for the most part. Don't worry about it, though. I'm sure she'll be delighted I've found someone of your background. Phone me when you've settled in your new house and I'll let the staff know you're to join us."

Now Dominique wished that Mrs. Filmore was available to introduce her to Sylvia Brussels. It would have been so much more comfortable than simply presenting herself to the unknown woman. Nervously, she asked Felice, "You're sure Mrs. Filmore isn't going to be in today?"

Felice gave her a sympathetic look. "She's in New York until Wednesday."

Dominique sighed and lifted the hand holding her purse. "If you could just point the way to my office, I'll put this down before I go to see Miss Brussels."

Felice stood up and came around her desk, shaking her head from side to side. "Miss Brussels will assign you an office." She put a hand on Dominique's arm in a gesture of camaraderie. "I wouldn't keep her waiting, if I were you."

Dominique tried to stifle her sense of disquiet. She took one last look around the reception area. Its gracious ambiance was reassuring. Then she turned back to the receptionist. Felice looked no older than her mid-twenties. Maybe this was her first job; it would explain her apparent fear of Sylvia Brussels.

"How long have you been working here?" Dominique asked.

"A year. I worked in a law office before, but was that ever boring!" Felice grimaced.

Dominique laughed. "You certainly don't look like the law office type," she said in a way that made it sound complimentary.

Felice smiled in acknowledgment. Then her expression turned serious. "Anyway, Mrs. Filmore is a sweetie. But" — she glanced at her wristwatch — "I'm keeping you from Miss Brussels. You'd better go on," she said gently. She looked up at Dominique with an expression of encouragement. "Last door on the left. I'll let her know you're here." She pointed down the hall.

Dominique lifted her chin and, with what she hoped was a relaxed gait, headed in the direction Felice had indicated. The hall was as carefully decorated as the reception area, Dominique noted, with fine prints and recessed lighting. The very atmosphere was soothing.

At the end of the hall, she stopped outside a closed door that announced, in brass letters, "Sylvia Brussels." Before Dominique knocked, she glanced down at her suit to ensure that every seam was in place. The understated Halston of navy silk was several years old, but a classic. Dominique was relieved that she could fit into it again, for she never could have afforded it now. Knowing that it had been tailored for her gave her confidence; she felt polished and professional-looking.

Dominique put a smile on her face and rapped on the door.

Silence. A few seconds ticked by. She raised her hand hesitantly. Should she knock again?

"Come in," said an impatient voice.

Dominique opened the door and stepped into a starkly modern space of chrome, black, and white.

Sylvia Brussels glared at Dominique over the top of her glasses. They were thick, black-framed affairs perched halfway down her pointed nose and contrasting harshly with her frosted blond hair. The glasses, though, matched the rest of her outfit: a flawlessly cut black silk dress, black sheer stockings, and black pumps. Sylvia had the ghostly complexion of a person who rarely saw the sun, the only touches of color provided by her crimson lipstick and matching nails. Everything about her was hard-edged and cold.

Determined to charm her into acceptance, Dominique took a step forward. "How do you do? I'm Dominique Parker."

"Right. The new girl."

Dominique tried not to flinch at the condescending phrase.

Sylvia sat back in her chair and gave Dominique a suspicious look. "You have some connection with Mrs. Filmore?"

"We have a mutual friend," Dominique said calmly. "I didn't meet Mrs. Filmore until the interview."

Sylvia shuffled some papers on her desk. "Right. In July. I was in Hong Kong." Her tone seemed to imply that Dominique had contrived an interview at precisely the moment when Sylvia was out of town. She plucked a piece of paper from her desk and ran her eyes over it with deliberation. Then she gave Dominique a piercing look. "It says here that you're from New Orleans. What's that accent?"

"French," Dominique replied, meeting her gaze steadily. "But I'm completely bilingual. I speak Italian and a little Arabic, too." She paused before continuing in a matter-of-fact tone. "Mrs. Filmore says that you do some work with embassies. I hope my languages will prove useful."

Sylvia sniffed and went back to studying Dominique's résumé.

Dominique shifted uncomfortably from foot to foot. It was unforgivable that this woman should leave her standing. "May I sit down?" she asked pleasantly.

Sylvia looked up, removed her glasses, and gave Dominique the fish eye. For a second, Dominique had the horrified feeling that her request would be turned down, and she was tempted to turn on her heel and walk out of the office. But she *had* to make Sylvia like her. Her job depended on it. Dominique forced an agreeable smile.

With a flip of her wrist, Sylvia finally said, "This won't take long, but go ahead."

Dominique realized she'd been holding her breath. She exhaled and sat, stiff and straight-backed, on one of the black leather and chrome chairs in front of Sylvia's desk.

Sylvia cleared her throat and folded her hands in front of her like a judge ready to administer a sentence. "I hope Mrs. Filmore warned you that this isn't a nine-to-five job. We work weekends and evenings and we don't get much time off."

Dominique said with composure, "I remember what it was like. I look forward to the challenge."

Sylvia's expression was cynical. "How long since you had a paying job?"

You know the answer, Dominique thought angrily, my résumé is right in front of you. Aloud, she said, "A number of years, but payment really has nothing to do with the effort I put forward. When I worked on Senator Patout's campaign or the Heart Fund ball, I tried to do as well as I did for Orman's."

Sylvia pursed her lips and began to lecture, "This is *not* the same — " But the ringing of the telephone interrupted her.

Felice's voice came over the intercom. "Mrs. Hamilton, line one."

"I have to take this," Sylvia snapped. She gave Dominique a dismissive wave of her hand. "Your office is all the way down the hall on the left."

◌ ◌ ◌

Mrs. Filmore's unobtrusive black sedan stopped in front of the high iron gates that so elegantly barricaded the entrance to the French embassy. Her driver lowered the window and announced his passengers, then the gates swung back and the car moved up the long, curving drive.

Dominique's pulse raced with anticipation as they drew near the main structure. The embassy looked like the country château of foreign nobility, its architecture distinctly European: light cornerstones on dark brick, leaded windows, and arched doorways. Set in a tree-dappled preserve in the exclusive Kalorama section of downtown Washington, the impressive acreage tumbled down a hill to Rock Creek Park, lending an air of splendid isolation to the property.

Mrs. Filmore turned to Dominique and smiled. "I've told them that you speak French and Italian. They're most eager to work with you." She looked past Dominique and fixed her gaze on Sylvia. Sylvia regarded her with an expression of attentive respect. When Mrs. Filmore was present, even Sylvia was subdued. "I think we can let Dominique play a leading role in this presentation. After all, it's the French ambassador's wife who organized the others. She'll appreciate the fact that we have a native French speaker on our staff," said Mrs. Filmore.

If Sylvia wanted to argue, she didn't show it, but Dominique suspected that it would kill her to remain in the background while Mrs. Filmore thrust Dominique into the limelight. Dominique regarded Mrs. Filmore with a look of trusting affection. She was the very picture of a Washington socialite, with her immovable gray pageboy swept straight back from her forehead, her aristocratic features (beautifully maintained with plastic surgery), and her discreet, almost stodgy, designer clothes. It was a look only slightly more contemporary than the

Queen of England's, but it was instantly recognizable as "Washing-ton elite."

Dominique was sorry that she saw so little of Mrs. Filmore. The office was more welcoming when she was present. But, despite her frequent absences, Mrs. Filmore seemed to have kept careful track of Dominique's progress in the firm. She had praised Dominique's work on her first assignment, the wedding of Senator McAllister's daughter. And she had called her assistance in the grand opening of the new Smithsonian exhibit "crucial."

"Kudos, dear. I don't know how we ever got along without you."

Now, after only three months with Capital Events, Dominique was being handed a leading role in a contract proposal to thirteen of Washington's most important embassies.

"It's not as though you're a novice," Mrs. Filmore told her. "The only reason you weren't made a project manager immediately was because we wanted to give you a chance to catch up on things," she explained cryptically.

Dominique knew that, in Mrs. Filmore's polite language, that meant she had been put through a trial period — and had apparently passed. If she handled this assignment well, she had no doubt she would be awarded the title of project manager. Then, who knew? Maybe account executive.

The embassies were to fund a gala in honor of the new members of Congress who would be elected in the coming week. The party would be held four months later, in February, 1973, after Congress reconvened. Each embassy possessed the staff necessary to host a gala on its own, but foreseeing turf wars, the group had decided to hire an outside contractor for the event. The contractor would do everything: conceive a theme, compile an invitation list, obtain a prominent member of Congress to serve as guest of honor, and, of course, work with caterers, printers, and all the others who provided services for such an event.

Dominique had handled large events before, but never one of this magnitude and complexity. There would be pitfalls, she knew, in reporting to a committee of thirteen.

The car rolled smoothly to a stop. Mrs. Filmore made no move to get out until the driver held open her door. Dominique followed her as Sylvia got out on the other side.

Mrs. Filmore turned to wait for the blond woman to catch up to them, giving Dominique a chance to gather her composure. It helped that the late October day was so lovely, with just a hint of autumn crispness in the air. She watched as squirrels, startled by the humans in their midst, scuttled away through the golden leaves.

Dominique felt Mrs. Filmore tap her arm lightly, and they turned toward the front door. As they walked, Dominique nervously touched the Hermès scarf she had draped, with continental flair, over her black silk suit.

A butler opened the door, and the women stepped into a soaring hall that rose endlessly past the balustraded galleries of a spiral staircase. The dark, paneled walls were almost hidden by exquisite tapestries depicting medieval scenes. In the center of the floor was a round table of inlaid wood. Though it was as large as a dining table, it appeared small in the vast space. Upon it rested a four-foot-tall arrangement of fresh flowers that looked like something out of a rococo painting.

Dominique suddenly realized that she hadn't been in such an interior since her youth in Egypt. Here was a richness that could only be acquired through centuries of collection. Though the building itself was not, of course, so venerable, it was furnished with treasures of the French empire.

Sylvia gave the butler their names. Then the women were led into a long salon containing several groupings of delicate antique furniture. A petite fiftyish brunette with an ultrastylish short haircut came toward them. She was wearing a bright red suit that was unmistakably Chanel.

"Ah, Madame Filmore, thank you so much for coming." The brunette presented a graciously outstretched hand. "I am Michelle de la Croix." The wife of the French ambassador.

Dominique liked her for not using her title of Countess. She smiled as the woman turned to her.

Mrs. Filmore put a maternal hand on Dominique's arm and said, "This is one of our associates, Dominique Parker. As I told you on the phone, not only is she a former citizen of your own lovely country, but she's an expert on large galas."

The Comtesse de la Croix widened her eyes in delight and rattled off a welcoming phrase in French. Dominique replied in the same language, but then switched to English, in deference to her two superiors. However, the comtesse continued to address most of her remarks to Dominique. It was clear that she felt comfortable with her. So did the other ambassadresses, who seemed to recognize in Dominique a person who shared their background. Dominique chatted briefly with the Italian ambassadress in her own language, then won points with the British ambassadress by relating amusing anecdotes of her time with the Royal Air Force.

Mrs. Filmore beamed as she observed the immediate rapport between Dominique and the other women. Sylvia Brussels glowered.

When the presentation was over and the three were back in Mrs. Filmore's car, the older woman said in her usual understated way, "I believe we'll get that account." She gave Dominique a kindly pat on the hand.

And it turned out to be true.

More surprising was the announcement at the staff meeting a few days later that Dominique would be in charge of the event. Until then, Sylvia had assigned Dominique to work under a supervisor, clearly not trusting her to perform on her own. So when Mrs. Filmore announced the new assignment — while Sylvia looked on with an expression that held a blend of challenge and cunning — Dominique's joy was tinged with apprehension.

"I can't afford to make a mistake," she confided to Felice over lunch. They had taken a break from the office to go to the Greenery, a stylish restaurant of blond wood and ferns that specialized in vegetarian fare. The dusky-eyed woman nodded understandingly as she munched on her salad.

Dominique stabbed a piece of raw broccoli and regarded it with distaste before she bit into it. She wasn't fond of broccoli, but it satisfied her appetite. Thanks to her careful regimen, she now weighed less than she had when she'd married Clay. Her new slenderness suited her, emphasizing her high cheekbones and large eyes.

Felice took a sip of water and said, "You just watch your back." She leaned forward and lowered her voice. "And lock your desk."

Dominique's eyebrows shot up. "Lock my desk? Are you saying that Sylvia would actually go through it?" She shook her head with incredulity. "Why? What could she possibly be looking for?"

Felice shrugged. "Fishing expedition. She does it to everyone. She makes such a big deal about coming in on weekends and working late — you know, the whole martyr thing — but half the time I think she's searching through people's desks."

"What could she possibly find?" Dominique asked, truly bewildered.

"You'd be surprised what people keep in their desks," Felice said knowingly. "Résumés, past-due work, letters about problems that might have come up with a job, . . . lots of stuff."

Dominique still couldn't believe it. She had never in her life read another person's mail, much less searched through their things. "How can you be sure she's doing it?"

Felice gave a bark of mirthless laughter. "She makes no bones about it. If she finds something incriminating, she confronts the person with it. Makes up some feeble excuse about why she was looking through the desk. A woman got fired last year because Sylvia found an old bill from the caterer stuck in the desk drawer. The caterer had been complaining about not being paid, and the woman claimed to have submitted the bill to accounts payable. It's true that she made a mistake, but it would have been resolved. Then Sylvia found the bill and went crazy. Called her at home and fired her."

The story depressed Dominique. It was impossible for her to understand the motivations of a person like Sylvia. Why was she so sour? "I can't believe Mrs. Filmore supports this kind of behavior."

Felice shook her head. "Who's going to tell her? If someone does something wrong and Sylvia catches them, what do they possibly gain by confessing it to Mrs. Filmore?" She paused, then added, "Sylvia's tough on everyone, but she really has it in for you. If she could catch you in a mistake . . ." She didn't finish her sentence, but her ominous tone left no room for misunderstanding.

Dominique sighed. "I do a good job. I don't understand what she has against me."

Felice raised her eyebrows. "You don't?" She let out a short, sardonic laugh. "Jealousy, pure and simple."

"But she's my boss! And Mrs. Filmore seems to have complete faith in her. Depends on her to run the office . . . everything. Why should she be jealous of me?"

Felice gave Dominique a look of exasperation. "You're being dense. Don't you see? You're from the same world as Mrs. Filmore. Sylvia Brussels can never fit in like you do. You've got style and class and everybody likes you. And one day you just turn up on Sylvia's doorstep." Felice threw up her hands comically. "Sylvia hires *everyone* at Capital Events. But you just turn up." Her eyes gleamed naughtily and she leaned closer to Dominique. "Can't you see that Sylvia Brussels is scared to death of you?" Felice giggled, obviously enjoying the thought.

Dominique turned her hands up in a gesture of appeal. "But I don't want anything of hers. I'm just grateful to have a job. And if I do well, it's good for everyone in the firm, including Sylvia."

"If you say so, but I doubt she sees it that way," Felice said ominously.

Dominique was silent as she contemplated this. It was disturbing to think that someone she relied upon was hoping for her failure. Finally, she sighed. "Well, I just have to make sure I do a great job." She paused. "If I can get a good guest of honor — someone really important — that'll go a long way."

Felice took a bite of salad and nodded in agreement. "Guest of honor's the whole thing in Washington. Get a good name on that invitation and no one will dare refuse."

"You would think an invitation from thirteen embassies would be enough to bring in the entire Congress," Dominique grumbled.

"You know better than that," Felice said with a nod of emphasis.

Dominique twisted her mouth into a half-smile and recited in a weary voice. "Right. White House comes first in rank, then important senators and congressmen —"

Felice grinned. "Then big lobbies: American Medical Association, AFL-CIO."

Dominique laughed. "National Rifle Association!"

"Mmm hmm," Felice said. "And all the other moneybags. The Harrimans, Mary Lasker, . . ."

"And then all those lobbyists who take congressmen on junkets. Hunting, golfing, . . ."

"Hawaii, Bermuda . . . ," Felice said dreamily.

"And finally" — Dominique made a little flourish with her hand — "the embassies."

The two women burst into laughter.

"So. . . ." Felice put down her knife and fork and leaned her chin on her hand. "You know anyone with clout?"

Dominique patted her mouth with her napkin, then replaced it on her lap. She took a deep breath and let it out slowly. "I'm sure Mrs. Filmore does, but I have a feeling it would be better if I did this on my own." She met Felice's inquisitive gaze. "I know one member of the Senate."

Felice's face lit up. "An important one?"

"Ye-e-es." Dominique drew out the word. "He's chairman of one of the top committees."

Felice turned her hands up. "Can you get him?"

Dominique looked down and twitched the teaspoon that rested beside her plate.

Felice leaned forward, her palms on the edge of the table. "Well?" she persisted.

Dominique refused to meet her friend's probing eyes. "I don't know. I haven't spoken to him in a couple of years."

"Yeah. So? Were you friends?"

Dominique lifted one shoulder and let if fall. "Sort of. My ex-husband and I had him over a few times. I met him a long time ago. He was host of an event I organized when I was at Orman's. And I also volunteered for his senatorial campaign. We got to be pretty friendly."

"Oooh. Juicy!" Felice said with relish. "You mean you had the hots for him?"

"Of course not!" Dominique said more sharply than she intended. She shook her head with rapid little movements. Out of the corner of her eye, she saw the long white apron of the waiter. He reached for Dominique's plate and she was forced to sit back and meet Felice's eyes. She encountered a sly look.

"So . . . did he have the hots for you?"

Dominique blushed furiously. "No! I mean . . . I don't know. Maybe at first. A little. But he's married. Well, not any more, but he *was*." She stopped, aware that she sounded flustered.

Felice gave her a knowing look. She was silent for a moment, then a smirk appeared on her face. "You're a lousy liar," she teased.

Dominique wished the hot flush in her cheeks would subside. She cleared her throat and lifted her chin, determined to regain her composure.

Seeing her friend's discomfiture, Felice erased the smirk from her face. In a more serious tone, she asked, "Who is he?"

"Mark Patout." Dominique couldn't keep the pride from her voice. His was an impressive name in Washington. What's more, he was known for integrity in a city where that quality was rare.

"Mark Patout?" Felice repeated.

"From Louisiana," Dominique clarified.

Felice widened her eyes. "I *know* who he is. Everyone knows who he is! You're saying you could get him as guest of honor?"

Dominique turned down her mouth in a Gallic expression of uncertainty. "I don't know. That's just it. As I said, we were once friends."

Felice emitted a short, incredulous laugh. "No wonder you have the hots for him! He's divorced, powerful, and a hunk! What more could a gal want?"

Dominique's mouth dropped open in outrage. "I never said he was anything more than a friend!"

Felice rolled her eyes. "Uh-huh. Right."

"You don't have to be sarcastic." Dominique's voice softened. "If you'd ever seen my ex-husband, you'd understand why I wasn't attracted to anyone else."

"You still carrying a torch for Clay?" Felice asked sympathetically.

"Of course not!" Dominique immediately turned in her seat to hail the waiter. She made a writing motion in the air to indicate that she wanted the check. Then she bent down to pick up her purse.

"Hey . . . ," Felice said softly.

Dominique raised her head.

"Because if you *are* still carrying a torch for him, you've got to stop that right away. From everything you've said, the guy's a grade-A jerk."

Dominique's impulse to defend Clay was automatic. "Look, he fell in love with someone else, and that hurt me. But he's a lot better than some ex-husbands. At least he pays for a good school for Gabrielle. And my alimony's not so bad."

Felice snapped her fingers in front of Dominique's face. "Oh, wake up, honey! He's a millionaire with enough money to support you in comfort for the rest of your life, isn't he? If he'd done right by you, you wouldn't be working."

Dominique shifted uncomfortably. She didn't like to be reminded of the raw deal she'd gotten from Clay. It made her feel foolish. And yet, she had fought back to the best of her abilities. It was just that he — and his attorney — had been planning their strategy for months, maybe even years. And all the while she'd loved and trusted Clay blindly. It was too painful to admit.

"I'd probably go crazy if I didn't work," Dominique rationalized. She shook her head. "I never wanted a life of leisure in the first place."

Felice's expression turned hard. "That has nothing to do with it and you know it." She brought her fist lightly down on the table. "You always make excuses for him!"

"I don't." Dominique's voice was defensive. "I just see a lot of divorcées worse off than I." She paused. "Besides. He's Gabrielle's father. It doesn't help her if I act bitter toward him." She gave her friend a look of appeal.

Felice swept the air in front of her face with her hand. "You're too forgiving," she groused.

Dominique smiled wistfully. "When you have children, you'll understand."

CHAPTER 23 ∽

"DOMINIQUE!" Mark's warm, rich voice resounded with pleasure.

"Mark!" Dominique pulled the phone cord away from the kitchen wall and sat down at the little table in front of the window. A bowl of green beans rested there, waiting to be cleaned. But Dominique was too surprised to continue her work. Why had Mark called her at home? She had left only her office number. She swallowed and tried to recover her presence of mind. "Thank you for calling me back so promptly. I didn't expect to hear from you until tomorrow."

"Now, would that be any way to treat an old friend, not to mention the best volunteer I ever had?" Mark teased.

Dominique smiled and relaxed. She had expected him to sound more distant, perhaps more self-important. But he had the same ease about him as before — as though his conversation with Dominique were the only demand on his time. "I know you must be busy," she murmured.

His voice dropped a register. "Don't be silly," he chided her gently.

Dominique could hear the smile in his voice. She curled one of her legs under her and leaned back comfortably in her chair. "It's nice to talk to you again," she said, meaning it. "I guess you know we're living here now."

"We?" Mark's voice sounded sharp. "Someone told me that you and Clay . . ." He didn't finish.

"I meant Gabrielle and Mother and I," Dominique said hastily.

There was an uncomfortable silence.

Mark was the first to speak. "I'm sorry. It must be difficult for you."

Dominique could feel his sympathy for her. Had his own divorce been as painful? Dominique attempted a light laugh, but it came out sounding abrasive. "It was a shock," she confessed. "I'm still a little . . ." She sighed. "It's hard to get used to."

"When did you move up here?" Mark asked.

"Late July, right after we finalized the separation agreement."

"Nice birthday present," Mark said dryly.

Dominique stopped short, not certain she had heard correctly.

"August fifth, right?" he asked.

"How did you remember?" Dominique asked, stunned.

"I remember the important things," he said lazily.

Dominique glowed with pleasure. It had been so long since she'd been at the center of anyone's thoughts. She laughed, this time genuinely. Then she remembered the purpose of her call and her voice became more businesslike. "As delightful as it is to talk to you again, I'd better confess that I'm calling to ask a favor."

"I'm glad," Mark said immediately. "I owe you one." He paused for a second. "Correction. I owe you at least ten or twenty."

"You don't!" Dominique protested, her voice affectionate. "What Clay and I did for your campaign —" She stopped abruptly. There it was again. Clay and I. Why couldn't she expunge him from her speech? "What *I* did," she amended, "I did because I believed that you were the best person for the job. And . . . and I had fun."

"Well, I'm glad, but I still owe you. Now what's on your mind?"

Dominique picked a green bean out of the bowl in front of her and absently snapped off the stem as she explained about the embassy-hosted "Welcome to Washington" party. "I thought about having it at that new Kennedy Center, if we could possibly get it. I have an appointment to meet with their public affairs person."

"So you're planning a big ball?"

"Not only that. I want to find out what play is scheduled to run that evening and ask for a special performance. I hope I'm far enough in advance so they won't have sold tickets to the general public."

"Sounds great!" Mark said enthusiastically.

"That's not all." Dominique's eyes sparkled as she was drawn into explaining her concept. "For earlier, I have another idea that I think will make the event unique. Practical, anyhow." Dominique frowned.

"I hope the sponsors won't think it too commercial." She hesitated. "Maybe I could test it on you."

Mark chuckled. "Go ahead."

"Well, it occurred to me that when I first moved here, I had no idea where anything was. Most of the stores in Georgetown are expensive little boutiques. I wanted to know where I could find the best super-markets, health clubs, doctors, shoemakers, dry cleaners — and not have to pay Georgetown prices." She lowered her voice conspiratori-ally. "You know, the taxes in Virginia are half what they are in D.C. You just take a five-minute drive over the bridge and you've already saved a little money." Her tone became more brusque. "But that's not the main point. Newcomers just need to know where things are."

"I agree. So what are you going to do? Print guides?"

Dominique grinned. "No. That would cost my clients money. But what if we set aside an area at the gala where local businesses can have display tables? They could open charge accounts or just hand out information."

"You mean an exhibition area? You think the embassies would like that image?"

Dominique laughed. "You sound skeptical, and I don't blame you. But what I have in mind is very discreet — not cardboard booths draped in red, white, and blue." She paused. "The room would be completely separate, maybe even on a different floor from the main event. We'd set up attractive writing tables — the kind you'd see in a bank or a very nice hotel. The people manning the desks would be in black tie. And we'd have waiters circulating with champagne. Maybe some harp music." Dominique paused. "You know, it occurs to me that those businesses would probably be willing to cover the cost asso-ciated with using the Kennedy Center."

"They'll probably compete for the privilege!" Mark sounded as ex-cited as Dominique.

"So you like the idea of having businesses there?"

"Now that you've explained it."

Dominique beamed. "And, of course, the ball itself will have the best of everything. The Iranian embassy is providing the caviar; the French, the champagne; flowers from Holland — they all want to make it as lavish as possible."

"Sure. It's a chance for them to showcase their countries and get off on the right foot with new members of Congress."

"Then . . . you have no problem with being the guest of honor?" Dominique asked, a little shyly.

"Dominique, for you I'd be the guest of honor at a tractor pull."

Dominique laughed. "Thank you. You've encouraged me!" she said cheerfully. "I can't wait to present the idea at the staff meeting tomorrow."

"I'm sure they'll love it," Mark said warmly.

"I'll let you know. Otherwise, the concept may have to be something different."

There was a brief, awkward silence.

Mark cleared his throat. "Listen, Dominique, I'd like to see you before then. How about getting together for a drink?"

Dominique's heart raced. Was it possible that Mark still felt toward her as he once had? She shouldn't jump to conclusions, she warned herself. Maybe he was just being kind to an old friend. Dominique knew he felt obligated to her. But how did she feel toward him? She loved talking to him on the phone, just as she always had. But was she attracted to him? In need of ego gratification? She wasn't certain of the answer — she only knew that she would very much like to see him.

"I'd like that," Dominique said warmly.

"Great!" Mark sounded genuinely pleased. "How about" — Dominique heard pages turning — "next Wednesday at six? I'll pick you up in front of your office."

Wednesday. Not a weekend. Drinks, not dinner. Dominique's racing heart slowed. Mark was probably just being friendly, after all. She said, "Fine. And you don't need to pick me up. Why don't we just meet in the lobby of the Madison Hotel? That's a halfway point. I'll try to have a blueline of the invitation by then."

There was a momentary silence, as though Mark didn't understand the reference. Then he said, "Oh. Oh. That would be great. Okay, I'll see you then."

怀 怀 怀

Mark replaced the receiver, noting the damp print his palm left on the instrument. He felt like a schoolboy after an encounter with the most popular girl in class. He had felt that way ever since his secretary had handed him the message slip with Dominique's name on it. He had read with disbelief the return phone number in Washington. Laying

aside messages from the deputy secretary of commerce, a fellow senator, and two important lobbyists from Baton Rouge, Mark had immediately dialed the number. He had dialed it himself, not wanting to
depersonalize the call by having his secretary place it for him. Unfortunately, there had been no answer at Capital Events. Dominique
must have gone home. Where did she live, Mark wondered? He called
information. What city please? the operator asked. Mark hadn't a clue.
After several tries, the operator located a D. Parker in Georgetown.

Dominique's wonderful voice was the same. Even if there had been
nothing else alluring about her, that accent would have been enough,
Mark thought. Talking to her made him feel somehow more complete,
as though she had awakened his emotions from a state of hibernation.
It wasn't that he didn't have women friends. Although he had long
ago left behind a disillusioned Nina, there had been others. But no
one had evoked in him the response Dominique had so many years
before. And though he hadn't seen Dominique often over the years,
each time he did, he felt that same reawakening that made his emotions toward other woman seem shallow by comparison.

What was it about Dominique that attracted Mark? He wished he
knew. So many times he had tried to shake free of it. He had never
imagined himself the sort for unrequited love, and he had never depicted it that way to himself. Often he went months without thinking
of her. So why hadn't he fallen in love with someone else?

Mark laced his hands behind his head and sat back in his chair as
he thought about it. His secretary buzzed the intercom. He leaned
forward, clicked it on, and said, "No calls now, please."

He swiveled his chair one hundred eighty degrees so that he faced
the window. The view was impressive: the white dome of the Capitol
brightly illuminated from below. It was rare that Mark paused long
enough in his busy day to admire it. Now, as he sat staring out the
window, he barely noticed it. His thoughts were on Dominique. Each
encounter with her provided a new surprise, a new trait to be admired.
When Mark's secretary had handed him the message slip bearing Dominique's name, he had surmised immediately that she had begun a
new life. It was brave of her to move her family to Washington, away
from everything and everyone she knew.

Then, when he heard her "Welcome to Washington" idea, it delighted him that she had lost none of her creative flair. He could sense
in her the same energy that had been such an asset to his campaign.

These traits Mark could list as justification for his attraction to Dominique. But in reality, her effect on him was the result of inexplicable chemistry. He read her name and his heart beat faster. He heard her voice and a thrill surged through him. And when he actually *saw* her . . . He tried to conjure an image of her. His mind didn't take him to their most recent encounter. Instead, he remembered her as she'd been on that first day, her hair glinting in the sun, her eyes closed, lost in a daydream.

Mark closed his own eyes as he thought of Dominique. What could possibly have compelled Clay to give up such a woman? Mark frowned as he thought of her ex-husband. What a son of a bitch! He took his young girlfriend to all the parties to which he had once taken Dominique, not even trying to conceal the fact that he had left his wife for her. Mark had heard the talk when he'd been home for Mardi Gras. There had been chuckles of commiseration from the men, a resigned expression from the women.

Mark felt the stirring of an ancient instinct — one that made him want to protect Dominique. Logic told him that she was fending for herself, but logic had nothing to do with Mark's feelings for her.

CHAPTER 24 ∽

"THIS isn't a convention! We can't have display booths!" Sylvia said scornfully.

All twelve people around the long cherry conference table — the entire staff of Capital Events — turned to look at Dominique.

"I absolutely agree," Dominique said serenely. "And we need to address that by having strict guidelines on dress and decor in the display area. We can pull it off in a very elegant way." Dominique explained the ambiance she envisioned. "But most of all, we want this night to be unique. These new members of Congress are going to be feted by every lobbyist, law firm, and interest group in town. They'll be invited to an infinite number of lovely balls. The Ambassador's Ball, the National Symphony Ball, White House balls, charity balls, and, in a couple of years, the Inaugural Ball." She held up one hand and ticked off the items on her fingers as she spoke. "If we can actually provide something more than a good time — a service, if you will — I think our evening will be a standout." Dominique looked around the table for assurance, and saw a few nodding heads. She continued. "The service area won't be foisted on the attendees, but I'm willing to bet they'll exploit it to the maximum. Plus, I think we can get the businesses to pick up a lot of the expense of holding the event at the Kennedy Center, so we'll save our clients some money." She looked pointedly at Sylvia. She held her eyes, ready to drop her bombshell. "Besides, I'm sure Senator Mark Patout wouldn't have agreed to be guest of honor if he didn't like this idea."

There was a murmur of surprised excitement. Everyone began to speak at once. Dominique looked at Mrs. Filmore. The older woman sat back in her chair at the head of the table, her hands steepled under her chin. She said nothing, but her eyes gleamed.

Across the table, Felice caught Dominique's eye and gave her an almost invisible nod of approval. The younger woman had been promoted from receptionist to executive assistant of one of the company's top account executives. And she had become a close friend — and an important sounding board — for Dominique.

Finally, Mrs. Filmore leaned forward and rested her hands on the table. The room fell quiet. "Sylvia?" she said.

No one spoke. The only sound in the room was the staccato tapping of Sylvia's pen on her notepad. Then the blond woman exhaled loudly and sat forward in her seat. "Mark Patout will make an impressive guest of honor. Congratulations." Her voice was grudging, and she didn't look at Dominique. She removed her glasses and met Mrs. Filmore's gaze directly. "And since Dominique here is so experienced in these matters, I think we should give her the opportunity to oversee this project on her own, should our clients agree to it. Of course, I'll negotiate the terms of the contract, as usual." She cast a tentative look at Mrs. Filmore.

Mrs. Filmore sat forward and dropped her hands to the table. She fixed Dominique with a thoughtful look. "Let's see how the embassies react. The manner in which you propose to handle this has considerable style. Practicality, too. But I wouldn't want to push our clients into something they're uncomfortable with." She paused and turned her gaze to Sylvia, her expression pointed. Everyone else at the table swiveled their heads in the same direction. "Sylvia will accompany you on your meeting with the ambassadresses. In that way, there can be no question of misinterpreting their reactions."

Dominique knew she should feel victorious, but she felt instead like an animal being lured into a trap by a delicious tidbit.

&co; &co; &co;

Dominique closed the folder on her desk and glanced out her office window. It was almost dark already. Only an hour to go until cocktails with Mark. She should start getting ready. She had told Gabrielle and Solange that morning, in a nonchalant way, that she would be late for dinner because she was having drinks with a client. Gabrielle had innocently accepted the explanation, but Solange's eyes had flared with curiosity. Dominique, however, offered no further explanation. If she did, they would pester her with a barrage of questions. There was nothing to tell, really. Dominique and Mark were just old friends. It was silly to think he could be interested in anything more. He was an important senator and, since his divorce, one of Washington's most eligible men.

Dominique pulled her purse out of her desk drawer and stood up. She felt rumpled after a day's work and wanted to freshen her makeup. As she moved down the hall, she paused at Felice's door.

Her friend looked up, a wide smile on her face. "Tonight's the night?"

Dominique looked skyward in pretended exasperation. "Don't make a big deal. It's just cocktails."

Felice laughed. "Cocktails with Senator Mark Patout. Alone. That's a big deal, in my —" She came to an abrupt stop and her smile disappeared as her gaze shifted to a point over Dominique's shoulder.

With a prickly feeling in the back of her neck, Dominique turned to find Sylvia's hostile gaze boring into her.

"I want a word with Felice," said the blond woman dismissively. "In private."

Dominique stepped out of her way, trying not to look flustered. Sylvia made her feel as though she'd been caught red-handed, when she hadn't done a thing! In a small act of rebellion, Dominique poked her head into Felice's office and said pleasantly, "Good night. I'll see you tomorrow."

Sylvia's head snapped around and she glared at Dominique.

"Good night, Sylvia," Dominique said in the same musical tone. She continued down the hall to the ladies' room, not waiting for a reply.

With a jaunty flourish, she swung her hip into the door and pitched it open. Then she opened her purse and set to work on her face. A little gray eye shadow, some of the pale coral lipstick that was so fashionable, a touch of peach blush. Satisfied, she put away her makeup kit and pulled out her comb. Her hair was cut in a loose, shoulder-length style that made the most of her natural waves. A flick of her wrist was all that was needed to bring it to life. She dropped her comb into her purse and prepared to close it. Then, at the bottom, she spotted an atomizer of perfume that she hadn't used since Clay left her. Dominique was momentarily stymied. What message did she want to send? Certainly not one of overeagerness. She gave up on the perfume and refastened her purse.

Back in her office, she debated leaving at once. It would be nice to walk to the Madison, get some fresh air. On the other hand, she could put in another twenty minutes at her desk, then take a taxi. There was certainly enough work. Opting for the second choice, she replaced her purse in its drawer and pulled open the folder in front of her. It was the file on the embassy gala. Dominique smiled as she recalled the Comtesse de la Croix's enthusiastic reaction to her idea of involving local businesses in the event. Sylvia had been closemouthed throughout the meeting the day before, and even more so since then. But it had been a delicious victory for Dominique.

Just as Dominique was thinking of her, Sylvia appeared at the door of her office, her face grim. Dominique looked up in surprise. Sylvia usually communicated with her by memo. What did she want? Quickly, Dominique smoothed her features into an expression of polite expectancy.

"There's a problem at the Cosmos Club," Sylvia said in clipped tones.

"Mary's event?" Dominique mentioned the name of one of the account executives as she glanced at her watch. "Isn't that due to start in an hour?"

"Yes. You'll have to go over right away."

Dominique half stood. "Oh! But I have plans. Can't someone else go?"

Sylvia raised one eyebrow. "I'm sorry about your plans," she said in a way that indicated the opposite. "I can call Mrs. Filmore and ask her who else we might send."

Dominique straightened and squared her shoulders. Don't threaten me, she wanted to say. Instead, she snapped, "Why would you do that? I thought these decisions were yours."

Sylvia looked taken aback for a moment. Then her eyes narrowed and her mouth clamped into a thin, hard line. "I need people I can count on in emergencies. Who'll change their plans when necessary. Maybe you don't understand that about this job."

Tight-lipped, Dominique replied, "I understand very well." She wanted to tell Sylvia exactly what she thought of her: that she was malicious and petty. That Dominique knew she was only trying to spoil her evening because she was jealous. Dominique bit the inside of her mouth lest she say something she would regret. She couldn't afford to lose this job!

She leaned forward and snatched the phone from its cradle. "I'll leave right away," Dominique said woodenly. "I need to make a call first." She glared at Sylvia until the other woman nodded and left the threshold.

ᕲᕲ ᕲᕲ ᕲᕲ

Gabrielle curled her finger over the top of Dominique's morning paper and confronted her mother with an expectant look. "Mom, you promised we'd go look for my Christmas present."

Dominique couldn't help laughing at her daughter's impatience. She put down the paper and glanced at Solange. A conspiratorial look passed between them. Solange had already bought Gabrielle a blouse and the album on her Christmas list: Carole King's *Tapestry*. Dominique had promised the girl a pair of shoes, jeans, and a sweater.

"I'm tired," Dominique teasingly complained.

Gabrielle groaned. "You're never tired!"

Dominique yawned elaborately. "I may go back to bed. After all, it's the weekend." She gave her daughter a sidelong glance.

"Mom! Christmas Eve is tomorrow!"

Dominique opened her eyes wide. "It is?" She looked outside, as though the bright morning sunshine contradicted her daughter's words.

Solange laughed. "Stop torturing the child!" she said in French.

Dominique pushed back her chair and stood up. She stretched as she gazed out the window. Frost sparkled over the little herb garden, now a winter brown, but the ivy draping the back wall was still deep green.

"Okay," Dominique told Gabrielle. "Unload the dishwasher while I dress."

For once, Gabrielle scrambled to her chores.

Dominique smiled as she watched her. Then she turned to Solange. "Join us?"

Solange's expression turned secretive. "No, thank you. I still have some Christmas shopping to do. I believe I'll take a walk down Wisconsin Avenue and see what I can find." Solange loved that busy strip of Georgetown. She had found a sidewalk café, Au Pied de Cochon, where she would go in the afternoons for an espresso and a chat with the French waiters, all of whom adored her.

Thirty minutes later, Dominique and Gabrielle were in the car headed toward a mall in the Virginia suburbs. They chatted happily until Dominique pulled into the parking lot of Montgomery Ward. Then Gabrielle's eyes widened in horror. "Mom, I don't want to get my stuff here!" she cried. "Everyone at school will think I'm weird!"

Dominique clicked off the engine. "Why?" she asked coolly.

"Mom!" Gabrielle said with exasperation.

Dominique turned to her daughter and said gently, "Gabrielle, I know the girls at school come from wealthy families, but try to understand our situation. It's not like when your father was with us."

Gabrielle tightened her lips in an unconscious imitation of Clay. "I don't see why we had to move away from Dad!" she cried. "None of this would be happening if we were still in New Orleans." Every so often, Gabrielle had these outbursts. Dominique understood the girl's distress, but the episodes were painful for her, too.

Dominique's voice hardened. "It *was* happening when we were in New Orleans. Why do you think I had to sell the house?"

Gabrielle hesitated a moment, then said in an accusatory tone, "Dad said you wanted to start fresh."

Dominique's eyebrows shot up in astonishment. Clay was twisting the truth to make her the villain.

Gabrielle narrowed her eyes and studied Dominique, her expression unforgiving.

Dominique gritted her teeth. "I was perfectly content where we were. Your father has given you the wrong impression."

Gabrielle made a sound of disbelief and turned her head away.

Dominique drew in her breath, too outraged to speak. Her palm itched to slap the girl. "Don't turn away from me like that, young lady! And don't ever make that sound — like you think I'm lying." Her voice was steely. "I've never lied to you and you know it."

The girl's head snapped back to face Dominique. "Then why won't you tell me exactly why you and Dad split up?" she hurled. "You never have, you know!"

Until now, Gabrielle had naively accepted the fiction — put forward by Clay — that Marie had somehow materialized after the separation. Dominique had never contradicted it. But, for the first time, Gabrielle was asking a direct question. And Dominique wasn't prepared to shoulder the blame in order to preserve Clay's image. In a voice that was deadly quiet, she said, "You've met Marie."

Gabrielle shook her head, panic creeping over her features. She didn't want to accept the truth. "No, I mean, why did you and Dad decide he should move out? I know he met her after —"

Dominique held up a hand like a person stopping traffic. "Just a minute!" Her eyes glittered with rage. "Your father," Dominique said in a brittle voice, "left me. I never wanted him to." What a coward not to own up to his actions!

Gabrielle's mouth dropped open. The roses in her cheeks faded abruptly to white. "But . . . I thought . . ." Dominique saw confusion in Gabrielle's eyes as the girl fought against the revelation. Then her expression grew dark. "He lied!" Her cry betrayed her disillusionment. Parents weren't supposed to lie! "He cheated on you and then he lied!"

The sight of Gabrielle's misery made Dominique's anger collapse. She reached for her daughter, her heart aching in sympathy. Gabrielle had only recently discovered a Clay who was more patient and pliable — more fun. But a Clay who was false! Who had lied to her just as he had lied to Dominique. Oh, but the circumstances were different! In spite of Dominique's disgust with Clay, she was convinced he had lied to Gabrielle to preserve the father-daughter relationship. And she had to persuade Gabrielle of it. The girl was old enough to know the real circumstances of the split, but was anyone so mature that they were not hurt by a parent's dishonorable action?

Dominique hugged her daughter close, and Gabrielle clung so tightly that she almost squeezed the breath from her.

"Your father was afraid you'd think less of him, that's all," Dominique murmured.

Gabrielle straightened abruptly, though she continued to grasp her mother's upper arms. Her face crumpled with disgust. "I hate him!" she declared vehemently. "How could he do that to you?" Her eyes filled, but she blinked back the tears.

The expression on Gabrielle's face re-ignited Dominique's own fury at Clay. At that moment, she could have shot him with no remorse. She didn't trust herself to answer her daughter. She could feel the venom poised to flow out of her.

Gabrielle's mouth started to tremble. She bit her lip and fixed Dominique with a determinedly hard gaze, as though bracing herself.

Dominique couldn't bear to see Gabrielle's eyes turn cynical. She was too young! There was all the time in the world for disillusionment. Why did it have to happen now, when Gabrielle was so impressionable? And yet, why should Dominique find excuses for Clay's inexcusable behavior? The blow he had dealt Dominique wasn't confined to adultery. He had torn her life apart.

Dominique burned to empty her heart to Gabrielle, to someone. But in the long run, that would most damage Gabrielle herself. "Gabrielle, I know it's hard to understand, but what your father feels for me now — the fact that he left — doesn't take away from the love he feels for you." She put her hand under her daughter's chin and looked into her eyes. "You know that, don't you?"

Gabrielle jerked her head back. "Why are you protecting him?" she cried. "He cheated on you! We had to sell our house and move up here. Why don't you hate him?"

I do! Dominique wanted to shout back. The words were on the tip of her tongue. She was so tempted. She could avenge herself by turning Gabrielle against her father. It was Dominique's only means of retribution. Clay had robbed her. She could rob him, and in the process, assure the loyalty of her daughter. She would no longer have to put up with stories about Marie's accomplishments or Clay's wonderful new life. Gabrielle would hate them both.

Dominique's body was tense with the strain of suppressing her thoughts. She had a hand on each of Gabrielle's upper arms and she could feel the slender limbs under her fingers. Suddenly, she realized she was clutching them too tightly. They were so delicate — not yet grown. Gabrielle was still a child, after all! She was lost and confused by a rupture she couldn't understand. What could be more despicable than to rob her of the only anchor left in her life — her family. Her parents. Both of them.

Dominique slid her hands down the length of Gabrielle's arms and took her daughter's hands. She gazed into her eyes, and knew that the girl's anger was nothing but bravado. Gabrielle was frightened — badly frightened. She had been raised to believe in certain principles, and one of the very people who had raised her was defying them. That made him bad, didn't it? Gabrielle's own father, whom she had always believed to be fundamentally good, now appeared to be fundamentally bad. Weak. Selfish. A liar. If that was possible, then who was there left to trust?

It was too much of a burden to inflict on Gabrielle. Why don't you hate him? Gabrielle had asked, loyally prepared to do so herself.

"Gabrielle," Dominique said gently, "I don't hate your father, because we have a lot of good memories together." She paused. "And . . . we have you."

CHAPTER 25 ∾

DOMINIQUE lifted the hem of her gown and stepped off the escalator into the monumental corridor that was the Kennedy Center's Hall of Nations. Enormous, colorful flags from many countries were suspended overhead, lending a ceremonial flourish to the grand space. Along the white marble walls were placed long tables to be used for the cocktail buffet. Dominique drew close to one of the tables, examining the centerpieces provided by the Dutch embassy. They were three-foot-high compositions of fruits and flowers — masterworks of artistry.

But Dominique could afford only a moment's pause. She was to meet Mark at six-thirty and there was still so much to check! She felt dwarfed as she made her way down the hall, around a corner, and into the wide lobby that served the Kennedy Center's theaters. She automatically looked toward the bank of vermilion doors that would later be thrown open to admit the guests to a special performance of *Cabaret*. A rush of adrenaline coursed through her, as it always did before a big event, and her step quickened. She hurried around the corner and into the Hall of States, also hung with flags. Good, the tables were already set up, as they had been in the other corridor. Waiters scurried about with trays of food, ice, and cutlery.

At the opposite end of the palatial hall was the bank of doors Mark would be entering. Dominique glanced at her watch and saw that it was almost six-thirty. Her pulse hammering in her temples, she made her way down the endless concourse.

❧ ❧ ❧

Mark glanced for the umpteenth time at the clock on the dashboard. Dominique was to meet him at six-thirty at the main entrance of the Kennedy Center, but Mark had been so eager that he had arrived fifteen minutes early. He didn't want Dominique to know that, though, so he circled the block, then eased into a parking space a few seconds away from his destination. If he stopped in the drive in front of the center, a parking attendant would take his car. So he would wait until six-thirty. Maybe even a little longer.

Impatiently, Mark drummed his fingers on the steering wheel. He tilted the rearview mirror down and studied his bow tie. He could never get it quite straight. His friends' wives teased him about that, claiming that he needed a wife of his own to tie it for him. He smiled wryly at the thought. Nina had never possessed the touch of maternalism that caused women to perform such tasks for their husbands. With a sigh, Mark gave the black silk cloth a tentative tug at one corner. For a moment, the tie straightened, but as soon as he released it, the corner tilted up and the tie was askew again. Mark felt a thin line of sweat form on his upper lip. He considered undoing the bow and starting over. Or would it only end up worse? He decided to leave it.

Mark reached up to return the mirror to its former position, then hesitated with his hand on the frame. He wasn't a man who usually spent time looking in the mirror. Even when he shaved, his mind was elsewhere, but he suddenly found himself wondering if Dominique would be pleased by what she saw. He brushed his fingers through his hair. Should've had a haircut, he thought. He always let it go just a little too long before cutting it. He studied the lines around his eyes and his mouth. Did he look older than his forty-four years? It was hard to say. The lines were definitely there. His mobile face and constant smile had caused that.

So be it, Mark thought. That's who I am and there's nothing to do about it. Some of his congressional colleagues had ever-so-discreetly opted for plastic surgery as a means to remain young in the eyes of constituents. Mark shrugged and flipped the mirror back into place. That sort of thing wasn't for him.

He took another look at the clock. Mark's heart raced as he realized it was time. He started the engine and pulled into traffic, anxious now lest he keep Dominique waiting. The gala started in just half an hour. He saw the traffic signal ahead turn yellow and stepped on the gas just in time to avoid the red. Then he pulled into the Kennedy Center's drive and handed the keys to the parking attendant.

He turned to the heavy glass doors. Behind them he saw the outline of a female form. His step faltered. Suddenly he was assailed by doubt. Now that he was to finally see Dominique, would he still feel the same? Was she changed? Embittered? Could she possibly be as attractive as he remembered?

He had been waiting for this moment since the day Dominique had phoned him in October. What had been the real reason for her last-minute cancellation of their cocktail date? Had she been trying to put him off? It had taken all his willpower not to call her when he'd returned from the holiday recess two weeks before, but he'd known she was busy with the gala.

Mark rubbed his tongue against the roof of his mouth. It was disagreeably dry. He hesitated one more time before the door and nervously fingered his tie. The female form inside moved closer. He took a deep breath and resolutely stepped through the doors. When he emerged on the other side, he abruptly stopped. He tried to focus on the figure before him.

For one confused moment, it was as though he had been transported back in time. In the soft light, Dominique looked no older than on the first day he had met her. The brighter lights from the central hall many yards away outlined her body, but her long black velvet gown and the shadows of the foyer created an illusion of mystery, as though she were not quite real. Something near her face sparkled, throwing off colored beams. Mark stood where he was and watched Dominique move toward him.

She was speaking to him in that enchanting musical accent. Her hands were stretched forward in greeting. She came nearer and he inhaled the light perfume that seemed uniquely hers: flowers and spice. Then she turned her face up to his and he saw the flash of her smile.

Mark's feelings toward Dominique, which he had firmly suppressed over the years, burst to the surface of his consciousness. He wanted to reach forward and touch her face, to cup it in his hands. He wanted to pull her into his embrace.

He closed his arms about her. He felt her arms go around him. He lowered his head to hers, his eyes focused on her lush mouth. He was going to kiss her, just as he had always wanted to. He was going to show her how much she meant to him. He forgot propriety, the past, their friendship.

As he drew closer to her, she ever so slightly turned her head and kissed his cheek. "Mark, how good to see you again!" Dominique's voice was affectionate, there was no mistaking it. But it didn't have the husky note that he had been imagining. There was nothing at all romantic in her manner toward him.

The realization jolted Mark back to reality. He blinked as her scented hair brushed against the skin of his face. He was confounded by her proximity, yet his social training told him that something was required of him. Something mundane and hearty and appropriate.

"Dominique, how are you, it's been much too long!" Mark heard his voice as though from a distance. It sounded right. It just didn't feel right. It wasn't at all what he wanted to convey.

Dominique disengaged herself from his arms, but held on to his hand. Mark allowed himself to be guided forward. She was chatting about something. He couldn't quite focus on her words. In a moment he would get his bearings, regain control. But every nerve in his body seemed perilously close to the surface of his skin. With hypersensitivity, he felt the touch of her palm against his.

They stepped onto an elevator.

"You're awfully quiet tonight," she laughed.

He forced himself to smile back. How could she be so relaxed? Didn't she feel the electricity between them? It was impossible that such a strong emotion was one-sided. Or was it? Hadn't it been one-sided in the past? Why had he expected it to change?

In the harsh light of the elevator, Mark thought he saw a few signs of the difficult times she had recently endured. A faint crease at the corner of each eye. A subtle wariness of expression. When she wasn't smiling, her mouth settled into a line that was more firm than before, as though she were determined to . . . what? He wasn't certain.

The elevator stopped and Dominique led the way out. She turned and looked over her shoulder at Mark. He noticed the youthful, confident squareness of her posture. He thought about the emotional battering she had suffered at Clay's hands. It seemed she had survived; not only survived, but bounced back, not unscarred but, in a way, stronger than before. He remembered the quality that had first drawn him to her: the vivid force that emanated from her. It was still there. Had grown in power.

Once more, he felt himself plummeting toward hopeless en-tanglement.

ᢙᢗ   ᢙᢗ   ᢙᢗ

The moment Mark stepped through the door, all Dominique's anxiety about the gala melted away. He wore the same irresistibly charming smile she remembered. A smile that enfolded her and conspired with her and drew her to him with a magnetic pull. A smile that said noth-ing in life is *that* serious.

She watched Mark's eyes light up as he focused on her, and she felt herself glow in return. He admired her, he genuinely admired her! He was a man surrounded by power, a man who could have his pick of virtually any beautiful, accomplished woman in America — and he ad-mired *her!* It made Dominique's confidence soar.

Almost at once, she reined herself in. He was, after all, a practiced politician. It was his job to engage people, make them feel important and, yes, admired. And he was so good at it! Her giddiness ebbed away.

Then Mark wrapped her in the warmth of his arms and — she couldn't help it — she clung to him in return. Oh, it felt good to be hugged! To smell the male scent of soap and shaving cream and — something that was exclusively Mark's — a freshness that reminded her of a morning walk in the woods. Not as overpowering as cologne, just a nice, clean smell.

She looked up at him and saw his face come toward her. Their lips were about to meet. But they had never before kissed on the mouth. He mustn't think she had done it on purpose! She was suddenly ter-ribly aware of her newly single state, and her pride asserted itself. She didn't want to be perceived as one of the countless women who threw themselves at Mark. She turned her head and lightly pecked his cheek. She didn't see the look of disappointment on his face.

He continued to hold her and she wanted to be held, but instead she stepped back. She looked attentively at him as she chattered about inconsequential things. Why did she always envision him as handsome? He wasn't really. She compared him to other men she'd known. Strictly speaking, he wasn't as handsome as Clay or Stephen

Hampton. Yet he transmitted kindness, humor, warmth, and — Dominique blushed as she thought it — sexiness. She wondered what it would be like to kiss him, not as a friend, but as a lover. She was surprised by the strength of her feelings. She had never before allowed them to stray so far into forbidden territory. During her marriage to Clay, she had firmly assigned Mark the category of friend. Despite the initial chemistry between them, she had irrevocably drawn the line. It would have been disloyal to do otherwise. Now, the necessity for boundaries was erased. Dominique's sensuality, long suppressed, came alive like a flower turning to the sun.

ॐ ॐ ॐ

By seven-thirty, the Hall of Nations overflowed with people, the hubbub of their conversation resounding off the marble walls. New congressional wives, initially a little bewildered, soon gravitated toward the "Welcome to Washington" room, where they relaxed with soothing harp music as soft-voiced "consultants" told them about their new city.

The crowd was a hodgepodge of styles, representing as it did every state in the union. New Yorkers wore the latest fashions — dresses with cutout midriffs and plunging necklines. Midwesterners ran the gamut from flowered print chiffons to no-nonsense simplicity, while New Englanders stuck to navy and pearls. The embassy community was clearly distinguishable from the rest. The women were either impeccably chic or festively arrayed in native dress.

At eight, handsome young men in black tie directed guests to a seated dinner on the top floor, giving the workers below a chance to clear the area of the debris from the cocktail buffet. Candlelit tables for eight, decorated with yet more Dutch flowers, were placed strategically about the room so that guests could enjoy views of the Potomac River.

Dominique sighed with relief as she overheard the guests rave about the dinner, an ambitious joint effort by several embassy chefs. There was sautéed fresh foie gras from France, creamy risotto in saffron from Italy, stuffed roast loin of lamb from Greece, cheeses from Switzerland, and pastries from Austria. Dominique herself was too nervous to eat. She shuttled back and forth from the great halls below to the dining room, ensuring that everything was moving along smoothly. On her last trip, she returned just as dessert was being served. The orchestra had begun to play, and a few couples swayed on the parquet dance floor at one end of the room.

Dominique noted that Sylvia Brussels was firmly ensconced at one of the tables, chatting as she enjoyed a cup of coffee and a cigarette. As Dominique passed by, she heard Sylvia accept the congratulations of the German ambassador. Dominique tried to shrug off her annoyance. After all, Sylvia *was* the company's top executive — apart from Mrs. Filmore, who had already departed earlier in the month for her annual trek to Palm Beach. If Mrs. Filmore trusted Sylvia enough to leave the company in her hands, she probably *did* deserve a lot of credit.

But a little voice inside Dominique reminded her that Sylvia had stayed as far away as possible from tonight's project. She sighed to herself. What did it matter? At least the woman was happy. For the first time, Dominique saw a genuine smile on her face. It was not directed at Dominique, of course, but that didn't matter. Sylvia could not deny that Dominique had proved her worth. That was the important thing.

After dinner, Dominique circled the room to check that dishes were being promptly cleared. As she passed the head table, where Mark was also seated, he caught her by the wrist. Dominique felt a charge go through her at the contact.

"Do you have time for a dance?" he asked.

Dominique looked quickly about the room. Did anything need her attention? People were laughing and chatting, toasting new friendships, and enjoying the glow of good wine and good food.

Dominique smiled down at Mark. "Just one," she said. As they passed Sylvia's table on the way to the dance floor, she could feel the woman's gaze burning into her. In view of Dominique's duties that evening, she could have found an excuse not to dance. But, she rationalized, that wouldn't be very polite. And the fact was that she wanted the dance. Just one, that was all.

It was a waltz — the rather sentimental "Fascination." But the words, crooned by a honey-voiced brunette in a sequined gown, suddenly resonated with meaning.

Mark carefully placed his hand on the velvet covering Dominique's waist — a little higher and he would have touched her bare back. As it was, his body heat radiated through the material. It made Dominique's nerves tingle with awareness. She felt as though she were on a tightrope. One wrong move and she would stumble to an unknown fate. At all costs, she had to avoid looking into Mark's eyes. Eyes that lingered on her face, her hair, her bare shoulders. She should try to make small talk, Dominique told herself. To look casual. But she was mute with tension.

Mark, too, was silent. He could smell the perfume rising from Dominique's skin. Tantalizing, erotic. He wanted to bury his face in her hair. He wanted to lead her away from the others, to be alone with her.

They whirled about the room, effortlessly attuned to each other's rhythm. The slightest movement of his hand told her when to turn, when to pause, when to move forward. This is how it was meant to be, he thought. Except . . . except she wouldn't meet his gaze. She looked over his shoulder, at his tie, his hair, anywhere but his eyes.

"Dominique . . . ," he said. His voice was soft, appealing. If he said her name, she would have to look at him.

And she did.

Dominique, feeling strangely tentative, looked up from under her lashes. She expected to see the familiar laughter in Mark's eyes, but for once they were serious. Her heart raced as she saw the determination there. She opened her mouth to speak. Then, flustered, closed it again. His unexpected intensity disconcerted her. She tried for a light laugh, but it sounded false. There was no place for it in the atmosphere between them. Her smile faded and she gazed squarely at Mark. His eyes pulled her in. She hadn't the power to look away.

As the last note of the song faded, Mark held Dominique firmly in his arms. For a second, they stood that way. Then, reluctantly, he let her go.

Even after they stepped apart, their eyes remained locked.

Mark had to speak now, to seal the moment between them, before it faded from her memory, before she could shrug it off. "You'll see me again, won't you?" he asked. His voice sounded raspy, as though he were speaking for the first time that day.

Dominique thought of all the reasons why she shouldn't. He was her friend. This would complicate their relationship. He might be trifling with her. It was a momentary attraction. She couldn't bear being hurt again. She was better off on her own.

She looked into his eyes and said, "Yes."

ꝏ ꝏ ꝏ

Monday morning, and Dominique basked in the praise of a circle of co-workers. They were intoxicated by the success of the gala and what it would mean to the company's revenues. In the quarter hour before the meeting officially began, they clustered around Dominique, balancing cups of coffee and doughnuts as they patted her on the arm or shook her hand.

"I hope you saw the society page yesterday!" Felice told her. "You should cut it out and frame it!"

"It was on the TV news, Saturday and Sunday!" exclaimed another co-worker.

Dominique, flushed with gratification, thanked them. Best of all, she knew that Sylvia Brussels had to be pleased, despite the fact that the woman had avoided speaking to her on Saturday. In the rush and confusion of the good-byes and final cleanup, Dominique hadn't noticed the omission. Then, shortly after two a.m., she had turned to look for Sylvia and found her engrossed in conversation with a diamond-draped platinum blonde whom Dominique recognized as one of Washington's rich young matrons. Dominique knew that Sylvia would not welcome an interruption, so she had finished her business and gone home.

Now Sylvia was forgotten as Dominique laughed with her co-workers and relived the victories of the gala.

"Did you see the line at the realtor's table? That was a stroke of genius!" said Frank Collier, one of the firm's two male employees.

"The dinner was divine!" said the catering manager.

Dominique barely had time to respond to one compliment before another issued forth.

Suddenly the atmosphere in the room changed. One by one the voices of praise fell silent. Dominique saw that the others were looking at the door, and she turned and looked also, her neck already beginning to tense.

Sylvia's petite frame seemed to fill the doorway like a beacon of ill-boding. When all eyes were on her, she strode into the room and dropped a pile of folders heavily on the conference table. "Let's begin," she ordered in a crisp voice. She opened one of the folders and propped her glasses on her nose. "First order of business: the reception for the Yves St. Laurent boutique."

The meeting passed brusquely, efficiently, and without a word about the gala. At the end of the hour, Sylvia snapped closed the final folder and stood. "Thank you. That's it," she said, and marched from the room.

Dominique and her colleagues exchanged stunned glances. Dominique felt hot with embarrassment, though she knew she had the support of those around the table. With her silence, Sylvia had undermined Dominique's entire effort.

"Well . . . ," breathed Felice. She gave Dominique a look of commiseration. "You can be sure that Mrs. Filmore knows how wonderful the gala was. I mean, we had as much media coverage as a state dinner at the White House."

Dominique nodded feebly, trying to take comfort in the words.

One by one, her colleagues rose from their chairs, murmuring about appointments and work to be done.

Dominique remained seated, too shocked and hurt to move.

Felice came behind her chair and put a comforting hand on Dominique's shoulder. "Hey, don't take it personally. She's one of those people who can't get a compliment past her lips." She patted Dominique on the back.

Dominique stood up slowly and smiled at her friend. "You're right. . . . I should just ignore this. Not let her get to me."

"That's the spirit!" said Felice, beaming.

"We'd better get back to work," Dominique said in a disheartened voice.

Felice gave her a philosophical look. "How about drinks after work?"

"Pardon?" Dominique was distracted, her mind still on Sylvia. "Oh, oh sure." She paused, gathering her bearings. "Six-thirty?"

Felice made a thumbs-up sign and left the room.

Dominique watched her go, then sat down again, her mind unable to let go of Sylvia's insult. Dominique had thought that surely this time Sylvia would have to acknowledge her worth. But it was suddenly clear to her that nothing she could do would please her boss. Dominique's insides churned with tension. Even more stress-inducing was the knowledge that she couldn't afford to displease Sylvia. If only Mrs. Filmore were in the office more! If only Dominique had been at the firm a little longer, she could have searched for another job. But such a short stay — after a hiatus of a decade — wouldn't look good on a résumé.

Dominique was trapped and she could think of no way out. She stared blankly at the table in front of her. After a moment, her eyes focused on the newspapers one of her colleagues had brought in. It was open to a page full of photographs from the gala. Dominique reached forward and pulled it toward her. Her spirits lifted as she read the captions. The evening had been an unqualified success! Nothing Sylvia did or said could take that away from Dominique.

With an air of resolve, she gathered up the papers and put them under her arm. She knew from reading the articles that her name was mentioned in none of them. But the clients knew she had been responsible, as did the dozens of people she had worked with to put on the affair.

Dominique's chin was high as she headed to her office. Just as she reached it, the phone rang. She threw the papers on her desk and hurried to answer.

"Senator Patout on line three," the receptionist told her.

Dominique inhaled sharply. Her heart pounding, she pressed the flashing button before she even sat down. "Mark, how are you?" She wanted to sound welcoming, but moderate. She kicked closed her office door, then brought the phone cord around the desk and sat down in her chair.

"What a great night! Everyone up here is still talking about it!" Mark sounded like a little boy at the circus.

"It wouldn't have worked without such an esteemed guest of honor," Dominique teased lightly. Then, in a tone of sincere gratitude, she said, "I don't know how I can ever thank you for your help." She smiled into the telephone.

"You can have dinner with me on Wednesday."

A short, tense laugh escaped Dominique. The thought of actually going on a date again made her apprehensive. And yet, she enjoyed being with Mark — had always enjoyed it.

"Wednesday?" she repeated. "That . . . that sounds fine."

"Good! I'll pick you up at your place at seven."

A wave of panic swept over Dominique. What would Gabrielle's reaction be? Resentment? Outrage? Jealousy? And Solange? She'd probably be pleased, but full of unwanted advice. Dominique was tempted to say that she would meet Mark at the restaurant.

"Dominique, are you still there?"

Dominique swallowed. She wouldn't be cowed into hiding her actions from her family. If they had objections, it was better to know now. "Let me give you my address."

∽ ∽ ∽

"Wednesday!" Felice squealed. "He didn't waste any time."

"Sssh!" Dominique quickly looked around. They were just emerging from their office building, and Dominique scanned the people around them to ensure that there were no familiar faces. When she saw there were not, she relaxed.

"Let's run!" Felice said, pulling her coat around her. "It's freezing!" She began to trot in the curious, mincing way of women in high heels.

Dominique kept pace beside her, shivering as the wind sliced into her. "Where are we going?"

"Let's go over to Nathan's. I have my car today."

Dominique halted abruptly. "Nathan's? That singles bar?"

Felice, a few steps ahead of her, jerked to a halt. She turned back to her friend with a startled look. "Haven't you been there? It's just a few blocks from your place."

Dominique didn't move. "I know." She met Felice's curious gaze. "It's just that . . . I've never been to a bar like that without a man."

Felice's expression was, for a moment, frozen with disbelief. Then she twisted her face into a half-smile, put her hands on her hips, and said, "What are you telling me?"

Dominique was amused at her friend's reaction. She took a few steps forward until they were standing side by side. With a gesture of her head, she indicated they should resume walking. "I mean . . . ," she said with deliberation, ". . . that I never went to a bar unescorted." A smile curved her lips. "That's not the way things were done in New Orleans. And when I was young . . ." She let out a merry gasp indicating that such a thing would have been absolutely taboo.

"Are you saying you don't want to go?" Felice's tone was challenging.

"Mmm . . . no," Dominique said obliquely. She gave her friend a sidelong glance. "But . . . what's it like?"

Felice's eyes sparkled. "Exciting! Music, a couple glasses of wine, and, most of all" — she looked at Dominique as though gauging her reaction — "men."

Dominique's eyebrows shot up. "And what do you do with these men?"

Felice gave her a smug smile. "What*ever* I feel like, baby!" She turned her face so that she was looking straight into Dominique's eyes. "You were tied down to that sorry husband of yours for too long." Her smile turned wicked. "But you got divorced just in time to enjoy the sexual revolution."

ᘒᙆ ᘒᙆ ᘒᙆ

Dominique's evening with Felice came back to her as she stood indecisively before her open closet. At Nathan's two nights before, women had perched on bar stools in everything from braless knit dresses to leather miniskirts. They had looked sexy, provocative, commanding, and — Dominique couldn't help thinking it — a little predatory. Dominique didn't want to transmit any of those impressions on her first date with Mark.

After much riffling through her wardrobe, she settled on a soft black sweater-dress and crushy suede boots, an outfit that was fashionable, but by no means blatant. When she emerged from her room, she found her mother waiting for her at the foot of the staircase.

As Solange looked up at Dominique, two frown lines creased the space between her eyebrows. "You're wearing that?"

Dominique kept her voice even. "Yes, Mother, I'm wearing this."

Gabrielle, hearing their voices, emerged from the kitchen. She cocked her head and looked uncertainly at her mother.

Dominique studied her daughter's face apprehensively. Gabrielle had said little when Dominique had announced her date with Mark earlier. In fact, she'd immediately changed the subject, as if she had not heard. Was it traumatic for Gabrielle to view her mother as an eligible, single woman? Dominique knew the girl liked Mark, but in the role of Dominique's suitor?

Dominique met Gabrielle's eyes. "What do you think of this outfit?"

Gabrielle's face was closed. "Okay, I guess."

"Why don't you wear the red?" Solange's tone was wheedling.

"Mother!" Dominique said with exasperation. "The red is too dressy."

Gabrielle broke in, engaged in spite of herself. "I read in the society page that La Bagatelle is supposed to be a real cool restaurant. I think people get dressed up to go there." She shrugged as if to say, Of course, I couldn't care less what you wear.

Dominique tried not to show her relief at her daughter's tacit acceptance. *Don't get excited. There's still a long way to go before Gabrielle's comfortable with this. Handle it carefully.* When she spoke, it was in a casual tone, as though they had this sort of discussion every day. "I know La Bagatelle's reputation." She adjusted the high collar of her dress. "And I think this outfit is fine for a Wednesday night." She gave Gabrielle a nod of acknowledgment. "But if it were a weekend, I'd agree with you."

"Hmph." Solange sniffed. With a haughty expression, she turned and went toward the sofa. She sat down and draped her skirt around her legs with elaborate care.

Dominique smiled. "You don't want me to look desperate, do you?"

Gabrielle gave her a look of adolescent sarcasm. "Yeah, right! Like someone's going to think you're desperate."

Dominique brushed Gabrielle's cheek with her hand as she passed by her into the living room. "Thank you for the compliment, dear." She settled into the easy chair near the couch.

Gabrielle came over and perched on the edge of the chair. It was an automatic gesture and Dominique was afraid to regard it with too much optimism. But at least Gabrielle wasn't hostile. A few seconds of silence ticked by. Dominique held her breath as she waited for her daughter to break the tension. This was all so awkward! Finally, Gabrielle said, "Mark's nice." The remark was offered in a cautious tone. She wasn't sure about the situation, her manner implied, but she liked Mark.

Solange gave Dominique a queenly nod. It was clear that she wanted to add something but was biting her tongue.

Dominique smiled at her mother, then looked at Gabrielle, her smile turning wary. "I wasn't sure you two would approve of my going on a date. . . ."

Gabrielle's face grew somber, her inner struggle evident. "I know Daddy made you sad." She paused and averted her eyes. She picked at an imaginary thread on her jeans. "I don't want you to be lonely."

๑๑   ๑๑   ๑๑

Mark raised his glass of wine in a toast. "To our reunion," he said, his eyes radiating warmth.

Dominique felt a sharp pang as she remembered all the times Clay had toasted her — toasted their love, their marriage. She blinked and tried to focus on Mark, her thoughts suddenly cynical. How many other women had *he* brought here? He was so charismatic that she doubted that many women could resist him. Did he intend for her to be just another conquest? Dominique unconsciously squared her shoulders, determined to regard Mark as an old friend, nothing more. It was safer that way. For her, at least.

Their conversation began on a light enough note. Mark again complimented her on the gala. "You brought the New Orleans spirit with you," Mark said. "Washington events tend to be all alike. People are a lot more interested in making contacts than they are in having fun."

Dominique gave him a wry smile. "If I hadn't developed such a good working relationship with Michelle de la Croix, I don't think I could have persuaded the firm to go for some of my ideas." She laughed. "Sylvia Brussels was against the showing of *Cabaret*. She thought the evening would go too late."

"She's the skinny blonde who never smiles?" Mark asked, waving away the proffered menus.

"That's the one," Dominique said dryly.

Mark gave her a sympathetic look. "She seemed pretty high strung."

Dominique looked skyward. "If you only knew." She sighed. "My job would be wonderful if it weren't for her. I love what I do, but she always finds something to criticize." She paused thoughtfully. "She must be a very unhappy woman, and I suppose I should feel sorry for her, but I'm afraid I'm not that big a person."

"Why not quit?" Mark's tone was casual.

"After only seven months? That wouldn't look too good on a résumé. Besides, Mrs. Filmore —"

"Hold on right there!" Mark held up his hands. "I don't mean another job. I mean start your own business."

Dominique couldn't help but smile at Mark's eagerness. Of course, he wasn't being realistic. "Mark, I'd have no idea how to run my own business. Where would I put my office? How would I get customers? Who would keep things organized for me? Right now, I have a secretary and can call on any number of staffers for big events. I could never afford that if I started my own business."

Mark refused to be discouraged. He leaned forward to make his point. "You'd get a loan," he said, as though it were all so simple.

Dominique fixed him with a sardonic look. "I can't even get a credit card! Every account we had was either Clay's or a joint one. I have no credit history of my own."

Mark frowned and sat back. For a moment he said nothing, and his expression turned pensive. Finally he asked, "Don't you have any assets you can sell?"

Dominique shook her head. "I sold them all. I have a little cash but, frankly, I'm afraid to touch it. You never know. . . ." Dominique thought of Clay. What if he decided to stop paying her alimony and she had to go to court all over again? What if an emergency arose? She couldn't invest her savings in such a risky proposition.

Mark tilted his head to one side and said slowly, "You're a paradox."

Dominique knit her brow. "What do you mean?"

Mark put his hand under his chin and rested his elbow on the table so that he was staring straight into Dominique's eyes. "You're one of the most competent people I've ever met, yet you're worried about making a living. You've initiated tremendous changes in your life, yet you shy away from more change. You have very clear ideas of right and wrong, yet you're forgiving when someone does something wrong to *you*."

Dominique stared at Mark, surprised that he had spent so much time thinking about her character.

The waiter appeared at Dominique's side with a menu. She breathed a sigh of relief, glad of the interruption. It was better to end the disquieting conversation.

After they had ordered, Mark sat back in his seat and folded his hands over his stomach. "Dominique. . . ."

Dominique looked at him apprehensively, sorry she had brought up the subject of her job. The restaurant was a romantic place, with dark-salmon banquettes and peach walls designed to cast a flattering glow on female guests. Why not simply enjoy the pleasure of being there, Dominique thought? Stay away from stressful topics — and thoughts.

Mark continued. "As I said, you're one of the most competent people I've ever met. You're certainly the hardest working. And I'd consider an investment in your new business an advantageous proposition for me."

Dominique's eyebrows shot up. "Wait a minute!" she said firmly. "You act as though I've agreed to this thing in principle. I haven't. For one thing, where would I get clients? I'm not going to steal Mrs. Filmore's. Plus, I don't have any knowledge about —"

Mark held up an index finger. "Let me interrupt," he said. "You've raised a few decent objections and one ridiculous one."

Dominique frowned at the word. She began huffily, "I don't think any of my objections are —"

"Where would you get clients?" Mark cut in, his tone frustrated as he mocked her question. "Do you think maybe that I have one or two contacts? And could steer them your way?"

Dominique was effectively silenced. She looked down at the tablecloth. Mark made it sound easy. But, of course, it wasn't. What did she know about running a business? If she failed, she would have no way to repay Mark. She *couldn't* take his money. It was antithetical to the new goal she had set for herself: independence.

"Mark," she began, her voice warm. "I appreciate your trying to help. And I appreciate your listening. But the time isn't right for me."

Mark leaned forward and propped his elbows on the table.

Dominique saw the disappointment in his eyes. She felt the need to offer an explanation. "I've had so many changes in my life this past year. . . . I'm just starting to feel settled. I'm not ready for another big disruption."

Mark dropped his hands and sat up straight. "You've always been strong. Don't let that Brussels woman dictate the circumstances of your life." He tapped the table softly for emphasis. "You're a survivor. You'll land on your feet."

"Mark," Dominique said softly, "if I accepted your loan, I wouldn't be standing on my own feet. I'd be relying on you."

Mark shook his head vehemently. "No! Don't you see? *You're* the one who would make it work. And when it did, you'd be free!"

Free. The word rang out in the murmur of the restaurant. How wonderful to be free. Seen in that light, Mark's offer sounded tempting. But she couldn't let herself be seduced by it. Dominique shook her head slowly. "If the time ever comes that I choose to go into business for myself, I won't do it by borrowing from a friend." She met Mark's eyes with an earnest expression. Then she reached forward and covered his hand with hers. There was a tingle of electricity where they touched, and the shock of contact jolted her. She withdrew her hand at once. Shyly, she said, "You're a good friend."

Mark leaned forward and grasped the hand she had just pulled away. "More than that, I hope."

Dominique studied Mark, trying to gauge his seriousness. His eyes creased at the corners in the perpetual smile that was unique to him. Was he just flirting? He seemed to be moving fast toward intimacy — an intimacy that Dominique wasn't certain she was ready for.

Mark saw Dominique's uneasiness and released her hand, frustrated. He knew that beneath the surface caution was hidden a woman of tremendous courage and resourcefulness. How could he bring her to the forefront?

With a sigh, he raised his hand to summon the waiter. For now, it was time to back off.

After dinner, Mark suggested a stop at Mr. Smith's, a Georgetown piano bar. The atmosphere in the dark little cavern was raucous and fun — much too noisy for substantive conversation. So they listened to the music and laughed at the singers. By the time they emerged at midnight, Dominique was feeling relaxed.

She grinned as she folded herself into his minuscule MG. "This gets harder with every glass of wine."

Mark laughed and closed her door. As he swung into the driver's seat, he said, "Yeah, but this car's a classic — a fifty-nine MG. One of my last bachelor flings. She has almost two hundred thousand miles on her." He patted the steering wheel affectionately. "She's been all over the state of Louisiana with me. All my campaigns."

Dominique's brow furrowed as she tried to recall his senate campaign so many years before. "This is the same little green car you had then?" She ran her hand over the leather-covered dashboard. "It's in perfect condition. You'd never know it was fourteen years old."

Mark started the engine. "I give her a lot of tender loving care, so I'm hoping she'll be around for a while. Even if she broke down completely, I don't think I could ever get rid of her."

Dominique found it endearing that Mark displayed his sentimentality without embarrassment. She remembered Clay's insistence on a new car every other year. Mark's stout loyalty seemed more admirable. He was so likable!

Nevertheless, the evening ended on an awkward note. As Mark

pulled to a stop in front of Dominique's house and turned toward her, she had a sudden moment of panic. This was too much like a date — the sort of date she'd had when she was a teenager. The whole thing suddenly seemed undignified. It didn't feel right to be sitting in a car in front of her house, wondering what would happen next.

Before Mark could say a word, Dominique gave him a friendly kiss on the cheek, and in a rush of words thanked him for the evening and slid from the car. "Don't bother getting out," she said. "I'm sure everyone's asleep, and I don't want to make any noise."

Mark stared at the empty place beside him, befuddled by Dominique's haste. Just before she closed the door, he had the presence of mind to call out her name.

She hesitated, then lowered her head and looked in at him. She seemed so uncomfortable that Mark couldn't help smiling. He guessed that this was the first time since her divorce that she'd been out with a man. That made him feel good, as though she'd broken a rule for his sake. "I'm not going to bite," he joked.

Dominique watched his expression turn jolly. There was nothing remotely threatening about him. So why was she acting like such a fool? "I know," she said with a self-deprecatory smile. She regarded him fondly. "I had a wonderful time, Mark." She paused. She wanted to tell him how much she appreciated his concern for her, how very special he made her feel, but the words stuck in her throat. "Well" — she took a step back and prepared to close the car door — "thank you."

"Dominique," Mark said, his voice hardly more than a whisper.

Her eyes were topaz candles in the moonlight, the only distinct feature on her shadowed face.

This is just the beginning, isn't it? Mark wanted to ask. But it was premature; Dominique was already so skittish. He fell back on the mundane. "I have a speech in Baton Rouge, so I'll be away this weekend, but can we get together next Wednesday?"

Dominique gave him a melting smile. "I'd like that."

⚭ ⚭ ⚭

"Tell me every detail!" Danielle demanded.

Dominique could envision her settling in for their Saturday morning call. She was probably curled up on the living-room sofa in one of her velvet and lace robes, a cup of coffee at her elbow. Dominique smiled and leaned against the kitchen counter. "About what?" she asked with comic innocence, knowing that Danielle had only one thing on her mind: Mark.

Danielle laughed. "I've been in suspense since Wednesday. Don't draw it out!"

"Wel-l-l . . . he came in and said hello to Mother and Gabrielle." Dominique spoke softly, not wanting to awaken the others. When she finished, she would wake Solange and put her on the phone with Danielle.

"How was Mother?" Danielle asked, her tone dubious. "She was so eager last Saturday, I was afraid she wouldn't let Mark out the door until he'd asked you to marry him."

Dominique snickered softly. "If anyone knows feminine wiles, it's Mother. With Mark, she was the picture of nonchalance."

"What about Gabrielle?" Danielle asked in a worried tone. It was clear she envisioned childish fits of jealousy.

Dominique's voice filled with affection. "She'll be all right. At first, things were a little stiff, but Mark charmed her."

"He could charm anyone!" Danielle said. She lowered her voice confidentially. "He'd be a wonderful catch."

"I'm not interested in 'catching' anyone," Dominique said sternly. "I've had it with marriage and I don't want to be burned a third time. I'm a lot better off on my own." Dominique had expected Danielle to contradict her but, surprisingly, she didn't.

"You may be right," Danielle said in a small voice.

Dominique was astonished. "Is something wrong between you and Ron?"

"No, no," Danielle said quickly. She paused. "I don't know. He's talking about early retirement." Another pause. Then, in a downcast voice, she said, "We can afford it, I suppose. . . ."

"That's good, isn't it?" Dominique asked, confused.

"No!" Danielle cried. "He's ending my life before it's even begun! He's not even fifty and he wants to go off to Florida or something and live like old people! And what am I supposed to do if I don't want to?" Her voice rose in distress. "I mean I love Ron and the girls, but I feel like I've missed something and I don't know what it is!"

Dominique felt helpless in the face of her sister's malaise. "You mean romance?"

"Noooo!" Danielle said scornfully. A pause. Then, thoughtfully, she said, "Well, maybe." Another moment of reflection. "Noooo."

"Maybe your feelings have nothing to do with Ron. Maybe you're just bored. What about getting a job?"

Danielle sighed. "Who would have an over-forty housewife with no experience?"

"You never know until you try."

Danielle made a sound of disbelief. "And just what am I qualified to do?"

Dominique pursed her lips. "Hmmm. I don't know . . . work in a store?"

"And stand on my feet all day? Ha! No thanks."

"What about a bank? You're certainly familiar with those," Dominique teased.

"As what? A teller? Again on my feet all day. I have corns."

Dominique threw up her free hand in resignation. "You find fault with every suggestion!"

"I'm realistic," Danielle said primly. For a few moments, the sisters didn't speak, then Danielle asked, "Anyway, what about you? How's your job?"

Dominique smiled resignedly. "It would be wonderful if it weren't for Sylvia Brussels. I think she's trying to drive me crazy so I'll quit." She hesitated. "You know, Mark tried to talk me into starting my own business."

"You told him about Sylvia, I gather." Danielle said the woman's name in a flat tone.

Dominique sighed and pushed herself off the counter. "I'm afraid so." She went to the coffeepot and poured herself a fresh cup. The comforting steam wafted up to her as she took a sip. She put the cup down on the kitchen table, then sat down before she continued. "Actually, what he said made sense, except that I would have to borrow money to do it."

"What do you need money for? Can't you just work out of your house?"

"Well, I've been thinking about that," Dominique admitted. "But, in my business, image is important. I need an office and an assistant, at least."

"How much would that cost?"

"There's a building over on Wisconsin Avenue that has five hundred square feet for lease — two good-sized offices. I stopped by on

my way home from work Thursday. It's a pretty building, newly reno-
vated. A law firm just bought it and the space is connected to theirs.
So that means that my clients would come in through their reception
area, which is nice. Brass and mahogany — you know, the men's-club
look. Right behind the receptionist's desk, there's a circular staircase
that leads up to the law library. The place reminds me of Henry Hig-
gins' study in *My Fair Lady*."

"I love that!" Danielle exclaimed.

"Also, they'd let me use their copying equipment for a small fee.
But, of course, I'd have my own phone lines and a plaque with my
company's name outside the building. The managing partner said he
would let me have it for five hundred dollars a month."

"Heavens! You're seriously considering this, aren't you?"

"You sound skeptical. You think it's a bad idea?"

"I . . . I don't know. You've only thought about this for a couple of
days. You should be careful. You don't want to rush into something
you'll regret."

Dominique began, "If you never take a chance —"

Danielle interrupted her with laughter. "I know, I know how you
are." She paused. "But where would you get the money?"

"I have that money from the sale of the house and things. I even
sold my jewelry and furs, though I didn't get nearly what they were
worth. Anyhow, that would be a start. And I thought I'd try to
borrow —"

Danielle interrupted her again. "But those are your life's savings!"

Dominique sighed. "That's what makes me hesitate. In any case,
it isn't nearly enough." She stared out the window. A squirrel was
making its way up the side of the old willow oak. Dominique absently
fixed her gaze on it.

"Then you're at a dead end, aren't you?"

"Maybe." Dominique fretfully wound the phone cord around her
finger. "But I thought I'd at least talk to my bank."

"I wouldn't hold out too much hope," Danielle said. "Banks are
only willing to take risks on known quantities."

Dominique was surprised at how much the words distressed her.
She hadn't realized how much she was beginning to count on the idea
of owning her own business. "All I can do is try."

Danielle brought up another problem. "Where would you get
clients?"

"I thought about that. I called Michelle de la Croix at the French embassy yesterday. . . . I think I told you that we've developed a nice working relationship."

"You're moving so fast! I thought this was just an idea. Don't be too impulsive, Dominique. Be careful!"

"I prefer to think of myself as decisive and efficient," Dominique joked with mock hauteur. Then, more seriously, she said, "Anyhow, I have to research this, don't I? How can I make a decision without an idea of my potential income and expenditures? There's nothing to be learned from mulling over a theory. And, once I decided to look into this, why delay?"

"Okay, okay, I see your point," Danielle admitted. "So what did Michelle say?"

"Well, she has no contract with Mrs. Filmore, because the embassy staff handles most events. But the French president is coming for a state visit in five months and she was going to hire us for some of the out-of-embassy events just because I'm French." Dominique lowered her voice. "She was actually glad I might leave. She likes Mrs. Filmore, but she can't stand Sylvia Brussels. And Sylvia's the one she has to deal with on contracts." Dominique took a deep breath. "So I'd have that job to begin. It's not a steady contract, but . . ." Her words faded.

"Would that bring in enough to support you for the first six months?" Danielle's tone betrayed her doubt.

Dominique was silent a moment. "It wouldn't leave much cushion," she confessed. "But if I had a client like that, I know I'd get others. In the embassy community, Michelle is a trendsetter." Dominique had an answer for every argument of Danielle's. The concept that had begun to form just three days before was becoming an entrenched idea. "Mark said that I could stay busy if I did nothing but organize political dinners, like I used to do for him. Members of Congress are always doing fund-raising events. And Mark has a lot of influence in Washington, so I know that if he recommends me, I'll get work. After that, it's up to me to prove myself."

"But aren't you scared to start this with only one client? And not even a long-term contract, but an *assignment?*" Danielle asked incredulously. "It sounds crazy to me!"

"How can I sign up clients when I'm still with Mrs. Filmore?" Dominique's words spilled out with urgency. "I have two very powerful people on my side. And in Washington, it's all *who* you know. If I can just get started, I know I'll do a good job and the whole thing will take off!"

There was a long silence as Dominique waited for Danielle to react. Finally Danielle said, "Well, if anyone can make it work, you can."

Dominique loosened her grip on the receiver. Until that moment, she hadn't known she was clutching it so tightly. "Thanks for saying so . . . ," she said softly. But Dominique wanted more from Danielle. She wanted her sister to be as excited as she was. She wanted an unqualified vote of confidence.

Again there was a lull in the conversation. It was clear that Danielle's misgivings prevented her from offering stronger encouragement.

Dominique was disappointed and a little hurt. "Well . . ." Her voice was downcast. "I'll go and get Mother for you. Don't say anything to her about this yet."

"Okay," Danielle said. "Bye."

As Dominique started to put the phone down, she heard her sister's voice calling to her. She quickly brought the receiver back to her ear. "Yes?" she said.

"Dominique . . . I just wanted to tell you . . . I admire you for doing this. . . ." She paused, as though she had something difficult to say.

Dominique waited in silence for her sister to continue.

Danielle drew in her breath. "I wish I had your courage," she said wistfully.

෨ ෨ ෨

The first day of spring bloomed warm and sweetly scented. Washington's parks were transformed into fields of daffodils. Saucer magnolia and cherry trees were poised to burst into flower, their buds already decorating the branches with an impressionistic haze of pink.

Dominique emerged from her house with a jacket slung over her shoulders. A few steps down her walk, she stopped, surprised by the morning's bright warmth. How glorious! Closing her eyes, she inhaled deeply. There was a dewy freshness in the air that made her feel as though she were awakening from a long winter hibernation. With a carefree laugh, she turned back to the house and unlocked the door. From the threshold, she leaned in and tossed her jacket on the sofa, then pulled the door closed again.

The temperature was even warmer when she passed through her wooden gate into the street. There, the leaves from overhanging trees were less dense and the sunlight splashed over the sidewalk.

"Where do you think you're going?"

Dominique spun around. "Mark!" she cried, "what are you doing here?" Never, in the month they'd been dating, had he dropped in unexpectedly.

He leaned on one shoulder against the brick wall that surrounded her house. "Playing hooky," he replied with a grin.

For the first time, it registered that he wasn't wearing a suit, but rather blue jeans and a plaid shirt that brought out the limpid green of his eyes. He was so brimming with masculine appeal that Dominique was, for a moment, held rapt. "Well" — she blinked, hardly knowing what to say — "it's nice to see you."

He drew close to her and put a finger under her chin. "You want to play hooky with me?"

Dominique made a sound that was half laugh, half gasp. "I can't possibly." She put her hands to her chest, as though her working clothes proved her statement.

Mark looked disappointed. He took her hand and said, "Come on. The office will survive one day without you." Seeing her about to protest, he continued, "Call in sick."

Dominique shook her head quickly. "I don't like to lie. Besides, I have a million things to do." She hadn't told Mark that she was seriously pursuing the idea of starting her own business. That each lunch hour was spent either visiting banks or — when they turned her down for a loan — revising her business plan. She knew if she brought up the subject with Mark, he would try to talk her into accepting his money. So she kept quiet.

Mark crossed his arms. "You can work tomorrow." He smiled and the dimple at the side of his mouth creased irresistibly. "It's too beautiful today." He leaned close to Dominique and said in a low, persuasive voice, "Stop arguing and go change."

It was a delicious idea. Simply skip work. Enjoy the wonderful spring day. Dominique often worked late and on weekends, and not once had she called in sick. Maybe one day off wouldn't hurt. Her eyes danced with excitement as she asked, "What do you have in mind?"

Mark gave her a mischievous look. "It's a surprise. Wear jeans."

"All right!" She turned to go into the house, then turned back. "Do you mind waiting in your car? I'd feel a little uncomfortable if Mother knew. . . ."

Mark began to back toward a mud-spattered black Jeep. Where was his MG? "It'll be our secret," he said in a stage whisper.

After she had called the office and changed, Dominique stealthily escaped the house and ran down the walk like a young girl, almost giggling with the joy of her naughtiness. Mark was double-parked outside the gate and he had taken off the Jeep's rag top. Dominique hopped into the passenger seat. "That's a great idea!" she enthused. "It's actually hot today."

Mark turned toward her as she got in. He caught his breath. A halo of sunshine outlined her strong profile, set off by her tight ponytail. Her features had an aspect of nobility, despite the simplicity of her blue jeans and cotton shirt. Mark smiled and said softly, "You look so beautiful that way."

The expression in Mark's eyes made Dominique's heart stand still. All at once, she was excruciatingly aware of his nearness. She had the urge to reach out and caress his cheek. And then to kiss him. What would it be like?

In the half dozen times they'd been out, she had avoided any displays of intimacy, and on two occasions their "dates" had been family outings with Solange and Gabrielle. There had been hand-holding and light kisses on the cheek. But Mark had clearly sensed that she wasn't ready for more. And he had expressed no sign of impatience. Never had he attempted contact Dominique did not want. But now, suddenly, she wanted it. She could feel her color rising as she thought about it. Embarrassed, she turned to look out the window.

With a furtive smile, Mark withdrew his arm from the back of her seat and started the car.

Dominique remained silent as he drove, spellbound by the sudden change in the mood between them. Mark's admiring expression a few minutes before seemed significant, like a snapshot in a photo album. Dominique couldn't put it out of her mind. She felt expectant, tense in a way that made her senses come alive. She commanded herself to relax. Better not to spoil things by overanalyzing them. Why not simply enjoy the beautiful day? It was nice to let herself be driven to an unknown destination, to be free of decisions.

In a few minutes, they were crossing Key Bridge, with its double row of old-fashioned light posts. "Welcome to Virginia," said the sign at the end of the thoroughfare. Mark steered the car onto the George Washington Memorial Parkway. The road looked like it was cut from the forest. Dominique gazed through the thin spring foliage at the Potomac River. It moved lazily over jutting boulders, its surface reflecting the blue of the sky.

They had not gone far when Mark took an exit that led to a parking area.

"Teddy Roosevelt Island!" Dominique cried with pleasure. "I've been meaning to come here with Mother and Gabrielle, but I never got around to it." A national park, the miniature island was little more than a stand of unspoiled woods in the middle of the Potomac River. It was reached from the parking area by a wooden bridge.

Mark turned off the engine and came to Dominique's side, holding open the door for her. She took his hand and got out.

"I have to get something from the trunk," Mark said. Dominique followed him and watched as he brought out a picnic cooler and blanket.

"A picnic!" She smiled with delight. "It's been years since I've been on one."

Mark grinned at her reaction. "Aren't you glad you came?" he asked.

"Very," Dominique said as she took the blanket from him. So absorbed was she in their preparations that she forgot her earlier tension.

They crossed the wooden bridge in comfortable silence, the only noise the thudding of their sneakers on the planks. At the end there was a path covered in dried leaves.

"There's no one here." Dominique's voice was subdued, as in a museum.

"Except on weekends, it's pretty quiet," Mark said as he took the fork to the right. "I come here sometimes to fish."

Dominique laughed. "What do you catch?"

"Perch and catfish." He grinned. "Good eating, just like home."

Dominique could smell the river, could almost feel its essence tingle inside her nose, cool and marshy.

They rustled along for a few more minutes, then the path began to curve to the left. "We're coming to the north side now," said Mark.

"Do we have a destination?" Dominique asked playfully.

"My yacht!" Mark announced proudly, pointing through the forest to the shoreline.

Dominique squinted in the direction he was pointing. "I don't see anything." Trees and fallen logs obscured the view of the water.

"You will." Mark veered off the path and — carefully holding the branches clear for Dominique — led the way to the water's edge.

Leaning on its side in the mud was a battered green canoe.

"O-o-oh, I see. Your *yacht*." Dominique chuckled.

Mark comically puffed up his chest. "Pretty proud of her, I don't mind saying."

He looked adorable in the silly pose, Dominique thought. "And is she seaworthy?" she asked with mock seriousness.

"*That*" — Mark paused dramatically — "is what we are about to find out."

Dominique burst into laughter. "How long has it been here?"

"Through the ages!" Mark intoned like a documentary narrator. Then he looked at his wristwatch. "Actually, since about a half hour before I kidnapped you."

"You brought it here this morning?"

"See all the trouble I went through for you?" Mark jested.

Despite his light tone, Dominique was touched. It *was* a lot of trouble.

Mark bent down and righted the boat. "You know how to get in so it doesn't tip?"

Dominique looked hesitant.

Mark smiled. "Never mind. Just get in here and I'll push it into the water."

"Oh, no!" Dominique protested in embarrassment. "I'll be too heavy!"

"A little thing like you?" Mark said in an exaggerated southern drawl. He made a motion indicating she should get in.

Dominique grasped the sides as she tentatively reclined onto the wooden plank that served as a seat. Mark gave the canoe a shove and soon they were floating over the glassy water. Mark showed Dominique how to coordinate her paddling with his. At first Dominique was too slow, and the canoe's nose kept heading in to shore. Mark laughed and told her how to correct the problem. Dominique couldn't help thinking how irritated Clay — perfectionist that he was — would have been in the same situation. Dominique would have grown tense trying to please him and, ultimately, given up after an angry exchange.

Mark's approach was the opposite. "Doing great!" he called up to her. "You've got it!" In reality, she wasn't improving much, and the nose of the little boat was still headed toward shore.

After a while, Dominique lifted her oar from the water and let it dangle. Their progress was much quicker that way, she noticed. They went all around the island, exploring little inlets and hidden coves. They saw a turtle on a log and, nearby, an egret.

"So beautiful!" Dominique exclaimed as it spread its wings and with barely a splash floated off the water.

A few minutes later, Dominique pointed excitedly. "Look!" A brown-and-white mother duck paddled near shore, six ducklings in a row behind her.

Mark smiled. "There's bread in the cooler." He spoke softly so as not to disturb the creatures. "Let's feed them." He lifted his oar out of the water and let the canoe drift.

Quietly, he opened the cooler and located a plastic bag. Dominique watched as Mark crumbled the bread into pieces tiny enough for the ducklings. Then he released it on the water. After a few cautious forays, the mother duck eagerly plunged toward the bread, the babies lagging a little behind her. Mark beamed at the scene. When the ducks had eaten every bit, Mark turned to Dominique. "How about you? Are you hungry?"

"Starving!"

"Then you should start paddling," he joked. "We'll hit ground in no time."

"That's cruel!" Dominique pretended outrage, but her broad smile let him know she wasn't insulted.

Indeed, they did reach shore quickly with Mark paddling alone. He hopped out and dragged the canoe out of the water so that Dominique's feet wouldn't get too muddy. Afterward, they trooped a short way through the forest and back onto the path.

"There's a nice big grassy area near Teddy Roosevelt's statue," Mark said over his shoulder. After a few minutes, the trees began to thin and Dominique spotted a broad, circular meadow. The center lay in full sun, the perimeter in dappled shade created by the new spring growth on the trees overhead. Directly opposite them was a bronze statue of Teddy Roosevelt.

"It looks like it's just going to be us and him," Mark said with a satisfied smile. "Where do you want to sit?"

Dominique looked around the cleared area trying to decide among a variety of enticing spots. "How about under that tree?" She pointed to a rough-barked maple whose leaves were just beginning to unfurl.

"Looks good."

After they had spread their blanket and sat down, Mark pulled from the cooler a bottle of white wine, a variety of cheeses, crackers, and chicken sandwiches.

"You thought of everything!" Dominique said.

Mark looked into the cooler with a frown of puzzlement. "There's something else," he said in a preoccupied voice.

Dominique watched in amusement as he searched through the ice.

"Aha!" he crowed, pulling out two frozen Snickers bars. He gave Dominique a look of mock gravity. "You *do* like these, I hope."

Dominique grinned. "Love them."

Mark pretended to wipe sweat from his brow. "Phew! As long as we have Snickers in common . . . That's very important, you know." He carefully laid them on top of the ice, then closed the cooler.

Dominique couldn't seem to stop smiling. Everything Mark did seemed agreeable — either funny or polite or thoughtful.

Dominique held the two chilled wine glasses as Mark poured the golden liquid into them. When he was finished, Mark clinked his glass against hers. "To our future," he said softly. He gave her a searching look.

Dominique's eyes locked with his as she brought the glass to her lips. The wine exploded on her tongue in a cool shower of fruit and oak and butter. It was one of those rare moments of perfect beauty. The smell of spring, the sweet current of air that rustled through the trees. Mark's green eyes, bright and expectant. His smile.

Dominique stared at him, her gaze lingering on each of his features. Suddenly, time and movement stopped. In that one breathless second, she was captured by the electricity that surged between them.

Mark sat immobile, his gaze fixed on her, suddenly tense, waiting. His magnetism was inescapable. Dominique felt as though she were being pulled toward him. She had no will of her own. Hypnotized, she moved forward until her face was close to his. She could almost taste his lips, feel their flesh. Every nerve ending strained toward him.

For an instant she paused, vibrating on the edge of motion. Then, ever so slowly, she reached for him. Her palm brushed the springy hair on the back of his neck. Brought him closer. She felt the warmth of his breath, of his skin. And then she kissed him.

ᖶ ᖶ ᖶ

Ten days later, on a Saturday morning, Dominique sat at the breakfast table in a dispirited mood. At her elbow was a smartly bound navy-blue folder: her business plan. The banks she had visited had praised it, as well as Dominique's impressive background and determination. But, they said regretfully, she didn't have the contracts necessary for a loan. Even if she had, one banker gently told her, her lack of personal credit would have made it almost impossible for him to convince his board to approve a loan.

Solange, sitting across the table drinking her coffee, remarked, "You seem glum. What's wrong?"

Dominique sighed and looked down at the plan. "I suppose I should tell you . . . I've been thinking of starting my own business. That is," she added ruefully, "if I can get a loan, which, so far, doesn't seem likely." She watched her mother carefully, not sure of what reaction to expect. Would she be skeptical, like Danielle?

Solange's eyes widened with pleasure. "That sounds interesting. You could make a lot more money than you do now. Besides" — she sniffed — "you wouldn't have to report to that awful Sylvia." She looked up at the ceiling for a moment, then back at Dominique. "Yes, I think it's a good idea," she said breezily.

Dominique wondered if Solange understood what owning a business entailed. How involved had she been in running the cotton business in Egypt? Had it all been left to caretakers? Dominique wasn't sure. What she *did* know was that Solange had almost never gone to the office near the Port of Alexandria.

"Why do you need a loan?" Solange asked, confirming Dominique's doubts.

What good was Solange's approval if it was based on nothing more than the pleasant sound of the idea? Dominique rubbed her temple fretfully. "I need an office and a business telephone, stationery, and cards. Someone to help me."

Solange looked skeptical. "That sounds expensive. Can't you install an extra telephone line here and work out of the house?"

Dominique shook her head regretfully. "How can I have an employee here? It's crowded enough as it is."

Solange looked down at her coffee cup. She was silent for a few moments. Then, in a solemn voice, "I could go back to New York. You could use my room as an office."

"No!" Dominique said at once. She was surprised at how strongly she rebelled against the idea. "I don't want that." Dominique fixed her eyes on her mother's. It occurred to her that she needed her — or at least wanted her — for moral support.

"But we have to be practical —" Solange started to lecture, then she stopped. The stiffness went out of her posture and she gave Dominique a grateful look. "May I see that?" She pointed at the business plan.

Dominique shrugged and slid the packet across the table to Solange. She wasn't sure her mother would understand it, not because it was in English — business terms were almost the same in French as in English — but because she doubted her mother's familiarity with such documents. "I don't see any way to improve it, but all the banks have said no." She didn't mean to sound so hopeless. After all, she still had a job. It wasn't as though her family's livelihood depended on her starting her own business. On the contrary, it might be jeopardized by it. But, somehow, she had worked herself into a high pitch of excitement over the plan, and the idea of simply going on at Capital Events was defeating.

She gave Solange a wan half-smile and waited for her mother's response.

Solange simply nodded, then lowered her head and stared thoughtfully at the report. After a moment, she asked, "Where did you get this rental figure? It seems low."

Dominique explained about the law office nearby.

Solange raised her eyebrows, clearly impressed. "That's a bargain." She went back to studying the document. "What about this figure for investment capital?"

Dominique inwardly winced, expecting condemnation. "The money from the sale of the house and things."

Solange looked up, her expression concerned. "And that's not enough?"

No warnings? No criticism of Dominique's use of her life's savings? For a moment, she was too surprised to reply. "Uh, no. You see, I need at least a year's cushion." She frowned. "After all, our livelihood will depend on this."

For several minutes, neither woman spoke. Dominique found herself forgetting her own problem as she studied her mother. Solange was normally so argumentative and determined. Clearly, she knew more about business than Dominique had initially thought. Why wasn't she urging Dominique to try other avenues? Why wasn't she berating her for not going about things differently?

But Solange remained quiet, her expression studious as she went over the plan.

Mollified, Dominique tried to summon words of optimism, but she could think of none. She would simply have to put aside a little money each month until she had saved enough to leave her job. Or perhaps she could come up with an alternative plan. Dominique cradled her cheek in her hand and tried to think creatively.

She was concentrating so intensely that the sound of her mother's voice startled her.

"We have the jewelry," Solange said quietly.

Dominique heard the words, but they didn't immediately register.

Solange seemed to understand this, for she elaborated. "The diamond bracelet, the rings, the whole lot that I took out of Egypt. If you sold it, you'd have enough."

Dominique dropped the hand that held her face and sat upright in her chair. She shook her head vehemently. "That's out of the question — it's everything you own!"

Solange gazed seriously at her daughter. "The jewelry will be yours one day. Anyhow, it's much too elaborate for these times. We should sell it," she said decisively.

Impossible! Dominique thought. Solange treasured the gems, wore them proudly at every opportunity. These were not jewels kept in a safe-deposit box and only brought out once in a decade. Solange donned her rubies as casually as the youngsters on the street wore peace symbols. Her emerald engagement ring never left her hand. And she eagerly pounced on excuses to wear her diamond earrings. She even found occasion to adorn herself with the glittering bracelet once or twice a year.

The jewels were Solange's link to a life that had long since disappeared. To sell them was to sell the family's past, its heritage. "Mother, how can you think of parting with them? They were *your* mother's. And Father's mother's. We'll never see workmanship like that again. And" — she shook her head — "they're part of you. Part of us." She finished in a sad voice. "You've always been so proud of them."

Solange averted her eyes, then pushed herself up from the table and brusquely moved to the coffeepot. Dominique half turned in her chair to follow her mother's movements. Solange poured herself a fresh cup of coffee, then returned to the table and sat down. She regarded her daughter steadily. "It doesn't pay to be attached to pieces of stone and metal."

Dominique knew Solange had more to say, but she appeared lost in thought. Her eyes had the distant expression they sometimes got when she spoke of Egypt before the trouble. A tremor went through the older woman, then her eyes focused once more on Dominique. She leaned toward her daughter, her expression ardent. "Those jewels — they aren't alive." She placed a hand on her chest. "We're alive! You need your freedom, and that jewelry can buy it for you. Believe me, aside from good health, there is nothing as valuable as independence!" Her words spilled out in an impassioned flow.

Dominique looked at her mother with astonishment. Solange's cheeks were flushed and her eyes glittered.

"But . . . what if I don't make a go of the business? What if we sell them for nothing?"

Solange's lips tightened into a decisive line. "That won't happen. Look at all you've done so far." She spread her hands expansively. "Your life fell apart not once, but twice, and both times you recovered and went on to new success."

"But, Mother," Dominique said with a grave expression, "I didn't have a choice then." She paused. "I don't feel comfortable taking the security you —"

Solange's palm slammed down on the tabletop. "Well then consider how *I* feel! You think I enjoy being indebted to my own daughter? All these years, I've depended on you and Danielle — mostly *you!* I never thought anything like this could happen to me. We had so much!" she cried, as though she still couldn't fathom the loss. She bit the inside of her mouth and turned her head away.

Dominique stared at her mother in disbelief. All these years, Solange had accepted their help as though it were expected, voicing gratitude only rarely. And, indeed, neither Dominique nor Danielle had expected gratitude. This was the culture in which they had been raised. One helped family. Suddenly, though, Dominique realized that Solange's insouciance was an act — an act designed to preserve her dignity. It was not in Solange's nature to cast herself in the role of poor relation, particularly when it would serve no purpose. Now, though, it *would* serve a purpose, and she was for the first time willing to admit what had gone unspoken for years.

In a bitter voice, Solange said, "I've just been a burden to you! Who in Egypt would have imagined things could change so?"

Dominique was immeasurably moved. She shoved her chair back and went to her mother's side. Then she knelt and enclosed Solange in her arms. "You don't owe me anything," she whispered. "You're my mother!"

Solange gently disengaged herself from her daughter. She splayed her hands on the tabletop and looked down at them. For several seconds she sat that way, her shoulders slumped, her eyes fixed. Then she straightened her back and, ever so slowly, took off her rings, all save her gold wedding band. She raised her chin and met Dominique's eyes with a look of dignified resolve. "You'd be doing me a favor to take them." She gently reached for Dominique's hand and opened it, then dropped the rings into her palm. Finally, Solange folded Dominique's fingers over the jewels and pressed her own hands on either side of Dominique's, almost as though in prayer.

Dominique's throat tightened. She didn't trust herself to speak. She put her head against her mother's chest and hugged her close. The older woman's arms closed around her, strong and warm.

CHAPTER 26 ❧

DOMINIQUE opened the manila folder on her desk, then pressed the intercom to her assistant. "Did you send the seating arrangement for the Capitol Hill luncheon to the Comtesse de la Croix?"

In the outer office, the secretarial chair squeaked. An instant later, a statuesque redhead rolled into the doorway. "She says it's fine. I've already sent a copy to the Secret Service."

Dominique gave Carter James a smile of approval. Thanks to Carter, the details of the French president's visit were largely under control. Dominique could count on her. "Make sure that Congressman Rosen's office gets a copy, too. And let's pray he doesn't have any changes."

Carter grinned. "Done." She used her hands to push her chair away from the threshold and was gone in a leggy blur.

Dominique had met the American University graduate student at a dinner party given by Felice. The two younger women took a class together in business administration.

"Pretty gutsy of Dominique to start her own business, don't you think?" Felice had proudly asked the group gathered around the dinner table. "I would've gone with her if she could afford me."

They'd all laughed, but later, Carter had expressed an interest in coming to work for Dominique. "I won't be as expensive as Felice," she'd said with a reassuring smile. "I just want experience in event planning. Felice has made it sound so interesting." At the time, Carter was supporting her night school classes by modeling in department stores.

"I'm sick and tired of threatening to spray innocent shoppers with perfume!" she had explained with a chuckle.

Dominique had studied the glamorous young woman dubiously. "This job would involve a lot of menial tasks."

Carter had nodded firmly and said, "I'm not afraid of that. It's the only way to learn the business."

Dominique had remained unconvinced. "How can you work full time if you're still in school?"

"I worked full time while I was earning my undergraduate degree, and I have to work full time while I earn my MBA," Carter said in a no-nonsense fashion.

That impressed Dominique and she had agreed to a one-month trial period. Now, almost three months later, Carter was virtually indispensable. Not only did she help with events, she ordered office supplies, paid bills, kept the books, and generally freed Dominique to pursue new clients and manage events.

Things had been very slow the first month, and Dominique had begun to worry that her funds would run out even sooner than she had projected. Then, one day, her name had appeared coupled with Mark Patout's in a Washington column.

No one created a greater stir at the glittering Italian embassy soirée last night than the very eligible, very attractive Senator Mark Patout. On his arm was a diminutive titian-haired mystery woman with a *très piquant* French accent. I don't need to tell you, Dear Reader, that all the bachelorettes were hoping she had just flown in from the Continent for a short visit. No such luck, girls (sigh). Turns out she's a former resident of the Senator's home state (giving a whole new meaning to the term constituent services). That's right, she's from that party capital, New Orleans, and she's moved to Washington to show us how to throw great galas. Until recently, she was at savvy Grace Filmore's Capital Events and now she's opened a shop of her own in Georgetown, Affairs to Remember. Could it be she's trying to tell us something?

Dominique was annoyed at the piece, until the calls started coming in. Mark Patout was a powerful senator and there wasn't a lobbyist in

Washington who couldn't immediately envision the benefits of hiring his "friend." Before the day was out, Dominique had firm commitments for two Capitol Hill receptions and one sit-down dinner in the Chevy Chase mansion of a prominent lawyer campaigning for appointment to the Supreme Court. These sorts of events didn't bring in a tremendous amount of money — not like huge galas held on behalf of charities or museums. Such established institutions didn't need to seek out Mark Patout's favor, so they were not the ones to respond to the column. But the smaller events were a start, and they paid the rent.

Mark, too, had referred several of his fellow legislators to Dominique, but from those she had secured contracts for only two campaign fund-raisers to be held in Washington. The other legislators had wanted events in their home states, and Dominique wasn't equipped for such work. How could she possibly travel to California, for example, when she barely had time to finish her work in Washington?

It had already become clear to her that she needed more help, but she didn't have the revenue to support it yet. As a result, she worked harder and longer than ever before in her life. Sometimes she felt a strange sort of panic, as though if she didn't finish everything she had to do each day, she would sink into a quagmire of overdue work from which she would never emerge.

Now, Dominique sorted through the message slips on her blotter trying to decide whom to call back first. Probably the manager of the Hay-Adams, the hotel that would host seventeen members of the French president's entourage. The most important, of course, would stay at Blair House, the U.S.-owned residence across from the White House, specially reserved for visiting dignitaries. Others would stay at the French embassy. Dominique wanted to ensure that those staying at the hotel felt in no way slighted. She had persuaded the manager to provide, gratis, several pampering touches.

As she thought of this, she smiled. She really *was* good at her job and, despite the problems, she loved being in business for herself. Mark, after all, had been right. She had to remember to tell him so when she saw him that evening.

Dominique picked up the phone and dialed the number of the Hay-Adams, then sat back and hummed a little melody as she waited for an answer.

౮౨ ౮౨ ౮౨

The delicious scent of roast meat wafted through the front door of Dominique's house. She looked at her watch and saw that it was only quarter to seven. Mark must have arrived early.

Her heart racing with anticipation, she unlocked the door. Laughter floated out from the kitchen. It was punctuated by the cozy sound of clanking pots and pans. Gabrielle was chattering rapidly in French, telling a story, while Mark and Solange interjected comments of their own.

Dominique paused, savoring the homey clatter. Someone turned on the tap in the kitchen sink. Solange asked Mark if she had sliced enough mushrooms. Gabrielle squealed as the oil on the stove started to sizzle and she was hit with a stray droplet.

Dominique closed the front door and moved through the living room, invisible to the others.

The three in the kitchen burst into laughter as Gabrielle reached the punch line of her story. Dominique tried to recall a moment in recent years when Gabrielle had shown such ease and happiness with Clay, but she couldn't. With Clay, there had always been pressure, anxiety to please. Mark didn't try to correct or improve — he relished people for who they were.

Dominique hugged herself and inhaled deeply, then, with a light step, hurried to join the others. As she opened the kitchen door, she was greeted with cries of pleasure. Such intense joy overwhelmed Dominique that she felt her heart would burst.

Gabrielle said, "Hi, Mom!" and threw an arm around her as Dominique wrapped her own arm around her daughter's waist. Gabrielle breathlessly launched into a repetition of the story Dominique had just overheard.

Solange kissed her on both cheeks, then resumed her mushroom slicing. She had about her the air of a woman with an important mission.

Dominique turned to Mark as she listened to Gabrielle's story with half an ear. His teeth flashed as he welcomed her from his position in front of the skillet. His shirtsleeves were rolled up to reveal the salt and pepper hair on his forearms. His tie, loose around the collar, was thrown comically over his shoulder to keep it out of the way. His wavy hair looked rumpled, as though he had bent down and risen a number of times.

Dominique let her eyes rove over him. She drank in the laugh lines around his eyes and mouth, his crooked nose, his broad shoulders, and the ever-so-slight love handles that were a testament to his enjoyment of life. Everything about him was comfortable and inviting. The lines on his face were the lines of a kind man, a funny man, a loving man. His looks would never inspire the awe that Clay's did, but they were far more appealing.

Dominique longed to put her arms around him, to nuzzle her face in his shoulder. But it was not their habit to touch in front of Gabrielle and Solange, so she contented herself with smiling at him.

For Mark, the noises around him receded to a distant hum. Gabrielle's chatter, the sound of Solange's knife against the cutting board, the sizzling oil — all of it became background noise. He looked into Dominique's eyes and saw the emotion he had awaited for years. He froze, spatula in hand, unable to move or breathe.

Dominique saw the response in Mark's face. It was like a miracle, the power she had to make him happy. And suddenly, making this gentle man happy was of paramount importance to her. She wanted to show him how much she cared. She wanted to allow him to enter the hidden recesses of her soul, wanted to share her thoughts and dreams with him. She wanted to forget about caution and courtship. She wanted only to acknowledge the love that burst forth from her like the crescendo of a symphony.

She took a step toward him. Their eyes met. It was as though they were speaking aloud, so clearly did they read each other's thoughts. Silently, Dominique confessed to Mark: I love you, too.

∽ ∽ ∽

Dominique listened for the sound of Gabrielle's breathing, regular and deep, then she closed the door of her daughter's bedroom. She turned and faced Mark where he stood at the end of the hallway.

"It's okay," she mouthed.

He came toward her and entered her bedroom.

It was something Dominique had never thought she would do. She didn't like the idea of making love with a man not her husband in the house where Gabrielle and Solange slept. Yet, tonight, Mark felt more like her husband than Clay ever had. Tonight it was inevitable.

Dominique shivered with anticipation — and apprehension — as she locked the door behind her. She was acutely aware of her lack of experience in comparison to Mark. What if she appeared clumsy, lacking in finesse? What if Mark was disappointed?

Mark studied Dominique's pale face and smiled reassuringly. He pulled her to the armchair in the corner of the room. "Let's talk for a minute," he said quietly.

Dominique let out a long exhalation of relief. She hadn't known what to do next.

Mark sat on the chair and pulled her onto his lap. Dominique snuggled against him and shyly rested her head on his shoulder.

A lone lamp burned on the night table, leaving their corner of the room in shadows.

"I love you, Dominique," Mark murmured. He nuzzled the hair near her temple.

Dominique raised her face to his. She saw the tenderness and desire in his eyes — and the love. Mark made her feel like the most beloved woman on earth. How could she doubt him? A blissfully liberating sense of trust chased away her apprehension.

Mark saw the change in her, and his face brightened. He brought his hands to Dominique's face and cradled it between his palms. The emotion that shined from his face was so intense that Dominique lowered her eyes. With a whispery rustle, Mark brushed the tips of her eyelashes with his lips. Dominique laughed at the fluttery sensation, then opened her eyes and gave Mark a grateful look. He knew just what to do to ease her anxiety. It made her heart ache with love for him.

Keeping his eyes fixed on hers, Mark lowered his head for a kiss, gentle and light. Dominique parted her lips and tasted the warm sweetness of his tongue. It tingled like spice. She kissed him there, where his lips curved upward, as though ready to smile, and there, on the dimple that appeared on his cheek when finally he did smile. She lightly stroked the side of Mark's neck with her fingertips and felt him tremble under her touch. His hardness strained against the softness of her thigh, but Mark showed no sign of impatience; he was content to let things progress at Dominique's pace. Dominique was unutterably moved by his combination of strength and vulnerability. He didn't hide the fact that she held his emotions in her hands, yet he seemed willing to trust her with that power. She had never known a person so open, so willing to give of himself.

As she met his eyes, the love between them was like a preternatural force that encapsulated them, blocking out the rest of the world. In her mind, Dominique said the words, Make love to me, though it wasn't in her nature to say them aloud.

But Mark reacted as though she had spoken. He gathered her close and gave Dominique a lingering kiss, then eased her from his lap and led her to the bed. They stopped at its edge and Mark pulled Dominique to him. For a moment they stood that way, their hearts pounding together. Then Mark kissed Dominique and his arms grew tense and hard as he wrapped her in his embrace. In unison, they sank to the bed.

Suddenly, they were both voracious to experience what they had so far only imagined. With a few deft movements, Mark freed them of their clothes. The cool air assaulted Dominique's nerve endings and she closed her eyes and shivered at the delicious feeling. Mark stretched out at her side, his elbow bent, his palm supporting his head. And for a long time, he didn't move. His regard swept over Dominique, as though to savor the fact that she was there. The heat between Dominique's legs turned into an ache and her breath grew short. She wanted to reach for Mark, but was held rapt in unbearable, immobilizing suspense — the kind that preceded an orgasm — yet Mark had not even touched her.

Finally, Mark stretched out his hand and delicately smoothed his fingers over Dominique's thigh. Goose bumps rose on her body. She remained breathlessly still as Mark traced the smooth curve of her arms, the smoother satin of her breasts. He circled his hand over Dominique's hips, then eased it between her legs. The hot eagerness she felt was like a distant memory stoked to unprecedented heights. She could bear the tension no longer, and she reached for Mark, bringing him close.

Mark looked down at her. In the dim light, she was rosy with arousal. Her eyes glittered beneath half-open lids and her lips, swollen from his kisses, invited more. She had always seemed so discreet, so self-contained. He had dreamed one day of reaching the passion beneath, and was rewarded as he watched ecstasy transform Dominique.

To Dominique, it seemed Mark was everywhere at once. He filled her and covered her. His soft, rhythmic touch made her come alive. He moved slowly, testing the effect on her of each feathery movement of his hand. His desire to please, and his restraint, freed her inhibitions. Now she wanted to give *him* pleasure, to see him forget himself as he was making her forget herself. She slid her hand over the wiry hair on his chest, then downward until she encircled his member, felt it tremble at her touch. With her legs, she enfolded him. Ready for him. As he entered her, she exhaled a long, shuddering breath. Dominique was awash with sensation, outside herself. At first they moved gently, then with ferocious impatience. Dominique's muscles grew rigid as the feeling held her in its thrall. Magnifying her pleasure a thousandfold was the awareness of their love. Their actions, their emotions, their tenderness were combining to *make* love. They were lost in each other — skin, muscle, touch, sensuality.

When Mark inhaled sharply and then, with a helpless tremor, climaxed, Dominique felt as though she were being filled with his soul. And, as the feeling sang around her and surged through her heart, she surrendered to it.

Afterward, they clung together in silence. Words weren't adequate to describe what had passed between them and so they remained mute, respecting its power. When their desire rose again, they came together quickly, their hunger fueled by their new knowledge of each other. They were insatiable, greedy as they had never been for the lovers who had gone before. Their inhibitions vanished as they breathed, tasted, reveled in each other. They wanted to possess and be possessed.

Finally, as the night sky began to lighten, they reluctantly moved apart, their fingers clutching each other even as they slid from the bed. Dominique threw her robe around her, shivering with the absence of Mark's warmth. But it was growing light — he had to hurry away.

With a sense of loss, she accompanied him downstairs, then stood at her front door and watched him pick his way down the uneven flagstones. When he reached the gate, he turned and looked back at her. The sky was still a deep, inky gray and Dominique could barely make out his features. But she saw the gleam of his eyes and she understood what they were saying to her. Her heart lifted out of her body, heavenward. She raised her index finger to her lips and lightly kissed it, then turned it in Mark's direction.

From the dark came his whisper, "I love you."

CHAPTER 27 ∞

IT WAS a deceptively crisp-looking Saturday morning, but Dominique knew that when she actually stepped outside, she'd be overwhelmed by the muggy August heat. She ran her fingers through her hair and stretched, reluctant to move from the cool kitchen. Then, bracing herself, she hurried out to get the newspaper.

Back inside, she settled at the table with a cup of coffee to await Danielle's weekly call. Just as she poured her second cup, the phone rang.

"Well, I did it!" Danielle announced proudly in response to Dominique's hello.

Dominique laughed at the cryptic statement, but her curiosity was piqued. "What?" she asked.

"I found a job!"

Dominique's eyebrows shot up in surprise. "You what?"

"That's right. I thought about how enterprising you were to start your own business. You inspired me!"

"That's wonderful! I knew you could do it!"

Danielle snorted. "It took a while. A lot of people just laughed in my face because I didn't have any experience. Politely, of course, but still . . ."

Dominique made a sound of commiseration.

"Finally, I thought of a way to prove I was qualified."

"Qualified? What kind of job did you get?"

"Financial planner at Pratt, Watkins."

Dominique's mouth dropped open. "You're kidding! The one with the ads where everyone —"

"Exactly," Danielle interrupted.

"But they're huge!" Dominique exclaimed. "How in the world did you do it?"

"Well . . ." Danielle was clearly ready to launch into the story.

"Wait!" Dominique cried. "Let me put Mother on the extension. She'll want to hear." Dominique put down the phone and ran upstairs to rouse Solange.

"Danielle's on the phone and she's found a job! Pick up the extension in my room."

Moving as quickly as a girl, Solange slid from her bed and grabbed her robe from the nightstand. A few seconds later, the three women were talking together.

"Mother, did Dominique tell you I found a job?" Danielle asked in French.

"*Oui! Mabrook!*" Solange answered in a mixture of French and Arabic.

Dominique smiled as she realized that she had never heard her mother say congratulations in any language but Arabic. "*Mabrook!*" was her cry on every happy occasion.

Danielle continued in French. "Well, everywhere I went, they told me that they wanted someone with experience. Of course, I had none. Then one day it occurred to me that I *did* have experience. I mean, I've managed my own portfolio. But I didn't realize how well until I put together a chart that showed my earnings over the past twenty years." She paused dramatically. "Do you know that I've outper-formed some of the best money managers in the business? I've aver-aged an annual growth of thirty-two percent. Recently, because of in-flation, I've doubled my money. Other times, I didn't do as well. But the average is still thirty-two percent. Pretty incredible when you compare it to a bank or bonds."

"Oh, Danielle, I'm so proud of you!" Dominique said.

"You were always so bright," Solange added adoringly.

"You should see the office . . . seventy stories right on Wall Street!"

"How long is the commute?" Dominique asked.

"Forty minutes. And the best part is, I get to buy a whole new wardrobe for work. I'm having the time of my life!" Danielle's voice soared.

"That's wonderful," said Solange. Then her tone became ominous. "How does Ronald feel about it?"

"He has no say in the matter," Danielle said flatly.

"He's not pleased, is he?" Dominique probed.

Danielle sighed. "Not especially."

"Well, . . . he'll come around," Dominique said.

"He'll have to," Danielle said in a tone that brooked no contradiction.

"How is he? And the girls?" Solange asked.

"Oh, Ronald's fine," Danielle said indifferently. Then her tone became enthusiastic. "The kids are great. I can't believe that Monique starts at Boston University next month." She sighed. "At least Lana's in Boston, too. Things are so crazy these days . . ."

"Give them my love," said Solange longingly.

"I think Lana may visit you before school starts, Mother," Danielle said. "If that's all right with you, Dominique."

"Of course," said Dominique. "She can sleep with Gabrielle, or we can pull out the living room couch, if she'd prefer."

"How is Gabrielle?" Danielle asked.

"Wonderful." Dominique's voice glowed. "She's going down to New Orleans next week for another visit with her father."

"And what about Mark? Is he still in the picture?"

"Oh la la!" Solange broke in with a laugh. "He's here almost every evening."

"Never mind that," Dominique said with impatient good humor. "Danielle, when do you start your new job?"

"I started on Monday. I even have an office of my own. It's small, but the managers above me have bigger ones. I want one of those by next year."

"And you'll have it," Solange said confidently.

"I'll give you another report next Saturday," Danielle said, her voice bouncing with optimism.

"I can't wait. You're terrific!" said Dominique.

"*Mabrook, chérie!*" Solange cried once more.

❦ ❦ ❦

"That's marvelous news!" Mark gave Dominique a smile of genuine pleasure as he led her onto the wide porch of his old Victorian. His home was in Cleveland Park, a woodsy neighborhood at the edge of the District of Columbia. There was a distinctly southern feel to the area, with its sprawling, comfortable houses and its broad, tree-shaded yards. It was the kind of place where people took walks on summer evenings and grew their own herbs.

After Dominique's conversation with Danielle, she had thrown on a pair of shorts and a shirt and driven to Mark's house. One Saturday a month he washed his MG, and Dominique had fallen into the habit of helping him. Afterward, they washed her car. On this afternoon, they were invited to go swimming at the home of Mark's neighbors, a congenial couple, both professors at Georgetown University.

"Want some iced tea before we get started?" Mark pointed at a pitcher resting on a white wicker table.

Dominique smiled in agreement. She liked nothing better than to sit on Mark's wraparound porch and watch people go by. It was a friendly block, and Mark and Dominique often socialized with the neighbors. It was rare that he received an invitation that did not include her and vice versa.

Mark poured two glasses of iced tea and handed one to Dominique as he sat in the rocking chair beside hers. "I bet Danielle will be running the company in no time," he remarked with a chuckle.

Dominique was warmed by his interest in her family. To him, they weren't just acquaintances. He cared about them, and was willing to exert considerable effort on their behalf. She thought of the pool party he had hosted in his back yard for Gabrielle and her friends. "It's important for teenagers to feel like part of the crowd. She'll be the toast of her class after this," he'd predicted. And he'd been right. He was equally considerate of Solange. That summer, she had been fascinated by the televised Watergate hearings. Mark had personally escorted her to a session, and reserved for her one of the coveted chairs in the row behind the witness table.

Now, as Dominique's thoughts turned to her sister, she laughed. "Next time you see Danielle, be careful what you say," she joked. "She may try to talk you into letting her handle your investments."

Mark stopped rocking and his expression grew thoughtful. "Listen, if she does as well for her clients as she's done for herself, I'd have no problem with that. In fact, it's not a bad idea. That old duffer at the bank hasn't done anything creative in years."

Dominique held up a hand in protest. "I was kidding!" She shook her head. "Please. If anything happened, I'd never forgive myself."

Mark smiled. "I'd forgive you."

Dominique's eyes lingered on the easy upward curve of his lips. It made her sad to think that, after tonight, she wouldn't see him for several weeks. Congress had just recessed until Labor Day and Mark would, as always, return to Louisiana to be with his family and constituents. She put her hand on his forearm. "I'll miss you," she murmured. The words escaped her almost before she realized she'd spoken them.

Mark gave her a look of appeal, then put down his glass and stood up.

Dominique did the same and, side by side, they made their way to the driveway. They were silent as Mark turned on the hose and filled the waiting bucket with suds. But as they leaned over his MG with their sponges, he spoke. "I still don't see why you all won't come down to Louisiana. We have plenty of room at Belle Terre and the family would love to have you. My sisters would pamper you three like baby chicks."

Dominique's face grew closed. She bent over the hood of the car and spoke into it. "Mark, we've been over this so many times! I just don't want to go back. I know Belle Terre is miles from New Orleans, but Louisiana is such a small place and everyone knows you. We'd run into someone and —"

"So what?" Mark interrupted, his voice more imploring than angry. He stopped scrubbing and looked at Dominique. She raised her eyes to his. "So what if Clay finds out we've been seeing each other? That bast—" He stopped short and took a deep, calming breath, then he continued in an even voice. "Clay doesn't deserve your consideration."

Dominique shook her head. "You know it's not because of me. I just don't want him questioning Gabrielle. He might make her feel odd about us."

Mark held Dominique's gaze. "It wouldn't be a problem if you married me," he said quietly.

Dominique stood motionless. She didn't want anything between them to change! It was perfect as it was. "Mark, I . . . I don't know what to say," she stammered in confusion. Panic rose in her as she remembered the devastation of her previous two marriages. She wasn't ready to try again! Not yet. She shook her head. "It's too soon," she said emphatically.

"Soon!" Mark looked up at the sky, his expression exasperated.

"We've been seeing each other for six months!" He threw his sponge in the bucket and came to Dominique's side. He grasped her free hand in his. "Why are you acting so surprised?"

Dominique had no answer. She knew Mark loved her. For that reason, perhaps, she didn't question the direction of their relationship. It seemed solid and secure.

As though reading her mind, Mark said, his voice downcast, "Do you realize that you've never told me that you love me?"

Dominique gave him a startled look. It had been on the tip of her tongue so many times. But she had always stopped at the crucial moment. She was afraid to say it, though she couldn't articulate to herself why. "You know how I feel," she said in a low voice.

Mark gave her a hurt look. Then he leaned back against the car and crossed his arms. Dominique would have to make the next move.

She looked up at him. "You *know* how I feel," she repeated softly. She stared down at the yellow sponge in her hand, dripping onto her sandaled feet. Why couldn't she say the words?

Mark pushed away from the car and took a step toward Dominique. With one hand, he reached forward and touched a strand of her hair. Then he dropped his arm to his side. "I still remember the first time I saw you."

Dominique gazed silently at him. A few beads of sweat glistened on his forehead. She wanted to wipe them away, to offer him comfort.

He continued in a soft, hypnotic voice. "I've loved you for such a long time. All these years. All the time you were married to Clay." He shook his head. "I would see you sometimes over the years. . . . You . . . Clay—" He halted abruptly and turned his head away. Then he looked back at Dominique. "I didn't want to be attracted to you, you understand."

Dominique nodded, infinitely moved. Of course he didn't want to be. Mark wouldn't pursue another man's wife. She felt admiration well up in her. She loved his sense of right and wrong. There were never shades of gray with Mark. Never the easy rationalizations with which Clay so adeptly justified his actions.

"And when I heard you'd divorced, . . . I thought . . . another chance." Mark stopped and clamped his lips together, too overcome to continue.

Dominique wanted to wrap him in her arms. He was always so cheerful that she sometimes forgot the depth of feeling of which he was capable. Now he was confessing something he had carried in his heart for years. It was an offering to be cherished.

Mark saw the emotion written on Dominique's face, but saw the hesitancy also. "Dominique, I didn't intend to ask you today — this way —" He pointed at the soapy car. "I wanted to plan something wonderful." He made a weary gesture of dismissal, then fixed her with an expression of entreaty. "But it kills me that you don't trust me enough to believe we can make this work —" His brows drew together. "And that you can't even say how you feel," he concluded bitterly.

Dominique reached forward and placed her hand on Mark's. She thought of all he added to her life. The prospect of living without him seemed unutterably bleak. Yet she wasn't ready to remarry. She was still convalescing from her divorce. Its repercussions had changed every part of her life. She had just begun to feel stable again. That was due, in part, to Mark. He gave her a sense of belonging. She once again fit into a society that seemed to congregate in groupings of two, and his love was like a soothing poultice to her bruised self-esteem. He offered refuge and comfort when she was overwhelmed with the difficulties of her new life. And, most of all, Mark accepted Dominique's love — though she could not speak of it — with infinite delight and gratitude, as though it were a priceless treasure.

But Clay's abandonment had been a rude shock, and a strong motivator. Dominique never wanted to depend on anyone again! And she was building a business that, one day, she hoped would provide her with that freedom. Now it required all her effort, all her concentration. She knew that the urgency would be gone if she married Mark. On the horizon, she saw the person she was striving to be — the life she was striving to make for herself. She wasn't there yet, though, and she wasn't ready to subordinate her efforts to marriage. She was afraid she would lose herself.

Dominique wrung her hands tightly and lifted her eyes to Mark's. "Mark, I can't say yes now. I'm scared. There are things I need to work out. Please, please understand," she implored, "that I'm not saying no for all time. I just can't rely on anyone else right now."

"But why not?" Mark persisted, his tone one of frustration. "I want to be part of your life. Why won't you let me?"

Dominique leaned forward and grasped his arm. "I want you in my life, but there are things I have to do for myself." Her voice was filled with emotion. Her eyes gazed into his, begging for his understanding. "If you can just wait a little longer . . ."

Mark looked at her with despair. "Dominique" — his voice was intense, rasping — "say it. Please."

But she did love him! Her heart burst with it. Why was it so hard to put into words? Mark wasn't like the others. She could trust him. So with the plummeting feeling of a parachute jump, Dominique closed her eyes and whispered, "I love you, Mark."

CHAPTER 28 ∽

WASHINGTON sprang to life after Labor Day. Congress returned from summer recess and the town buzzed with renewed excitement about Watergate. There were resignations, convictions, talk of President Nixon's impeachment. And there were parties, charity balls, fund-raisers.

As Dominique had predicted, her handling of the French president's visit in July had launched her reputation. Unfortunately, Washington was a ghost town in August, so she hadn't been able to capitalize on her success. However, now that fall was here, the phone at Affairs to Remember was beginning to ring again.

On this September morning, though, the first call for Dominique was from her friend Felice.

"Welcome back! How was the beach?" Dominique asked.

"Can't *wait* to tell you," Felice purred.

"It sounds like you have a secret," Dominique said, intrigued.

"You won't believe it!" Felice's voice was buoyant.

Dominique leaned forward in her chair and rested her elbows on her desk. "You met someone!" she breathed.

"Remember that guy my mother tried to fix me up with last Christmas? Charles Jackson?"

"And you refused!" Dominique crowed, guessing the rest.

"Let me tell you. He's gorgeous. Looks kind of like Billy Dee Williams. Columbia graduate. Radiologist. And the most wonderful beach house you've ever seen. *Plus* a brownstone in Manhattan."

"Good heavens! How old is he?"

"Thirty-nine," Felice said victoriously. "Just perfect."

"Is there anything wrong with this paragon?" Dominique joked.

"He hasn't asked me to marry him," Felice said wryly. "Yet."

Dominique leaned back in her chair and laughed. "And you have a solution?"

"Yes," Felice said with determination. "He's too much of a catch. He must have to beat the women off with a stick. And" — she dropped her voice — "I don't think I'm the only one he's dating. So-o-o . . . I'm going to play it cool. He's asked me to visit him in New York this weekend. I accepted, but I'm going to cancel a couple of days before."

Dominique clicked her tongue in mock disapproval. "You're terrible!"

"I'm smart," Felice said with conviction. "He needs to miss me." She paused. "And I'm not going to answer my phone this week." She giggled. "He'll think I'm busy every night!"

Dominique let out an incredulous gasp. "What if you scare him away?"

"I won't," Felice said smugly. "This'll work. You'll see."

"I don't know . . . ," Dominique said skeptically.

"Look, you might be older than me, but I have more experience with men," Felice said knowingly.

Dominique laughed. "I suppose. Well, as long as you're 'going out' every night this week, why don't you come over for dinner tomorrow?"

"I'd love to! It's been ages since I saw Gabrielle and Solange." She chuckled. "I'll bet your mom agrees with my strategy on Charles."

"I'm sure," Dominique said wryly. "I'll see you at seven."

As soon as Dominique concluded her call, Carter appeared at the door, her face glowing. She pirouetted to Dominique's desk and dropped a pink message slip in front of her boss. "The Corcoran Gallery of Art called while you were on the phone! They're planning a big kickoff for a new photography exhibition in March." Carter dropped her voice confidentially. "They said the Comtesse de la Croix recommended you."

Dominique eagerly seized the message slip bearing the name and number of the Corcoran representative, Cecilia Bernhardt. The Corcoran Gallery of Art took in an entire city block opposite the White House. The magnificent Beaux Arts structure housed world famous works of the nineteenth and twentieth centuries. On occasion, it also held photography exhibitions. Dominique pictured its endless concourses of marble and pillars, its graceful winding staircase. What a place for an event! And what a coup to be able to claim the institution as a client. This could be the break that would transform her business from an uncertain proposition into an unqualified success.

Two days later, Dominique stood in the grand foyer of the Corcoran, marveling at the towering space as she waited to meet Cecilia Bernhardt. She turned at the tap of high heels on the marble floor. A stately woman with pure white hair approached with an energetic stride. As she drew closer, Dominique saw that her face was barely lined — she could have been any age from forty to sixty. Dominique extended her hand and encountered the firm grip of Cecilia Bernhardt. In a glance, she took in the Italian silk scarf, the tailored gray suit, and the Bruno Magli shoes. As the woman released her hand, Dominique noticed that her unvarnished nails were clipped to a short, practical length, but beautifully maintained.

"Mrs. Parker?" Bernhardt spoke in the cultured tones of the East Coast elite. "I've heard marvelous things about you. You have a strong advocate in Michelle de la Croix."

Dominique's pulse raced. She wanted this job! "I can't imagine a more impressive setting for an event. I'm eager to hear about it." The words echoed in the vast chamber.

Mrs. Bernhardt smiled. "Let's go upstairs. I'll show you what the planning committee has in mind."

Dominique followed her to a bronze staircase made for grand entrances. Up they went, past dreamy Gainsborough portraits and romantic Turner seascapes.

"The photo exhibit is in black-and-white," the older woman explained.

Dominique immediately thought of the black-and-white balls made famous by Paris' Ecole des Beaux Arts. The Corcoran was a setting of similar grandeur and the theme would work there. Her mind began expanding on the plan even as she listened to Mrs. Bernhardt.

The other woman slowed at the entrance of a large exhibition space. It contained paintings dating from the 1950s to the current year. "The exhibit will be here. Usually, we set up the food downstairs or in the main concourse of this floor." Bernhardt turned and waved in the direction of the long hall. "But what often happens is that people spread out too much and the party ends up with a rather empty feel."

Dominique did a three-hundred-sixty-degree turn. "I can see how that would be." She faced Mrs. Bernhardt squarely. "I'll come up with a solution," she assured her.

Mrs. Bernhardt looked pleased. Then her expression grew more serious. "I think it only fair to tell you that we've invited two other firms to bid." She looked Dominique directly in the eye. "One is the public relations firm we already use. They've just formed an event planning department."

Dominique's heart sank. If the firm was already connected with the Corcoran, then they surely would be given special consideration. On the other hand, if they were only starting out in the event planning field, she would have the advantage of experience.

"The other is Elite Catering. We've used them before and been very pleased, but we aren't quite certain they can handle the whole job."

Dominique didn't see how they could. There were many facets to an event, food being just one. She *knew* her firm was more qualified. "I'm sure my proposal will be competitive," she said in a confident voice.

Mrs. Bernhardt nodded. "Let's discuss this more in my office. I'll give you a list of specifications." The woman lightly touched Dominique's arm to indicate the way.

Dominique spent an hour and a half with Mrs. Bernhardt, and by the time she left, they were on first name terms. Dominique liked Cecilia's style — businesslike, but not cold. As they parted, the older woman said, "I look forward to working with you." And she smiled as though she truly meant it.

∽ ∽ ∽

A driving November storm slammed sheets of water against the closed window of Dominique's office. It was near midnight and Dominique was dropping with fatigue, but she kept her focus on the work spread across her desk, trying to ignore the storm's furor.

"More coffee?" Carter got up from the floor and stretched. She carefully stepped around the binders on the carpet to approach Dominique's desk. They contained finished portions of the Corcoran proposal. The two women had spent the entire day preparing the fourteen copies necessary for the board, and Dominique was now drafting the cover letter. Carter reached across her desk and picked up her boss' mug.

Dominique sighed and rubbed her sore eyes. "I'm going to float away, but I need coffee to stay awake."

A sonorous clap of thunder shook the building, and Dominique shuddered.

Carter looked at her. "You hate storms, don't you?"

Dominique gave her a sheepish look.

Carter laughed and brought her the full mug of coffee. "Is that ready to type up?" She pointed at the draft Dominique was working on.

"I suppose," Dominique said wearily. "I've edited it so many times that I don't know if I'm making it better or worse. I wish we could afford one of those memory typewriters so you wouldn't have to keep retyping the same thing."

"At the business school, they're even using computers for stuff like this," Carter commented.

"Computers!" Dominique exclaimed.

"You never have to retype. You can edit and print as many copies as you want."

"What a time-saver," Dominique said wistfully. She needed more people, but she also needed better office equipment. If only she could get this contract!

ல் ல் ல்

The item in next morning's paper was a blow so unexpected, so damaging, that Dominique could only stare at the column in disbelief.

Everyone's dying to see who the Corcoran's going to pick to organize its big gala in honor of top photographer Harlan Wilkie. Word is that the new Affairs to Remember was front-runner, but there've been whispers about how firm president Dominique Parker gets her contracts. Everyone knows that she's *very good friends* with powerful Louisiana Senator Mark Patout, and sources tell us that the connection is her biggest business asset. It's not that he does any arm-twisting, but the "friendship" is no secret. And, Dear Reader, you know as well as I that there isn't a Washington player who won't snap at the chance to win favor with a high-ranking senator.

Sniffs one former associate of Dominique's, "All museums get federal grants. Obviously, Dominique is going to have the advantage over another firm, even if she's less experienced and less capable. If I were a competitor I'd want to know as much as possible about how that contract is awarded."

And how does lovely Dominique respond? Hard to say, since at press time, she hadn't returned our call. As for the senator, we couldn't keep his receptionist on the phone long enough to take a message. "He doesn't respond to gossip items," she told us. Yes, but, but, hold on a minute — "I'm sorry. That's his policy." Click! Well, Dear Reader, there you have it. Don't say I didn't give them a chance.

Dominique gripped the newspaper, her nails tearing into it. She remembered the phone message. It hadn't been left by the gossip columnist, whose name everyone knew. It had undoubtedly been an assistant. Dominique groaned at her mistake. She had thought it was, as usual, a salesperson trying to talk her into a subscription; the circulation department called at least once a week since she'd started her business.

Dominique was trembling with rage, humiliation, regret — her body ready to do battle. But with whom? The gossip columnist? The woman was only doing her job by printing a tip from Dominique's "former associate." Sylvia! It had to be Sylvia. What other "former associate" would say such a thing!

With shaking hands, Dominique pushed herself up from the table and hurried to the phone. She fumbled with the receiver, then dialed Felice's number. The other woman answered at once.

"Did you see the paper?" Dominique asked without preamble.

Felice sounded almost as agitated. "What are you going to do?"

Dominique's voice was ragged with frustration and anger. "What am I supposed to do? How do I fight something like this? Dammit, Sylvia's not even competing for this contract! Why won't she just leave me alone?"

"I told you . . . ," Felice moaned, "she's a miserable person. Don't look for sense in her actions. She can't stand the fact that you don't depend on her anymore — that your business is doing well."

"Well?" Dominique's voice grew shrill. "I can barely afford to pay Carter. I work nights and weekends. Except for the French embassy job, I've only gotten a few lousy little contracts. And who's going to want me after this?" Her voice cracked.

"Calm down, calm down, Dominique," Felice said soothingly. "Let's think. . . ." There was a moment's silence, then Felice suggested, "Why not call the reporter? Get her to retract this?"

"There's nothing to retract!" Dominique cried. "The whole piece is based on a quote from Sylvia. Anyhow, what's to deny? Mark and I *are* seeing each other. He *has* recommended me to people."

"But the way it's written twists everything," Felice said bitterly.

Dominique was silent as she tried to think. Finally, she said in a dull voice, "I can't let this go without a response, even if it draws out the whole episode."

"What are you going to say?"

"That's not even the point." Dominique's tone was despairing. "What's this going to do to my business?" She felt like collapsing in bed and weeping. She felt like locking herself in her room until the news grew stale. "And what about the Corcoran? They just got my proposal yesterday. Sylvia timed this perfectly!"

"Are you going to call them?"

"I don't know what I'm going to do!"

"Have you talked to Mark?"

"I called you first. I thought maybe you would know something —"

"You know how secretive Sylvia is. She never tells anyone anything." Felice paused. "I wish Mrs. Filmore weren't in Italy. *She'd* tell the reporter how good you are!"

Dominique's voice dropped. "Can you get me a number where I can reach her?"

⟱ ⟱ ⟱

Mark watched Dominique come through the revolving door then emerge into the lobby of the Mayflower Hotel. He expected to see a downcast expression — he knew she was deeply upset about the gossip column that morning. But instead she wore a look of expectation as she scanned the seating areas. When she spotted Mark, a happy smile appeared on her face.

Mark's heart thumped as he saw the change. It was exactly how he felt about Dominique. Without her, things seemed dimmer and less alive. With her, problems seemed less important. He rose to meet her, hands outstretched. His skin tingled with anticipation of her touch. When she drew close, he smiled into her eyes, and she, in turn, embraced him with hers.

She tilted her head in expectation of a light kiss. Mark had the urge to wrap her in his arms and hold her close, but mindful of the room full of people, he restrained himself. At the contact of her lips on his, chaste though it was, Mark's pulse quickened. She always had that effect on him.

A waitress appeared to take their order, bourbon on the rocks for Mark, a glass of red wine for Dominique.

Dominique began to speak even before the waitress turned to go. "I called Mrs. Filmore in Italy. I hate to think of the phone bill — it's going to cost a fortune! But she said she'd call the reporter. She's really the only one in Washington who can credibly deny that article."

Mark frowned. "What about Michelle de la Croix?"

Dominique looked troubled. "I don't want a client involved in this. Besides, when I talked to her today, she said, 'These Americans make such a fuss about love affairs. It's all so provincial.'" Dominique laughed. "All I need is for her to say something like that. It won't help my case at all!"

Mark couldn't suppress a smile.

The waitress returned with their drinks and they clinked their glasses together.

"To better times," Mark said.

"I'll drink to that," Dominique said wryly.

Mark reached for Dominique's hand, which lay on the arm of her chair. He entwined his fingers in hers. "Did you talk to the Corcoran?"

Dominique shook her head. "No. . . . What could I say? To defend myself, I either have to lie about us or criticize Sylvia. Either way, I won't look good. But I'm hoping Mrs. Filmore's denial will put an end to this once and for all."

"What did she say about Sylvia's behavior?" Mark asked with a scowl.

Dominique gave him a resigned half-smile. "Her exact words were, 'Oh, dear.'"

Mark raised one eyebrow. "That's all? 'Oh dear'?"

Dominique shrugged. "What do you expect? That she'll fire her? She depends on Sylvia."

"I expected a little more outrage!" Mark spoke in a huffy tone.

Dominique wore a resigned look. "We have no proof. It suits Mrs. Filmore to believe there's some doubt about Sylvia's role." Dominique waved her hands as though to dismiss the subject. "Anyhow, I'm sure Mrs. Filmore will make a glowing statement and, hopefully, that will be that."

Mark looked doubtful. "I suppose any comment from me will just fuel the fire?"

"Absolutely! Especially since you never talk to gossip columnists. If you make an exception for me, we'll never hear the end of it." Dominique shook her head vigorously.

They stewed in frustrated silence for a few moments. Then Mark turned to a happier topic. "Well, you said the Corcoran loved your ideas. This'll blow over."

Dominique's expression brightened. "Yes, Cecilia was excited about the black-and-white ball. It's traditional, but still different for Washington."

Mark nodded, his eyes alive with interest. As a member of the Senate, he was used to relying on his staff, so he appreciated Dominique's ability to conceive an idea, then execute it with elegance and efficiency. She was remarkable! He watched as she spoke, her hair bouncing with each gesture, her eyes sparkling with excitement. He had the sudden urge to take her in his arms, to kiss her beautifully shaped lips. But Dominique was absorbed in the discussion of the Corcoran contract. Mark let his fantasy slip away and instead focused on what she was saying.

"This would be such a wonderful job! The Corcoran knows exactly whom they want to invite and Congressman Yancy has already agreed to host it, so there won't be anything for me to do other than organize the event itself." Dominique's expression turned grave. "I hope Sylvia hasn't ruined my chances. If I could get this job, I could hire another person, maybe even Felice. Carter and I just can't handle —" She stopped in mid-sentence, regretting the words immediately.

The couple had assiduously avoided the subject of Mark's loan offer, but Dominique's mention of her financial situation gave Mark grounds for bringing it up again. Now he wore an I-told-you-so look.

Mark saw the warning in Dominique's eyes, but went on anyhow.

"You're holding back the growth of your business by not accepting my help," he said sharply. He was hurt that Dominique still refused to fully trust him — for he interpreted her refusal as a lack of trust.

Dominique gently placed her hand on his arm. "Let's not open this can of worms again," she appealed to him. She looked down and added quietly, "Especially in light of that gossip column."

"Dominique." Mark's tone was softer now. "If we were married, gossip wouldn't matter."

"How can you say that?" she asked with exasperation. "It would be all the worse because the connection to you would be even stronger. It would confirm everything in that column!" Dominique paused and her expression turned gentle. She leaned forward and took Mark's hands. "If I were ready to remarry, none of this would matter, but it's too soon. I've told you that. The divorce has only been final a few months. I'm trying to get my business off the ground and" — she shrugged — "now this thing's come up."

"It'll blow over by next week," Mark said impatiently. "But how long are you and I supposed to go on like this?"

Dominique drew back, releasing his hands. "You act as though what we have now is unendurable. What's wrong with it?" Of course, she knew the answer. Mark wanted a commitment that she simply wasn't prepared to give. Couldn't he understand that she was still recovering from the terrible blow of her divorce? She felt uncertain of her future, of her ability to make her business work, her ability to take care of her mother and Gabrielle. And, deep in her soul, she felt that this was her final chance to prove herself. How many false starts had there been? How many times had she struck out on the road to independence only to be sidetracked? She remembered the girl she had once been — twenty-one, eager to free herself of her mother's stifling presence. But her love affair with Stephen had become the watershed event of her adventure, and she hadn't attained independence at all. And later, when she had left Anton, she had launched a successful career. But, once more, she had fallen in love and been absorbed into the life of another. Dominique had played the "what if" game many times, and she knew that good things had resulted from both episodes. But she couldn't let her love for Mark cut short her promise once more. When she committed herself to him, she wanted to do it from a position of strength, not weakness. Not until she felt certain she could stand on her own would she feel free to irrevocably unite her life with his. If he'd only be patient!

Mark answered in a voice that was controlled, but insistent. "This isn't enough. It's not a real commitment." He saw Dominique's expression turn to one of alarm. He paused. Did he really want to pursue this discussion? Maybe he should back off and smooth things over. He didn't want to anger her, or scare her away. It was already a tense time for her. He massaged the bridge of his nose with his thumb and index finger. He told himself to suppress his disappointment, to just let things lay. But it was as though the words were fighting to come out. Before he even quite realized it, he said, "You're looking at this in the context of your past, Dominique. You're acting like you can't pursue your own interests if you marry me. I'm not like Clay or your first husband. I'm not trying to take away your independence. I'd never want to do that." He shook his head. "I want for you the same things you want for yourself."

Dominique studied his beloved face. Mark meant so much to her. She loved him, truly loved him, but a part of her was frightened by the feeling of powerlessness, of dependency that it gave her. By his importance in her life.

Mark saw Dominique's turmoil. He took her hands in his. "Think of it, Dominique. We could be there for each other every day. That means something to you, doesn't it?" His eyes were boyishly hopeful.

Dominique melted at his expression. Never had a man offered so much of himself to her. He *was* different. "Of *course* it means something," she reassured him.

Mark smiled and squeezed her hands. "Imagine sleeping together every night, telling each other our problems. Everything married couples do." Mark paused. He edged forward in his chair. His entire posture transmitted urgency. Then his words tumbled out in a rush. "Dominique, how can you not want the same?" His heart ached at the thought that his emotions might not be reciprocated.

The need in his eyes was wrenching. Dominique turned her head away in distress and stared at the brass doors at the end of the lobby. A laughing couple paused just inside. The man faced the woman and affectionately brushed away a lock of hair that had blown across her face. She smiled up at him, handed him the package she was carrying, and said something to him. He nodded and, shaping his mouth into a whistle, made his way to a table as she headed toward the ladies' room. The easy companionability of the scene struck Dominique. They loved each other, just as she and Mark did. It was lulling to observe. She felt herself being seduced by the idea of marriage to Mark. The companionship, the comfort. Her muscles relaxed at the thought of giving in to it.

Then, with a jolt of realization, she brought herself sharply to heel. Her throat tightened as though someone were squeezing the breath from her. The events of the day had made her feel shaky and insecure. And she couldn't allow herself to give in to her momentary weakness! Marrying Mark would be the path of least resistance. Once secure, would she still fight for her business, her reputation? Or would she lose herself once more?

"Mark." Dominique's voice sounded muffled and distant to her own ears. "I'm just not ready to get married."

Mark's face darkened. He stared silently at Dominique.

Cold apprehension gripped her. Why was Mark looking at her so strangely?

"Dominique . . ." His voice was somber. "I can't wait forever for something you may never agree to." The decisive look in his eyes suddenly gave way. Mark's face softened. "How much time is long enough for you?" He could be patient if only she would promise an end to his waiting.

Dominique reached forward and covered Mark's hand with hers. He was so open and appealing — his love so clearly written on his face. It hurt Dominique to disappoint him. But it would be even more abhorrent to mislead him. How to answer? When would she know for certain that she could take care of herself and her family? When would the fear and insecurity that imprisoned her fade?

Without realizing it, she shook her head in the negative. Her mouth turned down sadly. "I can't honestly say," she said in a voice full of regret.

Mark grasped her hands. He opened his mouth to respond. He was almost at the point of begging her. Begging! But what was there left to say? Her expression was set. She had made up her mind.

Mark dropped her hands as he recognized the look. Whatever she felt for him, it wasn't enough. He was helpless in the face of her rigidity. He, who had always been able to charm and convince, was completely without resources. He felt as though he were traveling a dark road to an unknown destination. There was no end in sight, and he could no longer endure it.

Dominique's expression turned to one of shock as Mark stood up with a jerky movement.

She, too, stood abruptly. Her purse dropped to the floor, but she ignored it. She stretched her hand toward his. "Mark . . . listen . . . ," she pleaded.

He drew back sharply to avoid her touch.

Dominique was aghast at the action. Mark had recoiled from her! "Mark!" she repeated, her voice rising in alarm. "We can work this out!"

Mark looked down at Dominique and it took all his willpower not to draw her to him. He wanted her in his arms. He wanted to tell her that he would continue to love her on whatever terms she set. But he felt a heavy pressure on his heart, as though someone had laid an iron weight on his chest. It prevented him from speaking.

Dominique gazed in despair at Mark. He looked stony, immovable, foreign to her. She wanted to thrust away the barrier, to bring Mark back to her. She couldn't bear this cold stranger. "I love you, Mark," she said, her voice resonant with feeling.

The words jarred Mark. "Whatever you mean by that, it's obviously not the same thing I do," he said.

Dominique blushed like a person disgraced. Mark had given generously and completely of himself, but she had been incapable of doing the same. She looked down at her feet. For the first time, she noticed that the contents of her purse had spilled onto the rug. She stared at them, not making a move.

Mark felt protective tenderness well up in him as he observed Dominique's slumped shoulders. His eyes traveled to the springy waves on top of her head, an incongruously lively note in the heavy atmosphere. His fingers wriggled involuntarily with the urge to caress them. He fought the impulse and clenched his fists tightly. He waited for her to speak. If she gave him a sign of encouragement — any sign at all . . .

Dominique stood silently, her eyes downcast. She felt Mark's gaze on her — could sense the accusation in it and could think of nothing to counter it. Her heart twisted in pain at the thought of living her life without Mark. She remembered the loneliness of the first days without Clay and knew it would be a thousand times worse this time, for Mark had given a thousand times more of himself. He had filled her life as Clay had never done. He had loved her as no one had ever done. She wanted — no, ached for — a way to hold him. But she knew he would not accept a promise without conviction.

Wearily, with an air of defeat, she knelt and slowly picked up the contents of her purse. Had this been any other moment, she knew that Mark would have rushed to pick up the items himself. The thought made her feel heartbreakingly lonely. Through blurred eyes, she watched his feet step back from her line of vision. She deliberately slowed her movements. She concentrated on placing each item in its own compartment of her purse. She wanted to immerse herself in the methodical act, to forget the reality of what was to come. She wanted to remain kneeling on the floor, to collapse against the soft chair and bury her face in her arms. But when each item was in place, she automatically clicked her purse shut. For a moment, she did not rise. Her posture was that of an old woman, exhausted after an activity that would not have troubled a younger person. Then, reluctantly, and with great effort, she pushed herself to her feet. She stood immobile and tried to gather her strength. An illogical, unfounded shred of hope kept her eyes on the patterned rug before her. Until she raised her eyes and looked around the room, she could still try to convince herself that Mark was there.

"Excuse me, ma'am," came the voice of the waitress. "Will there be anything else?"

Dominique turned hollow eyes to the young woman. As though observing a movie about two strangers, she saw the waitress' expression turn to one of concern. "Is anything wrong?" a voice asked her.

Dominique heard herself say, "No, no, thank you. I'm just leaving." How calm she sounded. How normal. How had she managed to make that voice emerge?

Dominique turned away from the waitress and looked about the room. She felt sick and disoriented. Where was she to go next? She couldn't quite remember. Everything seemed murky and out of focus. Only one fact was clearly imprinted on her mind. Mark was gone, as she had known he would be.

ᘒ ᘒ ᘒ

The next day, the newspaper had this to say:

> Well, Dear Reader, the fuss over one itsy-bitsy column! We've been taken to task for implying that Dominique Parker's Affairs to Remember owes its success to . . . well . . . an

Affair to Remember. Socialite Grace Filmore, owner of Capital Events, tells us that Dear Dominique is one of the most capable event planners who ever worked for her. And she called from Italy to tell us so!

Says the *très distinguée* Mrs. Filmore, "Everyone in this field has social connections. One can't get along without them. Dominique's friendship with Senator Patout doesn't account for her success. She has almost twenty years' experience in event planning and she's just wonderful at what she does." So there.

As for the cause of the brouhaha, Mrs. Parker shrugs off nasty innuendo. "Whoever made those remarks to you was trying to damage my reputation, but lacked the courage to do it in public. I pity anyone who feels that kind of jealousy. In any event, I question the validity of sources who want to remain anonymous and you should, too."

Dominique could barely muster a feeling of satisfaction at the column. Yesterday, it was all she could focus on. Today, it seemed unimportant in light of her break with Mark.

Her heart was too heavy to explain to her family what had transpired with him. Instead, she invented a Senate fact-finding mission to Australia, confident that neither Gabrielle nor Solange would discover the truth for some time.

As the days wore on, Gabrielle and Solange both noticed that Dominique seemed glum and edgy, but they attributed the mood to Mark's absence and — unknowingly cruel — teased Dominique about it. It took all Dominique's will to smile weakly at their jokes. She felt instead like bursting into tears. A hundred times a day her hand reached for the phone. Her fingers had learned the touch of Mark's number and itched to move that way. It required physical effort to restrain herself.

The only palliative for Dominique's suffering was work. She immersed herself in it, staying at the office late into the night. And each morning when Dominique entered her suite, she reminded herself, "This is what you wanted. This is why . . ."

The ringing phone was torment. It was Carter's job to answer it, and Dominique had to fight the urge to snatch it up as soon as she heard it. Dominique invariably held her breath and cocked her ear as Carter greeted callers. When she heard Carter laugh and joke, her heart beat faster. Could it be Mark? Then Carter would buzz her and announce Felice or Danielle or another familiar name. Dominique's stomach would plummet with disappointment and she would have to force herself to be cheerfully welcoming. In truth, she felt like shrieking, "Don't tie up the line! Mark might be trying to get through!"

Then, one Sunday morning, Felice called her at home with news that made her both happy and melancholy. Dominique knew at once it was something monumental, because Felice never awakened before eleven on the weekend and it was only nine o'clock. Dominique herself was still in bed.

"Charles asked me to marry him last night!" Felice chortled.

Dominique's spirits soared at the news. "That's wonderful!"

"I want you to be a bridesmaid! June first. Please? I promise no ugly flowered dresses." Her voice turned dreamy. "I'm thinking of doing everything in ivory. The flowers, the attendants, everything. Except" — she sounded a cautionary note — "none of those awful white tuxedoes for the men." She sighed and bubbled on. "It's going to be strictly traditional. Very elegant. What do you think?"

Dominique laughed. "I can't imagine anything nicer. Where will it be?"

"We've already checked on the National Cathedral. There's a chapel available that day. And for the reception, Mrs. Filmore's offered her place."

"Good heavens! How elegant."

"So you'll do it? You'll be a bridesmaid?"

"I wouldn't miss it," Dominique said warmly.

After she hung up, though, the feeling of good cheer abandoned her. She looked at the empty pillow next to hers and thought of Mark. It had been two weeks since she'd seen him and she missed him to the point of physical pain. When she crawled into bed at night, she was sharply reminded of her loneliness. In the dark silence, she tortured herself with the memory of Mark's arms about her. And, despite her fatigue, she found it difficult to sleep.

CHAPTER 29 ᥱ

MARK Patout wheeled sharply and stared at the woman disappearing down the hall of the Dirksen Senate Office Building. The hair was unmistakably Dominique's! His heart pounded as he reversed his course and followed the woman's clicking heels. Then the absurdity of his action struck him. What would Dominique be doing in the senate building? He slowed and watched the woman turn into an office. Her profile was pert, with classic Irish features and a generous sprinkling of freckles. Nothing like Dominique.

Mark's face fell. He stood motionless in the hallway as people milled about him. For a moment, he forgot his destination as he thought of Dominique. He kept hoping he'd run into her, but he never did. Soon he would be going home for the holidays and, of course, there'd be no chance of seeing her there. He rubbed his face bemusedly and, with a slow step, turned and headed for his office. No point in hurrying. There was little he looked forward to — the zest was gone from his life. He was still mourning Dominique, though he hated himself for his weakness.

Mark entered his office through his private door, bypassing the waiting room full of lobbyists and constituents. Normally, Mark made it a point to greet them all, but he didn't feel like smiling and acting cheerful today. Dammit, seeing that woman had taken it out of him.

He slumped into his chair and stared at the message slips on his desk. After a few moments of brooding, he picked them up and half-heartedly flipped through them. Lobbyists. The governor of Louisiana. Buffy Coleman, a prominent Washington hostess and fund-raiser. She was trying to introduce him to new women, now that she no longer saw Mark with Dominique. What a social coup if her match-making succeeded!

With a noise of disgust Mark threw the pile of papers back on the desk. He wondered if he would ever see Dominique's name on one of the little pink slips. He was tempted to call her. Always tempted. But what was the use? He wanted one thing, Dominique another. The next move had to be hers, no matter how much it cost him to hold back. But would she ever make that move? Did she miss him? Or was she already seeing other people? Was she so afraid of marriage that she would remain single for the rest of her life? Mark's heart twisted at the thought.

If only he could get over the pain and longing, he could live without her love. He had lived all his life without it and had been reasonably content. He had enjoyed women, felt deeply affectionate toward some, been wildly attracted to others. There had been no depth to his feelings, and that had been supportable — even desirable — for a man who wished to devote his life to politics. But now there was the pain. Eventually, he knew, it would have to stop. But when?

Mark fingered the pile of message slips on his desk, fretfully tearing at the corner of one of them. He had almost destroyed the top third of the paper when he realized he needed it to return the call. He looked at the name on the slip. Buffy Coleman. Probably calling to invite him to a dinner party. With Christmas just two weeks away, the social season was at its peak. Buffy would want to introduce him to yet another attractive woman. Mark predicted that she would be too young for him, but avidly interested nonetheless. A U.S. Senator had that effect, he thought cynically. Then he sighed. Maybe a flirtation, some friendly companionship, would help him fight his way out of the blue murk of depression. He was tired of being lonely. Tired of longing for something he couldn't have.

He picked up the phone and, with a desultory tap of his index finger, dialed Buffy's number.

∽ ∽ ∽

Carter beamed as Dominique walked into the office, a container of yogurt and a plastic spoon in her hand.

"You won't believe it!" the younger woman said breathlessly. "Just after you left for lunch, the Corcoran called."

Dominique halted just inside the door. Her heart thudded so hard that she felt it in her throat. "Cecilia Bernhardt?"

"Yes, and she asked you to call as soon as possible. She said she has a one o'clock lunch."

Dominique automatically glanced at her wristwatch. "It's already twelve thirty-five!"

Without bothering to remove her coat, she hurried into her own office. She sat down at her desk and dialed the number. As she listened to the ring of the telephone, she nervously bit her lip. She was relieved when Cecilia answered her own line.

The other woman greeted her warmly. "I'm glad you caught me," she said.

Dominique beamed at her tone. She would enjoy working with Cecilia. They'd hit it off right from the start. She waited expectantly for the other woman to continue.

"Dominique, I can't tell you how impressed we were with your proposal. Everyone on the committee thought it was exceptionally well thought out." There was a silence that seemed endless to Dominique. She gripped the telephone receiver tightly.

Cecilia continued. "But I'm sorry to tell you that the committee decided to go with our public relations firm instead."

Dominique stopped breathing. Her mouth went dry. How could it be? The public relations firm had just opened its event planning division — they had almost no experience! And Cecilia had loved Dominique's ideas — had understood immediately what Dominique was trying to accomplish. For her part, Dominique had done everything she could to keep the plan's cost down, to make her proposal the most attractive. She thought of the long, wearying evenings she and Carter had spent in the office. What had gone wrong? Struggling for calm, Dominique said, "Can you tell me why?"

"Well . . . I . . ." There was an uncomfortable pause. "It was a variety of factors."

Suddenly, Dominique understood. Sylvia! That damned newspaper column! Crimson rage flooded her vision. She closed her eyes and clasped her free hand to her forehead. The pulse at her temple throbbed against her fingers. Dominique wanted to scream at the hapless Cecilia, How could you believe that trash! Instead, her throat tight, she asked, "Did the rumors about me and Senator Patout have anything to do with it?"

Cecilia answered with her usual serene deliberation. "We know your capabilities are genuine."

What the hell did that mean? Dominique pressed the phone to her ear and sat very still, concentrating hard on Cecilia's words.

"Certainly, we don't lend credence to malicious gossip. But . . ." Cecilia faltered. "You see, our artists often rely on government grants. I'm sure you understand that even the *appearance* of undue influence —"

"Yes," Dominique cut her off. She couldn't listen anymore. It was nauseating, infuriating, outrageous. But the worst part was, she couldn't blame the Corcoran for its stance. Had she been on their board, she might have reached the same decision.

Cecilia's voice dropped. In a soothing tone, she said, "Personally, Dominique, I'd have liked to see you get the contract. And I hope you'll compete in the future. People have such short memories. But this thing was so recent. . . . You see what I mean?"

Dominique could sense her genuine sympathy. But what good did it do, she wondered bitterly? On the other hand, why burn her bridges? In truth, this woman regarded her kindly. In an even voice, Dominique replied, "I understand. Of course, I'd be honored to compete again. Perhaps I can call you in a few months to discuss your plans for the future?"

"That would be wonderful." Cecilia sounded relieved.

As soon as she hung up, Carter, her step tentative, appeared in the doorway.

Dominique shifted her gaze to the young woman.

Carter's expression fell. "You don't need to say anything. I can read it on your face."

Dominique stared at Carter, not really seeing her. "I didn't realize quite how much I'd been counting on that job." She thought of the new staffer she'd wanted to hire, the coat she'd wanted to buy Gabrielle for Christmas, the bonus for Carter.

"Dominique, you look absolutely frazzled. Maybe you should take the afternoon off." The younger woman's brow creased with worry.

"No!" Dominique said sharply. She shook her head. Then in a

weary voice, "We have a million things to do." There was the opening of the new boutique next week, just in time to capitalize on Christmas shopping. There was the fund-raiser for Congresswoman Parnell at the beginning of February. They were small jobs. Little money. But enough to keep her business afloat. She couldn't afford to let things slide just because she was disappointed.

Carter watched her with a look of deep concern.

Dominique gave her a reassuring smile. "It's discouraging, but I suppose it's all part of doing business."

Carter smiled back. "Anyhow, we have plenty to keep us busy."

"But" — Dominique scowled — "we still need more business."

"More business but not more work!" Carter laughed.

Dominique joined in her laughter. She was beginning to feel a little better. Work energized her. And she liked the feeling of control it gave her to be her own boss. Even with the disappointments and stress, she was glad she had started her own business. Now if only she could turn it into a living!

∾ ∾ ∾

"Lunch tomorrow? That would be delightful." Dominique smiled into the phone at Michelle de la Croix. Over the course of their relationship, the Frenchwoman had become as much friend as client. But today, the ambassador's wife was all business.

"I have a proposal for you. I've been thinking about it for some time, but I was waiting for the holidays to be over."

Dominique's curiosity was piqued. Another assignment? Her heart beat faster. Aside from the pleasure of working with Michelle, she could use the money. Congress wouldn't be back in session for another two weeks, stores were caught in the January doldrums, and everyone was tired from holiday entertaining. She didn't expect any new contracts until February, at the earliest.

They met at Sans Souci, the famous power-lunch spot across from the White House. Michelle, of course, knew everyone on the staff, and Dominique was shown to the other woman's table as though she were visiting royalty.

The comtesse greeted Dominique with kisses on both cheeks as the waiter poured white wine from a bottle resting in an ice bucket. After he had left them alone, the women launched into machine-gun rapid French. They discussed the holidays, their families, the cold weather, and the famous columnist seated at the table next to theirs.

Finally, Michelle leaned forward and fixed her gaze on Dominique's face. "How is your business?"

Dominique knew that the first rule of commerce was to act confident. She lifted her chin and said, "Fine, thank you. My clients have all been pleased and I've gotten a number of referrals." Her jaunty tone wavered a bit as she added, "Of course, the first year is always difficult. . . ."

Michelle gave her an understanding look. "I was sorry to hear about the Corcoran contract. I thought surely you would get it." She sighed. "I suppose my recommendation wasn't as influential as I thought."

Dominique protested, "I wouldn't have even been considered if it weren't for you." She shrugged philosophically. "I'll try again. They'll give me another chance."

Michelle frowned. "It's ridiculous that all this happened over something so trivial. And the irony is that you're not even seeing Senator Patout any—" Michelle stopped in mid-sentence. And then she did something Dominique had never imagined was possible. She blushed. Michelle's pale Gallic skin never betrayed a hint of blush, except where cosmetically applied. She epitomized sangfroid. But now her brow creased in a pained expression and her face flooded pink.

The women stared at each other in stunned silence. Michelle was the first to recover. "Forgive me." Her eyes reflected genuine regret.

Dominique found it almost unbearable to look at her friend. Her ears burned with humiliation. She stared at the tablecloth, unable to think of a response. How did Michelle know? Who else knew? "Did he tell you?" Dominique blurted out. How could he embarrass her that way?

"No!" Michelle said at once. "He would never deliberately hurt you." She leaned forward and covered Dominique's hand with hers.

Dominique raised tortured eyes to Michelle. "Then . . . how?" she whispered.

Michelle averted her gaze. "We attend many of the same parties. I've seen him and . . ." She paused, obviously ill at ease. "You weren't with him, so I drew my own conclusions."

Dominique's eyebrows went up, her expression puzzled. "But he's always attended plenty of receptions alone."

Michelle slumped in her seat. She looked down, then lifted her glass and took a long swallow of wine.

In a voice that was deadly quiet, Dominique said, "How stupid of me. He obviously wasn't alone."

To Michelle's credit, she derived no thrill from imparting the news. "Look," she said, meeting Dominique's gaze squarely, "if it's over between you, you must expect this sort of thing. Senator Patout is one of the most attractive men in Washington."

Dominique nodded, not trusting herself to speak. Of course, Michelle was right. Had she expected Mark to remain alone? Yes, she had. Or at least she had hoped he would. To be truthful, she had *counted* on it. What a fool! She pictured Mark's face, with its charming one-dimpled smile. Women melted at the sight of it. How could she have thought he would remain alone? Oh, God, what had she done? She raised her eyes, sick with regret, and met Michelle's concerned gaze.

Dominique tried valiantly for a smile and only half succeeded. Lowering her lids, she asked, "What was she like?"

Michelle gave her friend a pleading look. "I don't know. Dark hair. Young."

Dominique's lips tightened. She searched Michelle's eyes. "Beautiful?"

Michelle turned up her palms. "In a hard sort of way." She shook her head. "You're far more attractive."

Dominique was touched by the other woman's loyalty. Her eyes softened. "Your prejudice is showing." Then, all at once, it struck her. Young, brunette. Beautiful, in a hard sort of way. She sounded like Clay's wife! A knife twisted in her gut. How could she go through this again? How could she stand it? *But you caused it, this time. You drove him away.*

"Dominique, is there no chance for reconciliation?" Michelle asked.

Dominique shook her head vehemently. *Just like Clay's wife.* It was a stuck record playing in her mind. She couldn't stand to be hurt like this twice.

But what if she called Mark? Told him she'd marry him. Would it be too late? She wanted to race to the phone and do just that. But, of course, she couldn't. Couldn't marry him in a panic of emotion. And then, suppose she humiliated herself for nothing, as she had done with Clay? Her memory flashed to the day, two years before, that Clay had left her. Dominique begging him to stay. Clay's cold, flat eyes dismissing her, anxious to get away. She had never known such humiliation.

It wouldn't happen twice! Dominique took a deep, ragged breath. Her face turned to stone. "I'll get over Mark," she told Michelle.

The other woman met her eyes. There was a long silence. Finally she said, "I know you will."

With hands that shook ever so slightly, Dominique picked up the menu and opened it. Not a word on the page registered. Without looking up, she said, "What do you suggest?"

Michelle's voice came back poised, casual, as if nothing had happened. Playing along with Dominique's face-saving act. "I always have the sole."

Dominique closed the menu. "That sounds fine." She lifted her wine glass and took a sip. Then another.

Michelle spared Dominique from talking to the waiter by ordering for both of them. That done, she launched into a monologue about the repairs necessary at the ambassador's residence — inconsequential chatter designed to allow Dominique time to recover her composure.

After a few minutes — and a few more sips of wine — Dominique found herself smiling as Michelle told an anecdote about waking in the middle of the night to find the roof was leaking — straight into their bed. "From the outside, the building is magnificent, but oh la la, we don't dare look in the attic!"

By the time the waiter brought their entrées, Dominique was able to concentrate on the discussion, and even inject a few comments of her own. As Michelle promised, the sole was delicious, the golden wine refreshing, and by the end of the meal, Dominique felt genuinely better.

"I'm glad to see you smile again," said Michelle as the waiter placed tiny cups of espresso before them. She pulled a cigarette from her red lacquered case and lit it. "I originally asked you to lunch to discuss a subject I hoped you'd find pleasant," she said ruefully.

Dominique tried for a chuckle but, from the guilty look on Michelle's face, she wasn't sure she succeeded. Wanting to ease her friend's qualms, Dominique leaned forward and said teasingly, "Don't keep me in suspense."

Michelle exhaled a puff of smoke and said, "Were you aware that we will return to Paris on the first of May?"

"No!" Dominique cried. "Why?" She hated to lose her new friend and, equally important, a good client.

"It's routine," Michelle explained. "Ambassadorships are not indefinite. We've been in Washington for four years, and the president has asked my husband to return home now."

"Will he be assigned somewhere else?"

Michelle smiled. "Washington is the highest post any diplomat can attain." She paused and her smile turned mischievous. "However, once a diplomat has attained that position, he may be 'promoted,' if you will, to the president's cabinet." Michelle looked down and said with quiet modesty, "My husband has been named minister of trade."

Dominique was excited for her friend. "You must be so proud of him!"

Michelle tipped her head in acknowledgment. "Thank you. And, as much as we love Washington, we are looking forward to going home. Our family is there. And our country place."

Dominique knew that by "country place," Michelle referred to the count's ancestral estate in the Loire Valley — a seventeenth-century château with five hundred acres of vineyards. She shook her head. "It sounds heavenly, though I'm terribly sorry to see you go."

Michelle studied Dominique in silence. Finally she said, "I shall miss you as well." She paused. "Unless . . ."

Dominique smiled. Michelle was undoubtedly going to invite her to spend some time with them in the summer. She probably couldn't afford it, but the gesture was nice, just the same.

Michelle put her index finger to her chin in a thoughtful pose. "I would like you to come with us."

Dominique stared, uncomprehending.

Michelle smiled and continued. "My husband will find it necessary to host many foreign delegations, especially from the United States and the Arab nations. He, of course, will have an aide to arrange formal meetings. But we will also be called upon to entertain — to host many events, both in Paris and at the country place. And I will have to arrange excursions for the families." She paused. "You have lived in Egypt and America, but you're a French native. And you are a most capable event planner, much more so than the social secretary who serves the embassy here." She laughed. "I am desperate to have you join my staff. You would be perfect!" She gave Dominique an appealing look. "Please say yes."

Dominique was aghast. "Michelle, you can't be serious! I just moved to Washington. I have my family here, my business."

"Your mother and Gabrielle will be better off in France," Michelle replied breezily. "After all, you say your mother's French is better than her English and your daughter is already fluent. And" — Michelle held up her index finger — "you can be certain that Gabrielle's education in France will be superior to what she receives here." She made a noise of derision. "In America, the children watch too much television and the schools are too permissive. There is no intellectual life.

"Aside from that, think of what an adventure it would be to move to Paris. You've said many times that you love the city," Michelle reminded her. She lowered her voice. "Your salary would be most generous. And, don't forget, in France, vacations are mandated by law. A month in summer, a week at Christmas. You'd have much more leisure to spend with your family. All your health care would be taken care of and, ultimately, you could retire with a government pension."

"You mean resettle there? Never return to America?" It was hard to take the idea seriously, it was so outside the context of her current life.

Michelle shrugged. "If you wished to return to America, there would be many opportunities during holidays. Ultimately, you could do so permanently, if you wished." Michelle gave Dominique a sly smile. "But you would likely remarry. In this position, you would meet many eligible men. And remember, the French do not share America's obsession with youth," she said disdainfully. "A woman is not interesting until she is at least thirty-five."

Michelle made it all sound so tempting, so easy, but it wasn't. "Even if the schools are better in France, I can't move Gabrielle again. It's disruptive. In the fall, she'll be going into ninth grade — her last year of junior high." She shook her head. "I can't do that to her."

"But in France, the structure is different. She would be changing schools in any event and all the students would be new." Michelle paused, looking thoughtful. "Why don't you ask her how she feels? Maybe the prospect of moving to Paris would be exciting for her."

Dominique looked dubious. "But Michelle, that's not the only objection." How could she make this woman of privilege understand? She picked up her cup of espresso and drained it, bracing herself. "I'm honored that you want me, but I've made a life for myself in Washington. I've started a business." She gave a self-mocking smile. "I'm not saying that either one is a smashing success. But . . . it takes time to make things work."

Michelle's look was sympathetic. "I know how hard it's been. But what do you prove by persevering in the face of such difficulty? What's holding you here?" She gave her a look pregnant with meaning.

Dominique flushed, but said nothing. The more she denied that Mark had anything to do with it, the less Michelle would believe her.

The countess went on. "I could understand if you had no other alternative, but . . ." She turned up her hands in an expression of bafflement.

Dominique smiled at her friend's pragmatism. Abstract ideals weren't important to Michelle, only the bottom line. "It's true my business hasn't made me rich, and I've had disappointments. But it's very important that I stick to the course I've chosen." Without realizing it, Dominique's hands had formed fists of determination. "It would take too long to tell you all the things in my past that have brought me to this point." She paused, and her gaze intensified. "But I *have* to prove I can make a life for myself. A life *and* a living."

Michelle made a sound of impatience. "My dear, your idea of independence sounds like enslavement to me." She lifted one delicate shoulder. "After all, what is independence? If you have money and your health, you do as you wish." She fixed Dominique with a severe look. "If you take the job in Paris, you'll have enough money for independence."

Michelle's arguments sounded so logical. Dominique could easily picture herself in the job Michelle described. And moving to Paris sounded glamorous. Why refuse such a wonderful opportunity?

Because it meant surrender, and the very thought panicked Dominique. But how could she explain that to sensible, practical Michelle? She gave her friend a sidelong glance, feeling cornered. Aside from the personal relationship, Michelle was one of her most important business contacts. To simply refuse her outright would seem rude and ungrateful.

Michelle rescued her from having to devise a diplomatic response. The woman signaled for the check and said offhandedly, "Think about it. Talk it over with your family. In the end, I'm sure you'll be persuaded."

CHAPTER 30 ∞

THE YOUNG woman's long, dusky hair spilled over Mark's chest as she slid on top of him. She was beautiful, eager to please.

Mark closed his eyes as he slid into her. She began to move, ever so slowly. Almost at once, Mark could feel the pressure build. It had been two months since he'd been with a woman. Been with Dominique. He tried to push the thought from his mind. Alexa Martinelli deserved better than that. She was an intelligent, accomplished girl. Woman, he corrected himself. A Justice Department attorney, she had pursued Mark with singleminded determination from the first moment they'd met at Buffy Coleman's dinner party. She had been perfectly straightforward about her desire to sleep with Mark. At first he was put off — almost shocked by her forwardness — then amused and, finally, intrigued. She offered herself so freely, promised so much.

Mark slid his hands over her silky buttocks. They were hard and taut as a young boy's. But Mark wasn't interested in young boys. He couldn't help comparing her streamlined muscles to Dominique's voluptuous curves. He opened his eyes and gazed at Alexa's perfect bone structure. She had it all, Alexa did. Everything to impress and ensnare a man. What's more, Mark knew she was falling in love with him. With him or with her image of the senator from Louisiana? Mark wasn't certain, but her devotion was obvious. The little gifts, the notes, and, most of all, the look in her eye. It was tantamount to worship. She was so young.

Mark kissed her, his touch full of affection — and desire. But what about love? Could he love her? Mark glided his hands up the length of her elegant thighs.

Alexa ground her hips into him and Mark caught his breath, trembling on the edge of release. She was every bit as delectable as she'd promised. Every bit as accomplished. He closed his eyes again. Tight. Brought his hips up. Hard. Then, with sudden ferocity, he flipped her on her back and pounded into her until he reached a shattering climax.

∞ ∞ ∞

"Paris!" Danielle sighed wistfully into the telephone. "I envy you."

Dominique laughed. "There's nothing to envy — you've achieved your dream. I'm still struggling."

"So stop struggling. Michelle de la Croix is offering you a way out."

Dominique sighed and pulled her velvet robe — a Christmas present from Solange — tighter. The kitchen was Saturday morning quiet, her mother and daughter upstairs asleep. She kept her voice low so as not to wake them. The last thing Dominique wanted was for Solange to get on the extension and add her argument to Danielle's. Solange hadn't stopped lecturing, sermonizing, cajoling since Dominique had told her of Michelle's proposal two weeks before. To hear Solange, Paris was the promised land, Michelle's job the golden fleece.

Gabrielle, on the other hand, was of two minds about the move. "I like my friends here," she said, "and it's not like I *want* to move or anything, . . . but *Paris!*" Dominique had secretly hoped that Gabrielle would be vehement in her opposition to the move. That would have put the issue to rest. Instead, the girl's reaction only added to Dominique's indecision.

The problem, Dominique thought sourly, was that Gabrielle had been raised on the idea that Paris was the ultimate paradise. Glamour, lights, beauty — that was the Paris Solange had spoonfed her granddaughter. And it had been confirmed when Gabrielle had accompanied her father to France, for Clay and Marie had chosen the best hotels, eaten in the best restaurants. Gabrielle had been dazzled by the euphoria that permeated the trip.

As if reading her thoughts, Danielle said, "The fact that Gabrielle is willing to move should tell you something. Even she probably understands that this is a once-in-a-lifetime chance."

"But so is owning my own business," Dominique countered.

"Look, Dominique, let's be frank, if it were making you rich, that would be one thing, but —"

Annoyed, Dominique broke in. "I just got a new account this week — a department store opening. The boutique I did in December was so pleased that they recommended me." She paused. "I feel like my business is starting to take off." It was hard to keep the enthusiasm from her voice. She knew Danielle probably thought she was deluding herself, but she wasn't. The January doldrums were over. It was the first week of February and the phone was starting to ring again.

"Even so," Danielle argued, "Michelle is offering you the kind of security you'll never have working for yourself."

"Security has always been more important to you than independence," Dominique shot back, "but not to me." She regretted the harsh words immediately. She was striking out at Danielle who, after all, only wanted what was best for her. "I'm sorry," Dominique said. "I shouldn't have said that."

"Why not?" Danielle asked casually. "It's true enough. I've always been the saver. You've always been the spender. I've always been cautious and you've always been impulsive. That's why I don't understand why you won't take this opportunity." She spoke in a frustrated tone. "It's such an adventure! It seems tailor-made for you."

There was something in that, Dominique thought. And she could easily picture herself in the role Michelle had described. "Just walk away from my business?"

Danielle sighed. "I don't know. It depends on your reasons for starting it. I guess that's what you have to think about. But just do me a favor. Promise me that you'll seriously consider Paris."

"If I weren't, I wouldn't have told all of you about it."

ɡᴏ ɡᴏ ɡᴏ

Dominique studied the monthly bank statement and shook her head. It was a good thing the check from Harrison-Fletcher department store was due any day now. The deposit on the contract for the spring opening would carry her through the rest of February and March. She wondered if the mail had come yet. She would call the receptionist downstairs and see. As she reached for the phone, it rang. Dominique picked it up and a familiar voice, one she couldn't possibly mistake, said, "Dominique." No question mark at the end.

Dominique blanched. "Clay," she said flatly. His calls never brought good news.

"You don't sound pleased," he joshed, his voice oozing with good fellowship.

Dominique wanted to retort, Why should I be? But there was no point in insulting him. When Clay set out to charm, he detested being rebuffed. Dominique tried for a casual tone. "I'm just tired. I've been working long hours." She couldn't resist the opportunity to throw a dart of guilt his way.

"Are things going well?"

"Reasonably." Dominique's tone was clipped. She didn't want him to get the idea that she no longer needed the check he sent each month.

Clay's voice deepened, transmitting affection. "How's Solange?"

His air of intimate fondness at first annoyed Dominique. Then she remembered that he had always truly liked Solange. She relented a little. "Very well, thank you. I was worried that she'd miss New Orleans, but she's made new friends here."

Clay snickered softly. "You always worry too much," he said, his voice retaining its affectionate undertone.

"I have a lot to worry about," Dominique said tartly.

Clay laughed again, as though she had made a joke. Dominique recognized that it was his way of smoothing things over. But, to Dominique's surprise, instead of changing the subject, he actually addressed her statement. "We ought to talk about that," he said, his tone soothing.

"Where should we begin?" Dominique said dryly. He wanted to talk about her worries? Since when? With a shock of realization, she was transported back through the years of their marriage. It was as though she were high up in an airplane surveying a landscape in which she had always lived. The perspective was entirely different, and she saw things she had never seen before. He had never occupied himself with her concerns. Never, not in all the years they'd been together. She suddenly remembered her first date with Mark, how she'd confessed her frustration with Sylvia Brussels. They had spent almost an hour discussing her work, her future, her life. When had Clay ever paid so much attention to her interests?

Clay's voice dropped another register. He said huskily, "Why don't we start over drinks tonight?"

"Tonight?" Dominique was stunned. "You're here?"

"Just for one night. Business." He paused. His voice became wheedling, yet smooth as silk. "I have a lot to tell you."

Dominique didn't like the sound of that. It didn't matter that his tone was friendly. She had learned not to trust his outward demeanor. Her hand tightened on the phone. What if it had something to do with Gabrielle? Or the alimony?

"I can see you for an hour at five-thirty," Dominique said.

"Great!" Clay said. "I'll meet you in the lobby of the King George Hotel."

Dominique didn't like the bar there. It was dark and gloomy. But it was close. Why argue?

~ ~ ~

Dominique brushed her hair until it glowed, then applied fresh lipstick and powder. She had changed from the flats she wore in the privacy of her office to brown suede high heels that complemented her butterscotch silk dress. She knew she looked good, but was annoyed that she cared. With a glare of irritation at herself in the mirror, Dominique snatched her handbag from the counter and stalked out of the bathroom. She was undeniably agitated, aflutter with a mix of emotions. She wanted to impress Clay; she couldn't help it, but she did.

Dominique exited her building and turned in the direction of the hotel, a block away. The air was rich with the threat of a storm. Snow or rain? Dark, lumbering clouds blew across the sky as a strong wind contorted the trees. It made Dominique feel jittery and uncomfortable.

It was soothing to step into the heated dimness of the hotel bar a few minutes later, even if it wasn't her favorite place. She paused just inside the door, blinking until her eyes adjusted to the light. She surveyed the crowded room, looking from the circular, polished bar to the mahogany tables that surrounded it.

She saw Clay before he saw her. He was attractively tan and turned out in an impeccable dark blue pin-striped suit. His hair had a little white at the sideburns, but was as luxuriant as ever. Dominique had almost forgotten how handsome he was. In the room full of gray businessmen, he stood out like a star.

Dominique squared her shoulders, lifted her chin, and walked smoothly across the carpeted foyer. She was gratified to see Clay's eyes light with surprise and admiration. He hurried from behind the little table and came toward Dominique, arms outstretched. "You look marvelous!" he cried too loudly.

She had intended to greet him with a dignified handshake, but he ignored her proffered hand and wrapped her in a bear hug so tight that it hurt her ribs. "It's great to see you," he murmured against her hair.

Dominique was surprised by the extravagance of his greeting, yet relieved that he was so friendly. Their last meeting had been a hostile one in the office of his lawyer.

Dominique laughed uneasily and extracted herself from his grip. Without realizing it, her hand went to her hair. She smoothed it, then dropped her hand limply at her side. She felt awkward and uncertain.

Clay, brimming with confidence as usual, clutched her firmly by the elbow and led her to the table.

He held up his hand to the waitress, who immediately appeared at his side, a look of adoration in her eyes. "Yes, sir?"

"Our usual, Dominique?" Clay asked. A martini already rested on a napkin in front of his place.

Dominique shook her head rapidly. Didn't he realize that she had only drunk the gin concoction to keep him company? Martinis had never been *her* favorite. "No thanks! I've given up mixed drinks. I'll just have a white wine spritzer." She looked at the waitress as she said the words, but Clay repeated them as though she had given him her order to transmit. That had been the way they'd done it before.

After the waitress left, Clay settled back in his seat and turned his winning grin on Dominique. "I can't get over you! How much weight have you lost?"

Dominique, to her dismay, blushed. She said in what she hoped was an offhand manner, "I don't know. A lot."

Clay scanned her with an expert eye. "Size six again?"

Dominique hesitated, then said, "I'm not sure that's any of your business." She had meant the words as a rebuke, but her voice sounded coy to her own ears.

Clay threw back his head and laughed and Dominique found herself laughing with him. She didn't know what to say next. She thought of telling him that he looked good, too, but decided against it. She was sure that he already knew it.

"I like your hair that way." Clay held up his hands like a picture frame. "A little longer."

Dominique's arm jerked involuntarily as she automatically moved to raise her hand to her hair, but this time she restrained herself. She didn't want to appear to be preening under his approval.

The drinks came, and the presence of the waitress gave Dominique time to recover her composure.

Clay raised his glass and said, "Let's drink to" — he appeared to think the matter over — "good memories."

He was trying to win her over. But why, Dominique wondered?

Clay took a sip and continued. "Aren't you even going to ask how I am?" He assumed an expression of mock injury.

"You seem prosperous and fit," Dominique said coolly.

Clay's face turned serious. "You used to know me better," he said wistfully.

"That's not my job anymore. It's your wife's." Dominique was surprised at how matter-of-fact she sounded.

Clay leaned forward and took Dominique's hand from the stem of her glass. He covered it with his own. "Dominique," he said huskily, "I hurt you badly, didn't I?"

His touch felt familiar, yet oddly inappropriate. She pulled her hand away and placed it on her lap with the other. "Why bring that up?" she said, her voice strained.

Clay hung his head. "I owe you an apology. I was an idiot! And" — he fixed her with an earnest look — "I was cruel."

Dominique agreed, but she didn't like the pitiable portrait he drew of her. She met his eyes squarely. "I've recovered," she said crisply.

Clay looked down and said quietly, "I see that. You've really come into your own." He paused, then brought his eyes back to hers. "I almost feel I did you a favor."

Dominique let out an ironic laugh. "Please, Clay." How typical of him to try to absolve his guilt.

"Really." He lowered his voice and leaned forward. "You're very sexy this way."

Dominique was startled by his expression. It held a languid suggestiveness. It reminded her of when they'd first met. She had thought him impossibly attractive then. And now? She had to admit, he still was. He had a manner of looking at her that was somehow . . . arousing. He was stirring the embers of old, buried emotions.

"Clay," she asked uncomfortably, "why did you want to see me?"

Clay straightened in his seat, but once more lowered his head. He twirled the stem of his glass between his fingers. "Dominique, sometimes we all do things that are . . . regrettable, I guess you'd say."

Dominique clutched her hands together tightly in her lap. What was he getting at? What more could he do to her that he hadn't already done? She remained silent, in an agony of suspense.

Clay looked squarely at her. "And I hope that people can be forgiven, at least once in a lifetime."

Dominique swallowed and moved her head in a barely perceptible nod. She wondered if Gabrielle had·given Clay a hard time during her most recent visit. Perhaps she had turned against Marie. But the girl hadn't mentioned any trouble.

Clay spread his hands in a gesture of helplessness. "I made a big mistake with Marie." He gave Dominique a look of appeal. "Things aren't working."

Dominique froze. Her heart thudded. She could almost hear it, pounding and pounding. She held her body perfectly still. "That's unfortunate." Her voice was barely louder than a whisper.

Clay shook his head and dropped his eyes. I was wondering if" — he paused, tore off a corner of his cocktail napkin — "if you still had any feelings left for me."

Dominique stared at him, unbelieving. Clay wanted her back! How often she had dreamed of this, yearned for it. She remembered the day he left her. She had implored him to stay. She had humiliated herself. Later, she had fought the urge to commit an act of vengeance, for fear of irrevocably alienating him. She had not wished to hate him, for if she hated him, how could she possibly allow him back into her life? At the bottom of all her actions had been the hope that he would return.

Now he was offering himself to her. He was as appealing as ever. More so, now that he was in the role of supplicant. This was the man with whom she'd fallen in love. So why didn't she feel joyous? Victorious? She didn't even feel relieved. Only suspicious. Yes, he was attractive. He still affected her physically. But was there any more to it than the titillation of impressing an old flame?

Playing for time, she asked, "Are you divorcing Marie?"

Clay shifted uncomfortably in his seat. He cleared his throat. "Well, you see, we never formally married. We told everyone we did for Gabrielle's sake. But frankly" — he regarded Dominique with a conspiratorial look — "I was never certain I . . . had done the right thing in leaving you." He dropped his lids with an air of embarrassment.

Then why force her from her home? Why cheat her on the settlement? Why brush her off like an annoying insect when she begged him to stay? It was a moment of blinding clarity for Dominique. This was an act! Nothing but an act! Clay didn't feel remorse — only regret that he had thrown away something that he later realized was valuable. He didn't care about the damage he had done Dominique, except as it affected her feelings toward him. He was like a greedy little boy who, having won a coveted prize, no longer valued it.

Dominique's eyes flashed as she said, "You seemed convinced at the time that you were doing the right thing!"

"I don't know what came over me." Clay's expression was sheepish, almost mischievous. As though he were guilty of no more than a harmless peccadillo!

But he had driven Dominique to the point of contemplating suicide. Was he so self-centered that he failed to recognize the monumental upheaval he had created in Dominique's life?

Dominique squeezed her hands so tightly that the veins on her wrists stood up.

Clay looked humbly at her from under his brows, as though ready to accept whatever punishment she meted out. At the same time, a certain playfulness in his expression transmitted confidence that once she had upbraided him, she would forgive him. He was so accustomed to getting his way with her that he seemed incapable of envisioning another outcome.

Dominique almost pitied him. For the first time in her life, she saw that he would never grow up; he would always be a grasping little boy. He would charm his way into women's hearts. But he didn't truly have the capacity to love.

All at once, Dominique thought of Mark. Of his genuine concern for her. His tender caring. His generosity of spirit and his wisdom. His values, his love of family, his unshakable principles. Oh, she missed him! She could hardly stand to think of it.

Dominique picked up her handbag, shoved her chair back from the table, and stood. "Clay, I'm leaving," she said, too upset for civility.

Clay looked up at her with an astonished expression. "Leaving?" he repeated.

Dominique pushed the thought of Mark from her mind and focused once more on Clay. He looked incredulous. "Go back to Marie," she said bluntly.

Clay's face turned a deep red. He sprang to his feet. "You don't understand. . . . I'm asking you to marry me again!"

"I understand," Dominique said in a tone of overtaxed patience, as though addressing a child, "and my answer is no."

"But — but," he sputtered, "why?"

So many accusations came to Dominique's mind. So many judgments. So many harsh truths. But they didn't provide the answer to his question. She felt an exhilarating sense of liberation as she replied, "Because I don't love you anymore."

೦೦ ೦೦ ೦೦

Dominique hurried from her meeting with Clay to her home a few blocks away. The encounter had left her with a feeling of anger, but also with energy and resolve. It would be interesting to tell Solange about it. She wondered what her reaction would be? Would she think Dominique stupid to reject conciliation with Gabrielle's father? Or would she cheer her on, once more urging the move to Paris? Solange was wily. Dominique could imagine her turning the encounter with Clay to her advantage. She would argue that it was best to sever all ties with the past, move to Paris, and be truly independent of Clay.

Dominique sighed. Maybe she would keep Clay's visit to herself. Why stir up another argument? She had promised Michelle an answer by the end of February. Until then, she preferred to weigh her options in peace. She kept telling herself that she should simply say no. That she wasn't even seriously considering the move. But then Solange and Danielle would start on her again. And their arguments made sense. The lure of Paris was becoming very real.

Dominique unlocked her front door and closed it quickly behind her. She removed her coat and put it in the closet.

Where was Solange? Dominique looked for a light under the kitchen door. She started as her gaze landed on a dark form in the living room: Solange sitting perfectly still in the armchair. A dim wash of gray from the windows cast a shadow on her immobile face.

Dominique's heart stopped. She threw her purse on the couch and hastily approached the older woman. "Mother, what's wrong?" she cried.

She noticed, for the first time, that Solange was dressed to go out, her handbag at her side.

Solange raised stricken eyes to Dominique. "Danielle called a little while ago. . . . I tried you at the office, but you'd already left."

Something had happened! A thousand possibilities sprang up in Dominique's mind.

Solange continued in a monotone that, more than anything else, revealed how upset she was. "Ronald is dead."

A chill went up Dominique's spine. That wasn't possible! Ronald was young. Not even fifty years old.

"He was in a car accident."

"But . . . that can't be. He takes the train to work!" Dominique was uncomprehending, as though by arguing, she could alter the facts.

Solange shook her head. "Not today. He had a business trip." She sighed deeply. "Danielle is . . ."

Dominique kneeled down and stared into her mother's shocked face. "Danielle is what? Is she all right?"

Solange said, as if in a trance, "I have to go to New York."

"But of course. We all have to go!" Dominique cried. "Now. We have to go now." She reacted automatically, her mind in high gear with the need for haste. "Oh no! Where's Gabrielle?"

Solange looked up at her daughter. "She's upstairs packing. I wanted to take care of everything so we could leave right away. My suitcase is done. I put yours on your bed and started to pack, but you need to check that I remembered everything."

Dominique looked at her mother in wonder. "You shouldn't be lifting those suitcases!" she chided her.

Solange pushed against the arms of the chair and rose ponderously. "I wanted to be ready. We have to go to Danielle."

Dominique stared at her mother.

"Go on! Finish!" Solange commanded her.

Dominique did as she was told.

By nine that evening, they were in Danielle's ultramodern home, blinded by the whiteness of the living room — the carpet, the sofas, and the drapes. The only contrast was provided by the women in black who milled about the room speaking in hushed voices. A little apart sat Danielle, a small dark figure on the capacious white sofa. Her head was bowed and she was frowning, as though concentrating on a difficult problem. Her arms were folded across her stomach and she had one hand pressed to her lips.

Solange was first through the door. She hurried to Danielle's side more quickly than she had moved in a long time. As she approached her, she opened her arms.

"Maman." Danielle's voice sounded hollow and bewildered, as though she did not understand the occasion for Solange's visit. She rose and clutched her mother, then buried her face in her fleshy shoulder.

"Gabrielle, take the bags in the other room, please," Dominique whispered absently. She was focused on her mother and sister. She wanted to embrace Danielle, but felt oddly shy about intruding between her and Solange. A moment later, though, Danielle lifted her face and extended her hand to her younger sister.

Dominique came forward and took the hand. She looked questioningly at her mother, expecting to be excluded. But Solange simply pulled the two sisters down on the couch, arranging it so that Danielle was in the middle.

Solange studied Danielle minutely. After a moment she said, "You should cry, *chérie*, it will make you feel better."

Danielle shook her head impatiently. "I . . . feel so . . . strange. Like I'm lost or . . . or dreaming." She covered her face with her hand. "This doesn't seem real."

"Where are the girls?" Dominique asked, concerned for her nieces. Monique, in particular, had been close to her father.

Danielle inhaled deeply, then let out her breath in a slow, tremulous stream. "They're flying in from college. They should be here soon."

Solange and Dominique nodded slowly.

"Ron and I were married almost thirty years," Danielle said forlornly. She fixed her gaze on Dominique. "I complained a lot, didn't I?"

The expression in Danielle's eyes alarmed Dominique. Danielle was usually so confident and flippant. She seemed always to know exactly how to please herself. Now, her look held uncertainty and loss, both of which were normal under the circumstances. But there was something more, too. Was it remorse? Dominique couldn't tell. She only knew she wanted to reassure her sister.

Dominique murmured, "People complain. You weren't serious."

Danielle averted her eyes and stared straight in front of her. "I wanted to leave him. Do you remember?" Her upper lip quivered slightly. She tightened her mouth in an attempt to stop the movement.

Dominique looked quickly at Solange. Had their mother known that? But Solange didn't appear to see her glance. She was intensely focused on Danielle's face. Now she spoke. "The loss of a husband is always worse than you anticipate, even though you may not have been in love with him anymore."

Danielle turned her head sharply to her mother. "You know, it's so peculiar, but I don't think I ever stopped loving him. There were times when I was furious, and then later" — she looked briefly at Dominique — "bored. But now . . ." Danielle shook her head and her eyes filled with tears. Solange fished a handkerchief from her purse, but Danielle gently pushed it away saying, "It's not fair to cry." Her voice was hard, but it was clear that under the brittle surface, Danielle was wrestling with her guilt.

Dominique looked at her, horrified. "He wasn't a saint, either! You gave him almost thirty years. You should cry if you feel like it."

Danielle closed her eyes. "You're right," she admitted wearily. "I'm being a martyr because I don't really know what else to be. I feel . . . stranded. I" — she shrugged helplessly — "don't know what to do. I never really wanted to be alone." Her gaze was tortured as she said to Dominique, "I don't know how you stood it after Clay left. I don't know how I could have thought I wanted to be divorced and alone."

But the choice was no longer Danielle's. Dominique shivered at the unexpected finality of it. She took her sister's hand and squeezed it.

Then it was Solange's turn to take command. She gathered Danielle into her arms and gently pressed her head to her shoulders. "Cry, *chérie*," she crooned as she stroked Danielle's hair. "Cry. And after, you will feel better."

And, finally, Danielle did. She cried for the loss of something she had long ago forgotten she possessed.

CHAPTER 31 ∾

ALEXA Martinelli rested her head against Mark's chest. It was dark in his room. They'd just made love and she was in the mood to talk. "What if I were to get pregnant?" she asked.

Mark raised his head and looked at her. "What do you mean?" he asked with alarm.

Alexa gave him a sly smile. "What if I told you I wanted to have your baby?"

Mark pushed himself up, forcing her to sit up, too. He was too taken aback to hide his shock. "Are you pregnant?"

White teeth flashed in the dimness. "No, silly." Alexa's voice was loving. "But didn't you ever want children?"

Mark sighed and relaxed against the headboard. "Once. Nina said she didn't want them right away." He shrugged. "In retrospect, I guess she never wanted them at all. But I came from a big family — always thought I'd have a house full of kids." The words conjured up a mental image of Gabrielle. Their relationship had been satisfying, affectionate. With her, he had felt a bit like a father. He missed her. He missed the dinners the four of them would have in Dominique's warm little kitchen.

Alexa grinned. "It's not too late, you know. I'm only twenty-eight." Her voice turned husky. "I could give you a house full of kids."

The conversation was getting uncomfortable. To hide his dismay, Mark laughed and put his arm around her. "I'm too old for that."

Alexa pulled away in protest, her shining hair swinging into her face. Impatiently, she tossed her head. "Only forty-five! Lots of men become fathers at your age." Her voice turned flirtatious. "There's *nothing* over-the-hill about you, darling."

Her insistence was disturbing. "Alexa, you wouldn't do anything foolish?"

She laughed mischievously. "You mean, to trap you? Why — would you marry me then?"

Mark turned to look directly at her, and the expression in his eyes left no room for misunderstanding.

攉攉 攉攉 攉攉

"Please don't leave me." Danielle looked up at her mother.

Solange stood behind her daughter's chair, her hand resting protectively on Danielle's shoulder. Danielle reached up and covered Solange's hand with her own.

From her place on the sofa opposite, Dominique listened as her eyes traveled around the living room. In the days before the funeral, it had been overflowing with callers. They had brought with them the consoling warmth of friendship. But the funeral was over, and the room looked abandoned and forlorn. Wilting flowers filled it with the cloying scent of rot.

Dominique turned her sympathetic gaze on Danielle. Her sister was more herself now. She was eating again and, that morning, for the first time, she had made her bed before Dominique could do it. But it was clear she was disturbed by the notion of being alone. Monique and Lana were upstairs packing to return to college. They had wanted to stay longer, but Danielle had bravely insisted that they go back to school.

"They'll just brood if they stay here with me," she'd confided to Dominique.

"Why don't you come home with us?" Dominique asked Danielle. "Stay as long as you like."

Danielle looked as though she were considering the idea. Then she sighed, "I can't take any more time off. I've already missed almost two weeks of work."

Dominique stared at her. "But surely they understand —"

Danielle shook her head vehemently. "I can't risk losing the job."

Her grim-faced intensity told Dominique that there was no point in arguing. Danielle wouldn't come.

Dominique understood. The job was now Danielle's anchor, her link with the world of the living. She would recover her old confidence more quickly once she was working again.

But Danielle wasn't ready to be alone yet. She wanted Solange to stay with her.

Dominique tried to gauge Solange's reaction. "Mother?" she asked. "Would you like to stay?"

Solange tightened her grip on Danielle's hand. "A little while, just until Danielle feels better. She needs me now."

Dominique felt a momentary sadness. It occurred to her that Solange might prefer to stay permanently with the daughter who, after all, had always been her favorite. Solange hadn't mentioned the Paris job even once all week. She was completely absorbed by Danielle. Dominique studied her sister. Even in her unhappiness, she looked superb. Dominique didn't doubt that she would one day remarry. And then what would Solange choose to do?

Dominique smiled understandingly at her mother. "When you're ready to come back, let me know. Wherever I go, there'll be a room waiting for you."

Solange's eyes shined back at her. "I know. Thank you." She paused. The corners of her mouth turned up and she said, "You're a good daughter."

Dominique looked straight into her mother's eyes. She stood up and took a step forward. "Oh, Maman! I'm going to miss you." She closed the gap between them and wrapped the older woman in her embrace. Her mother's arms gripped her with surprising force. They held each other for several seconds.

Then there was a thump on the stairs. Solange and Dominique stepped apart and looked up to see Gabrielle descending, dragging the suitcases beside her. "That's everything." Gabrielle's usually boisterous tone was hushed, in deference to her aunt.

Dominique looked up at her daughter and was struck by a torrent of emotion so strong that she felt a sob catch in her throat. She swallowed and dabbed at her eyes with a tissue. She mustn't weep. It was important for Danielle that she restrain herself, otherwise they would all start crying.

Dominique bent to her sister and encircled her neck with her arms.

She placed her cheek against Danielle's sweetly scented one. She saw the tiny grains of powder on Danielle's face, and suddenly felt like laughing. Danielle was wearing makeup for the first time since Ron's death!

Dominique kissed her sister good-bye, then rose and, once more, clutched her mother close.

ϾϿ ϾϿ ϾϿ

Dominique and Gabrielle arrived at La Guardia just as the ten o'clock shuttle was leaving. Dominique shrugged with resignation. "Well, we have an hour. Let's go to the Sky Club. I can use your father's name to get us in. At least we can stretch out."

The sunny, comfortably upholstered room was so much more cheerful than the waiting area in the general concourse. Dominique and Gabrielle ordered diet sodas from the bar, then went to sit near a window. Gabrielle quickly finished her drink, then got up to search the magazine rack.

Dominique stood up, too. "I'm going to the ladies' room. I'll be right back."

As she washed her hands, she checked her makeup in the mirror. She pulled out her cosmetic case and powdered her face, then ran a brush through her hair. Finally, she applied coral lipstick and studied the effect. The color was flattering with the cream wool suit she wore.

When she emerged from the rest room, the bright sunlight momentarily blinded Dominique. She stood still until her eyes adjusted, then looked around the room to find her place. There was Gabrielle, a stack of magazines on her lap. Dominique smiled and moved through an assortment of seating areas toward her daughter. She was almost there when she paused to allow a couple to pass in front of her on their way to the bar.

The woman murmured, "Excuse me," with a decidedly English accent.

At the sound of once-familiar tones, Dominique looked up. A man followed, excusing himself also. He smiled at Dominique and she politely smiled back. He was one step beyond her when his step faltered. He did a sharp about-face, then stood immobile. Curious, Dominique turned toward him. Her eyes met his. And locked. In the background, she heard the woman's voice. "Stephen!" she said. "Are you coming?"

Dominique gripped the back of a chair for support and stared fixedly at Stephen Hampton.

He took a step toward her.

Again, the woman spoke. "Stephen? Whatever is the matter?"

"Is that you, Dominique?" the man's voice was strained with shock.

Dominique could scarcely articulate a reply. Even to her own ears, it sounded faint. "Stephen. . . ." It wasn't a question. There was no question. Then Dominique saw the woman over his shoulder.

Stephen followed her gaze and turned. "Oh . . . oh, forgive me, dear." He took the woman by the elbow. His face flushed then turned pale. "Serena, this is someone I used to know in Egypt," he said vaguely. "Dominique Avallon —" He suddenly stopped. "I beg your pardon, I'm sure you've a married name."

"Parker," Dominique said woodenly.

Hampton continued, his voice stronger now. "Mrs. Parker used to work for the RAF in Egypt."

The woman studied Dominique from head to toe. "Ah yes," she said, "Ismailia, wasn't it? For whom did you work?"

The woman's clipped tone helped Dominique recover her poise. She arranged her features in a polite mask. She smiled graciously at the woman. "No one in particular. I was in the typing pool." Dominique tried to discern a resemblance between the long ago photo on Stephen's desk and the woman before her now. Yes, the bones were the same. And the cool, measuring eyes.

"Well. . . ." Stephen shifted nervously. "It doesn't seem quite right just to say hello and move on. We were going to have a cup of tea. Would you care to join us?"

Dominique looked from one to the other. The woman said, "Yes, do. We have hours to wait for our connection. Such a bore. Unless, of course," she paused in a manner weighted with meaning, "one runs into old friends."

Dominique studied the man before her. He was still handsome, but he looked worn and somewhat defeated, not at all the dashing hero she remembered. "I'd like to join you, but my daughter, Gabrielle —" She stopped, a little confused.

"It's okay, Mom, that would be cool."

Dominique turned, surprised to find Gabrielle directly behind her. They all sat down in a grouping of chairs and ordered drinks.

Egypt was hardly mentioned. Stephen told of the places he had lived since the Suez crisis. Dominique described her business in Washington. Gabrielle and Serena barely said a word.

All the while, Dominique wondered why Stephen had stayed married to the woman he had professed to no longer love — a woman who had been unfaithful to him. She watched the interplay between them. Dominating it was the tone of irritable affection that many long-married couples adopt.

Dominique tried in vain to associate with the man before her the burning, all-encompassing love she had felt at twenty-one. She remembered desperate unhappiness, ferocious passion. But none of it seemed remotely connected to this Stephen Hampton. There was nothing left of that old fire.

Stephen, in turn, searched Dominique's face. She felt it. Wondered what he was thinking. But her curiosity had limits. She would never know the answer, and she found it did not matter.

They had one cup of tea, then it was time to go. Dominique held out her hand to Serena and felt the cool, limp contact in return. She turned to Stephen and held out her hand as Gabrielle said good-bye to his wife.

Stephen leaned toward Dominique and kissed her on the cheek. In her ear, he whispered, "I'll never forget Ismailia."

Dominique gazed into his eyes. They seemed desperate with a message she couldn't read. Regret? Melancholy? Nostalgia? She didn't know: they were the eyes of a stranger.

She shook his hand. "Good-bye," she said.

Dominique and Gabrielle hurried to the gate, but unnecessarily. There was a line of people waiting to board, and they were at the end of it.

Dominique stood on tiptoe and looked impatiently at the ground attendant checking tickets.

She felt Gabrielle's gaze on her and turned to face her.

Gabrielle smiled. "You know what, Mom?"

"What?"

Gabrielle's voice was quiet with wonder. "You've still got it."

Dominique blushed. "Don't be silly! What are you talking about?"

"That man. He was in love with you, wasn't he?"

Dominique shrugged and looked away. "I don't know. It was so long ago."

"*I* know," Gabrielle intoned. "Because he's still in love with you."

Dominique looked in her daughter's eyes and saw the admiration there. "Oh, you're imagining things," she said with a little laugh. But she was pleased. Not by Stephen's admiration, but by Gabrielle's.

ᕲ᠑ ᕲ᠑ ᕲ᠑

Dominique was quiet during the flight home. Seeing Stephen made her reflect on what he had meant to her. Why hadn't she been at all attracted to him? Though she wouldn't admit it aloud, she agreed with Gabrielle that he appeared to still love her — at least to carry the memory of his love within him. The look of resignation he wore caused Dominique to wonder if their affair had been a highlight of his life.

Yet, that wasn't so for her. So much had happened since then. She smiled as she thought of it. She had been so young. So romantic! How had she rationalized their affair?

Not until Anton had she learned about consequences. She shuddered as she remembered the desperate isolation of her time with him, the harsh months afterward. But in those months, she knew, she had for the first time taken responsibility for her own fate. Then she had fallen in love with Clay. And, bit by bit, she had succumbed to the life prescribed by him, by her upbringing, by New Orleans society. She had done it of her own free will, glad to have found her place after losing the one she had had in Egypt.

Dominique stared at the vast blue sky outside and thought of Mark. To him, she wasn't an accouterment, but rather a person apart. A person to be valued on her own terms, on equal terms. Why hadn't she been able to make that distinction? She had fought so hard for her independence that she had failed to recognize that she had won. She thought back to the night, right after the separation from Clay, when she had considered suicide. On that night, she had taken back her life. Since then, she had rebuilt it. Rebuilt it so that it was hers. And she knew Mark would never ask her to give it up. He, of all people, would understand why she intended to say no to Paris. That no matter how enticing the opportunity, she couldn't give up what she was building in Washington. The process might be long and laborious, but she *was* succeeding. And Mark had encouraged her every step of the way.

So why was she denying herself the happiness of being with him? She had nothing to fear from him. Her heart expanded as she envisioned his good-natured face. He would never intentionally hurt her. He was not the sort of person to do that to anyone. He was tender and kind. He was, and had always been, her friend.

She closed her eyes and pushed her seat back. Mark was her friend, yes, but he had taught her about passion, too. He made her feel relaxed, yet wildly excited. What an odd congruence of emotions! It was what people searched for all their lives. It was the very meaning of love. Not even with Clay had she felt that particular harmony. And yet, she hadn't cherished its uniqueness.

Regret, so bitter she could taste it, filled her. Was this what Danielle was going through? Why was it that people didn't realize how lucky they were until it was too late?

Like snapshots in an album, memories of Dominique's times with Mark began to flash through her mind. Vividly, she recalled lying with him in his canoe as he sang "Old Man River" at the top of his lungs.

She remembered another time. Mark had run out of gas and had wanted to push his car to a service station perhaps a half-mile away while she steered. Mark had labored for a quarter of the distance before he'd commented how hard going it was.

"Maybe I'll just go get the gas and come back. I thought this would be easy, but there's more of a grade to this hill than it looks," he'd remarked with puzzlement.

It was then that Dominique discovered she'd forgotten to release the hand brake. She'd admitted it with trepidation, expecting the sort of angry outburst she was used to from Clay.

Instead, Mark had broken out laughing, and he had made Dominique laugh, too.

The crackle of the intercom broke into Dominique's thoughts. The flight attendant instructed them to place their seats in the upright position. Dominique obeyed, then turned her gaze back to the window. They flew over the Washington Monument, then the Lincoln Memorial, then the Capitol. Traffic around the Capitol was congested. Watergate, of course, was keeping Congress busy.

Dominique knew that Mark was there, a few miles below. Her heart contracted at the thought, then she forced it from her mind. She was just making herself sad.

With a *thump*, the plane landed. After Dominique and Gabrielle claimed their luggage, they made their way through the jostling crowd to the taxi stand outside.

The taxi that stopped for them was overheated, but the warmth was comforting. Dominique leaned forward and gave the driver their address, then sat back and gazed out the window. Across the Potomac River, almost directly across, was the Capitol.

The driver fought his way through the traffic at the airport, then took the ramp onto the Fourteenth Street bridge. "You want to go M Street or the Parkway?" he asked over his shoulder.

Dominique thought for a moment. Suddenly she said. "Neither! Take me to the Russell Senate Office Building." It was a crazy impulse, but impossible to fight.

Gabrielle snapped her head around in astonishment. "But —"

Dominique's look silenced her. "I'll explain later." To the driver she said, "After you drop me off, take my daughter to the address I gave you before." She handed him enough to cover both fares.

Gabrielle stared at her, mouth open.

"You'll be okay for an hour or so, won't you?" Dominique asked Gabrielle.

"Of course," Gabrielle said with adolescent defensiveness. "I'm not a baby!"

Dominique laughed, then pulled her close and hugged her.

"Mom!" Gabrielle wriggled away, embarrassed, but smiling.

Dominique leaned forward in her seat, willing the taxi to go faster. Faster, before she lost her courage. Her heart was pounding with apprehension.

As the driver pulled up to her destination, Dominique patted Gabrielle's hand and said, "See you later." Then she charged out of the vehicle and into the building.

Her heels clicked noisily in the hall. She concentrated on the rhythm, refusing to focus on what might happen in the next few moments. If she thought about it, she would lose her nerve.

And then she was outside Mark's office. She stood in front of the open door and watched the two receptionists field an incessant flow of telephone calls. She took a deep breath and stepped in.

"Hold please," said a receptionist into the telephone. She looked up at Dominique and her eyes widened in recognition. Dominique did not recall ever before having met her, but it was likely the young woman had seen photos of her with Mark. "May I help you?" the young woman asked, her expression worried.

Dominique took a step closer to the desk. She thought her heart would burst from her chest. "Yes, please. I'd like to see Senator Patout, if he has a moment. I'm Dominique Parker," she added unnecessarily.

The woman nodded. "Please have a seat," she said dubiously.

Dominique sat down in a brown leather armchair in the corner of the room. Immediately, she sprang up again. She was too nervous to sit. She looked at the receptionist to whom she'd spoken. The young woman had turned her back and was speaking softly into the phone. The other receptionist continued to answer the ringing lines. Dominique couldn't hear a word the first one was saying. Then, catching herself, she turned away. What would the woman think of her staring that way!

She sat back down and fiddled with the handle of her pocketbook.

Her eyes found the carved wood door that led to Mark's office. It looked thick and impenetrable. She watched for the turning of the brass knob.

The young woman put down the phone and turned to say something to Dominique, but it immediately rang again. She held up her index finger as though asking Dominique to wait, then she picked up the phone.

Dominique felt unnaturally warm. She wanted to take off her coat, but, somehow, she found she couldn't even make that easiest of gestures.

When would the receptionist get off the phone and tell her what was happening? The woman had turned away again, and Dominique wondered if she was avoiding eye contact with her. Suppose she had something embarrassing to tell her? Suppose she was going to say that Mark was unavailable?

Dominique had the sudden urge to flee. She stood up and went to the receptionist's desk. She'd leave a note. Mark could call her if he wanted to — if he hadn't fallen in love with the dark-haired young woman. This wasn't the time or place —

His door opened. He stepped out quickly, a look of surprise and expectancy on his face.

Dominique gazed at him, the dear sight of him. Had it only been three months? She wanted to run to him. To throw herself against his chest and feel his arms around her. But she stood rooted to the spot in front of the receptionist's desk.

Mark's face lit with happiness. "Dominique?" His voice was uncertain.

An effervescent, soaring feeling took hold of her. It seemed as though there was no one in the room but the two of them. "Mark," she blurted out, "am I too late?"

Mark stared at her, his expression all at once serious. Was it shock she saw there? Rejection? Regret? Why didn't he speak?

Suddenly the phones stopped. Every line was flashing, all callers on hold. The receptionists no longer pretended to ignore the scene. They gazed, transfixed, at Dominique and Mark.

As though suddenly remembering an appointment, Mark looked at his watch. Then he raised his eyes to Dominique and gave her his irresistible lopsided grin. He relaxed with one shoulder against the door jamb and crossed one leg in front of the other. "Why, no," he said, "I've been waiting."

5/95